# The Poet of
# ❖ Loch Ness ❖

# The Poet of

# ✤ Loch Ness ✤

Brian Jay Corrigan

THOMAS DUNNE BOOKS

St. Martin's Press

New York

THOMAS DUNNE BOOKS.
An imprint of St. Martin's Press.

THE POET OF LOCH NESS. Copyright © 2005 by Brian Jay Corrigan. All rights reserved. Printed in the United States of America. No part of this book may be used or reproduced in any manner whatsoever without written permission except in the case of brief quotations embodied in critical articles or reviews. For information, address St. Martin's Press, 175 Fifth Avenue, New York, N.Y. 10010.

www.stmartins.com

Design by Kathryn Parise
Photograph courtesy of Heather Saunders

LIBRARY OF CONGRESS CATALOGING-IN-PUBLICATION DATA

Corrigan, Brian Jay, 1957–
    The poet of Loch Ness / Brian Jay Corrigan.—1st ed.
        p. cm.
    ISBN 0-312-32931-8
    EAN 978-0-312-32931-0
        1. Triangles (Interpersonal relations)—Fiction. 2. Ness, Loch, Region (Scotland)—Fiction. 3. College teachers' spouses—Fiction. 4. Tour guides (Persons)—Fiction. 5. Americans—Scotland—Fiction. 6. Married women—Fiction. 7. First loves—Fiction. 8. Poets—Fiction. I. Title.

PS3603.O7725P64 2005
813'.6—dc22
                                                                2004065659

First Edition: June 2005

10  9  8  7  6  5  4  3  2  1

*For Damaris, my love*
*Constance, my life*
*and*
*Lenore, my hero*

*Love is not jealous.*

A course more promising
Than a wild dedication of yourselves
To unpath'd waters, undream'd shores, most certain
To miseries enough; no hope to help you,
But as you shake off one, to take another;
Nothing so certain as your anchors, who
Do their best office if they can but stay you,
Where you'll be loathe to be. Besides, you know
Prosperity's the very bond of love,
Whose fresh complexion and whose heart together
Affliction alters.

—*The Winter's Tale*
Camillo IV.iv. 559–67

# Acknowledgments

❖

Many thanks to the North Florida Writers, FCCJ, and to the organizers and judges of the Florida First Coast Writers' Festival, where this book won first prize. Thanks also to the Josiah W. Bancroft panel, who selected this book for their premier award. Warm thoughts and thanks to Howard Denson, and special thanks to David Poyer and Lenore Hart Poyer—exceptionally talented and generous people indeed. Bless you.

For their words of encouragement, strength, love, and patience through the writing of this book, I wish to thank foremost my wife, Damaris, and mother, Constance. My thanks also go to Mitchell S. Waters, my agent, whose strength and belief in this book is nothing short of heroic. Thanks also to Dave Barbor, Jamie Lovett, Sheldon Bernstein, Mark and Kathy Corrigan, Deborah and John Alderman, Kim Kennedy, Michele and Jerry Bruce, Dr. Sally Allen, and Dr. B. J. Robinson for their unflagging interest and commentary—and to Dr. Peter Green for his friendship, good company, brilliance, and also for the use of his translation of Archilochus for this book.

Heartfelt thanks to my editor, Marcia Markland, for her patience, unerring good taste, humanity, happy voice, and belief in this book.

And also for the valiant efforts of Diana Szu, many thanks. Thanks to Olga Gardner Galvin for her care and insight.

Thanks to Mephistopheles, my black moggy and good angel, who patiently occupied my lap during the entire process of writing and editing this book.

Thanks to the two hotels where initial drafts were completed: The Sir Christopher Wren in Windsor, and the Rubens Hotel, London (with special thanks to Dave)—for their continued warmth, good fellowship, and hospitality.

Thanks and eternal admiration to the good people of Invernessshire and St. Andrews, Scotland, for your hospitality, good sense, and genuine kindness to a daftie Yank. Thanks for never once rolling your eyes when the subject of the "monster" was broached. Surely you are the patron saints of patience. Alban forever.

Special thanks to my friends in Drumnadrochit, Scotland: to the staff at the Loch Ness 2000 Exhibition Centre and especially to its director, naturalist Adrian Shine, for all of their help with the ecology of the loch; to Willie Cameron for his bonhomie, wit, and knowledge of the sightings; to Heather and Donnie Fraser for sharing their magnificent view; to Duncan MacDonald-Haig of Borlum Farm for the use of his horses Ceilidh and Blossom; and most especially to Fiona and Ross Urquhart of the Glenkirk for their assistance, generosity, hospitality, friendship, and memorably excellent breakfasts (with no hint of ptomaine, Donnie).

And thanks to you, rare reader. Dying breeds are the noblest of all.

B.J.C.
Drumnadrochit, 2004

# The Poet of
# ❖ Loch Ness ❖

# Prelude

✤

## LOCH NESS

"Put his hand in the water, Aidan," the old man said.

The flat-bottomed boat rocked softly on the silken black swells that rolled from one side of the loch to the other. The boy regarded the old man with amusement.

"Why should I put his hand in the water?" he whispered, not to wake his father.

It was June, past midnight, and the moon was new. Only stars picked out the skies and showed where the surrounding hills began their slow plummet to the water's edge.

"Because, lad, if you dip his hand into the water while he's sleeping, he'll bepiss himself." The old man nodded several times to indicate his sincerity.

Aidan could see the old man's features by the yellow-green glow of the lamp they had suspended from a pole off the front of the little boat. The lamp would bring the fish up, the old man had said. They'll think it's the moon shining down. It was the best way to lure fish, he had assured the boy and his father.

1

The father, Andrew Macgruer, slept peacefully in the narrow bow by the pole. He had put in a long day and had decided he did not want to go fishing. He'd kept it to himself, though; the boy was so eager. The old man, formerly his professor of medieval studies at St. Andrews, was now just a close friend, a retired intellectual with some time on his hands. The recent heart attacks had encouraged him to get out and enjoy his few remaining years.

"Go on," he coaxed the lad. "Carefully."

Aidan inched up to his sleeping father and caught his shirtsleeve at the elbow. He lifted it over the edge, like an experienced puppeteer, and the arm slid under the surface to the elbow. Aidan then slid back to his place in the boat.

"There now," the old man said.

"How long before he does?" Aidan whispered.

"It all depends." The fish had not been biting as predicted, and this seemed appropriate sport until they began.

He violated his own rule about talking in the boat, bored. "Has your father really seen the monster?"

Aidan shrugged. "He says he has, then he says he hasn't. He's told me it's just for the tourists. It's a way to make a few pounds, leading them out to where they can look."

The old man shook his head sadly. "Is that all he does now?"

"No, Mr. Carlisle," the boy said earnestly. "He writes still."

"But he disnae publish." The old man slipped his pipe between his teeth and rekindled the dead flame in the bowl. "Does he publish?"

"Only writes."

A deep swell rolled under the boat, raising it gently before dropping it into the well noiselessly.

"Bloody hell!" Andrew started up from where he was sleeping and snatched his hand up from the water.

"Did you bepiss yourself, Father?" Aidan said, laughing at the prank.

"I did not," Macgruer said. "You're too close to the shore, Carlisle."

"I'm not."

"You are. I just dragged my hand across bottom."

"We're a hundred yards from shore," the old man said and sucked his pipe.

"I tell you I just touched cold silt. How fast are we going?"

"We are sitting still."

"We're not. We're moving and fast. You'll run us aground, man."

"You were dreaming."

"I'll show you who's dreaming." Andrew Macgruer slipped his hand back into the loch up to the elbow, then leaned out of the boat and sunk down to the shoulder.

"See? It's better than a half mile deep just there. Go ahead and reach a little further then."

Macgruer sat up and lay back in the boat. "I tell you, I touched bottom."

"I'd say you hit bottom, Andrew. The lad says you're earning your keep off tourists now. What happened to teaching?"

"I was one of the cutbacks, ken?"

"That's ages ago, Andrew. There's been other positions since."

"Not for poets."

Carlisle pulled at his pipe quietly. There was no use arguing. Andrew Macgruer was stubborn and would have his own way in everything.

"I can hear the water on the shore close by," Andrew said.

"Nonsense," Carlisle said. But when he listened, he heard it, too.

Aidan closed his eyes, though the darkness made it nearly unnecessary, and listened. At first, all he could hear was the gentle clank of the tin lamp rocking on the pole, but then he heard the quiet plash of water against shore. It was nearby.

"It's over there," he said and pointed, opening his eyes.

The water under the lamp was gray-green, like the skin of hard-boiled egg yolk. It danced and wrinkled, stirred by retreating waves from the shore. Then the quiet gurgle of water grew silent.

They looked to where Aidan had pointed. Andrew unhooked the pole and swung the lamp over the side of the boat. All they could see was open water. Another swell raised the tiny boat and bounced it gently into a gulf, rocking the three.

"How could the shore just vanish?" Aidan said.

Carlisle had stopped pulling on his pipe. He stared at Andrew.

"Nae," Andrew said to his old professor. "Don't even think it."

"I hear it again," Aidan said. "The shore's over there." He pointed to the other side of the craft.

Andrew swung the lamp. It glinted off of something in the mid-distance; maybe fifty feet off starboard, but the glint vanished, as did the sound of waves lapping. The boat heaved again.

"It's swimming under us," Carlisle said.

"Don't be daft," Andrew said, but Carlisle didn't respond. His eyes were fixed on a spot above Andrew's head.

Andrew turned and saw it.

In the soft glow of the lamp, a form could just be seen, slender and slick, glinting like wet rubber. It stood six or seven feet above the surface, only a lighter shadow against the blackness beyond.

Carlisle grabbed for the oars and began pulling heavily against them.

"Hey!" Aidan protested. "We'll lose the rods."

"Let them go," Carlisle said. "Let them go."

He pulled again and again at the oars, turning the craft slowly until the feeble light no longer picked out the image in the water, placing it aft. He then tugged hard at the oars.

"Easy," Andrew warned. "Let me take the oars, man. Mind your heart!" But Carlisle wasn't listening.

Andrew saw a wide, flat object slip past the side of the boat like a half-submerged stone, perhaps a meter long. The thing's head. The boat raised on the swell.

"It's got in front of us again."

"The light," Carlisle gasped. "It's attracted to the light. For God's sake, put it out."

Andrew fumbled with the pole and bounced the lamp off into the water. It sizzled as it hit and blackened the world as it died. Andrew heard the metallic clank as the bow struck it, and thrust his arm down to retrieve it, chasing it under the water as it sank away from his groping fingertips. Then he touched something else, the silken, taut flesh he had mistaken for silt only minutes before. Cool to the touch, like the water around it, but smooth and slick. He jerked his hand out of the water.

"Lamp's gone," he said and rolled onto his back in the boat.

Carlisle had stopped rowing.

"What is it, Carlisle?" Andrew said. "Why are we stopped?"

He couldn't see in the blackness.

"Mr. Carlisle's fallen onto me," Aidan said in the dark. "I think he's sick."

His heart. Andrew knew it must be his heart. He crawled across the little boat, groping, until his hand touched his old professor's trousers. The pant leg was wet and warm. Carlisle had lost control of his bladder. Andrew pulled the old man up and felt around him desperately, searching for his throat, a wrist, somewhere to check a pulse. He put his fingers up under the old man's jaw and felt. The pulse was weak and thready, hardly there at all. Then what pulse there was vibrated and ceased under Andrew's fingers.

"Carlisle," Andrew said. "Not out here. Not now."

"What is it, Father?" Aidan said. "What's happening?"

"Didn't you see it?"

"See what?"

Andrew sat cross-legged in the darkness with Carlisle across his lap and felt the rocking of the boat slow and stop. The beast had sounded, swimming down into the black depths of the loch. Macgruer buried his face in the old man's quiet breast and wept.

# Chapter 1

# April

## Michigan

*The crocuses have come out again. They've tunneled up (from the wood chips I laid about the beeches and elm) like resolute pioneers of the dawning year. They always remind me of eggcups somehow. Strange. I invariably think of them as hearty, durable, and my association of them with eggs or anything so fragile seems to relinquish my most romantic notions of the springing season. Life is not fragile, only love.*

*We set out today for Scotland, for Loch Ness. Everything is packed away like nuts. We won't be here again for six months, and Perry suggested we store everything away in boxes to fend off the dust, the mice, the cockroaches. Nothing will fend off cockroaches, of course, but the activity was filled with purpose and hopes. That always makes an activity seem worth doing.*

*Perry helped. He's always so good to help. In many ways, Perry is an ideal husband. Many ways, not all.*

*So we have wrapped and folded and boxed and taped until it seems that we are moving away forever instead of just the six months.*

*I don't mind.*

*I am not going to miss Larchmont.*

*I am not going to miss Michigan.*

*I will not miss weekends, or television, or baseball. I will not even miss the house.*

*I will not miss the weekly rites that crowd the calendar but not the life.*

*And I will not miss the college lowering in its shady crevasse along Lake Niack like some unhappy woman waiting in a bus terminal, eternally waiting—waiting in bored expectation of nothing she cherishes, nothing she hopes for, nothing she finds congenial. Obligatory waiting.*

*The three-hour drive into Detroit is yet to come; we will listen to a book on the tape deck. I have a whole selection. I collect them up for when I'm gardening. I treasure McKellen's* Odyssey, *but that is too long; it will never end by the time we've reached the airport and will leave us for six months on the island of the Cyclops.*

*Can't have that.*

*I have decided even while thinking about it: Miranda Richardson's reading of* Enchanted April. *How perfect. I love Miranda, I love the story. And in some ways, this is my enchanted April, after all. Not off to Italy but rather to Scotland, my Scotland, which to my mind is every bit as full of life and love as any Tuscan castle or vineyard leased by the month.*

*It has lived in my mind like ivy, Scotland, growing untended these seventeen years. I was away there for my junior year in college and have come to think of it as my only real home.*

*St. Andrews looms now in my imagination like the sea-swept islands of Homer, vast and mythic. I'm sure I never thought so back then. But how full a vision becomes when it is dwelt upon and cherished, how ripe when perspective and years creep under the skin of remembrance.*

*And now, oh now, St. Andrews and Scotland ring in my memory like Troy, magnificent and tragic.*

*Sorry to say, we are not going to St. Andrews, alas. This is Perry's trip, Perry's grant, Perry's plan, Perry's money.*

*It is a lot of money. I don't know precisely how much. I'm not certain Perry knows. He's like that, scattered. Sometimes he says twenty-five thousand dollars, sometimes twenty-five thousand pounds, as though there really isn't much difference, but of course there is. He isn't always exact about the twenty-five thousand, either. At first he thought it was only fifteen thousand, but he's amended that.*

*Perry's like that.*

*It is not strange for a professor to be scattered a bit. It fits the absent-minded image, after all. He never forgets an anniversary or birthday, love him, but he has something of an ongoing struggle with what happened yesterday, how it might influence today, and what he's to do tomorrow. I have completely given him up on questions of the weekly garbage now and take it out myself each Thursday. Perry cannot be trusted with diurnals.*

*But he remembered my birthday last month. He will remember our anniversary, too. We will celebrate our thirteenth wedding anniversary in Scotland.*

*Scotland was my grandmother's home. I visited her grave yesterday, swept away the new-fallen pollen on the stone and arranged her flowers. She loved flowers so. She taught me to love them, too. She taught me so much gardening and dreaming that sometimes the two seem to be the same thing. She also taught me something about men.*

*"Men are lovely wee creatures until they think you think so."*

*I sat quietly with her for hours, recollecting her stories of home in the Highlands. It was not long, however, before I was recalling our conversations about Perry.*

*"Is it a divorce you're after?" she wanted to know.*

*"No, I can't stand the thought of being without him. Perry's such a dear man."*

*"You love him?"*

*"Yes—"*

*"I hear reticence in that yes, Perdita. What's the matter, child?"*

*"It is hard to love a man and not love him enough, to respect and like him without fully enjoying his company or conversation. He is good, I know, but he irritates me sometimes. It is a mild irritation that collects up like the waxy residue of soap until I want to—I don't know what."*

*"Ach," she said. "Weel, there is no adequate remedy for random irritation."*

*It is true. There is only a creeping but endurable discontent and ennui that comes with the final realization that one is not unhappy, but that is the best that can be said.*

*"Is it enough not to be unhappy and nothing more?" I once asked her.*

*"It is enough to be content," she replied.*

*"I don't know how to be content."*

*"Then your trouble's no' your husband, my dear."*

*She was right, of course. Perry's tried to make me happy and I him. When I was so ill and so frightened, he was there every minute. It left my poor heart weak, and Perry has been patient with me, walking slower when I needed him to. He still smiles at my jokes though he never really understands them. We have tried. Indeed we have tried to make one another happy. But after nearly thirteen years of trying without success—without unconditional success, that is—what can one do?*

*Grandmother would doubtless say, "Try a wee bity more."*

*Huff.*

*So this is his trip.*

*And we won't be going to St. Andrews but rather to Iubhar, on the south-eastern side of Loch Ness. It is funny in its own way how things work out, how we get what we ask for but not what we want.*

*I used to beg Perry to take me to Scotland those first few years we were married, to take me to St. Andrews or out to the Highlands to traipse the heather. At first I was too ill, then when I recovered it was too expensive, too far away, or always too something that amounted to gentle refusal.*

*I long to leave America. In many ways, I blame America for making people like Perry. Democracy, with its lowest-common-denominator mentality, works to stifle good men like Perry. It levels them, clones them like white mice, presses them into cookie-cut corporate Christians, all blanched wheat and refined sugar. No ginger, no snap.*

*Perry is content with feeling guilty for being white and male. These to him are aspects of race. I think Americans threw away race, national identification, when they confused it all with skin color and the direction of parental migration. Race is a matter of mind and shared experience and not, please God, pigmentation or ethnicity.*

*I want to be somebody, not simply a part of some thing.*

*I am Perdita only.*

*So I will not miss America, Michigan, Larchmont, or Lake Niack.*

*I will only miss the white, the yellow, and the purple crocuses. They will bloom tomorrow, I'm sure. But tomorrow I will be somewhere over the Atlantic.*

*Everything that is just opening here will be dead when I return. All of these ripening buds, filled with the liquor of life, will be crisp, brown litter when next I see them, only a soft, deathly crackle under my feet, and I will have never seen their passage through this world.*

*But I remain, as always, optimistic.*

*To my mind, these buds are like Scotland: ripe with life, perdurable, green, and growing. Oh, Scotland! Its roots dig deep into history—my history, not my family's history, my own—sucking up the juices that have pooled in me, never stagnant: the deep, selfish waters of my slumbering life.*

*So I will return to Scotland, but on Perry's terms.*

"We're not going to St. Andrews, then?" I said, unable to keep the disappointment out of my voice.

"No, dear," he said. "Loch Ness. Place called Iubhar."

He never noticed the trace of yearning that hung in my question.

He wouldn't, of course.

Perry lives in a world of direct questions and declarative statements; there is no tone for Perry: irony, sarcasm, disappointment, irritation, approval are all the same to him. He understands that such things exist, of course, but he understands only in the abstract. He knows people communicate with tone of voice, but he is tone-deaf to underlying meanings. I believe that is why he is such a timid conversationalist, like a blind man on a rifle range.

He will study the marine life of the loch: freshwater marine biology, flora and fauna. I don't think anyone is taken in, though. He is chasing his fantasy. Certainly he is. He was denied a place on the 1987 research team that went hunting for the monster. That was before I knew him, back when he made his one and only attempt to break his mold.

I would not say it to Perry, but I believe he is only a middling sort of scientist. Why else would he be stuck at a provincial college on Lake Niack? It has always seemed enough for him. That's Perry: enough, always just enough. Just enough money. Just enough time. Just enough laughter. Just enough love.

Just enough is not plenty, though, is it?

Scotland understands that. Scotland understands me. There it will be enough only to be everything I am.

# Chapter 2

✤

## LONDON

"Perry Miggs," the college professor said in answer to the customs officer's question. Heathrow Airport was crowded, and the officer pressed for time.

Perry's passport said he was fifty, but he looked considerably older. Thin hair, thick spectacles, and a long, narrow throat of loose flesh

"How long are you planning to stay, sir?" the officer said automatically.

"Six months." When the officer gave his passport a long look that Miggs interpreted as doubt, he added, "I'm leaving the end of September."

Perry Miggs would hardly be denied admission into the United Kingdom. There was nothing objectionable about him. He was as unobjectionable as a gelatin mold. The worst that could be said of him was that he was plain.

He was a spare man, lean and mousy. Regular in his habits and unimaginative, he was known around his biology department as "the other." His classes were unpopular. When all the popular classes had been filled by the most energetic young scholars, latecomers were obliged to sign up for "the other" class, the one taught by Miggs.

"I suppose," he confessed to everyone who knew him—the department chair, the secretary, his colleagues, and even Perdita—"I suppose I am a little colorless." He would raise his eyebrows at his observation and sigh—a sigh that said "little can be done about that, though." It was his explanation of himself, his summation.

He used colorlessness to explain his lack of ambition, his customary bewilderments, and his failure to secure tenure the first time. It was his explanation for failing to earn tenure the second time. And when the department chair informed him that he had finally won tenure on his third and final attempt, Perry Miggs said, "They only did it out of pity." His senior colleagues did not contradict him. It was true.

"Purpose for visit?" the customs officer said absently.

"Vacation," Perry said. It was easier than explaining the varied purposes he had for coming to the United Kingdom, and "vacationing" was ultimately the only real reason he had come at all. The purpose he had given his wife was too preposterous. He would embarrass himself in telling it to the officer.

"And you are traveling with your—" the officer hesitated as he looked at the youthful woman beside Perry Miggs. The officer usually said "companion," but this time he faltered.

His eyes had caught the young woman's. Most people in the customs line avoided his eyes. It was such a surprise to be confronted so pleasantly with a pair of sparkling blue eyes, almost green, that he completely lost track of his routine.

If Perry Miggs looked much older than his years, Perdie appeared much younger than hers. So though there were only a dozen years between them they seemed like father and daughter.

"My wife, yes," Miggs completed the officer's question quietly. It had happened before, many times. "We'll be in London for a few days before heading up to Scotland."

The officer gave a sharp, bureaucratic nod and passed the American couple through.

They went to a well-appointed inn up the Thames from London. Perry had arranged everything. He was an excellent planner. He showed no immediate sign, however, of moving on from there to Scotland.

The days passed slowly for his wife while Perry Miggs crept about London like a bewildered cat, poking into post offices, making inquiries, paying for everything in advance. He stopped in at a chemist's and, after some misunderstanding and explanation, purchased a large bottle of tablets. The chemist insisted on affixing a dire warning to the bottle.

"This is nothing to trifle with, sir," the chemist warned more than once. "Any mistake in the dosage, you understand, would be a dodgy thing."

"It is all right," Perry assured her. "I am a doctor of biology. I know how to handle toxins."

Perry's manner did not reassure her. He was ill at ease, self-conscious. The chemist hesitated, but he had produced the credentials he needed. She took his money and turned from the counter, trying to put her doubts away.

Miggs entered the red telephone booth outside the chemist's shop and dialed a number that he had called on the two previous days. He listened to a dead line for a long moment before he heard the gentle burping of the distant ring. The line rang four times before someone picked up.

"Hello?" Miggs shouted unnecessarily into the receiver. He was calling Scotland. "Is that Mrs. Shaw there? It's me again, Prof. Perry Miggs. Have you located him yet?"

"Yes, he's sitting oot the door, please hold the line."

Kira Shaw went through her front door to where the handsome man sat twirling his fingers through the tail of a ginger tabby tomcat that rubbed under his tented knees.

"Andrew, that call's come through for you."

"High time." He lifted himself from the ground with muscular dexterity, careful not to disturb the comfortable cat, and made his way to the telephone.

"Yes, sir?" he said into the handset. "Is this the professor that's been looking for me?"

"Yes," Miggs replied, "if you are Mr. Andrew Macgruer."

"I am. What's this aboot?"

"You are a difficult man to track," Miggs used his most cordial tone, filled with apology and self-deprecation.

"Am I? Why would you be tracking me?"

"I only mean, that is, I'm sorry," Miggs stammered in the telephone box, looking through the glass sides like a fish in a bowl. "I have started badly. I do apologize. I only meant to say that your friends there say you don't have a telephone."

"Nae," Macgruer agreed. "I dinnae care for them. They're intrusive. Besides, when am I ever home enough to answer one?"

"When indeed?" Miggs chimed up without really knowing anything about Andrew Macgruer or his habits.

"So, why have you been trying to reach me, Professor Miggs? Do I know you?"

"No, not in the least. But I know you. That is to say, I know *of* you."

The line was so quiet while Miggs awaited a reply that he was obliged finally to say "Hello?" into the receiver.

"So you know of me. What's there to know of me?"

"You were with one Prof. David Carlisle, late of St. Andrews University, last year. Is that right?"

There was another long pause on the line. Miggs began to repeat "Is that right?" when Macgruer broke in.

"Aye. Davey Carlisle died in my boat last June."

"David Carlisle of St. Andrews University?"

"Tha's right. He used to be. He was retired. What's this aboot?"

"I am with the Royal Geographic Society. I want to investigate the loch. Don't hang up."

"I was nae going to hang up," the Scotsman said, laughing slightly. "So you're with the Royal Geog and want to come up monster hunting?"

"Only in part. You see, I'm a marine biologist."

He paused to allow his credentials to sink down.

"I didnae think you were a vulcanographer."

"No," Miggs said, laughing self-consciously. "Quite right. Not a vulcanographer."

"So what does all this have to do wi' me? And what does Davey Carlisle have to do wi' anything?"

"I understand you were guiding him on the loch when he died," Miggs said. His palms had begun to sweat, and strain showed in his voice. Subconsciously, he began to roll the brown bottle of tablets in his pocket like a worry bead.

"You understand wrong. We were fishing. Davey Carlisle was a friend of mine from my university days. He was over on holiday."

"You were not his guide?"

"Nae."

"But you do sometimes act as a guide," Miggs said, grappling with the situation awkwardly. "That is, Mrs. Shaw there said you sometimes act as a guide."

"That's right."

Miggs relaxed. "Right. Good. I wish to hire your services to guide me on and around the loch."

Macgruer laughed.

"What's the matter? Why is that funny?"

"You dinnae know me. All you ken is Davey Carlisle died in my boat last year. You're a Yank claiming to be from the Royal Geog. And you want to hire me to guide you around the loch. You dinnae even know if I'm any good."

"I— I assure you," Miggs stammered, not keeping up with the last of Macgruer's observations, "I am from the Royal Geographic Society. It is true I am an American, but I am here on a very handsome grant from the Royal Geographic Society. I want to explore the flora and fauna of the loch's ecosystem." He paused while Macgruer's observations finally sank in. "*Are* you any good?"

Macgruer laughed. "Nae, sir. I'm the worst guide you could have chosen. So you are no' interested in the creature at all; is that right, sir?"

Miggs choked, the moment seemed again to be slipping past him. "I— I didn't say that, no. I am interested in the creature. What do you mean you are the worst guide?"

"I mean I'm the only guide on this side of the loch. That makes me the worst. It also makes me the best. You dinnae seem too concerned about whether I am the worst, though."

"Of course I am. Are you any good?" Miggs tried to muster some resolve.

"Passable. But I dinnae know that I'm interested. I'm a private sort, you see."

"I can make it well worth your time." He was no negotiator. "I've been given quite a lot of money to do this."

"Fifteen pounds each time we go oot?" Macgruer said. He decided to test the tremulous man's resolve. "And that's payable daily whether we find anything or no', and nocht—that is, nothing—to be refunded at the end. Right?"

"All right."

"How long will you be wanting my services, then?"

"Six months."

Macgruer only smiled on the other end of the line.

"Do we have a deal?" Miggs said.

"I'd be a fool to turn it down."

"One other thing. Can you drive a really big ship?"

"Nae. No' if you mean one of the Cunard liners."

"Not that big. Something more like a thirty-eight-to-forty-foot rig."

"That's what you mean by a big ship?" Macgruer laughed. "Aye, I can handle that, why? Are you bringing one up?"

"No, Mr. Macgruer, I need you to take it up for me, along with my wife and me. It's in Pembroke now—that's in Wales. I'll pay to have you meet us there and sail it up the coast and then up the waterway from Lismore to the loch. I'll make all the arrangements, but you'll have to drive the ship. Can you?"

"I can pilot her up, right enough. Question is, do I want to. When do you expect me to do all of this?"

"On your schedule. The sooner the better."

"Meet me in Pembroke Monday next, then. It will take us several days to sail her up, so be sure she's provisioned for four."

"There will only be the three of us," Miggs corrected apologetically.

"I'm bringing my son, Aidan."

Miggs was worried at first, then flummoxed. "Are you married? You have a son? I— I mean, that is, how old— won't y-y-your wife object? I mean— why? Is he a sailor?"

"He's a ten-year-old boy. I am bringing him wi' me because he's never been on the Irish Sea. That's part of my price; Aidan comes along. You arrange to have us both in Pembroke Monday or I'm no' coming."

"Yes. Yes, yes, all right. I'll arrange everything. You . . . and the boy."

"Dinnae sound so worried. He's a good lad."

"Very well."

Perry Miggs hung up the receiver. He dug his hands into his pockets and meandered through London with only half an aim in mind. He came at last to the Royal Geographical Society.

He found a capacious armchair in the RGS foyer and settled himself into it. The docent, an aged woman with sharp heels and stray hair like steel, passed him several times before stopping at last before him.

"Yes?" she said in a businesslike but not unkindly manner.

Perry smiled at the professional woman rather helplessly.

"I am supposed to have a meeting with the Royal Geog people this afternoon."

"I see," the docent replied. "With whom did you have your appointment?"

"I'm sorry?"

"Whom are you meeting?"

"Oh." Perry shrank back into the cushions. "I'm not meeting anyone. I am only *supposed* to have a meeting here. That is, I mean my wife supposes I have a meeting. I haven't any meeting."

"No?" The firm woman relaxed her facade a little. There was

something charming about the little man in the armchair. He seemed exposed, intimidated, helpless.

"I wouldn't have my wife think I hadn't come here for the world," he explained.

"Is that important to her?"

"It is important to me," he said with a gravity that made the woman cock an eyebrow involuntarily. "She can't think I've lied to her. She must never think it. So if I really come here I can tell her I did. And she can believe it."

The little man smiled at the woman.

"I am about to do something—" he looked suddenly dark and severe. "I am about to do something kinda against the grain for me. Pretty much out of character. But it is a secret."

"Are you deceiving your wife, then?" the docent asked airily, hardly believing it.

"I said I would come here, and I did."

"But that's just a prevarication, isn't it?" she teased. "You were also supposed to meet someone."

"Yeah," Perry replied, troubled. "But I have met you."

The docent flashed a superior sort of look at Perry and shook her head.

"Still," he went on quickly, "I've been a long time getting things fixed up here in London. Too long. And now to wait until Monday for the boat—"

The docent did not follow his ramblings as he mumbled about High Street postal boxes and Highland appointments.

"But it's all been necessary," he concluded. "And I wouldn't have her suspect for a moment. If she suspected even for a moment why we're going to Scotland—why we are *really* going to Scotland— everything would be ruined. Just ruined."

"And why might that be?" The woman suddenly felt uncomfortable. She caught a glimpse of the brown bottle he was fingering. It had a red label with a skull on it. He was not nearly so helpless as she first thought, not nearly so innocent.

"Why would it be ruined?" Perry Miggs echoed. He looked up suddenly and snapped, "I want to show her—" he stopped abruptly, the fire flitted away behind the owlish spectacles. He shrugged.

"I just want to show her, that's all."

# Chapter 3

❖

Andrew Macgruer awoke early that Sunday morning and dressed:
rough linen shirt, waistcoat, and a tartan plaid wrap of Hunting
Fraser design. He slung a rough pack across his back. It was laden
only with necessities: two linen shirts like the one he wore, shoes and
stockings for the streets of Inverness and when he met the American,
food enough for the long walk up the loch into town, and the note in
the blue envelope. His dirk was at his side, and his personal things
were in his sporran.

He tickled the marmalade tabby under the chin as he left his home.

"There's moles and mice aplenty, cat," he said to the tom. "Make the
best use of them. I'll no' be back until week's end."

The tomcat arched along Macgruer's bare legs, curling its tail
around his knee. His purr rumbled in the darkness of morning and
filled the clearing in front of the house with a sense of insular sanc-
tuary.

"That's a good lad," Macgruer cooed to the muscular animal.

Macgruer lived in a bothy up in the ragged woodland cliffs that
climbed into the Monadhliath range. Below him lay the tumbling village of Iubhar, a scant armload of houses and outbuildings clinging to

the wide furrow leading out of the loch like a half-drowned mariner just pulling himself ashore. Through the midst of Iubhar ran the *grá*, a sweetwater stream that tumbled down the mountainside toward the loch.

The sun was only dawning beyond the Monadhliath Mountains as he set out. It lightened the sky and painted the far opposite shore of Loch Ness with thin tendrils of gold. But Iubhar, the *grá*, and his cottage were still bundled in night.

He stripped the dead twigs from a fallen branch as he traversed the slope leading down and used it for a walking stick. The brindled marmalade tom followed him for a quarter mile until he was distracted by the scurry of rodents among leaves. Macgruer worked his way to a woodland path and from there to the main road up the southeastern bank to Inverness.

The main road is scarcely traveled during the week proper, but on Sunday in the early morning it is nothing more than a wide, paved footpath, and Andrew Macgruer walked down the center of it without a thought to vehicles.

Inverness was a journey of eleven or twelve miles from Iubhar. Macgruer would make good time if he arrived by ten o'clock. He wanted to arrive early. He needed to. He would have to find a public washroom and groom himself, as he always did around city people. He would have a light wash, put on one of the fresh shirts in his pack, and brush out his wavy auburn hair and ragged beard. The long tartan wrap, an ancient *breacan an fheil,* would have to be rewound, too. He would turn it to the city side, the side that had not been picked and pilled by the woods. He would throw it over his shoulder, wrapping it around his waist and securing it with a belt from which he would rehang his sporran and dirk.

He would find his usual washroom and drench, scrape, and rewind himself until he shone like a copper platter. Only then would he present himself to Meg.

All of his preparations were necessary because he was about to kidnap his son.

He waited, polished and presentable, outside the Presbyterian Church where he knew they would be that morning.

He watched the congregation spill into the streets of Inverness, hollow-eyed people trudging past the posted sermon notice, LOVE IS NOT JEALOUS. Aidan appeared beside his mother at the church door, his hair plastered down until it almost appeared as if someone had painted the color onto a knob. Very proper, very confined—wholly Meg's boy. Meg passed a few comments with the minister before turning to see her former husband in the street.

"Hello, Andrew."

"Hello, Meg."

"Have you eaten yet today?" she asked with a mixture of consternation and concern.

"Breakfast."

"Come on, then. I'll buy you a proper lunch. I promised Aidan we would eat in town today, besides. You'd best come along now, before someone thinks you've been set here by the tourist board for photographs."

"Someone already has," Macgruer said, grinning through his beard. "Three times while I waited."

"Bloody tourists." She did not approve of Andrew Macgruer's life choice, could not live with it, certainly. But she understood him—moderately—and appreciated his reasons. The thought of him being diminished like that, made picturesque and quaint, angered her vaguely. She did not know, though, whether she was angry with the tourists who photographed him or with Macgruer for letting them. "Come on, then."

They went to a modest shop around from the church and ordered lunch.

"You're looking well, Andrew," she said at the table.

"And you."

Margaret Macgruer was attractive at thirty-six, a petite school-teacher with aspirations only to rear her son and teach geography to the yearly crop of eight-to-twelve-year-olds that crowded through the school door every fall.

"What brings you to Inverness today?" she asked.

"I've come to take young Aidan fishing." He was hope-filled and boyish in the request, and made Meg smile.

Aidan sat bolt upright with anticipation. Meg looked compassionately at her son.

"Oh, I don't know, Andrew," she said. "It's a full week for him at school. They're having an important comprehensive examination on Friday. I think it would be best if he used this day for study."

She stroked her son's face, wiping away the disappointment she found there. He was a polite boy and did not protest, but his feelings were clearly hurt.

"We could bring his school books along," Andrew said. "I can help him study while we pass."

"No, Andrew. I don't know." She was wavering. Both Andrew and Aidan sensed it.

"Is it you dinnae think I'm up to tutoring him?" Andrew said.

Meg screwed up her face at him. Of course Andrew Macgruer could tutor Aidan. He was not only educated at the finest university in the British Isles, but he was also the smartest man she knew.

"It's not entirely that," she said.

"What then?"

"Are you planning to have him out the day?" she said. "Because I'll no' have you two going out in that little rowboat of yours."

When she had learned that they had nearly capsized last June while out fishing in the dark of the night, when Professor Carlisle had died on the loch, she had forbidden Aidan ever to go out in the boat again.

"There were extenuating circumstances."

"I understand," she replied. "And I am sorry for good Mr. Carlisle,

Andrew, but I just don't think it is safe to take Aidan out on the loch in that tiny boat. I won't have it. Promise me you'll no' go out on that boat."

"Verra weel, I promise."

"How then will you go fishing? Don't tell me Andrew Macgruer is about to sit along the bank with a bent pin and bit of cane. Or are you taking him angling?" Both suggestions struck her as preposterous.

"We'll go out on a hired boat somewhere down the bank."

"Where would you be getting the money for that?"

Macgruer fished a handful of notes from his sporran and laid them on the table.

"Where did you get all of that?"

"Murdering and thieving, mainly," he said. "The rest came from raiding the herds of my neighbors."

Aidan laughed behind his hand, his eyes dancing. Meg smirked at Andrew.

"Really?" she insisted.

"I've been hired on to guide some American on the loch next week. He sent this along in earnest."

"Another one?" Meg was clearly exasperated. "How many does that make through Inverness this year? Why can't they just leave it be? Even if there were a ferlie in the loch, what good will come of finding it? Bloody tourists."

"May I take my son fishing, Meg?"

Meg relented. "When will you have him home, then?" Aidan nearly burst with glee.

"Before his test on Friday, anyway."

"Andrew—!"

"All right. No later than nine."

"Six," Meg began the usual negotiations.

"Nine," Andrew said firmly. There was to be no bartering out his son's time today.

"Nine, then," Meg said. "But you will be careful."

She said it sternly, as though she had given nothing away, as though she were a hard negotiator getting her way. But nobody was fooled, herself least. How, after all, could she refuse a man who routinely walked eleven miles to be with his son?

"Of course we will," Andrew said. "Now, let's go around and pick up his school things."

Aidan's books, pencils, and pads were crowded into the pack with Andrew's extra shirts. Andrew also took the opportunity to pack fresh clothes for his son while Meg was not looking, and finished by leaving the note in the blue envelope on the kitchen table.

Aidan was not particularly surprised when his father walked with him to the train station. They had gone to Aviemore before to fish in the Spey, but it had not been a good outing. His father did not like river fishing. Nevertheless, Aidan thought they were going to give it another go. But when Andrew Macgruer did not offer to get off the train at Aviemore, Aidan grew curious.

"Where are we going, Father?" he asked.

"Edinburgh."

"Edinburgh!" Aidan was momentarily excited, then puzzled. "But that's hours away. We'll hardly be there before we have to come back. What kind of fishing is in Edinburgh?"

"We aren't stopping to fish," his father said.

"Then what will we do in Edinburgh?"

"We'll head on to Newcastle, then to York, to Manchester, and Birmingham. It will be dark by then, so we'll sleep there."

"What is in Birmingham?"

"The morning train to Cardiff that'll take us out to Pembroke. Ten hours today, five tomorrow."

"Mother's going to be furious."

"Verra probably."

"You told her you'd have me back before nine."

"I didn't say nine today," Macgruer said flatly.

"You lied!"

"No, Son, it is a wicked thing to lie. I told your mother the truth. She just didnae hear it. I told her I'd have you home for your examination

Friday. I told her I'd help you study. I told her you would be home afore nine. If I have you home at nine o'clock before your test on Friday, I will no' have lied."

Aidan accepted the explanation immediately and began to bubble in anticipation of his windfallen holiday. "Why are we going to Pembroke?"

"I've told you," Andrew said, then corrected himself, "I told your mother. There is an American wants me to guide him on the loch. He has a boat hired at Pembroke I'm to sail up for him."

"You said we were going down the bank from Inverness," Aidan said, catching up his father.

"Pembroke is down the bank from Inverness," Andrew replied. "A verra great deal of the world is down the bank from Inverness. You have never been on the Irish Sea, Aidan. You have never been anywhere but that small world at the point of the earth where nae one comes—nae one but the self-deluded and the mystery hunters. Only sad people go there, and desperate. There's nothing for a young mind to learn from sadness and desperation."

He unlatched his pack and pulled out one of his son's texts.

"Here are the facts and figures of life—our history and knowledge, Son. This is verra important to know, but it is only an anchor to life, no' life itself."

Andrew Macgruer laid his head on the chair cushion, his face close to his son's.

"I am a poor man, Aidan," he said. "I am poor by choice, though, and am proud to confront the day rather than meet it on the road like a stranger. But, because I am poor, I have nocht but myself to give you. This may be my one chance to give you a wee bit of the world. I hope and believe you are old enough to understand that, Son. The world is no' to be passed through but savored, broken open like eggs and sucked. I want to show you how, my lad, and this may be my only chance."

They worked on Aidan's studies for a while and watched the country speed past from their windows. They ate supper in the York station and saw the sun set between Manchester and Birmingham. They arrived late in Birmingham and slept at a Moat House overnight.

❖

*It is seven hours from London to Pembroke, four hundred twenty minutes. The last bit, Carmarthen to Pembroke, looks short enough on the map, but in reality it is a tortured one-and-a-quarter hours. The views all along the way are spectacular, I guess, but I couldn't enjoy them at all. There are such castles and splendors to be seen along the way, and Perry, equipped with his red book, was anxious that I should not miss a single medieval pile or glimpse of south-facing coastline.*

*Perry hardly needed the Baedeker's that day, however. There was a boy, he must have come aboard at Bristol, who proved a harbinger to every sight worth seeing. For every turret, every sea view (no matter how obscured by the rain that constantly fell during the final four hours of the journey), for every mark or patch or high place to be noted, he would appear like a Mother Carrie's chicken at the front of our car, staring in rapt satisfaction at the spectacle of whatever landmark had captured his attention.*

*He was a handsome lad with long chestnut hair parted sharply in the middle and a keen, intelligent look in his eye. That eye would remain fixed on whatever object had caught his imagination, and he would pass through the car toward the back of the train and out into the next compartment, never wavering. In another few minutes, I would see him dashing forward again, the spectacle having vanished from view from the back of the train, only to reappear at the next marvel of hillside or shrine.*

*I don't think Perry noticed the boy, though, entrenched as he was in the guidebook, his only anxiety to read the short description to me in time to glance up at the sight himself as it passed across our field of view.*

*But I was hardly in the mood to have my breath taken; I did not care to stare in mute wonder at Wales. Not Wales.*

*Perry spent the first leg of our journey, Paddington to Bath, being disappointed by the utilitarian train cars.*

*"I always imagined them differently, somehow," he complained. "All, I don't know, polished wood and etched glass with private compartments and*

*sinister characters with mustaches and linen suits, wearing hats and lurking about."*

*"You're thinking of Agatha Christie movie trains."*

*"Yes. She's English, isn't she? I never expected this on an English train. They're too much like— like—"*

*He'd arrive at a simile soon.*

*"—like New York or, or Detroit city buses, aren't they?"*

*"A little."*

*"I hope the boat thing is more—" he searched again "—appropriate."*

*"It must be. It's what they use at the Royal Geographic Society to do what you're going to be doing, isn't it?"*

*"I think so," he said, doubt creeping in. "I did tell them what I needed it for."*

*"Then it will be just fine," I assured him. "Enjoy the view."*

*I counted minutes while he counted castles.*

*Finally, on the final spur into Pembroke, he got up.*

*"Lav run," he announced. So far, it was the only British expression he'd assimilated. He'd heard it said precisely once at the inn restaurant. The man who'd said it was from Florida, but I didn't tell Perry. To his mind, he had gone quite native.*

*He kissed my cheek and left toward the back of the car.*

*In another moment, he was back, muttering, "Out of time," and we were pulling into Pembroke.*

# Chapter 4

✤

The light rain that had begun in Bristol continued to fall in Pembroke. I stood in the sheltering eaves of the harbormaster's hut while Perry went in to announce us to whoever might care to know we'd arrived.

He appeared a few minutes later, with a man dressed to the toes in black oilskins. He had a comically large umbrella and escorted Perry and me to the end of a dock to the little motor launch.

"She's been stocked as you requested, Mr. Miggs," the man said as he flipped the switches that woke the engines into protesting grumbles. The sea heaved white behind the launch, and the little motorboat staggered away from the dock like a morning before coffee.

The rain whipped across us, and the wind threatened to throw up the skirts of the umbrella, so we folded in the harboring canopy and braved the wet.

Our destination was a large craft anchored a few hundred feet away. It was a sleek vessel with a lean mast and antennæ like thorns bristling from its brow.

I know nothing of watercraft, less even than Perry, who knows little enough, so to say that the boat was a ship or a yacht or a cruiser or a yawl or a schooner would be all the same to me. If it stays afloat while I am aboard, and keeps its deck and masts pointed toward the stars, I am

31

satisfied to call it any sort of boat there is. So I will call this a schooner, mostly because I like the word—it trails across my tongue like lake breezes in summer—but also because I have always associated schooners with sleekness and polish, and that was my first impression of this craft.

She was an older vessel, scarred along her sides and faded into elegance along her wood and fittings. She rode on the chop like a lazy seabird, and I was amused to see that her name was Pelican. Her lazy liftings and fallings made gaining purchase of the short few rungs of her ladder difficult, but we managed to climb aboard, and while Perry checked everything below with the harbor man, I huddled under the umbrella on deck and shivered in the breeze lolling up from the sea.

The Pelican was "yair," I would learn that later from the harbor man when he came topside with Perry again; though I never would learn what "yair" meant, I gathered from his tone that "yair" was an admirable thing for a boat to be. I decided to make "yair" mean "fitted," for so she was. Her decks and rails were deeply polished. I think they might have been made of teak. There were dark lines, like pitch, between her planks, which somehow made her feel solid and firm. Her brasswork did not shine but rather glowed with a patina of age that reflected the cloud-crowded sky and black sea.

While waiting for the men to return to the deck, I listened to the wind spin around the mast and send her couplings dancing and clanging softly. I wondered idly if this is what it was to be lost at sea, becalmed, to be rocked and cooed into the depths of the ocean until life and water were one. It made me wish for islands and rock, and, when I opened my eyes again, I found Perry back on deck bidding the harbor man farewell.

I went below, out of the rain. Perry followed.

"We'll be casting off," he said, "or I suppose weighing anchor would be more precise, just as soon as our captain joins us."

"What are you doing?" I laughed at him as he staggered through our little cabin, grappling with his suitcase.

"I have brought a little— artifact. I got it back in the States."

He fished out a small cardboard box labeled "Brookstone" and opened it. Inside was an elastic band with a plastic bead sewn into its web. He strapped it around his wrist, the bead against his pulse.

"For seasickness. Can't take any chances."

I laughed. I had forgotten how we'd honeymooned on Mackinac Island, and he'd become sick on the boat over. I'd teased him for it: the marine biologist with mal de mer.

Mackinac took me back. It has been thirteen years. I was only twenty-five, he thirty-seven. It's hard to recognize him now from those pictures pasted in our album. That was before he'd lost all of his weight and his flesh had begun to sag and wobble.

He was a different man on Mackinac, so much younger, not only thirteen years but a whole lifetime younger. He was an ambitious lover, too. We were well matched. Nightly bouts of love, sometimes twice. It slowed after the honeymoon, of course. But still, four times a week wasn't odd for us, not during the first year.

We'd talked of children then, and I had planned. I would have liked to have had children with Perry. I would like to have Perry's children with me now, I think. Perhaps children would have helped keep Perry young and ambitious.

But I got sick then, and he was sick with worry over me. Then I got better. But he did not recover, and all his drive seemed to drain off with the flesh. His vitality dwindled away so quickly, so quickly.

"It works by accupressure," Perry said as he strapped on the seasickness bead. "I think it will probably work."

"You didn't get one for me?"

"Yes, I bought two, but you're never sick, are you? And I just might use the other one around my left wrist if I feel the need."

We laughed.

"And when are we expecting our captain?"

"He should be here at any time, really. If he made all of his connections, he should have joined our train in Bristol and been with us the rest of the way. I'm sure he'll be along soon. Meantime, I'm going to check around up in the— the— I don't know what to call it; bridge seems too grand."

"Pilot house? Helm?" I suggested, as benighted as my husband.

"Whatever," he shrugged. "There are supposed to be all sorts of electronic listeners and lookers and gizmos and stuff. I think I'll try to find the manuals and begin learning how to run them."

*"Take this," I said as he began out, and threw the other accupressure band to him. "Put it on so you don't lose it."*

*He smiled and scooted out, strapping the cuff to his left wrist as he went. "There're provisions in the— er— galley down there if you get hungry," he shouted in from the rain.*

*"Thanks."*

*I was a little hungry, so I went to the tiny area where the minia-ture kitchen heaved like a doll's house on the wave. I opened the play-refrigerator's door.*

*Ah, Great Britain!*

*I blessed the harbor man secretly. Here were the treasures of my year in Scotland: the sharp, rich cheeses, pickled this and that in tins and tiny jars, and the nutty brown ales I'd learned to love at university that year. How it all took me back. I wondered if the ale would still tingle on my tongue and feel rather than taste tart.*

*I opened one of the friendly, fat bottles and tipped it up so warily one might have thought I expected poison. I was that nervous. What if it was dif-ferent? Same bottle, same label, same everything. Perhaps it would expose my most secret misgiving that I had changed. The nutty brown ale suddenly loomed like some godawful examination, comprehensive and final, a test of my worthiness to enter upon this last leg of my journey back. A litmus.*

*It trickled past my lips and touched the tip of my quivering tongue.*

*It flowed in memory, a flood of recollection. I suddenly smelled the aroma of the North Sea again as it broke over the pier at St. Andrews, felt the rough stone of the West Port again. My body tingled as it had the first time I'd entered the crisp water at the Castle Bathing Pool.*

*I nuzzled the bottle, and large, foolish, grateful tears rolled from me. It was all still there. Every trace, every nuance of that magical year, so long buried in the back cupboards of my hopes, was whole, fresh, clean, and un-tattered by the moths of time.*

*I must have spent an hour with that bottle, savoring it by the drop, so afraid that this might be the last bottle of wonder, the final distilling of that cherished past.*

*I was dripping out the last, as cautious as a Père Gaucher, when a boy en-*
*tered the cabin. He was streaked with rain and looked like a drowned rat.*

*"Father said for me to wait below while we set out."*

*I swept up towels and wrapped them around the child, squeezing his hair*
*dry and polishing his clothes with the rough cloth. I hadn't stopped to won-*
*der who he was or who his father might be to tell him to wait below. I only*
*saw him shiver.*

*"Your father is the captain?" I asked as I scoured his head, rubbing in*
*warmth and out wet.*

*"Captain?" he said. "Father? Aye, I suppose he is." He smiled at the*
*thought. It concerned me that he did not immediately think of his father, our*
*captain, as a ship's master.*

*He was a handsome child, with wide eyes and full lips as red as his*
*cheeks, like pale apples against milk-white skin. His hair was a lustrous*
*brown that shone red as blood in places where the light struck. That hair*
*was so much like my own that I played for a moment with the thought that*
*he could indeed have been my own child. The ale had made me just that fan-*
*ciful; I thought again of Perry's children that were not to be, and on an im-*
*pulse I hugged this lovely little stranger to me.*

*How improper! What must this child think of the clinging madwoman*
*below decks? I caught myself at once.*

*"There now," I said and ran my hands up and down his arms to create*
*some warmth, covering up my outburst, "is that better? Warming up a bit?"*

*"Aye," he said, not the least perturbed, "thank you, miss."*

*I liked it that he called me "miss." It encouraged me to feel young, which*
*is desperately how I wanted to feel now that the engines were vibrating*
*below and I could sense that we were headed at last for Scotland, my*
*Scotland.*

*"What's your name?" I asked the boy.*

*"Aidan."*

*"Very well, Aidan, call me Perdita."*

*I took the towel from around his head, and his long hair fell into a natu-*
*ral part down the middle of his scalp. He was suddenly familiar.*

*"Why, you're the boy on the train. You were very interested in the land-scape coming in, weren't you?"*

*"Aye, miss, my father is showing me the world."*

✤

The rain continued to fall gently as the vessel rounded St. David's Head.

"We head out into open water from here until we hit Braich-y-Pwll on the north end of Cardigan Bay," Andrew said to Perry, who had found the equipment manuals and was studying them. "We should see it before nightfall. I'd like to hug the coast from there to Holyhead in case we need to put in along the way. We'll stop at Holy Island tonight; we should be there by ten or eleven at the latest. If everything is quiet tomorrow morning, we'll head out into open water again and stop at the Isle of Man for a rest. We'll leave again before nightfall and rest at Ard-lussa in the sound. We'll sail up the Caledonian Canal into the loch and go on into Inverness on Thursday."

"Why are we going all the way to Inverness?"

"I promised the boy's mother to have him back before Friday."

"Cutting it awfully close, aren't you?" Perry said. "I mean starting out Thursday morning from the other side of Scotland."

Andrew shrugged. "If we dinnae make it we dinnae make it."

"We could drive on at night, if you're in a hurry," Perry offered. "I don't mind."

"Can you sail?"

"No," Perry stammered, flustered.

"I thought not. I'll have to sleep sometime, won't I?"

"Yes," Perry said. "Of course you will. I'm sorry not to have considered that."

Andrew shrugged again. "It's no' important."

"Thank you."

"I'm nae great hand at open-water navigation, either," Andrew said. "Night would only compound our problems, and, besides, I want the lad to see a bit of the world, so we'll sail by daylight. Have you arranged our passage up the canal?"

"Yes," Perry replied. "I bought the six-month summer license by mail. No problem."

"We can make the passage in fourteen hours if we time ourselves right," Macgruer said. "Then we ought to be in Inverness by late supper Thursday, not that the lad's mother will be inclined to give us any when we arrive."

He laughed. Perry did not understand why.

Across the mouth of Cardigan Bay, Perry toyed with one particular piece of equipment he had been reading up on.

"It's some kind of sonar," he said to Andrew and Aidan, who had joined them. "There are three beacons, called transducers, housed on the bottom of the boat— the, er, hull. The beacons can triangulate any depth down to four hundred feet and follow an object. The manual was written by a fellow who used it to explore sunken ships from the surface down in the Caribbean."

"It just finds sunken pirate ships?" Aidan said.

"In a way, yes," Perry said. "They take soundings and reproduce an image on this television screen. That way, this fellow says, they can sail right over a shipwreck and the beacons will lock onto it and scan it even before the ship has a chance to stop, and they don't lose its position."

"Super!" Aidan said. "Can we give it a go?"

"Yes," Perry said. "I was just going to."

Perry pecked at the keyboard tentatively, checking the manual repeatedly as he did. But, though he was cautious, the screen only bounced and produced an INPUT UNRECOGNIZED message.

Perry cleared the screen and tried again. Again he failed.

"Here. Let me read the instructions aloud and let you type them in."

"Who? Me?" Aidan could hardly contain himself.

"Yes, why not?"

The operation was successful. In the next moment, the screen flipped twice, began to roll, and then balanced itself between the frames of the monitor. Random sparkles of white played across the screen like a light snowfall before the machine made an audible click and began to hum. Suddenly the screen was alive with a thin, white line snaking across; the beacons were tracking something. The display at the bottom of the screen read 47 METRES.

"What is it?" Aidan said.

"Well, let's try to see. There's a way to enhance once an object is located," Perry said and read the sequence of instructions to Aidan, who typed as he did.

The white snake clarified into an image, not quite photographic in quality, but obviously an image of a school of fish. The individuals could be clearly seen.

"There," Perry said, very satisfied. "The manual warned about the beacons locking onto fish, but I think it's kind of pretty. Very lovely in its way—not buried treasure or Spanish galleons, though, is it?"

Andrew said quietly, "It ought to be verra helpful in your researches."

"The manual says it can also record onto magnetic tape like a video camera," Perry said. "But I haven't any tape on the boat, and that's a shame."

Perry bent down to the monitor and examined the image.

"You see," he said to Aidan, "these are haddock, *Melanogrammus œglefinus*. If this were a better sort of picture you could identify them by the big blotchy patch just behind their gills. It's called Saint Peter's thumbprint."

"You ken all about fish," Aidan said, impressed.

"I teach about fish where I'm from."

"And it's about time you started learning something on your own, lad," Andrew said. "I promised your mother you'd study while you were out wi' me. Go on below now and get some reading in. I'll call you when we sight land again."

Aidan sighed. "Everybody's a teacher on this boat."

"Are— are you a teacher, too, Mr. Macgruer?" Perry asked.

"Used to be," Andrew replied. "Literature. And my former wife, the lad's mother, teaches geography, so the lad feels a little like he's never out of school. But whoever is?"

"He'll like it below, then," Perry said. "Perdita isn't a teacher at all."

"Perdita?" Andrew's eyebrows raised and his grip tightened on the wheel.

"My wife. I did tell you my wife was with me?"

"It's just that it's an unusual sort of a name."

Perry went below, where his wife was trying to read. Without asking if she wanted any, he warmed some tinned milk on the burner. He glanced around at her to make certain she was engrossed in the book before quietly tipping out two orange tablets from the brown bottle. He used the back of a spoon to crush them. He sprinkled the powder into the milk and stirred it in.

"Here's some warm milk," he said softly to her, pressing the glass into her hands. "It will help you sleep."

Cardigan Bay was a five-hour crossing. The vessel cut across choppy seas as the rain continued to fall. The day offered only slight visibility, but they passed Bardsey Island as the sun was setting and saw Braich-y-Pwll in the distance just before dark.

"A verra unusual sort of a name," Andrew whispered again as he dropped anchor.

# Chapter 5

✤

We seemed ages skirting through Caernarvon Bay between our meeting land again at Braich-y-Pwll and reaching Holy Island. The coastline slipped past us under the moonless, cloud-filtered sky, unrelieved by the welcome light of a landward home. We finally dropped our anchor and the monotonous engines muttered into silence. I was unable to sleep despite having a warm milky drink; my head ached with the engine sound, but I could dream perfectly.

Things will be different in Scotland. I will be different, too. In Scotland, I'm another person. Even my name changes there. In Larchmont, they call me PurDEEta and Perdie, but in Scotland, where every tongue is lapped in music and words flow as sweetly as water, I am always PÆRdita. It sounds like a dance, and I am never tired of hearing it said.

"Perdita," Perry's voice woke me. It was daylight already and bright under heavy skies.

I opened an eye to see Perry. He was sitting beside me, with our captain behind him, a handsome man with a rough beard.

"Am I disturbing you, darling?" Perry said.

"Not at all, I had to wake up anyway to see who was prodding me."

"Perdita, this is our captain, Mr. Macgruer."

I looked up at him, a smiling and pleasant-seeming man. I had a momentary impression of a rugby field, drenched in mud and struggling young men. I stared past the beard and into the eyes, brown as chocolate, and I recognized him. My heart leaped. It was too impossible.

His eyes were bright as fire, just as I had remembered them, and he stared down into me as a man staring into a deep pool.

"Surely not Andrew Macgruer?" I said as I held out my hand to him. I'm sure I must have bubbled like a schoolgirl with a crush.

I thought I saw his eyes puddle at the question. Was it just wishful thinking on my part? He looked grateful for a moment, but then he looked away. He looked up toward the deck. Was he drinking back tears? Odd. With a collected breath, he turned back to meet my eyes again. The fire was gone, the deep pool of tears, too. He was suddenly serene and reserved, distant as an oak tree in winter.

"Aye," he said quietly and took my hand. "I am Andrew Macgruer. I'm sorry— have we met?"

The question shook me, but I held onto his hand, allowing him to help me to my feet. "At university," I said. "At St. Andrews. I was there in my junior year. We had some classes together. Latin composition for one."

"Aye." I could tell from his response that he at least remembered the Latin composition.

"Perdita," I prompted.

"Perdita, of course," he said; some glimmerings began to creep through—not enough. "Perdita—"

"Leal," I gave my maiden name, still smiling, even cordial, though I was cold inside, in the very sink of disappointment.

"Perdita Leal! Yes, how foolish of me. How utterly stupid. You were Melanie's friend, weren't you? Melanie—" again he grappled for a last name, but this time he found it. "Melanie Torrence."

Melanie Torrence was a horrible creature I'd met on the flight over to Scotland. She was from Charlotte or Winston-Salem or some other tobacco-patch place, and I would hardly have called her my friend.

"Yes," I replied, for in truth I didn't know what else to say, not with Perry standing there. "Melanie Torrence's friend."

"Welcome back," he said with the cordiality reserved for strangers, and released my hand. "Welcome back to Scotland."

"Thank you."

I spent the rest of the morning brooding on the back deck of the Pelican.

"Nutty brown ale be damned," I muttered to myself as I watched the sea. Dark clouds were piling up on the western horizon.

I had remembered Scotland well enough—too well, I think. But Scotland had obviously not remembered me. How could Andrew Macgruer, of all men—of all Scotsmen—not have recognized me? Andrew Macgruer!

Perhaps he was only pretending. Yes, Perry was close by. There was that initial fire in his lovely eyes. That must be it. He could have hardly thrown his arms about me and cried. "My darling, at last you have returned," now, could he? Still, he might not have recognized me. It had been years. Or perhaps—I hated to think it—he had forgotten. Forgetting is an intentional act, I think, like dragging garbage to the curb in pails; it is a process, routine and effective, of doing away with what is no longer desired.

I struggled on the back deck between my disappointment, the blow to my ego, and my desire to pick up and go on as I had been ten minutes before seeing Andrew Macgruer again. But it was no use. Pride is the tenderest flesh and swells quickest when nettled. It won't be soothed; it can't be ignored.

I feasted on gall and spleen that morning and had no appetite for breakfast when Perry came to call me in.

"She says she isn't hungry," Perry Miggs said as he sat down to the cabin table. "I hope she isn't getting seasick."

"I think she looks like Mummy," Aidan observed before filling his mouth.

"Aye," Macgruer said after a moment's thought. "She does favor your mother a bit around the eye."

"How long will it be to the Isle of Man?" Perry asked.

"Between four and six hours if luck holds. It'll be a tricky crossing in open water, nothing like what we've had. The Irish Sea can be tricky."

"I thought we were already in the Irish Sea."

"Saint George's Channel. We'll be in the Irish once we round Holy Island."

"What makes the island holy?" Aidan asked.

"There was a monastery there once. Some say God was so pleased with the work there that He threw a moat around their monastery to protect them forever, and that is why it is an island and holy to this day."

"Is that true?" Aidan said, wide-eyed.

"As true as anything your minister preaches on Sundays," Andrew replied.

Aidan breathed "Smashing," and Perry smiled.

"Isn't it getting late?" Perry said. "Shouldn't we be getting on our way soon?"

"There's a storm blowing in. It wouldn't do to be in the middle of the Irish with an April squall rising. We'll sit it out here."

"I thought you were in a hurry to get to Inverness," Perry said.

"I am," Macgruer replied like a man in no hurry at all. "But I'll make what time I can when I can. There's no advantage in pushing forward now only to be pushed back."

They finished their breakfast, and Andrew sat down with Aidan to read through his son's lessons. They took frequent breaks to look through the tiny cabin windows and stroll the forward deck together.

"He loves that boy very much," Perry said to his wife on the aft deck.

"Yes, he does."

✤

*I watched the western clouds grow blacker and tumble through the sky toward us, bringing a storm. The pioneer clouds that drifted above dropped a light sprinkle that hardly washed the deck, and I let the tender rain find me where I lay.*

*A little after nine, Andrew Macgruer came and leaned on the railing beside me.*

*"I am sorry I didnae recognize you at first," he said with the easy grace I remembered so well.*

*"It's really quite all right," I said, but of course it was not all right at all. When he didn't speak, I continued. "It was a long time ago," I said, and "I could hardly expect you to remember," and "So very much has happened since that time," but, of course, all my apologies on his behalf rang hollow.*

*He continued through my blind stumbling to stare at me with a mixture of wonder and compassion that bordered on pity. It annoyed me. And, in annoyance, I finally picked up truth like a cudgel.*

*"No, Mr. Macgruer," I said in an angry whisper that Perry would not hear. "In point of final fact, it's not quite all right at all. It's all wrong, in fact. Here I've been, for the better part of the last twenty or so years cherishing, even worshipping my memories of Scotland—and you've figured very large in those memories, you should know. Very large. Eclipsingly large, as a matter of absolute fact."*

*He continued to regard me with the flat expression of earnest comprehension.*

*"I haven't any right to feel this way," I continued, trying to untangle myself from my feelings. "But you promised to write. You really did promise. You were going to write a great work of poetry for me, you said."*

*"I am sorry," he said again with the same level compassion he had said it before.*

*Infuriatingly honest. Blunt and honest as a mallet.*

*"Yes," I said and looked to sea. "Well, it doesn't really matter, does it? I'm sorry I was so—tactless." It was a weak word to use, but all my words felt inadequate just then.*

*He continued to regard me with that same dejected look, the mild compassion of a bystander at an auto accident.*

*"Look, I've accepted your apology. Please go away."*

*He did.*

*How I loathed myself then. I had said everything wrong. Everything childish and wrong.*

"Damn," I whispered, and with that word the rains began to fall.

I went below to Perry. He was worried that I had not eaten breakfast and insisted that I drink some juice at least, which I did, to humor him.

The winds picked up, and we rocked violently in every direction. Perry continually unstrapped and restrapped his wristbands, adjusting them and rereading the instructions. I could see he was growing ill with the thrashing about. He turned pale, then green, on the bed of our little cabin.

By four o'clock, the worst of the storm seemed to have passed. The motors under us began to growl, and I could feel us moving forward. Poor Perry, how the movement threw him into new waves of misery.

The rains were still pelting, and I wondered aloud why we should have to sail through such weather.

"He has a promise to keep," Perry was barely able to whisper in his agony.

Finally he began to heave, and I grabbed the first convenient vessel I could find. It was the enameled washbasin Andrew had used last night for his shirts. Perry vomited into the enameled bowl again and again; the sight of his own vomit sickened him worse, and he vomited yet again until there was nothing left to vomit. Then he heaved without effect until he was too exhausted even to do that. I wiped his poor head with a cool cloth and spoke gently to him, but he only fixed his eyes on the floor, unrelieved by his purgations.

"Poor lamb," I whispered to him and kissed his forehead to give him strength. "Poor, tender lamb. Hold on now, darling, we'll be at the Isle of Man soon. You'll feel better then. Just hold on. This isn't going to kill you."

"That's what I'm afraid of," he muttered pathetically.

# Chapter 6

✤

Perry had not recovered by the time we reached the Isle of Man.

"I'll take him ashore tonight," Andrew said. "If he sleeps on land overnight he'll recover by morning."

He pulled up the little motor launch we were towing and brought it alongside the boat. He put Perry in it, and Aidan climbed down, too.

"Will you come along, Mrs. Miggs?" Andrew called up to me.

"No. I'm content to stay aboard."

"We'll be back tomorrow, then."

I watched them bounce through the waves toward shore. How that must have troubled poor Perry! We had anchored off a deserted area of coastline, and the three of them reminded me of explorers heading toward an uncharted land, uncertain, brimming with expectation and misgiving.

I brim, too.

I know now how poor Odysseus must have felt to see Ithaca, to come so close to home, only to be blown from his course by a storm and wander for ten years. At least Odysseus had a true-hearted Penelope awaiting his return. Not like me. No, not me. I have only a forgetful Scotsman.

✤

"There," Perry said as Andrew helped him out of the launch. "Terra firma. Here's where I belong."

"Why are you doing this to yourself, man?"

"Perdita would say I am doing this to fulfill my destiny. She's romantic that way. She believes we are all put here to do something particular, that things are meant to be. She would say that I'm doing all of this because it is what I was meant to do all along." He sighed deeply. "She might be right."

"But do you think it's right?"

"I don't know."

Perry walked away from the small camp to the edge of the water. He looked across the expanse to where the ship breasted the waves. He could see only the tiny cabin light. It reflected across the water, pointing at him across the surface like a thin yellow finger. She was in there, he thought, reading, perhaps. She liked to read before bed. How distant she seemed to him. How distant she had always seemed.

"How do you know?" Aidan said to his father at the camp. "How do you know if a thing you do is right?"

"You don't know, lad," Andrew said with a sigh. "You can only do what seems best. You can only consider deeply and act accordingly. There may be nae 'right' at all for all I know."

Andrew rubbed his fingers through the boy's hair, got up, and went to where Perry Miggs stood.

"So you must do this thing," he said to Miggs. "You've set your mind on finding monsters. Why bring your missus along?"

Perry continued looking out at the vessel. "In many ways, I'm doing this for her."

"It's no' my business, Professor Miggs, but the man you are is determined solely by the man you are and no' by the things you do."

"I do believe that, Mr. Macgruer."

"This is your adventure, no' hers."

"I've put it off as long as I could. I don't expect you to understand that."

Andrew Macgruer shook his head. "It's forty hours from here to Inverness. We'll have to set out by five o'clock if I'm to keep my promise and arrive by nine on Thursday. The storm set us back a bit, and I'll have to sail straight through. Let's get what sleep we can tonight." Andrew hesitated before speaking again, quietly. "Let me tell you something aboot women, Mr. Miggs. They are no' so impressed by pretentious display as we lads like to think they are. If you're doing this to make your wife love you better, you're best advised to go home and love her better."

Perry knit his brow in consternation as Andrew made his way back to the makeshift tent.

"One more thing to think on while you stand there," Andrew said over his shoulder. "Nessie has been looked for by every scientist, local, and tourist visiting the loch since nineteen thirty-three. Your chance of failure is almost assured. Is that what you'll be wanting your wife to take back home wi' you in September?"

"No."

The night was quiet. The men slept well, and Aidan, Andrew, and Perry were back on board by four a.m. Andrew started the great engines of the ship and set out. They skirted the Isle of Man and continued north.

Perdita awoke as the sun was rising over a rocky cliff.

"Where are we?" she asked when she came topside.

"That's called Galloway," Andrew responded.

"Scotland?"

"Southern tip. We're just heading into the North Channel."

"When do we stop?"

"We don't stop at all today. We travel straight from the Isle of Man through the canal. We won't touch ground again until Inverness."

By midafternoon they had sailed past the Mull of Kintyre, and by midnight they had cleared the Sound of Islay and turned east for the mainland.

❖

*I awoke early Thursday as we passed under a lighthouse. Andrew had been piloting all night and the day before, so I made coffee in the galley and took it up to him. We were in a narrow body of water now, bottlenecking in from the great sea behind us and into a slender passageway before.*

*"Where are we?"*

*"Loch Linnhe and the head of the Caledonian Canal."*

*"We've made good time."*

*"We're just on schedule. Everything slows from here, and there's the locks and bridges to contend with as we pass. We'll make good time to be at Inverness by nine o'clock this night."*

*There was strain in his voice. I was touched by his desire to keep his promise to Aidan's mother, to make good in front of his son. This was the man I remembered, gallant and honest. That part of him at least remained even if his memory had failed.*

*I had never seen anything so spectacular as this canal. We cruised along for hours, stopping from time to time to be borne up upon one of the locks. The engines ran easily, quietly along the waterway, and all was peace.*

*The scenery along the Caledonian Canal is more splendid than is to be found anywhere in the world. In places it is as wild and dramatic as the alps; towering cliffs and rocky crags belly into the water like overweight women at poolside easing themselves over the edge. In other places, the canal is no more than a narrow strip of water, level with each bank, and looks like a blue strip of grass idling through the green. In these places, the canal is so slender that one could toss a stone from either deck onto pasture lands and never fear its getting wet.*

*I felt Larchmont and London, the storms on the sea, and my own anxieties slip from me like the ancient mariner's albatross, to be swallowed in these calm and welcoming waters.*

"*Glen Albyn: the great glen of the Highlands. Grand, isn't it?*" *Andrew came up to me at the rail.*

"*Yes, it is.*"

*He grasped the railing before us and leaned on it. His wide shoulders bulged as they took his weight.*

"*Who's steering the boat?*" *I said, suddenly realizing that he had been our only helmsman.*

"*Look for yourself,*" *he said and nodded over his shoulder.*

*I looked into the pilothouse and saw Perry at the wheel. He waved at me, a ridiculous smile on his face, and bounced his fingers on his chest in a "look at me!" parody. I laughed and waved back to him. He put on a hat and struck an Admiral Nelson pose for my benefit, and I laughed again. Perry is such a lamb.*

"*Good morning! Good morning!*" *a chorus of tiny voices called my attention back over the railing. Five little girls gathered at the water's edge not twelve feet from us. Two more were running up from behind them, waving as they came. They were dressed in simple little frocks that fell to their knees, and they wore their hair long, some braided, some pulled out in pigtails, but most wore it full and falling about their shoulders: immaculately brushed hair that glistened and shone.*

"*Good morning!*" *I called back as Andrew did. We sounded like echoes of one another.*

"*Where are you bound?*" *one child cried, the one who trotted along the bank, keeping even with us on the foot trail there.*

"*Inverness, lassie,*" *Andrew called back.*

"*I have a brother there. Will you carry my hello back?*"

"*I will do that.*"

*She told him her name and her brother's.*

"*I'll tell him you're weel,*" *Andrew called to her, then he said to me, "She could ring him, of course, but people have been carrying messages up the canal for nearly two hundred years.*"

*I placed my hand on the railing to call to her. I laid it beside Andrew's, just touching him. It was an idle gesture, even casual. He could never know* whether I meant to do it, but he did not move his hand away, and I knew that was his choice.

"What are you girls doing?" I said to her. Her little friends were occupied at the water's edge, poking long sticks out under an overhanging clump of foliage.

"We're looking to be the queen of May!" she shouted back and, as if the revelation recalled her to her purpose, ran back to join her companions.

"Why aren't you lassies in school?" Andrew said.

"We're having lunch just now!" they chorused from over the back of the boat. I watched them for as long as they remained in sight.

"What did she mean about being the queen of May?" I asked Andrew.

"On Good Friday the locals weave wreaths from flowers and vines and throw them into the canal. Some of the wreaths can live for weeks floating there, some even flower. In the last days of April the young women and men go hunting the wreaths. If they find one that is blooming, they use it to crown their queen of the May Day celebrations. It's a pagan ritual, of course, held over from the wild days of auld Scotland, a fertility rite filled with fervor and passion. The queen of May ensures bounty and blessings on the land all summer long and up to harvest time, but the Christians have kept it on and found a way to make it mean Jesus—just as they always do."

He shook his head in mild consternation. Andrew had always been contemptuous of mindless, dogmatic devotion. That much of him had remained the same from our university days.

We passed the tiny town. The maypole was up, heavy and erect in the midday sun, trailing long streamers down its sides. A thick and leafy wreath sat at the top of the spire. It would slowly slip down the smooth shaft during the dance on May Day morn.

"It is May soon, isn't it?" I said, having lost all track of time.

"Friday," he replied. "Tomorrow."

The canal slipped out into another loch. I do not know its name, but it was a lovely expanse with hills crowding around it like aunts and uncles at a bassinet.

Aidan had been dipping the boat hook over the side for some time, playing *in the wake of the* Pelican. *He came forward just after lunch with a garland in his hand. It was an enchanting circlet of white and yellow buds, tiny and delicate.*

"Look what I've caught! It's the May Day wreath." He placed it on my head, still dripping from the loch. "You're our queen of May!"

"Thank you, Aidan. But I don't know how to be your queen of May."

"First, you must kiss all of the men."

"Then what?"

Aidan shrugged.

"You must make the land bloom," Andrew said from over my shoulder.

"I'll do what I can," I said and pecked Andrew on the cheek. If my kiss was cool, friendly if not downright obligatory, Andrew's reception of it was cooler still, as passive as stone. I let it pass, though, and kissed Aidan and went up to the pilothouse.

"You'll never guess," I said to Perry.

"Looks like you've won first prize at something," he ventured. "Water polo?"

"I have become Primavera, the May queen, and I am here to kiss you, encourage fecundity, and make the land bloom."

I approached Perry playfully, tarting up my part. I had intended to kiss him comically, but, as I put my arms about his neck, he wrapped his around my waist and pulled me to him. He kissed me tenderly first, then he kissed me a second time with passion. It was an awkward kiss filled with inexperience.

"Thank you," he said into my ear as he held me. "Thank you for coming up here. Thank you for coming with me. I know this seems to be all for me, but I am doing it for you mostly. All for you."

He backed up a step and looked into my eyes with deep, almost pleading sincerity. There were drops on his cheeks. Perry was no crier, no sentimentalist, and I guessed my May Day wreath had dripped on him. I wiped them away, though, as if they had been tears.

"You are worked up about Loch Ness, aren't you? I haven't seen you so emotional in years. Would you like to try it again? That kiss, I mean. We could think of it as starting a new habit."

"Do you know that?" he replied, ignoring my suggestion. "I've brought you here because you wanted to come back to Scotland—and, of course, for the other thing."

"Yes. Thank you, darling. But you have it all wrong. I'm the May queen. I should kiss you." I brushed him lightly on the lips. "Good luck, darling. I hope you find the thing you're looking for here."

"I hope so, too," he said and smiled, his eyes gleaming with delight at the thought of it.

Andrew went below for two hours' sleep, but he was up and at the helm before we reached Fort Augustus.

The Pelican slipped into the high, gray stone walls of the Augustus lock. She slipped in simply, naturally.

We rode the final lock to the level of Loch Ness. It groaned and whined before opening and pushing us out on a gentle current; we motored from the restrictive canal and out onto the wide body of water, a mile across at least, that stretched before us to the far horizon.

"Loch Ness," Andrew shouted down from the wheel, "the most mysterious place on earth."

Perry dashed from rail to rail, staring into the water from every side as though he expected the Loch Ness monster to be waiting for him at her front door.

As we reached the center of the enormous loch, Andrew cut the engines and showed us how to unfurl the sails. They bellied in a freshening breeze, and the good ship slid across the face of the loch like a fairy on ice skates. All was quiet but for the occasional snap of canvas in the wind. The water seemed to whisper around us in an unintelligible, Celtic tongue, telling secrets we could never understand.

It was darkening on the loch as we passed Urquhart Castle. Andrew pointed it out to us, a red and ruined outcrop against the western hills.

"And over there," he said, pointing to the shore opposite the castle, "is our final destination, Iubhar." We looked across the loch but could see only the trees and steep hills rising from the water.

It was nearly eight o'clock when we dropped anchor at the northernmost point of the loch. We took the launch to land. Andrew was anxious to return

Aidan to his home within the hour, and he left us there at the dock with instructions to meet here again later.

Perry worried. He usually worried on vacation.

And while he troubled himself over little nothings, I bent to the ground and caught up a handful of Scotland. It was a rich, loamy soil that I squeezed through my fingers as my heart pounded. It smelled fresh. It smelled real. It smelled old and familiar and full of life and promise.

"Home," I said down deep in my throat so Perry didn't hear.

I wasn't speaking to him.

# Chapter 7

# May

❖

## Iubhar

*Enchantment must be a joy delayed, and Nature is penurious. She saves up her treasures—enchantment, youth, love—and shares them only sparingly, for that is just wise husbandry.*

*I have leisure now and will study to be patient. She will enchant me in her time.*

*But until then, I will spend my days in this charming home up the embankment from the waters of Loch Ness.*

*This is the home of two sexagenarian sisters, this place Perry has found for us. It is a quaint home, all fresh-scrubbed floors and simple woodwork on the doors and old-fashioned patterned paper on the walls. Tables are plentiful in every room, and they seem to form part of a pixilated collection.*

*Drop leaves, piecrusts, and tip tops crowd about the rooms and huddle in every corner. Each table sports jaunty runners, some made of tapestry, some of lace that looks hand tatted, and on each runner there are arranged assortments of the most unusual and intriguing ornaments I have ever seen outside of a flea market.*

*Two sisters live here, Mrs. Reese and Miss Shaw. Caitlin Reese is the taller woman with the sterner eyes. Kira Shaw is shorter, rounder, and generally merrier. They are both in their sixties, I think, and Mrs. Reese is the younger sister, though appearances seem to indicate just the opposite.*

*Caitlin came back to Iubhar after an unhappy marriage to a man named Reese, a drunkard and a leech, to use her own description.*

*Shaw is the maiden name, and apparently Kira never married. Rather, she kept the home when her sister went into her married misfortune and was still here when Caitlin returned from the nuptial nightmare. I believe all of this happened decades ago. The sisters have lived in the large home together since, occasionally taking a lodger into the upper floors, for it is a many-storied house.*

*I say "lodger" and employ the singular because they apparently expected only one guest and were surprised when the two of us appeared at their doorway. The sisters had also apparently expected Perry before suppertime, and we did not arrive until after bedtime. They had not expected me at all.*

*Caitlin held me in an affronted glare while Perry explained to Kira that I had been intended all along, that he had perhaps forgotten to mention the fact, and he assured them more than once that we were long married.*

*"But it is only the one bedroom," Kira explained.*

*"That will do."*

*"It has only the one bed," Caitlin said with a judicial air. They were the first words she had spoken to us. She reminded me of a thick and somber sort of bird, a crow perhaps, or a raven: small, unblinking eyes and disapproval in her every gesture, her arms folded back like wings, her shoulders folded forward.*

*"Oh," Perry said. "Yes, I see. Is it a very small bed then? Because if it is, I could be happy on the floor or perhaps a couch or chair."*

*"The bed is large enough," Kira replied but seemed to hesitate.*

*"But there is only the one bed in the room," Caitlin amplified.*

*"Then that will do nicely," Perry responded.*

*The sisters exchanged a look I could not decipher; it seemed a troubled, embarrassed sort of look, as though an indelicacy had occurred or a vulgarity uttered. They seemed to agree between themselves to let the matter drop.*

"The rate we usually charge is twenty-five pounds per night for the room," Kira said as she scuttled behind the desk and opened a leather book filled with figures. Her tone indicated that she thought it was too much and that she half expected us to say so and object.

"Meals are extra," Caitlin said imperiously, without apology. "Five pounds per person."

"Aye," Kira confirmed and hesitated again. She was a woman of delicate sensibilities, very like Perry in her desire to keep from offending.

But her younger sister was made of sterner stuff. "We collect by the week in advance. And you'll have to order meals in advance, too, and pay for them."

"Aye, that's right," Kira added. "It's so we may plan our marketing for the week, d'ye ken?"

"Perfectly reasonable," Perry said. "But I would prefer to pay for the entire stay now and be done with it. Twenty-five per night is, let's see, a hundred and seventy-five each week to make the bookwork simple. We'll be here no less than twenty-one weeks, which is thirty-six hundred and seventy-five pounds. We'll want to take meals each evening at least, so that will be another ten pounds each day. That will add another fourteen hundred and seventy to the bill, so can we just make it an even fifty-five hundred for the summer? That will make the figuring simple enough."

The women watched in a state of disbelief as Perry peeled the bills from the roll of cash. He placed the money on the desk before them.

"I'm sorry about these small denominations, but I thought you might have trouble trading larger bills out here."

We had spent a wearying evening in Inverness while waiting for Andrew, by going from hotel to hotel, and ended up at a late-night currency exchange in order to change all of our remaining dollars to pounds.

"I don't want that much cash in the house," Caitlin said a little breathlessly.

"We'll have to take it up to the bank tomorrow," Kira said, hardly able to contain her excitement. I doubt she had ever in her life seen that much money at one time.

"I am sorry," Perry said. "I wish I had thought of that. How thoughtless of me."

"Not at all, Professor Miggs," Kira Shaw said.

"No need to apologize," Caitlin Reese agreed. "We will have to go in to market tomorrow. Saturday is our usual day. We'll also go by the bank."

"And," Kira said, displaying her delight, "perhaps we could contact Mr. Trent!"

"We'll discuss it later," Caitlin said.

And so we were ensconced in our rooms above the loch.

They are cheery rooms, not large, but warm and welcoming. The bedroom is crowded with the sort of bric-a-brac to be found in the lower floors. The bed itself is no larger than full, but that is large enough, as Perry and I are smallish people anyway. Besides the bedroom, there is a narrow hallway to a functional lavatory—a tiny cubicle with just the essential elements to make it a bathroom. And there is a sitting room at the front.

The sitting room is exquisite, a study in simple elegance—all russet drapes, antique wallpaper, and lace. It is surely my favorite room in the entire house. There is a wide table there with almost nothing cluttering it, just a basket filled with imported fruit on a bed of fresh flowers. And there is a window overlooking the dusty trail that passes through Iubhar as its main road. The road links a handful of houses and shops together, collecting the few inhabitants into what might be called a village. But there is something both welcoming and aloof about that road, about the whole view from the window.

All of Iubhar is welcoming and aloof, just like Scotsmen, friendly and private.

From that window I can see the steep hillside that rises up from the loch, though I cannot see the loch itself. There are wild trees on the hillside, tangled and surprised trees.

It is dark woodland, interrupted only by Iubhar itself, which has done nothing to civilize the forest around it.

I find myself growing whimsical at that window, staring into the woods, speculating on mythology and folklore. It is not difficult at all for me, when looking into that scene, to understand why the Celts believe the things they do about fairies, kelpies, and the other ferlies that add atmosphere and character to the twilight world of Scotland.

*Perry and I spent that first evening unpacking. Even though we had arrived late, I was much too excited to sleep. I was finally in Scotland, finally undoing my bags, finally settling after seventeen years. I was in a hurry to get on with it. I shook out my things, refolded and hung until the late evening sun had finally set and I had to light the room with the glow of a weak bulb.*

*How dowdy my things all looked in that light.*

*I had only two nice pieces: the yellow silk blouse and the spring acetate dress I had bought special for the trip. They were the last purchase I had made with our credit cards back in Larchmont before Perry wrapped them away and told me that we were now on the Royal Geographic Society's budget and should pay cash for everything.*

*The blouse and dress shimmered even in the inadequate light of the bedroom. They were fresh, sexy, new. All of my other things paled: mousey browns and muddy greens, substantial navies, dusty roses and dull creams. I could not picture my face floating above any of them; they were all so lifeless and drab. They were entirely like Larchmont and nothing like me, nothing like Scotland. These were the clothes of a middle-aged woman, a dismal, dreary, dingy, and discouraged woman.*

*Some of my clothes dated back thirteen years, nearly to the honeymoon. The crispness was all broken out of them; they were flaccid and cheerless and put me in mind of a chained prisoner hanging on a dungeon wall, forever hanging, with no hope of freedom.*

*"I need new clothes," I said abruptly to Perry. He had been very good to help unpack even though he was exhausted.*

*"You just bought new things back home." It wasn't protest or denial—not from Perry, goodness knows—but rather an observation, flat and practical, mixed with a mild request for confirmation.*

*"Yes," I sighed and stared into the half-lit armoire.*

*"And you packed so much."*

*"True."*

*How could I tell him that these clothes were cut for another woman's body, another woman's mind? These were the uninspired clothes of the uninspired wife of the uninspiring professor of biology. They held no riddle, no allure: terse clothes.*

*They were clothes that shouted "Yankee" even from their hangers. They proclaimed "tourist," "sightseer," "visitor."*

*They were inappropriate. They were wrong.*

*They whispered of the fall and of drying leaves, of bare branches and blackening bark. They were themselves like the desiccated humus of that russet season, crumpled and lifeless.*

*I could no longer live down to these clothes, to wrap myself in expected folds.*

*"We should have shopped in Inverness today, then," Perry said.*

*"I didn't know I needed to until now."*

*Perry laughed in his fatigue and hugged me.*

*"And now you know?"*

*"Just now that I get a good look at everything. It all looked all right in the closet at home—I mean, all right the way the paint on the walls is all right because it is invisible and not annoying. But everything looks different here somehow. They aren't all right at all. They are all wrong, I think." Perry only stared at me, so I repeated myself, "Everything looks different here."*

*"More visible and annoying than at home?"*

*"Yes," I said and laughed before kissing his cheek.*

*"What do you need?"*

*"Everything new," I blurted. "I need sturdy things. Slacks and heavy blouses with lots of pockets because I plan to hike around here—as much as I am able—while you're out on the boat. And I want some dresses for when you take me out to Inverness or across to Aberdeen maybe for a night—dining and dancing. I want some slinky, sexy things, too, and all Scottish, nothing American. I don't want to stand out here."*

*"You want to be sexy and not stand out?" Perry said and smiled at me.*

*"That's right." Perry is a very understanding man, but men simply don't understand. It's all about coupling, with men. I just wanted to feel sexy. I wanted to wrap myself in Scotland and never come out. That would be sexy.*

*"Yes, then," he said, "all right. Perhaps you can ride in with Miss Shaw and Mrs. Reese when they go marketing tomorrow."*

*That was all the hint I needed.*

*Next morning I loaded my new purse with cash from the upper drawer* of the dressing table and went down to the car. It was a cramped machine, faded red, with only a padded ledge in back for extra passengers to sit upon and no leg room whatever.

Kira Shaw was a careful driver, and we were nearly forty minutes driving up the narrow road into Inverness. We talked along the way, Kira, Caitlin, and I, and that is when I learned about Mrs. Reese's unhappy marriage. Mr. Reese had apparently turned Caitlin against the whole sex in general.

"A man may have his place," she said, "but I canna think where that may be."

I wanted to laugh, but she wasn't joking.

Inverness is an elegant little town, and, as we entered, a small army of people were working to set out forests of flowers and plants in the hundreds of tubs and hanging baskets all through Inverness's city center, dressing her up for the summer.

I understood how necessary that was, better perhaps than any other person in the whole city that morning.

I left my hostesses at the market and walked around to the shops in the high street. It was a wild and decadent experience, buying what I wanted and never stopping to count the cost. Of course, I never did anything like that. Although Perry had said I could spend until I saw the bottom of my purse, and that is precisely what I had intended to do, I ultimately shopped for the sales. One shop had tropical blends, all patch pockets and sand-colored khakis; they reminded me of African safaris, Bengal tiger hunts, Egyptian midnights, and I bought a complete outfit, including a flop brim canvas hat.

"Are you going exploring, then, this summer?" the shop woman asked.

"Yes." I beamed.

"And where are you bound?"

"South." I said. She was impressed, so I didn't bother to explain that I wasn't going very far south, only eleven or twelve miles.

In the next shop, I bought several clingy blouses and narrow skirts, and a summer dress with full skirts. They all shimmered in pale blues and pastel shades of yellow and red. They flowed like warm caramel about me and made me think of silken sails on Ægean winds. I bought a wide, bright sun hat there, too, and big sunglasses that reminded me of Audrey Hepburn. I bought four pairs of shoes, feeling increasingly libidinous for every pair after the first. And, at the end of two and a half hours, I had completely replaced thirteen years of accumulation. It would be a relief, a release, I thought, to return to the little room above the loch and quietly dispose of my old clothes.

I would repack these new things in the bags we brought from Larchmont. Not the old things at all. Those would remain here, mixing with the world I left and found again.

I bought too much, though, and was unable to carry the bags out of the last shop. There was a time I could have hefted the boxes and bags, I am certain, and borne them away on enthusiasm alone. But now I was older, more readily winded, and I had to leave everything in the last shop while I went to meet Miss Shaw and Mrs. Reese at the market.

Kira Shaw was an old-fashioned cook and had crowded the tiny automobile with fresh vegetables, meats, puddings, and the like, until there was barely room left for me and no room for the things I had bought.

"Oh, I am sorry," she said. "I hadna thought of your things. I was that taken up with the cooking and planning."

"You'll have to have your things sent on," Caitlin announced. "The food canna be left to spoil. We must go straight the way home now."

"After the post office," Kira said seriously. "We must inform Mr. Trent of our good fortune."

So I asked the shop woman to hold my things until I could arrange to have them picked up. She was very nice about it.

We made a short detour to the post office, where Kira Shaw posted a letter addressed to a Mr. Breton Trent of Aberdeen. She was very flustered and worked up as she dropped the letter in the box, but she only smiled broadly around the car and wrinkled her nose like a schoolgirl at us. She offered no further explanation to me, though Caitlin seemed to understand it all well enough, and disapproved.

When we arrived home, I found Perry had taken over my charming little table in the sitting room. The basket of fruit and flowers was laid on the floor, and he had spread out his charts and maps and notes and drawings.

*He looked like a tiny, gog-eyed accountant in the midst of his paperwork when I walked in on him.*

*"Back so soon?"*

*"Mm," I hummed as I glared. I didn't like it that he had a whole boat to himself and had decided to encroach upon the one area that I had staked out for my own. "It's been over four hours."*

*"Has it?" he looked at his wrist before realizing he had not put his watch on that morning. From the look of him, still in his dressing gown and morning stubble, he had opened his big portfolio of papers the moment I was out of the door. "That time flew by, didn't it? I thought you were going to buy something."*

*"It'll be sent over Monday. Why don't you go and have your bath now?"*

*He was apologetic, as usual, without need, as usual, as he tottered up and went into the bath. "Yes. Yes, I got wrapped up in things here after you left."*

*As he was running his tub, I carefully collected together the papers and drawings, Curtis Kane's pictorial book* Oceans of Prehistory: aquatic rep-tiles, *and his photographs, and Xerox copies. I zipped them back into the big, flat portfolio, and laid it all by the door for him to take to the boat the very next time he went. I then replaced my basket of imported fruit and fresh flowers and marked my territory by eating one of the apples.*

*Perry came out of the bathroom an hour later, shaven and dressed, and set about moving the bowl off and reopening the portfolio on the table.*

*"That's about the most peaceful place in the house," I said pointedly as he nullified my careful work.*

*"It is nice."*

*"I thought perhaps I would make it my place while we are here. I like the view out over the village and woods."*

*"Yes, it is lovely," he replied, giving the view a cursory glance. "That will be so nice for you."*

*"While you are on the boat, I mean, with your charts and things," I said, again pointing my tone, tingeing it with malice. "You will be out there work-ing, and I will have this area here all to myself."*

*"Mm," he said and nodded.*

*I glared at him. He was a few moments noticing. He hadn't caught my tone; I never expected he would, but he knew the look.*

*"What is it?" he said, suddenly self-conscious. "Do— do you want to come out to the boat with me when I work? Are you going to be too lonely up here, you mean?"*

*"No, dear, I just want a little niche all to myself. This is your trip, after all, and you have that nice, big boat all to yourself. Would it be too much if I claimed this little area with the table and window for myself?"*

*"No. Of course not. It shall be yours. I want you to have it."*

*"All mine. And without drawings of plesiosaurs or stratum maps littered about on it—just the basket with the apples and bananas and grapes on the flowers sitting here. Just like it was when you came out of the bath. Just like it wasn't when I came home. Just like it isn't just now."*

*"Yes, dear. All yours."*

*He went back to reading his notes and making marks on one of the charts, the really big one that resembled a huge blueprint of the shoreline around the loch. I gave up and tossed myself across the bed and began idling through the Condé Nast article on the Highlands I had brought with me. The walk around Inverness had tired me more than I had thought, and I fell asleep before I could finish reading the Ombudsman letters.*

*When I awoke, I was surprised to find all of my purchases gathered around the room. The big packages and small, all in their new-smelling wrappers and crisp bags looking just as they had when I abandoned them at the shop, huddled about the room like excited children home from an adventure.*

*Perry sat at my table in the sitting room. He had finally put away his things and sat smiling at me.*

*"You meant to tell me that you didn't want my things strewn about in here, didn't you?" he said. "You meant you wanted this table and window for yourself now, right?"*

*I flung my arms around him and kissed him.*

*"You went all the way into Inverness to get my things!" I practically squealed. It was the most thoughtful thing he had ever done.*

*"No," he said, coughing in his usual way when embarrassed. "Actually,*

Miss Shaw told Mr. Macgruer how disappointed you were about not being able to bring your things back, and he took their car up to collect everything. I only carried them up the stairs. But if I had known you had left your things, I would have gone to get them. You did buy a lot."

"Are you upset?"

"I am delighted. Show me what you've bought."

I spent the rest of the afternoon trying things on for Perry, who was most complimentary. He did try so hard to say something appropriate for each piece I showed him, but I have come to realize that men simply do not care about clothes. It is a sad fact, a bewildering fact, perhaps, but a fact nevertheless. And at last, with Perry's repertoire of compliments beginning to cycle like a looping phonograph, I gave up without showing him half of my new self.

Around seven, we went down to the dining room and ate with our hostesses. Kira had prepared a splendid and savory lamb with rosemary and small potatoes. Caitlin had made dessert, an egg custard without much sweetness or flavor.

We ate while Kira, a natural talker, regaled us with pleasant chatter about this and that and punctuated her observations with sincere declarations of delight that we were staying the "whole lang summer." We retired that night and slept deeply in the cool Scottish night.

# Chapter 8

✦

Andrew Macgruer could not sleep. He had not slept well for over a week, not since the two Americans—not since *she*—had come to Iubhar. He looked at the clock, three a.m., and tossed back his covers. It was time again.

He walked naked through the old crofter's cottage that served as his home, collecting up his clothes in the pale light of a waxing moon, and was still naked halfway down the hill into Iubhar. He pulled on his clothes with the ease of a man who knows he is the only waking soul in the woods. The marmalade tomcat came from the undergrowth and met him, following him along the *grá* and into the village.

Macgruer stopped only once. He stood for a moment under the eaves of Kira Shaw's house and looked up at the dark window on the second floor. He sighed a troubled sigh and then moved on toward the loch.

He pushed the launch into the water as the cat jumped in. He paddled out to the *Pelican* and came alongside of her. The cat remained in the launch while Macgruer climbed onto the *Pelican*'s deck.

He went down to the galley and took a handful of pickled eggs and a tin of sardines before making his way up to the cabin. He went through his nightly routine of turning off the tape in the scanner and checking the lock count on the computer. The machine had recorded twenty-seven objects passing under the *Pelican* since nine o'clock the previous evening. Macgruer wound the tape to each reading and previewed the recordings as he ate the eggs: school of fish; smaller school of fish; another school of fish, perhaps the first school returning this way again. It was the same litany. It had been thus every night for over a week. No monumental discoveries. Nothing spectacular. Nothing even interesting. Macgruer made a note on the tape of where the recordings could be found, Perry Miggs would want to view them himself, and then put another tape in the machine. He slipped the recorded tape into his belt before lowering himself into the launch.

He peeled back the top on the tin of sardines and laid it down for the cat before casting off and heading back toward shore. He had strong, hard arms, and the boat glided purposefully forward with every stroke. The water muttered lazily under him, the only sound to be heard in the hushed predawn.

He aimed the launch at the low strand expertly and allowed it to beach itself gently. The cat leapt from the bow and onto dry land as the boat rattled up onto the pebbles. There he sat to wash the sardines from his face as Macgruer pulled the boat onto the shore.

Andrew knelt by the water's edge and, stripping to the waist, bathed himself as the tomcat sat at a discreet distance and watched him incuriously.

Macgruer was almost finished when he heard the cat growl, a low, deep tone of warning. He looked around to see the tom arch his back and waddle backward, staring pointedly at some intruder Macgruer could not himself see.

"What is it, cat?" he whispered to his companion, but the cat only spun and bounded up the low terrace behind and disappeared into the brush above.

Macgruer stood and looked about him in the darkness, but he could see nothing.

"Hallo?" he said quietly. "Who's that, then?"

He remained still, naked to the belt and bare legged, with his shirt draped down about his kilt. The faint moon picked out the hard contours of his broad chest and muscular arms.

"Macgruer?" whispered a voice from the bushes at the back of the strand.

"Aye? Who's that?"

"It's me, lad," the old man said as he picked his way through the bushes toward Macgruer. "It's auld Grant."

"Grant?"

Adam Grant was known to everyone around the loch as "Mad Adam." He was a frail old wanderer who had been around as long as anyone could remember. He was now in his eighties at least. He was called "Mad Adam" for any number of his peculiarities, but mainly because he insisted that he spotted—and spoke to—the creature of the loch an average of once every second or third day.

"I might have kent," Macgruer said, "that you'd be the only other soul up and aboot at this time of morning."

"You were a bit of time under the Shaw's window," the old man said.

"I stopped there on my way down," Macgruer responded, returning to finish his bath.

"Why might that be?" Mad Adam said to himself. Macgruer did not answer. "Auld Kira Shaw has sent for Mr. Trent."

"I have heard." Kira Shaw had hardly made a secret of it.

"That would mean she's come into the money she's looked for all these long years."

"Yes," Macgruer said and chuckled. Mad Adam liked behaving as if he knew great secrets. He often claimed to hear them from the creatures of the woods and loch, but everyone generally knew he was a tireless busybody, who collected his information through gossip, eavesdropping, and outright spying.

"I have heard," Adam said grandly, "that she's collected up better than six hunnerd pounds."

"Have you?"

"Maybe as much as seven or eight," the old man tested.

"Aye," Macgruer said, "and maybe even more. I'm certain Caitlìn Reese is quiet enough about the exact amount if it's her you've been asking."

Mad Adam laughed. "I dinnae have to be asking Caitlìn Reese. The forest is full of ears and willing tales." He moved around to the launch where he could see Macgruer in profile at the water's edge. "Better than eight hunnerd, then, is it? Closer to nine hunnerd or even a thousand pound some would say."

"Better than five times that," Macgruer said. "They have a lodger staying through until September."

"But a thousand is no more than a guess of them that ken no better," Adam concluded. "I happen to know it is much more like five thousand pounds and maybe a bit more. That is surely enough to call back Mr. Trent."

"It surely is so," Macgruer agreed and stood.

"And so she has," Adam said wisely. "She has sent for Mr. Trent. She mailed him a letter a week back Saturday."

"And has she heard from Mr. Trent in return?" Macgruer asked.

"She has no'," the old man said. "Little enough in that, though. Breton Trent was never a lad quick to act. But," he continued, changing the subject, "you say the women have a lodger. I have heard they have twae guests and that you were the one tae bring them here."

"True, Adam, true."

"You brought them down from Inverness in that boat there," he said indicating the *Pelican*. "It's a monster hunter, is it no'?"

"It is."

The old man nodded gravely. "That explains it, then. She allahs kens when they've come around."

"Auld Nessie, you mean?" Macgruer said as he pulled his shirt back on and threw his tartan over his shoulder again.

"Aye, she's a wise auld girl is she."

"How d'ye mean?"

Mad Adam puckered his lips and raised his eyebrows in thought, then said, "I havna seen her once this past week or better. Tha's unusual."

"A full week?" Macgruer teased. "That must be some record for you."

"Aye. She allahs disappears when the monster hunters come. She kens, d'ye see? She kens."

"Small wonder. With all the electrics and sonar hum, it must sound like a brass band coming down the loch."

"Aye," the old man said and nodded his knobby head. "And why is it you are mucking about wi' it all this time, then?"

"There's a Yank," Macgruer explained. "He's given me a hundred and fifty pounds to guide him to her."

"A hunnerd fifty?" the old man said, impressed.

"Aye, just for the first few times. After that it will be fifteen pounds each time we go oot."

Mad Adam whistled softly. "And this Yank is here for the month?"

"All summer," Macgruer said. "He's no' planning to leave until September."

"That I've heard; that I've heard," Adam inserted quickly.

"So far he's been pleased to let her sit there at anchor, hoping Nessie will swim up below for a holiday snap."

The old man knit his brow. "He'll want to take her oot sooner or later."

"Aye," Macgruer agreed. He gave it a long thought before continuing, "But he's nae sailor. I dinnae think much will come of his summer researches."

"Is he the reason you're stopping under the window there each morning?"

"Nae," Macgruer replied. "He's brought his wife."

Macgruer sat on the pebbles of the beach and stared out onto the black waters.

"A bonny lass?" Adam guessed.

"I knew her, Adam, back at university."

"Did you?"

"Aye."

"And she is the one, is she?" Mad Adam laughed. "So oot here you've come—all the way out to Iubhar—to say farewell to all of that—that time before—and oot here it chases after you."

"Aye," Macgruer said. "That's the way it does seem."

"Weel," Adam said casually, "the past is like that."

"She's married, Adam." Macgruer stood. "And I want to have peace in my life."

"Aye. She's married tae the monster hunter." The old man leaned close to Macgruer. "So are you gane tae take him oot in earnest, then? Will you show this one where to find the auld girl—for the sake of his wife, this lassie you kent once at university, I mean? The lassie that split yer heart and tore yer soul? Will you show him Nessie for her?"

Macgruer stood and gave the launch a sudden jerk to be certain it was firmly on shore.

"Nae," he said with resolution.

# Chapter 9

✤

*Mornings here are best, I think, especially those mornings when Mrs. Reese bakes.*

*Caitlin is the baker and also the charwoman of the inn and comes up the stairs twice a week. On Tuesdays and Fridays she comes to collect our linens and straighten our room (which she does with such cold solemnity that I am forced to laugh behind my hand—and I suspect that she has begun to think I must have a respiratory problem).*

*The world is such a serious place to Caitlin Reese.*

*Caitlin is the chambermaid because she can come up the stairs and her sister cannot.*

*Kira Shaw has something wrong with her hips, which prevents her climbing the steep and narrow flight. So Kira is the washwoman and cook. She is also the gardener and has an herb garden neatly packed in around the back door of the house.*

*Caitlin uses herbs in her breads, and the house is almost constantly filled with the aroma.*

*Wednesdays are the special days here. On Wednesdays, Caitlin Reese is forbidden her baking and banished from the kitchen while her sister prepares* the delicacies for the midafternoon tea. Women begin arriving around one o'clock, and by three the front parlor is transformed into a social hall. The women are mostly from Iubhar or are former residents who have moved away to Inverfarigaig, Foyers, Lochgarthside, or Errogie on Loch Mhór. But they all return on Wednesdays and gather in the parlor to drink tea, eat, and talk.

Their conversation is of familiar things, people who have died, people who have moved away, the children, the land, the old days, the weather, and food. Recently the topic of a Mr. Trent has crept into the conversations, but I really do not understand the significance of Mr. Trent or why he should monopolize the tea-table tattle.

There is such a ritual of preparation each Wednesday morning. The cooking, dusting, swabbing, squabbling, are all neatly choreographed, but nothing compares to the final great ceremony: The Ordinance of the Tables.

The numerous tables that crowd about the various rooms are arranged every Wednesday morning like jigsaw pieces in a giant puzzle. It is the most extraordinary thing, how those tables all fit into place to make one solid, twisting labyrinth of tabletop through the main floor's rooms. Caitlín and Kira spin, dust, and adjust them in such a rigorous, well-practiced, and tightly orchestrated routine that you might set the whole performance to music. They are precisely like clockwork mechanisms in their dogged persistence toward their goal.

But I disdain all such routine. I have determined, since I am out of my home and country, to be also outside of time.

So I spend Wednesdays walking, as much as I am able to, in this hilly world (it wears me out so quickly), and otherwise sitting quietly on the front porch while the plinking and tattling of the tea party drifts through the open windows into the moist shade of the sleepy street.

It was on such a Wednesday, on a sour sort of morning that promised rain, that Andrew Macgruer called at the inn. I was on the porch earlier than usual, and the sisters were still arranging tables and squabbling inside when he appeared at the end of the street and ambled easily toward me.

"Is your husband in, Missus?"

"He is."

He looked hard at me for a long moment before looking away, toward the water. The blood flushed up in my cheeks involuntarily, foolishly. There was such a sudden sparkle in his eye.

"We'll be going into Fort Augustus this day," he said flatly.

"Will you?"

"Aye."

"That will be nice."

"Aye."

He continued to look away, toward the loch. He stood silently staring down the street for so long that I finally followed his gaze. The only thing moving in the street at that time of morning was a yellow tabby cat. Andrew seemed to be watching him.

"There's a pub there," he said suddenly.

"I see."

"You dinnae mind?"

"Why should I?"

"Some women would."

"Yes, some might," I said, trying hard to keep up my end, to keep him standing there with me. "That is, if they thought perhaps he should be doing his work instead."

Andrew squinted up through the tree limbs.

"It looks like rain, so there's no' much hope in sailing this day."

"So you'll have a drink and be home early?"

"We'll be sair fecht to do ocht else."

Andrew could speak the queen's tongue when it suited him. I couldn't understand why he chose the Highland dialect this morning.

We continued playing at small talk, listening to Caitlin and Kira piecing together their puzzle tables, waiting for Perry to emerge, until our talk dwindled into the sweet, adhesive silences that varnish personality and harden speech.

Perry finally came out, kissed me perfunctorily on the cheek, and walked away with my brawny, cold Scotsman.

*I watched the two of them disappear into the woods together, heading to-ward the water. I decided not to walk that day. It threatened such rain.*

✤

The rain set in on the loch early that morning and whipped the water into peaks.

MacCallum's Pub screwed down its windows, stoked up a fire, and settled in for a long spring lashing. The canal was gray and the loch beyond black and chopping in the stiff wind that blew through the Great Glen.

Rain slipped sidelong through the heavy air and beat on the thick panes of the little pub. The expected crowd was there, heavy-fisted men with the weary, lost look of manual labor about their eyes. They huddled over pints, shoulders folded.

"Why did you bring your wife along?" Macgruer said. The question was almost whispered into his pint, almost drowned in the froth.

Miggs furrowed his brow, but he knew he had no aptitude for read-ing underlying meanings.

"I— I didn't really have a choice."

Andrew put his elbows on the table and regarded the papers laid out there. "Gae on wi' your plans." Perry put his pint down carefully and continued outlining his plan for covering the loch.

Macgruer seemed to be listening this time, and Perry grew ani-mated. The men in the pub listened respectfully from their places as the professor described traversings and overlapping patterns and land-ings and samplings.

"Well, then," Macgruer said at the end of Perry's presentation, "you've got it all worked out, have you?"

"Yes. I am not good at much, I'm afraid, but I can plan. I have a good head at planning."

Macgruer slid his empty pint to the side of the table, indicating his need for another.

Perry took the empty glass to the bar and waited to catch the atten-tion of the barkeep.

A wiry little man took the opportunity of Miggs's absence to approach Macgruer. He was an old fellow of the pub, with a bulb nose and a toothless, protruding jaw.

"What's this then?" the old fellow said, pinching a corner of the charts lightly between his fingers.

"Monster hunter," Macgruer replied without emotion.

The old man's tangled brow rose on his forehead as his eyes squeezed to slits and his thin mouth widened into a ridiculous grin.

"Is he, now? Thought as much."

"Aye."

"Gallus auld gangrel," the old man muttered through his amused grimace, twisting his eyes shrewdly toward Miggs still at the bar. Macgruer knew the tone well enough. The old fellow's comment was as critical as he dared to be in public, as scathing as politeness allowed. "Is he doitit, then?"

"Nae," Macgruer replied without much conviction. "He's sound enough in the head."

"And so you're in frae the weather for your beer, the lowe of the grate, and mad talk of the monster, then, just you and your American friend?" It was a fair way to dupe a man out of a pint of beer. Perry returned with Macgruer's pint.

"So 'tis the auld girl you're after, then?" the old man said to Perry.

"Sorry?"

Macgruer interposed with an amused smile. "Miggs, this is Tam Turnbull."

"Buy me a pint, too," Tam said, inviting himself to sit, "and I'll yatter all the day aboot Nessie and what's been seen here and aboot, man."

"Yes," Perry replied, digging money from his wallet, "yes, I'd like to hear that."

"There's some will tell you auld Nessie is a whale or shark that has found its way down the river Ness, but she is no such a thing. The auld girl has lived in these waters now over thirteen hunner years. In our legends it was a fair bright day along about five sixty-five in the year of the

Lord when Saint Columba came upon men burying one of their fellows.

"'How did the man die?' asks Saint Columba.

"'Bit to the death by the monster o' the loch,' says the men.

"Now Saint Columba held no faith in their words, for he believed there could be no monster in the loch. That is, until he and his monks made to cross the river Ness. The good Saint Columba had come to the river's edge, and him and his men were pulling off their sandals for to cross, when the water boiled white in front of them and a great beast rose up from the depths. It made for the men on the shore, but Saint Columba cursed the ferlie with a blessing and drove it out of the river and down into the loch.

"What is your interest in her, sor?" Tam Turnbull suddenly turned his attention onto Perry.

"I am a marine biologist," Perry responded, surprised to be addressed.

"And you ken about creatures of the water?"

"Y-yes. That is, within reason."

"What ferlie of the water lives for thirteen hunner years and more?"

"N-none do."

"Ah!" Tam said and looked about the dark afternoon room, taking in the faces glowing in the firelight. "There is one. The kelpie lives forever, ye ken."

"Kelpie?"

"Aye, sor, the kelpie. She's a sea-witch sort of a ferlie that sometimes shapes herself in the likeness of a horse."

Tam slid his pint at Perry for a refill. Perry scuttled away to the bar as Tam called after him, "And that's what's in the loch, sor. Only this one's lost her fight, she has, since Saint Columba drove her back with that blessing. She only swims aboot, do you see, unable to do her mischief now under God's eye."

Perry returned with the pint and placed it down before the old storyteller.

"But she is seen regular, is she, by those that live along these shores.

Mary Maitland saw her. 'Twas a dank morning with the early fog lying low on the water. And there across the bay she saw auld Nessie lying up on the pebbles like she was taking the sun, but there was no sun just then, only the fog."

"Wh-what did it look like?" Perry breathed. "Did Mary Maitland say?"

"Aye," Tam replied seriously, "she did. The ferlie was some thirty or maybe fifty feet from head to tail, wide in the body and narrow in the neck like a man had threaded a snake through a turtle's shell. Only the body was soft and glistened in the morning dampness, and when she made for the loch she rose herself up on flippers like a sea lion and sort of hobbled and hopped to the water."

"But she saw the monster out of the water and walking on land?" Perry confirmed.

"Oh, aye," Tam said seriously.

"That's right," offered another man in the pub. "I heard tell up to-ward Dores a gynecologist saw her crossing the road with a sheep in her mouth that she'd caught in the field opposite."

He winked at his comrades. Tam gave the man an evil glare.

"Would it have looked anything like this?" Perry pulled out a sheet of paper as large as the portfolio. On it were a dozen pencil sketches sur-rounding a central drawing, all of a wide-bodied creature with a long, reptilian neck and a head roughly the shape of a horse's.

"What's this, then?" Tam exclaimed, amused almost beyond his ability to hide his mirth.

The men crowded in close to look at the paper on the table.

"That's not half bad," said one. "Did you draw that?"

"Yes," Perry replied. "I think it's what the creature looks like. I have combined what we know of the prehistoric plesiosaur with the eye-witness accounts I've read. I believe they coincide. I've taken some evolutionary changes into account."

"You think there's a dinosaur in the loch?" one of the men said.

"Yes," Perry replied. "I believe something like the elasmosaurus—that's a type of plesiosaur—is swimming in the loch. The horselike head is a likely evolution from the prehistoric animal, which had a skull that was already showing some elongation of the snout."

"You sound pretty certain of your facts, sor."

"I have evidence," Perry said. He pulled out a file folder filled with photographs and set them out on the table.

"Some years ago a team of scientists laid out a sophisticated network of cameras and strobe lights under the surface of the loch. They exposed hundreds of rolls of film, enough for a sixteen-hour movie, and they got these incredible photographs."

He displayed them proudly. They were gray and grainy photographs, displaying a mass of white dots forming hazy white silhouettes in the emulsion. Perry interpreted the forms for the men.

"Look at this," he said, laying a hand on an eight-by-ten of a leaf-shaped blur. "It's the monster's left front flipper. The creature swam very close to the camera, you see?" he traced the outline with his forefinger. "It is shaped like a wide diamond on a playing card. From this, scientists have named the creature *Nessiteras Rhombopteryx*: diamond-finned wonder of Ness."

The men stood by silently.

"And if it's a hoax?" Macgruer said quietly.

"Ah," agreed Perry "That's the problem. But look here."

Perry used his finger to circle an area on the lower left of the photograph. It was hardly more than a lighter-gray streak on a light-gray background.

"They've run this through the computer for analysis," Perry explained, "and the computer says that this streak here is another neck and head—a second creature. Why would a hoaxer go to the trouble of putting a second image in the water? You see, I think these photographs are genuine. I think there must be a whole colony of creatures in the loch."

"Oh, aye, then," said one of the men and winked at the others. "There could be forty or perhaps a hunner of them doon there."

"Aye," said another, "that'd surely explain it."

The rainy afternoon turned to rainy evening before Macgruer and Miggs made their way back out to the *Pelican*.

"Were they—" Perry said awkwardly as Macgruer started the engines, "were those men making fun of me?"

Andrew only hummed a noncommittal sound.

"I have trouble telling what people mean by what they say. I wonder, were they being—" he searched for a word "—sarcastic?"

"The lads like their fun."

"So they were . . . teasing me?"

"Aye," Macgruer said gently.

Perry nodded and knit his brows in thought.

"What do you think, Andrew?" he said after the boat was underway.

Macgruer considered his answer before delivering it. "I think a man should do what he feels he must and damn the world that laughs."

"But, I mean, do *you* think I'm a fool? Were you teasing me, too?"

Macgruer laughed. "Christ, Miggs, you are direct."

"I have to be."

Macgruer shook his head and laughed again.

"Were you?" Perry persisted.

"Aye."

Andrew Macgruer looked Perry in the eye and summoned up all of his conviction and sincerity.

"I think it is foolish," he said with soft kindness, "to be chasing phantoms and the like, because there's nocht—nothing—can come of it even if you find one. I think it is better to be and to let be. What's the use of dredging it all up? The things that are hidden, I mean. What good can come of it?"

"It's better to know, Mr. Macgruer. It's always better to know."

"Why is that, then?"

"Because," Perry said and then stopped, stymied. He stared out into the churning loch, the wind-swept, rain-pocked waters, for a long time before he continued. "Because love is not jealous." Perry rolled his eyes up to the ceiling of the pilothouse, deeply moved.

"You've had too much to drink."

"It isn't, is it?" Perry insisted, in some inner turmoil. "Love isn't jealous."

"Aye, Miggs, that's right. You just sit down afore ye fall down. We'll be home soon."

# Chapter 10

✤

*I dreamed of growing deep, of blooming with the Scottish spring and welling
with the new dawning year like a Celtic priestess renewed in the land of my
mothers. I dreamed of attaining that peace that accompanies contentment,
the bliss of fulfillment, the final enchantment.*

*I wavered on the threshold of enchantment like a peddler at the doorway,
laden with riches, unable to enter.*

*I suddenly knew the reason when I saw the boots. I had the answer all
along and had hidden it, slipped it away like mismatched socks in a drawer.
I had tucked it away, that answer. I had packed it back as far as I could,
hoping, no doubt, that it would go away. Hoping that it might just vanish
into that world where unwanted things go—the broken, ugly, ungainly,
awkward bits that collect in the junk drawers and closet shelves of life—
those obligatory baubles of the soul we no longer wish to keep but cannot
bring ourselves to scrap.*

*But Perry opened that neglected place in my mind, and the crumpled,
awkward answer tumbled into sight for me—no less ugly, no less ungainly,
and no less real than when I had stored it away there.*

*And poor dear Perry never meant to do it, I'm sure.*

*He only opened a box that he had ordered from town. He did nothing* more than pull out a pair of wading boots—olive drab, rubber-clad, hip deep. But the emotion those boots inspired shot through me like a fine, sharp fire. The back door of my memory broke open, and the feeling rushed in like a prickly flash of lightning. It arched and danced along my veins, glowing like corposant, and I knew what had kept me out of Scotland and Scotland out of me.

It was Perry. He had brought enough of Larchmont with him to keep me from immersing myself in Scotland.

"I have had a thought," Perry said as he allowed the boots to loll over onto themselves, broken-necked, like misshapen swans on the floor. "I am going trekking up the shoreline. Two weeks, I think, all to myself. I'll collect samples in my little jars like I did on Lake Niack at home. That will give me a basis for comparison, don't you think? I wish I had thought of it before."

"Catching minnows and mudfish in the shallows?"

"Yes."

"Isn't that a little like starting an ant farm as a prelude to an elephant hunt?"

Perry smiled in his uncomprehending way and nodded happily, just like he would on Lake Niack. I saw him clearly again, crouching along the shoreline by Widow Park Lane on the way to the college, dipping mason jars carefully into the water and scooping out little fish, collecting speci mens, his jellied knees tucked up under his armpits like some overgrown, obscene, olive-drab frog.

"I will start up the shoreline toward Inverness tomorrow, I think, and work my way down the opposite side to Fort Augustus next week. Two weeks, I think, might do it. I don't know though, it may take three. Ness is a bit bigger than Niack, isn't it?"

I had not changed.

I had bought new clothes and found a seventeen-years-dormant sensuality still alive within me, but despite all of that, I had brought what I was with me. Perry had seen to that. We'd packed Larchmont along with us.

"What a good idea," I heard myself saying to my struggling husband on the bed.

He stopped pulling and straining, the boots about his knees, and looked *at me through the hole formed between his crotch and the boots. He looked a bit like a narrow owl peeking out of a tree.*

*"Do you really think so?"*

*"Oh yes, I think it does a man good to get out in a strange place, perhaps lose himself in a thicket or two without his lunch. Builds character."*

*"Thank you, darling," he said with a deep appreciation. "I hoped you wouldn't mind."*

*"And what will you do with the* Pelican *while you take your perambulation of the lake?"*

*"Macgruer will still be here. I'll have him monitor the equipment, keep the log on the video. Not to worry, all's well."*

*"Mr. Macgruer is going to stay here?" My tone remained neutral, but I felt an unexpected shiver thrill through me at the news.*

*"Yes."*

*"And who's going to guide you around the lake?"*

*"Mr. Macgruer has a friend who will see after me—take me to the shallows and keep me close to . . . you know . . . necessaries: toilets and hot meals and such."*

*"And keep you from playing in the deep end as well, I suppose?"*

*"Oh," Perry replied seriously, "I wouldn't want to go into the deep parts at all. Might drown."*

*"Who is this friend of Mr. Macgruer's?"*

*"A man named Adam something—" His eyes widened and I could see that the elusive name had, at just that moment, slipped from his mind like a dropped bit of paper and slid under the dustier parts of his brain. He scrunched his face together and grappled with his wits like a man with one arm stuck under the sofa. He managed to retrieve it. "Adam Grant, that's it."*

*At last I had had enough. For Perry, there is only one approach when you wish to have a thing clearly understood. So I confronted him directly.*

*"Perry, dear," I said a bit sharply, "I don't think so. We have not come all this way so you can treat Ness like Niack. If you wish to embarrass yourself by puddling around Lake Niack, that is one thing, but you can't do it here. Not in Scotland."*

*"Oh," he said weakly, "I see."*

*Perry only wanted telling. He required certitude, the absolute declaration of intention. He needed that from time to time, a bellwether for his stumbling ideas, a lighthouse in his murky imagination. He knew it, too.*

*"You see," I murmured in his ear, kissing it as I did, "it's really not your very best idea."*

*"Yes," he said rather sadly, "I suppose it isn't."*

*Then he said something remarkable and altogether shocking.*

*"Still," he said, "I believe I am going to do it anyway."*

# Chapter 11

✤

*That pretty little schooner sits out on the loch now. Alone, it has been riding at anchor for three days without Perry. He's out in his shallows.*

*It rides on the water as if it is coasting in place, slipping along without moving, gliding on the picture postcard of eternity.*

*How long have I ridden at anchor, like her?*

*I came down to the banks of the loch today for the first time. Somewhere deep in my imagination, the schooner seemed to call to me, crying out for company, companionship, fellowship. I sat on the pebbled shore and watched the Pelican for, oh, I don't know. It seemed like hours and hours.*

*And I wondered how long I had been like her—swanlike and still, in my element and yet idled, becalmed. Forsaken.*

*Thirteen years. Can it have been thirteen years?*

*I had ridden at anchor for thirteen years, the years I had been married.*

*Perry was my anchor.*

*He'd tied me off in Larchmont and anchored me there as he'd anchored the Pelican on the loch. Left us to drift at our moorings, alone and untended, while he went searching the banks and shallows.*

*"Let him," I thought toward midday, when I had worked myself into a quiet boil. "Let him go hunt his efts and polliwogs."*

*I would remain behind, as always. The* Pelican *and I would remain behind this time and await his return from this ill-conceived excursion along the banks of Loch Ness.*

"Sometimes," *a voice came from behind me,* "sometimes you must no' want him to come back at all." *It was Kira Shaw. She spoke in her polite, tactful way.*

"You're right," *I admitted, hiding my guilt, feeling she had read my thoughts. I kept my eyes shut, face turned toward the sunshine, feigning indolence.* "Sometimes I don't."

*I turned and smiled at her.*

"You seem so peaceful and serene there," *she said in her beatific way.* "I nearly turned back to the house when I saw you. I hardly wanted to disturb you. How lovely for you to sit quietly and simply enjoy the day. Not like Caitlin, dear no. She canna sit still. I believe I could, though, given the opportunity of time. I believe I could sit. Were you in a dwam, Mrs. Miggs?"

"In a what?"

"In a dwam. I mean were you woolgathering?"

*I smiled, still not comprehending. Kira returned my smile sweetly.*

"Do you daydream?" *she said with a quiet sense of apology.*

*I laughed.* "Constantly."

*Kira laughed, too.* "So do I."

*She inched along the uneven pebbles toward me, walking carefully on her painful legs.*

"What were you thinking just then?" *she asked.* "Just then when I spoke, I mean, what was it on your mind?"

"Why do you ask?" *I responded, avoiding a confession of my uncharitable thoughts.*

"It's just that you seemed so very peaceful to me just then. Contemplative and, I really canna say, rather angelic and wise. There was such a look of— a look of the seraphic on your pretty face if you would know my opinion. I was wondering what thoughts could affect the face so, make it so pretty and so keen."

*I shrugged, flattered but rather ashamed that my insensitive thoughts had translated onto my face as anything so virtuous and attractive.*

"I was only idling."

"I didnae mean to disturb you, Mrs. Miggs, but you did say you enjoyed your gardening at home."

"My crocuses, yes. They should be all bloomed out by now."

"I think it is no substitute for your own fine beds, but I put my mind to working in that little herb garden of mine today—off the back door, ken—and thought, if you would like, that you could maybe keep me company. And maybe do a little clipping and scuttering aboot for me while we talked. Of course, we dinnae have to talk if you dinnae wish it."

"I'd love to, Miss Shaw."

Kira Shaw's garden was a fairyland of tiny buds and aromatic leaves tucked up under shrubberies and snaked around heavy tree trunks.

"This is so very charming, Miss Shaw. You must be proud."

"Aye, it is a quaint and quiet sort of a locality," she admitted with the air of a wholly contented woman.

She was full of restraint and marigolds, and we talked of gillyflowers.

"I call them carnations."

"Oh, no dear," she corrected me in the sweetest terms. "Carnations are the very large blooms that come around June and July. Gillyflowers are early middlings; the little ones are called pinks, you know. But gillyflowers are streaked with color.

"I love carnations, too, of course. They always remind me of cloves—the way they smell I mean—cloves and all that goes with cloves—holidays and punch and the like. And their crimps and colors are like Christmas paper, aren't they? Och, it is verra pleasant for me to catch that first whiff of carnation come June, what with the summer sun and warmth." She lapped me up in her sweet and sparkly smile. "I believe I'm just dreaming now, though. I have had all of the winter I care for and am so happy for the violets."

She was contentment to me, and I writhed inwardly that I could not achieve her state of simple bliss. What does it take to be like her—to dash away so easily to Christmas and cloves? Is simplicity something that grows with age, or is it the ripening and mellowing of discontent? I wonder if despair is tempered like the bitter whey that ripens into those exquisite British cheeses—Wensleydale, Cheshire, Gloucester, Stilton—names that always remind me of staid and respectable Mayfair families who push their prams around Kensington Gardens on warm summer afternoons.

I think not, however. I think despair is always only despair.

And I fear she was always like this: content, happy with life as she found it. And I fear that tranquility is ultimately something one either has or has not. If so, I am lost to peace forever.

I'd like to think peace is like popcorn or coffee, however, and smells much sweeter than it tastes. It's probably more like chocolate, though, and stabs to the soul like love. It is a mystery.

I poked away at Kira's garden and thought about it, forgetting for the moment that she was even there. I began thinking of Perry again.

"Science gives me a niche," Perry likes to say. "It is a comfortable little alcove—a fence against mystery."

Perry cannot bear a mystery.

Back on the airplane, while we hung like mistletoe from the sky, Perry stared at the ocean. I imagined that my marine biologist was gazing into his world below in much the way that astronomers peer into the heavens, imagining vastness, inspired by knowledge, and seeking after wisdom and infinity. But Perry only sat back in his seat and sighed deeply.

He had gone quite pale. The glory of creation spread out below him, and, instead of rising in flames like a phoenix reborn, Perry could only sputter and snuff like the flame of a penny candle, frightened by immensities.

"My goodness. It is awfully big," he had murmured to me.

"It is one of the defining characteristics of the ocean. I believe Webster's defines it as 'Wobbly, wet, and awfully big.'"

He did not catch the joke. "Jacques Cousteau is welcome to it."

"Except he's dead."

"Somebody else then."

I'm certain I would never feel that way. Were I a water creature like Perry, I would look out upon the vast Atlantic and think, "Mine, this is mine, and I am part of it." I would feel exhilarated, expanded, unfolded if I could see how much there was out there to swirl about islands and rocks before swimming into me, filling me, completing and finishing me with the knowledge and appreciation of so very much.

*But Perry only seemed to grow anxious at the sight of it.*

*The years of crouching in the puddle behind the college, rubber clad to the knee, had not kindled or sparked him at all. It had only limited him to the boundary of Lake Niack. So, instead of extrapolating the great from the small, he had only grown small himself.*

*It was then that I noticed Kira had stopped gardening. She was looking at me, and a wistful smile played sweetly on her lips. I was apparently looking angelic again. I returned her smile and asked, "And this is where you daydream?"*

*"Aye," she said with a bedeviled grin, "when I have the time and the inclination."*

*We worked for a long time, turning our talk to familiar things, plants mostly. I cleared my mind of Perry and lost myself in the richness of the soil and the fragrances of freshly turned earth, clear water, and life.*

*"It's difficult for you, is it?" Kira said, breaking into my reverie. "Being apart like this for the days Mr. Miggs goes up the way, that's difficult for you?"*

*"No," I said and smiled inwardly. If only she had the power to read my thoughts, she would never have asked.*

*"Nae," she confirmed. "That's love, ken, when the separation is endurable. When you know he's in the world and there's enough for you, that is love."*

*I felt the lump rise in my throat. How often over the past seventeen years had I secretly told myself that very truth. Only I had meant Andrew Macgruer, not Perry.*

*"Yes," I managed to choke out.*

*Kira cleared her throat and closed her eyes in concentration before speaking again:*

> *"Our two souls therefore, which are one,*
> *Though I must go, endure not yet*
> *A breach, but an expansion,*
> *Like gold to aery thinness beat."*

*"John Donne."*

*"Is it?" Kira seemed surprised. "I memorized it from my book of*

*world-loved poetry. Mr. Macgruer gave it to me. He is a poet, too."*

"Is he?" I said, but I knew it well enough. Andrew had been a fine poet at college.

"Oh, aye. He was educated at St. Andrews. It's one of his class books he gave me. That passage was marked. How odd that he should have marked that one bit of poetry. It is so appropriate."

"How is it appropriate, Miss Shaw?"

"I am in that position—the position of the speaker in the poem. I was in love, oh so much in love—many years ago—but we had to part. It is a sad thing to love and part."

"Yes."

"So it was strange that Mr. Macgruer would have marked that bit of poetry like that, as though he knew what solace it could bring a soul that loved in secret—alone, away, and apart."

The news of that marked passage gripped me and sent my poor, pained heart galloping. How I grasped at chance and hope: his textbook from school, she said, a passage of yearning love and separation. Perhaps Andrew Macgruer did not remember the wound of love I had left on him, did not remember it now, but I blindly grappled with the hope that he had once suffered for me as I have for him. To have been loved, I thought, is nearly as sweet as to be loved.

"Tell me," I said. "Tell me about when you were in love."

"Och," Kira said through a coy, sparkling grin that had probably melted men's hearts a quarter of a century before. "You would nae want to hear the daft ramblings of a foolish old and romantic woman."

"You are absolutely right," I said, "but I'd like you to tell me about when you were in love, which is nothing like that, I think."

"What a dear thing to say, Mrs. Miggs." Again she flashed her winsome and bashful smile.

"You may call me Perdita."

She froze in surprise at the suggestion before melting into a polite sigh.

"Nae," she said, shaking her head slightly, "I dinnae think I could do that, Mrs. Miggs."

"And why not, if I wish it?"

"It isn't entirely seemly. Besides, Caitlin would nae like it over much."

"Well, she can call me Perdita, too—or Perdie if she prefers."

Kira Shaw allowed herself a brief whoop of mirth at the thought of it before shaking her head again.

"Nae, nae," she said in a voice raised just above a whisper, "that she would never do."

"Ah, well—"

"But," she continued in her quiet voice, "if we might conspire together to be upon Christian-name terms only out here in the garden and only out of Caitlin's hearing, I think I should like that verra much. But you must call me Kira if I'm to call you—" she moved her lips in a pantomime of "Perdita," as though it held magic and was not to be bandied.

"Very well, then, you shall be Kira in your garden. And you will call me Perdita. And, Kira, my first imposition upon our friendship will be to ask you to tell me about him—your distant admirer."

Kira turned to clip some of the rosemary behind her, turning her back to me with a timid and uncertain smile. She set to the herbage with coy resolution.

"We've a good growth of pot-herbs started here," she said, changing the subject, "and I have hopes for the simples down the way. I've set aside a still room for them this year and am hopeful of a good growth."

She snipped and trimmed, and for a long time the only sound in the little garden was the shish of our clippers among the greenery. After some time, I realized that I was doing all of the clipping. I determined to fare forward through the herbs and let my hostess sit and think. I was rewarded for my patience.

"He was a young man of the village," she said at last. "Not over tall nor over handsome, but a good heart and a fair face all the same."

"Was his name Breton Trent?"

Her blush told me it was.

"There is nae great story to tell," Kira said in a quiet, matter-of-fact way that contradicted her words. "It is in the main a tale of flirtation, great hopes, and trivial promises."

"That sounds like love," I offered. My observation seemed to please her.

"Aye, I think so, too. I hope so anyway."

"So, what happened?"

"Och, little enough. We were namore but bairns when we started and namore but teenish when we parted. Twelve lovely summers of flirtation in all; gracious they were and genteel. Warm hands clasped, friendly words passed, a kiss now and again, some little bit more than affectionate, some little bit less than passionate; like the kissing of souls in paradise they were."

She lost herself in the memory of those kisses for a while and busied herself in the rosemary.

"We had a special place kent only to him and to me," Kira said almost to herself. "Would you like to know where?"

"Please tell me."

Kira jabbed her pruning snips toward the sky. "Up there. That was our special place."

"Heaven?"

"Nae, child, up there on the roof of the house." She repeated the jabbing of the snips, and I saw that she was pointing to the wide shoulder of roof extending out over the kitchen toward the loch.

"We were young and spry and could shin out across the roof from the attic window. We would sit there for hours and look out over the forest—over to the loch. Oh, you canna see the loch from down here; but up there, when the breezes blow fresh, you can see all the way to the castle on t'other shore. We could see the far castle with our young eyes. We held hands but seldom spoke. We were that comfortable in each other's company, though, that words seemed quite unnecessary."

In the next moment Kira had returned to the present. "I suppose you are to blame for putting me to woolgathering. You did so put me in mind of those days. I used to dream out over those waters with young Mr. Trent all those years ago just as you were dreaming today. I imagine that my own expression then was much like yours was today. I'd like to think I used to be as blissful in contentment as you seemed to me. I really do believe I was. Thank you, Mrs. Miggs, for giving me this peacefulness of heart today."

"Perdita," I corrected.

"Oh, forgive me," she teased, the joke on the absent Caitlin. "Thank you, Perdita."

"And he left?" I asked.

"Aye," she said, a little sadly. She stared up at the flat spot on the roof for a long time and seemed wrapped in her remembrances. With a collected sigh, she returned her gaze to me, smiled wistfully, and then busied herself among her rosemary again. "He went away, but no' without leaving behind a dear promise to return when he had made his fortune. He promised to come back home to Iubhar with his pockets breaking at their stitching with all the money he would make. He promised to come home and build a fair, fine belvedere up where we used to perch. He promised to build it and marry me up there when he returned."

Again, Kira was overtaken by a reverie. Her eyes began to mist and then puddle with the thought of it.

"But he never did come back?"

"Nae," she replied flatly, "never. He went to practice carpentry in Inverness, and he sent me a letter from Aberdeen some years later. Work had been difficult in Inverness, he said, and the money poor and meagre. He had hopes of better tidings in Aberdeen. He had by then finished his apprenticeship and wrote that he thought I would nae have to wait many years for him if only he could find establishment there. Caitlin had moved back in wi' me by then and told me to put away foolish notions. My Mr. Trent wrote to beg me to wait for him, but Caitlin said men were no' up to their words. She had been roughly abused by Mr. Reese, of course, and had little use for the whole sex. I didnae pay her much mind, adamant as she was, but the years came and passed on until I knew he had no' made his fortune at last, and I had overwaited my prime."

She remained motionless on her wide cushioned stool for several long minutes, poised over the rosemary, holding the open snips tenderly around a narrow stalk. At last she squeezed the handles gently and severed the tiny plant.

"I dinnae regret waiting," she said as she dropped the rosemary into her basket. "In some way I think it was like living with him, us both remaining true as we did and unmarried as we were. In saving ourselves for one another *we were as good as married I always thought. That's why I said what I did about being enough just knowing he is in the world somewhere. It has always been enough for me. It always has."*

While she spoke, I had busied myself with brushing some gray mold from under the motherwort. I was whisking briskly at a stubborn patch when I noticed Kira had stopped speaking. She smiled patiently as she watched my labors.

"You'll have a bit of trouble with that," she said, indicating the dark places under the plants. "That's the shade of the plant. You canna sweep away the shadows, dear."

We both laughed merrily at my foolish, dogged tenacity, and I felt all barriers between us dissolve.

"But now he is coming home?" I prompted, and the color rose to her face.

"Who would have thought that I would be the one to make my fortune and no' him at all? Aye, now he's coming home, Perdita, and I'll stuff his pockets with money until the seams break just as he always boasted he would return. And there's money aplenty to buy the lumber and necessaries to build that belvedere, and him a carpenter, too. I can make his every promise come true for him," she said before adding quietly, "for us."

Her resolve made me uncomfortable. I imagined Breton Trent grown old and embittered with failure or, worse, forgetful of his promises. I thought of Andrew, who had once promised to love me forever, with words strong enough to bind every saint in heaven, demon in hell. These Scotsmen can be terribly forgetful in love, I thought.

I resolved there in the garden that I would intercede at every opportunity with Mr. Breton Trent. I would see to it that he remembered his every promise; that would require me ferreting more from Kira. And I would see that he saw the advantage to himself in keeping those promises. I would, in brief, become Kira Shaw's good angel in love.

"And then in the evenings," I found myself saying, "after you are married and settled in your contentment, you and Mr. Trent, your husband, will sit out upon that belvedere and watch the loch again."

Kira blushed and tried to find an objection to my styling Mr. Trent her husband, but it was useless. We knew. I had read her hopes. In my own vain *desires for a Scotland I could never have, could never own, could never admit wanting, I had recognized her own aching need for her Breton Trent.*

"And perhaps," I continued, "one night from your rooftop you will see the creature of the loch herself. In the failing light of dusk she'll rise, and magic will be reborn."

Kira chuckled and shook her head.

"I think people of the loch are more complacent about the auld girl than anyone else in the world. Familiarity breeds complacency, it does, more than it breeds contempt. We are so verra familiar with the loch, and there is an end to all mystery. If she is there, let her be, and if she is not, why bother? That, I think, is the general attitude."

I shrugged. I didn't care about the creature. That was Perry's concern. That was Perry's career, and just now I was annoyed at Perry. I think I might have even been a little satisfied to hear Kira express doubt that the thing even existed. Perhaps, after all, it didn't. That would teach Perry to keep his priorities straight in the future.

The thought of Perry suddenly made me realize what Kira had first said to me on the pebbled beach.

"What did you mean awhile ago?" I asked her.

"When?"

"When you said that sometimes I might not want Perry to come back at all."

"I just meant I thought perhaps you would want Mr. Miggs to keep away for a good long time and let you stay in that peaceful world of imagining and woolgathering."

"But what an odd thing to say, when you know he's been gone now for three full days."

"Aye," Kira said and smiled a knowing smile. "Three days it is, but what of the nights, Perdita, what of the nights?"

"I don't know what you mean."

Kira nodded conspiratorially and hefted the basket to the other side of her gardening stool.

"I'm sure I would never breathe a word of it myself," she teased. "I think it is wonderful, mind, that you and your husband keep the same quarters. Isn't that rare? Very romantic and rare."

"Is it?" I had always assumed husbands and wives slept together as a matter of course. Kira obviously had other, more maidenly, ideas of marriage.

"I am intruding."

"Of course you aren't intruding. Please go on. What did you mean?"

"It's only Iubhar is such a little place, such a quiet and a little place, that secrets must be whispered very low or else they find no place to hide at all."

"Secrets? What secrets?"

"I haven't seen for myself, though I have heard the automobile," she said cryptically, confidentially, with a good-natured smile. "And Caitlin says she's seen him."

"Who?"

"Mr. Miggs."

"When has she seen him?"

"Of a night," Kira replied. "I think it is verra romantic of the two of you to court in the night like secret lovers."

"Is it?"

"The game is up, but I won't let on as I ken, dear, and Mr. Miggs need never learn that we are privy to his sneaking back here each night when all are abed."

"I see," I said, striving to keep up with her. "So you and Caitlin both know that Perry is staying away all day and sneaking back to meet me at night when he thinks you've gone to bed?"

She nodded and said, "But I'll never breathe a word to him."

"Good," I said with my most chipper tone, but inwardly I began to boil again.

Could it be that he had set me to drift here for nothing? And worse, could Perry really be staying somewhere so close that he could sneak back to the house each evening? That would be too much. I remembered how he had done the same thing once on a weeklong field trip; he had planned to circle a bay one summer with a research group from school and ended up remaining *at one spot too long. He had found some interesting crustacean or mudfish or something and ruined the entire trip. Complaints from students were filed, refunds demanded, reprimands placed upon permanent files, and he failed to earn tenure for the first time.*

*Could he have learned nothing then? Was he now doing to me what he had done to the college all those years ago? Was he out on unintentionally false pretenses?*

*But why sneak back every night? Kira did say every night. I resolved upon another thing in that garden that day. I would get to the heart of Perry's game.*

# Chapter 12

✤

I cherished a quiet vengeance in my bed that night.

I had slipped into my cream chinoise peignoir, the patterned silk I had bought in Inverness. It was thin as a butterfly's wing and soft as melting butter against my bare skin, and I had stripped myself nude before putting it on.

I gratified my sense of revenge by watching myself in the mirror as I slid the sheer fabric over myself. It was all quite narcissistic and indulgent, and I relished every sensuous moment. I was still firm in the bosom and narrow through the waist. Perry used to be most enthusiastic about my body; he still was from time to time.

And that was my revenge.

He would have gaped at me tonight if only he could have seen me.

I was livid all night and slept only fitfully. When I did sleep, I did so in angry, sporadic bursts. My dreams, such as they were, flashed in affronted parodies of indignant imaginings; no narrative, no allegory, only images of Perry—smug, docile, intractable, artless, derelict, and thoughtless—paraded through my half-waking dreams. Heartless images conjured from my wounded ego to feed my private resentment—images to fuel my anger.

I began to reconstruct my past that night.

Lying awake in my silken sheen of sex, I reexamined moments long forgotten: Perry arriving home late, neglecting a compliment, ignoring me in a dozen trivial ways. And these fragments of memory welled up, all the petty affronts to courtesy that had once passed unnoticed. Nearly unnoticed. They lived there still. In the quiet crypts where tokens of pain, like shards of glass, are preserved, they lived.

And in my restless slumbers, Kira's voice kept repeating, now ominous and fateful, "You canna sweep away the shadows, dear."

I would confront Perry when he sneaked back in for his sandwiches and milk, or whatever he was sneaking back in for. I would confront him with fire and ice, firing his lust, meeting it with my ice.


In the darkness of the late night, I was roused from my slumbering watch by the sound of a footfall under my window.

I knew it was Perry.

I slid out of bed quietly and glided down the stairway as light as a fairy, a sensuous, nearly nude fairy wrapped in a billowing, transparent gossamer woven of cobweb and lace.

I crept into the kitchen at the back of the house and waited for him to appear at the back door. The soft light glistened on my body, and I sparkled as though tiny diamonds had been sprinkled across my bare skin.

I floated in the uncertain light like a fantasy of sensuality, a dream of love in blue.

My part was simple. I knew my lines well: "Come to bed" when he had seen me; "Not tonight" when he had nestled in beside me.

Soon I began to wonder whether he would ever appear at the kitchen door. I sensed my carefully planned moment passing. I peeked out of the kitchen and saw him standing in the road under our bedroom window.

It was so like Perry to idle like this and ruin my designs.

But not tonight.

I sailed to the front door noiselessly, pulled it gently open, and slipped out onto the porch and into the friendly, flattering moonlight.

He stood in shadows, but I felt his eyes upon me.

"Did you think I wouldn't know?" I whispered into the night air. "Do you believe I couldn't sense your presence every night? You know you can't stay away from me."

He stepped out of the shadows into the blue light with me.

It was Andrew Macgruer.

My body tensed. I was at once startled, embarrassed, horrified, and thrilled. All at once I was aware of the trembling tingle of silk brushing against me, enveloping me in a tender, sensuous flutter like the throbbing race of anticipation.

His eyes were fixed upon mine, and he crossed to me deliberately. He was serious, masculine, and sincere, and I whispered inwardly, "Oh, God, don't let this be a dream."

He placed his wide, hard arms around me and pulled me tenderly to him. My own arms wrapped around him gently, gratefully. He held me for a long moment in the warm night before tilting my face softly up to his. He kissed my lips, a long, light kiss, and his breath was warm and sweet as balm, his lips as soft as the velvet of rose petals, his affection and longing sincere.

"I'm sorry," he breathed against my face with a depth of feeling that broke my heart.

He stepped back and brushed my cheeks lightly with the backs of his fingers, drinking me in with his eyes.

He cradled my head in his large, sensitive hands and pulled me to him again and kissed me harder, with passion, the way he had kissed me for the first time. My mind raced back to St. Andrews, the West Port gate, and to a time when I had been too shy to return his first kiss.

I did not make the same mistake now. I wove my fingers into his long hair and kissed him for all I was worth, a seventeen-years-waiting kiss.

We parted slowly, and he breathed a long, stuttering sigh that satisfied my every doubt of his warmth. He opened his large, intelligent eyes and looked deeply into mine.

"Welcome home, Pær," he said softly, calling me by the nickname I had nearly forgotten.

His eyes filled with mist and his face trembled slightly under my palm.

*He turned from me the next moment and strode away toward the loch, never looking back, leaving behind only the muscular orange cat that followed him everywhere.*

*The cat remained at my feet, arching his back against my bare calves, wreathing his long, soft tail around my legs, watching with me as Andrew disappeared into the blackness of the forest at the lane's end.*

*I bent to stroke him, but his tail was flat, like linen, and when I opened my eyes I was still in bed, the sheet coiled between my fingers.*

*"Damn," I whispered in my dark and lonely room.*

✦

"Are you going back again tonight?" Adam Grant said sleepily from the bed of leaves he had piled around himself.

"Yes," Perry said a little uncertainly, still groggy from just having awakened.

He had overslept.

It was growing rapidly toward morning. The nights are short in the Scottish summer, and he had to get back before the household was awake.

"Why?" Adam said, sitting up. "Why come all the way up the loch only to steal back of a night?"

Perry was fishing for his keys in his trousers even as he pulled them up his legs.

"I have to." In another moment, he stopped tugging on his pants. "What do you mean when you say *only* to steal back in the night? Do you think we've done nothing else than that?"

Adam fixed Perry with a long, hard look. "You're like nae monster hunter I've come upon, Mr. Miggs."

"I see," Perry began pulling his trousers on again. "In what way am I different? Do you think I'm more scientific, perhaps? Better in some way?"

"Nae, sor. You are the most peculiar sort I have met. What do you want to find here in the shallows and streams? The auld girl is out there in the deeps, sor."

"Yes," Perry said as he stood and fastened his belt. "Yes, I suppose she is."

He stared out into the night and watched the moon glint off of the water far away. He had spent the day taking samples from a stream high up a hill from the shore. The bracken and scrub had blocked their view of the loch nearly all day.

"Still, I want to be methodical, leave no stone unturned, no avenue untrod."

"That's what I mean by different. Most hunters are keen to get on wi' their cameras and suchlike, get a shot of auld Nessie for the papers and television. They never take their eyes off of the loch for a minute. But you—"

He began rolling up his blanket as he let his observation hang.

"What are you doing?" Perry said.

"I'm packing it in for the night and gane back wi' you."

"Are you?" Perry seemed mildly alarmed. "Are you going back with me? Why?"

"Morning's nearly here. Time to be getting up. Why is it you dinnae want me along?"

"I—" Perry hesitated. "I need to be intrepid. Quiet, you see? I wouldn't want Perdie to know I was sneaking back like this."

"Why not?"

"She thinks I'm a long way around the loch by now. She thinks I'm doing something very important and necessary. She doesn't really understand—this, this thing I'm doing."

"I dinnae understand it myself, Mr. Miggs."

Perry sat on the fallen log beside the car and tied his shoes. When he had finished, he stared blankly toward the water beyond the tangle of trees.

"I'm frightened," he said quietly.

Adam Grant stopped packing up his sleeping things and sat beside the wiry little professor. He slapped Perry on the knee to give him reassurance.

"It's no good," Perry continued. "I have planned it out so carefully, so meticulously, but I'm afraid that it will all fall apart—the whole summer, I mean. There are so many things to be taken into account, so many ways it could all go wrong that I'm afraid. Failure would be unendurable. I have failed already so often."

He turned to Adam and smiled feebly.

"So often," he repeated with resignation.

"And now," Adam interpreted, "you're afraid to begin for fear of failing. Aye, well, that's understandable. It's no reason, though. No' trying is the surest way to fail."

"I know you are right," Perry said, "but the strain is so great that I think I might collapse from it. I have disappointed her at every step, failed her at every turn. I don't know if I can take this pressure. It weighs on me, and I just want it to be all over. All of it."

Perry climbed into the little car, and Adam threw his kit into the back and crawled in.

"So why creep back to Iubhar and the lodging house every night?"

"I have to," Perry said. "It's all part of the plan."

"Weel, even if you do ken what you are aboot, and even if trailing up every current and flow has some sort of reason, I canna think of any explanation for sneaking back to the house at night."

"I—" Perry hesitated before climbing into the little car. He looked over the top at Adam and said, "I'm checking on my wife, if you must know."

Adam laughed an impolite, I-knew-as-much laugh that Perry did not comprehend, and they both slid into the car.

"So why not just bring her along with you?"

"Oh, no. I couldn't. She wouldn't. That would spoil it all. You see, I am not being honest with her." Perry pushed the gears out of neutral and began his way back to Iubhar. "I need your help in a little—er—deception of mine. My wife is a very sick woman."

"She does nae look sick."

"She is, though. And if it ever should happen that I can't be around to give her—to make her take her *medicine,* I wonder if you could see that she has it?"

"She canna take it herself?"

"No. No, Adam, she can't. She doesn't know she's sick. And—and I don't want her to know. So we have to give her the medicine in her food so she doesn't suspect."

He pulled the car off the road and stopped, then turned to Adam as he pried the brown bottle from his pocket. He had long since scraped off the red label marked "poison," and he tipped a handful of orange pills into his palm. He showed Adam how to crush them into powder.

"No more than two at a time or else she might—er—react. It has to work by building up slowly in her system."

Adam nodded his understanding, and Perry gave him a supply of the pills. "So you can look after her when I can't, okay?"

The car lurched up onto the road and growled away in the darkness of morning. They arrived in Iubhar after a brief drive. Perry doused the headlamps as the car came into town and rolled slowly down the hill toward the boardinghouse. He pressed the brakes carefully, and the little car squeaked to a meek halt.

"I need to go into the kitchen," Perry said sotto voce as he climbed carefully out of the car, being certain to press the car door gently, chattering it closed. "Please wait here in the car. I won't be more than five minutes, then we must return to the creek."

"To scoop out more muck?"

"Yes."

"All in aid o' this little deception ye've been telling me aboot?"

"Yes."

The old man shook his head wearily. Perry regarded him, hoping Mad Adam would prove an ally. Adam looked up through the windscreen as if he were about to speak, when he froze. His eyes widened.

"Sweet heavenly God," the old man murmured sincerely, "thank you for your blessing of eyesight."

Perry turned in time to see the vision of his attractive wife wafting like a naked angel on a cloud of silk. She was striding purposefully from the open door toward their car. She brushed past Perry, leaned into the open driver's-side window, and pulled the keys from the ignition.

"Now come to bed," she snapped at her husband and stalked back toward the house.

Perry followed obediently after her, leaving Adam Grant smiling broadly in the car.

That night Perdita made passionate love to her husband, and they both overslept their breakfast while Kira smirked and grinned about her morning chores.

"'Tis a fair thing," she muttered cheerily, "married love."

# Chapter 13

# June

"You dinnae know how to work the equipment," Andrew observed. There was an odd desperation in his voice.

"I have read the manuals, Mr. Macgruer, and what I don't know I can teach myself," Perry replied.

"You must take me with you. You hardly know your way around the loch."

"I've had some practice excursions," Perry replied with an ingenuous optimism. "I think I can drive her. It shouldn't be too difficult."

"You—you won't know where to look for her," Andrew said. "You need a guide."

"Mr. Macgruer," Perry said seriously, "I have a plan."

"What is it?"

Macgruer was skeptical, but more, he was worried.

"You know the saying that the loch never gives up her dead?"

"Aye."

"It's true. The cold waters inhibit the bacterial action and keep the body from bloating. That's why nothing ever floats here. That's what I was looking for along the shore last week. No dead fish. Nothing washed ashore. Everything sinks. I don't think I'll need a guide,

Mr. Macgruer, because, you see, no one knows where the bodies are—not even you."

"What did he mean?" Mad Adam Grant said when Andrew met him back on shore and reported their conversation. "What did he mean aboot knowing where the bodies are?"

"He's no' looking for Nessie," Andrew explained. "He thinks there's a whole colony of creatures down there. If he's right, there will be some dead'uns. That's what he's looking for with that sonar array under the boat. He's going to map the entire bottom of the loch and find the skeletons if he can. He's going to find her, Adam. He will find her."

"Maybe he will," Grant said. "But you say he canna work the machine?"

"No' yet," Andrew said. "There's a trick to it he has no' got by rote, has to read the book."

"Then put your fears away. I have had a measure of the man. He will no' be long at it before he despairs and does nocht. He has the seeds for his own failure in him. He lacks the dreamer's ambition, Andrew. He lacks the fire and spirit. He is weak-willed."

"How do you mean that?"

"I mean it is a shameful thing for a man to treat his wife as Mr. Miggs treats Mrs. Miggs." Adam Grant held out a fistful of cash. "Can you imagine," he continued, "asking to have his lovemaking done by proxy in this way. He has a weak will, Andrew Macgruer, and his pretty young wife deserves better."

"What has he asked you to do?"

"Never you mind, Andrew Macgruer; never you mind. But I'll say this to you, and I'll say it to you once only. If I were a man of half my years, I would nae let that pretty, lonely woman pine away without the comfort of her husband—or her lover."

"I've washed my hands of her, Adam."

"You've washed off only the painful memory," Grant responded. "There is a sort of fate at work, isn't there? In all your pagan thought you ken that everything happens to purpose. There are no accidents. Your purpose is before you, waiting and ready."

"Why are you encouraging this, Adam Grant?"

"Everything has taken us to this moment, has it no'?"

Andrew hesitated in thought before bending to stroke the marmalade tabby.

"Daft," he said before striking off into the forest up the *grá*.

"Aye," Adam muttered to himself. "There is nothing so daft as desire."

✦

*It was Wednesday again and Kira and Caitlin were doing their parlor trick with the tables, readying everything for their afternoon fête, filling the household with the warm steam of pie and herb bread. I did my best trying to keep from invading the routine of the household.*

*I sat at my window all morning and watched the curtains flutter in the warm summer breeze. Mainly I daydreamed and felt listless amid the aroma wafting up the stair into my hermitage.*

*"Mrs. Miggs?" a voice cried up to me in the late morning. I looked down and saw Adam Grant in the road.*

*"Yes, Mr. Grant?"*

*"Will you come wi' me this day?"*

*I wanted to ask where we might be going, but he turned immediately from the door and began up the road toward those twisting woods that I wanted so to discover, so I followed him.*

*I thought, as we made our way from the village and into the hills, "This is what it is to follow mindlessly, to follow as the children who capered after the Pied Piper." Mine was a shuffling piper, however, who probably had not capered for many a decade. His only music was the rattling rasp of his old lungs against the steep climb.*

*I asked twice where he was taking me. I tried to tell him that I had a weak heart and should not exert myself too much. I was curious about the basket he carried, however, so I followed on and held my questions.*

*"All right, then," I said when we had gone far, "where are you taking me?"*

"Here," Adam replied. He put the basket on a flat stone beside me, where I rested, and said, "Lunch."

I opened the basket, expecting brown bread and perhaps a block of rough cheese. I was surprised to find a white pot of Keiller's "famous tayberry conserve," ripe brie, brown ale, and two tea roses, one red, one white.

Odd coincidence. It was a meal I remembered well.

The first picnic I had ever gone on with Andrew Macgruer was a luncheon of Keiller's tayberries, brie, and brown ale.

"Wild berries for nature," he had said, "and brie for culture."

"And the nutty brown ale?" I had asked.

"That's for you," he had said and laughed. Then he added seriously, "It is the color of your hair and the spice of your lips." Then he picked two flowers, red and white; one for love, the other for eternity, he said.

We had walked that long-ago day, too.

It was the first time I had been taken down to the pier. I had been there many times before, but that was the first time I had been escorted and the first time I had ever really seen it in all of its majesty. We watched the North Sea crash about the shore before walking through town. He stopped me under the West Port gate and kissed me. He cupped my face in his hands and pressed his lips to mine tenderly.

I was so awkward, I didn't know what to do with my own hands, so I pressed them into the rough stone of the archway behind me. The roughness of stone reminds me still of that first kiss in Scotland, and I often recalled that kiss as I worked in my garden at home, unearthing little rough stones and replacing them with flowers.

"You dinnae like it, Mrs. Miggs?" Adam Grant said.

Lost in reverie, I had not yet unpacked the food from the basket.

"Why are you doing this?"

"You like to walk. I've shown you the best path to see what you will. Do you see that wee crofter's bothy set behind the mead?"

He pointed up the opposite hill at a wide swath of grass running up into a forest. In the forest, I could just make out a cottage.

"I see it."

"That is the home of Mr. Andrew Macgruer, Mrs. Miggs."

"Did he send you?"

"You would like that, would you no'?"

"How do you know so much about me?"

"I dinnae know much aboot you at all, lassie, but I want to. I want to know you," he said mysteriously, "before it is too late."

He then smiled and pinched his eyebrow in gesture of farewell before leaving me alone to find my own way back to Iubhar.

The next morning was the tenth. I awoke alone in my bed. Perry had left for the Pelican early, while it was still dark, and had disturbed me only a little with his fussing about in the room.

I awoke to find that my table beside the window was crowded with flowers, red and white—spilling over with them, in fact. Large armloads of flowers crowded the tabletop and piled the floor around it like some Eastern miracle, and their fragrance filled the whole upstairs with the scent of summer.

I stayed upstairs all morning arranging the flowers in the little vases and pots I found, decorating the bedroom, and did not go downstairs until late.

I did not venture into the wonderland of Scotland that day but rather went around to the kitchen door to see if I could find Kira.

"Dinnae go into the kitchen," Caitlin said in stentorious tones from the parlor. "You've missed breakfast."

"Sorry?" I said, peeking around into the room that Caitlin was cleaning.

"You have missed your breakfast already," Caitlin repeated without looking up at me. "Dinnae go into the kitchen."

"I wanted to see if I could help."

"No' in the kitchen," she said brusquely. "Stay oot of the kitchen during the cooking hours. If you would be helpful, you may help me in here. Miss Shaw is not to be meddled with during the cooking hours."

She was in earnest and even looked a bit distressed.

"Thank you for the flowers this morning."

"What flowers?"

"There is a lovely array of wildflowers in my room, all red and white. Didn't you put them there this morning?"

"I put nae flowers in your room."

"Then who—?"

"No' me."

In a little while, Kira came into the room. I sensed the chill between the sisters. Something had happened, something serious.

"Did you place flowers in Mrs. Miggs's room this morning, Miss Shaw?" Caitlin said with an edge in her voice.

"I placed nae flowers," Kira said dismally. "And why would you think I would be putting flowers in Mrs. Miggs's room, Caitlin?"

She sounded defensive and wounded.

"Because it is the sort of romantic nonsense you've been up to all along, isn't it, Miss Shaw?" Caitlin was positively poisonous, pronouncing each word distinctly, precisely, with an overabundance of malicious cordiality.

"I dinnae see what is nonsensical about romance, dear," Kira said to her sister. She looked at me, and I could see that she toyed with the idea of drawing me into the fray, looking for an ally. She abandoned the idea, though, with a shake of her head, and turned again to her sister, who was aggressively polishing a table.

"I said," Kira continued, "that I dinnae see the nonsense—"

Caitlin snapped around and silenced her sister with a look.

"We've not done talking of this," she said hotly. "But for the moment and for the sake of hospitality we will leave it be."

"I have some things to do today," I said tactfully. "I may be some time coming back."

"Thank you," Caitlin said sharply. "We'll no' wait a meal for you."

"Yes," I continued. "I had a lovely time sitting by the loch some weeks ago. I discovered such a charming little place afterward, too. I think I may go there today. It was a bit of a fairyland."

"Enjoy it," Caitlin said with no hint of good wishes.

"Thank you. Good morning."

I went straight out of the house and was not far before I heard Caitlin's voice raised. I could not make out the words, but the tone spoke of anger, hurt, perhaps even betrayal. Kira, I supposed, was responding in the long silences that punctuated Caitlin's tirade. Kira would not raise her voice, I knew.

*I remained idling in the herb garden behind the house, hoping that Kira would remember that we had gardened here on the day she had found me daydreaming by the loch. I began to think that perhaps she had not picked up my hint—or perhaps she did not wish to meet me. But, a little while after the unpleasant voice had gone quiet, she appeared at the kitchen door.*

*She smiled at me, but much of the luster was gone from her accustomed joviality.*

*"What is it, Kira?" I had positioned myself deep in the woods at the bottom of the garden and out of sight of the house.*

*"Caitlin is fair put out." Kira had the air of a beaten woman, exhausted and exasperated.*

*"What about?"*

*"She believes I have done a foolish thing, Perdita." I was glad she remained on familiar terms with me even in this distress.*

*She wrung her hands in her apron for a long time before speaking again.*

*"She found out aboot the money," she said at last.*

*"What about the money? What money?"*

*"All the money that you and Mr. Miggs paid to stay here." Kira rolled her eyes up as though seeking divine inspiration, but it became readily apparent that she was drinking back the flood of tears that she had hidden from her sister.*

*"What of it?"*

*"Caitlin thinks we'll no' see it again."*

*"See it again? Why? What's happened to it?"*

*"You remember I told you all those weeks back about Mr. Trent returning?" she began, hesitantly. "I wanted so to have him return as he had promised, with his pockets breaking with money, that I mailed him a cheque for all that we had remaining in the bank. I of course told him where the money was from and what I wanted him to do wi' it. You see, it was all a sort of a loan, I thought, and Mr. Trent would give it right back to me when he got here. That is, after he'd flashed it about to show everyone how well he had done. Caitlin thinks I've been foolish in trusting him wi' so much money."*

*Kira shook her head.*

*"She's not overfond of men anyway," she added rather unnecessarily.*

"I always thought that it might be the money keeping him away. He had left with such promises and grand boasts, do you see? He just could nae come home again wi'out a rich cache to prove he had no' failed. I thought the money would bring him back all the quicker."

"When," I said carefully, "did you send it?"

"Back when he first wrote in reply to my letter and said he was coming back."

"Did he write to you that he needed the money?"

Kira seemed shocked. "Nae. It was all my own idea. Caitlin thinks it was Mr. Trent asking for it that made me send it, too. But it was all my own idea."

"When was Mr. Trent supposed to be here?"

"Yesterday, the ninth," she replied, struggling with her emotions. "I thought it would be grand to have him walk in wi' all of Iubhar there in the front parlor, walk in like a pasha and his pockets wide wi' money."

"When did Caitlin find out," I said, "find out about the money?"

"Yesterday morning. The cancelled cheque arrived from the bank."

"So he's cashed the check," I said softly.

"Almost as soon as it arrived. Weeks and weeks ago."

"Oh, Kira." I could not help myself. The discouragement in my tone was too much, and Kira broke down and wept in her herb garden for a long time while I sat helplessly patting her shoulder and wishing I could find some words of comfort.

"Of course it is all too bad," Kira said. "I've disappointed everyone."

"How, everyone?"

"We shan't have enough now to continue serving these grand meals. I've stumbled at every turn."

"Never mind that."

"But I did it for love, Perdita, for love. That must tally on some account."

"It does," I assured her. "It does."

"But, of course, that is neither pot nor pan to Caitlin. She has nae use for love, and weel you ken. That is why she was so cross about the flowers in your room."

"You did put them there then?" I said, a little disappointed.

"Oh, no. I didnae put them up there. That was the first I had kent of

*them, but Caitlin thinks I'm that foolish to be placing flowers and me no'
able to climb the stairs."*

*"Then if you didn't put them in my room, and Caitlin certainly didn't,
then who—"*

*"Surely it was Mr. Miggs."*

*"No, he wouldn't—" I began, but caught myself."Yes, yes. It must have
been."*

*I knew it could not be Perry, would not be Perry. Perry would have no
reason to send me flowers today. But then again, nobody would. It was no
special date.*

*"Just a minute. Did you say yesterday was the ninth?"*

*"That's right."*

*It suddenly came clear to me.*

*Today was June tenth.*

*June tenth. I had almost forgotten the date, had almost let it slip away
entirely.*

*I'd left Scotland on June tenth. Seventeen years ago to the day, Andrew
Macgruer left an important rugby game, one I thought he would never miss,
to meet me at the airport and hold me for the last time.*

*He had again given me two roses then, one red, one white, and reminded
me that they meant eternal love.*

*The red and white flowers I had found in my room this morning sud-
denly bloomed in my imagination, and I was filled with an aching. I fancied
there in Kira's færie garden that the enchantments of Scotland were finally
finding me.*

*"What was that?" Kira pulled me from my reverie. "Did you hear that?"*

*We sat listening for a moment before we heard it again—a shrill whistle.*

*"It canna be," Kira said, wheeling around the tree.*

*On the roof of the house, God only knows how he got up there, was a
bow-legged little man in a blue suit and battered hat. The jacket sleeves
came only to his mid-forearms and the pants were a size too wide, but he
stood in a jaunty attitude, his thumbs tucked up under his lapels.*

*"Good morning, Kira darling," the whimsical fellow called. "I'm sorry to
have been delayed for the day, but here I am at last."*

"Breton Trent," Kira said, her hand clasped over her breast, "as I pray for salvation from flames."

"And I have a bit o' something for you, darling," he said, opening his jacket and pointing to the inside pocket. "Look at how she bulges, eh?"

He wiggled a fat envelope from the narrow, threadbare pocket and tossed it down to us. Kira retrieved it and opened the flap.

"Every penny," she cried. "Every penny of it is here!"

She dashed away at once into the house, the envelope clutched to her bosom—off to vindicate Mr. Trent to Caitlin.

"Isnae that just like a woman?" Breton Trent said to me. "Toss her a bit of cash and you might just as soon fire a pistol. They're off just that quick. What's your name, then?"

# Chapter 14

❖

Breton Trent was a jaunty, devil-may-care little man. His bagging trousers were battered and patched. His bowler hat was broken in the crown and wrinkled all along the brim until there was hardly a brim worth the name. His shoes, once black, were rubbed raw, and his thready jacket pinched him.

But there was something beyond his disheveled clothes that bespoke elegance. Perry was immediately taken with Breton Trent.

Trent had stayed over for supper. He was open and disarming in conversation, said what he thought and made no apologies for himself. He was like a breath of south wind for Perry, this man who refused to speak in the riddles of intonation and insinuation. Trent's jokes were funny, his observations pithy; his every frank opinion was filled with wit and perspicacity, and, most important to Perry, everyone in the room understood him as Perry understood him. That was rare.

Despite Perry's pleasure, the evening was not pleasant.

There was tension in the room over supper. Caitlin Reese was too innately polite to allow her hostility to find direct expression, but her every look was filled with rancor, her every phrase tinged with reproach. Perdita saw at once that Caitlin's celebrated animosity toward the male sex was not exaggerated. This was, in fact, the first time since Caitlin Reese had returned to Iubhar that a man had sat at her mother's table as an unpaying guest of the house, and she quite clearly did not like it.

She seemed to blame her sister, Kira, for having invited the interloper, and there had been an ugly scene whispered over steaming kettles in the kitchen before supper.

"You must think ma heid buttons up the back, Kira Shaw." Caitlin slapped the wooden spoon hard against the heavy kettle. Had she been a more emotional woman, she would have been on the verge of tears. But not Caitlin. Tears were a luxury she could no longer afford. "You'll be having him big up that wart on the roof of the hoose you've been yammering efter a' these years. Your belvedere, is it?"

"It'll be no' so expensive as we'd thought it."

"Expense be biled, Kira Shaw, we agreed no' tae have it put up. We agreed."

"We never did, sister. You namore than laid oot the law as you'd have it, and I namore than said I understood that there was the law as you'd have it. I never said it was as I'd have it."

"That's it lying open then, is it?" Caitlin spewed. She knew that ultimately she would have to capitulate. Kira was the elder sister. Caitlin was the prodigal daughter returned. She knew well enough that she could win only if Kira allowed her to bully the question, which usually she did. But this was a different question. This was Mr. Breton Trent. Caitlin decided to fall back, retrench, and stand her ground about the belvedere in a later skirmish. This current battle, she could see, was lost.

"Weel enough, then," she said. "Gang your own gate. You can put a bit of howtowdie before him this night, but we have no' finished discussing the belvedere, Kira Shaw."

So it was that supper was a dour affair.

But all that Perry could see that evening was that Breton Trent was a wonder. Despite his ragged clothes and the hard-worn face of a rugged, taciturn man, Trent was glib and spoke freely. He was un-guarded, entirely comfortable, and carefree. He was a gifted storyteller, able to spin interesting tales out of the most mundane happenings. He was youthful in his approach to life and had an open honesty and a re-freshing, if puerile, sense of humor.

He continued relating his tales well into the meal. His tales dove-tailed one into another like an ancient epic of the common man with comical effects added on. ". . . His name was, let me think now. We called him Sammy Sausage because he was a daffin auld doolie, but that was no' his real name. I was up laying on a roof; and a fine steep roof it was with a gabling that pointed up to the sky like steeples o' the kirk. I was laying on the roof, as I say, wi' ma spikey shoes and knee pads on to keep me frae rolling off that roof, ken? I was nailing up the roof and Sammy Sausage was doon a' t'other end wi' the tar crew. They were spreading on the hot tar—steaming and bowffin it was oot in that sunshiny day. He was making a habble o' the job, was Sammy Sausage, taking no care at all wi' the tar brush, when all a' once he cries oot, 'Here, I've gone and ruint ma shirt!'

"I lookit over at him and there he had a great, steaming clart o' tar on his shirt. 'Flype it,' I cried over to him. 'I'll no' be working wi' a man that canna handle his brush. Give that shirt a flype.' Sammy didnae know what I meant by 'flype it,' so I told him to turn that shirt inside oot so the foreman would nae see. He stripped off and gave the shirt a flype and slid it back on afore that great lump of steaming tar had ony chance at all to cool.

"You could hear it hiss against his chest from the street, so you could.

"Up he jumps again on that steepy sort o' roof, looking to tear off his shirt again, do you see? And all the time he's crying, 'Mary mother o' God!' so loud that the whole crew stopped to see what was ailing him. Now Sammy was no' on his feet a moment afore ma Good Lady Gravity takes her part. Over he pitches like a rolly-bottom doll, and doon the roof, bang goes his heid on the guttering, and oot o' sight he drops like a weight o' lead with a surprised sort o' look painted on it.

"He was still lying in the bushes, bubbling like a baby, when we broke it off for lunch. He was no' so bad hurt, though. He'd split a half dozen tree limbs coming doon, so he was no' the worse for the cuts and scratches. But the dampt fool didnae pull off his shirt lying in the bushes all that time, waiting for some one of us to come and help him oot and feeling sorry for himself the while, and all the time that bit o' pitch cooling against him. In the end the doctor had tae cut that great hard clart o' tar off him wi' a knife."

Perry laughed and struck the table with his palm. He had never heard such a clear example of fun.

About Breton Trent there was a subtle air of gentility; his work-roughened hands were graceful in their way, his gestures cultivated and polished, charming. And while his sensibilities and tales were of the schoolyard and woodshop, his manner and form knew the way to the high street.

"I wanted to be a musician," Breton Trent told Perry the following day.

Perry had invited him out to lunch on the *Pelican*. They had opened several bottles of ale between them and were beginning to feel companionable, altogether chummy, and rather rosy.

"I wanted to play music, Mr. Miggs, music to charm children and melt the hearts of fine ladies. I used to close ma een and see a crowd o' people. They would be listening to ma music, almost in love wi' me for playing it for them. That would have been the life I would have weaved oot for myself."

"Why aren't you? Why aren't you a musician?"

"I am, Mr. Miggs. It is something you are or are no'. I am a musician. Music lives in me and kindles ma fires. But you're asking why I am no' a musician to pick up an instrument and play for ma crowds."

He held up his left hand. Half of his little finger was missing.

"I cut it off when I was no' but a birkin with a heid full o' plans and no' enough sense to watch what I did. Learning the carpenter's trade was I. One fautit moment wi' the saw and the carpenter trade was all I could do. Och, but once upon a time I could play the violin as sweet as a bird can sing, Mr. Miggs. It was tae be ma everything, but I missed it all oot by a wee inch o' finger."

"I am sorry."

"I believe I'd have been a great man in music, efter all. I believe I could have been for all o' that. I dinnae miss so much the chance at fame now, not so much. I do miss the quiet times I might have spent playing sweet and lovely to myself, though. A room wi' oot music, Mr. Miggs, is loneliness itself.

"After a time I smashed up ma violin into a load o' brock. Oh, I used to have a temper. I wish I had no' done that, though, breakin' up ma violin. It was like killing off a bit o' myself, but I was that angry. I ken I wanted to kill a part o' me. But I killed off the better part, and let the worser alone. I took to drinking and forgetting myself. I woke up one day in Aberdeen, the braw bit o' my life spent already. And I realized that day that I could gae on as I'd been or gae back tae the way I was. And I put all o' the bitterness away then, all o' the pain, all o' the disappointment, and the hunner thousand bits o' blame I'd let pass for personality. I just let it gae.

"And when I let it gae a ferlie thing happened. I suddenly found the braw young man I'd been—waiting there, he was, waiting to be me again. I wrote off the thirty years past as bad debt and would nae carry them a step further, for, you see, the only real damage a body can do himself is to keep carrying the injuries along.

"I'm no' a violinist wi' oot a finger, do you see? I am a musician whose music is all o' the inside. That is what I am."

"And you have no regrets?"

Trent smiled. "I am no' proud o' all I have done, Mr. Miggs, and I am sorry for much that has passed in ma life. But I have nae regrets for who I am."

Trent closed his eyes and sighed deeply. "I can still dream it, though, can I. Still in my night-waking mind I can lift the violin to my chin and play so shocking sweet that the angels weep and demons repent themselves of sin. I regret perhaps what I have nae got, but I do no' regret who I am today."

"I wish I could say the same."

"How do you mean? What have you tae regret, Mr. Miggs?"

Perry shrugged. "Almost everything."

"That's a heavy humph."

"Do you," Perry said after the two had looked out over the loch for a long silent time, "do you find this place romantic, Mr. Trent?"

"Aye," Trent said with a deep satisfaction. "I do. I grew up here, and you might think I would grow tired of it, that it might lose its charm to me, but I hinnae and it disnae. I fell in love here. There's a thing that disnae leave a man. Why are you asking?"

"I want Mrs. Miggs to be deliriously happy here before— I'm not a romantic sort of fellow. I don't know how to be, really. But I want to fill her life with romance just this once. That's what I meant when I said I regretted everything about my life. I have been such a— such an altogether inadequate husband to her."

"Demanding is she?"

"You say a man can change just like that, just walk away from thirty years and be the man he was. I think some can. If you have a strong constitution and a strong will, maybe you can. You can just wad up the rubbishy parts of your life and toss them away.

"Perdita could do that. She's like that. Strong, I mean. Emotionally strong, anyway. I'm kind of afraid, though, that it's me that's the rubbishy part of her life."

"That's just havering."

"Sorry?"

"Nonsense, I mean, Mr. Miggs."

"No," Perry sighed. "No, I think it is perfect sense. Absolute sense. I have been a disappointing, rubbishy kind of a husband. I've never meant to be. I suppose I've gotten kind of lost in it all. Now I don't know how to get back. That's why I came out here. I think I might be able to make it all right out here."

"Oot here on the loch, you mean?" Trent said, growing groggy with the ale. He was beginning to dream peacefully of his old violin.

"Yes, out here on Loch Ness. That's why I wondered if you found it romantic here. I would like to have Perdie think I had brought her someplace romantic. Everything depends on it."

"Aye, weel, there are no' many women who would nae find it so. The Highlands are gey bonnie."

Trent closed his eyes and let the boat rock him and the sun warm him.

"I hope so, Mr. Trent," Perry said after he had sat awhile in thought. "I've had to make decisions, you see, a long time ago when we were first married. She wanted children. But children just weren't in the cards, what with one thing and another—Perdie the way she is and all, you see? So I— I had a procedure. It didn't look like she'd ever recover, so I had myself— operated on. It seemed a good idea at the time, firing blanks, no children. But I didn't tell her. Pretty soon, making love was kind of like lying to her, making a promise I never meant to keep. So I just quit, just quit making love. She never complained. But I think she missed it. I think she was trying to be nice about it all. But it's still hard to live with the lie."

Perry's nose had reddened and begun to run. His eyes clouded with tears.

"It isn't something I can just wad up and throw away, you know? It isn't like a finger for a violinist, Mr. Trent. I can't just be a father on the inside. And I can't live with that."

Perry had been looking out across the wide loch, watching the day cruisers and pleasure boaters as he spoke. He turned and saw that the rumpled little Scotsman had fallen asleep in the warm sun.

"Ah—well," Perry patted Trent's arm, "my secret's safe with you anyway."

# Chapter 15

✤

"Do you mind too much?" Perry said to me at breakfast that Saturday.

"Mind?" I said. I had been playing at a crossword. "Do I mind what too much?"

"That I want to go out on the boat today."

"But it's Saturday. I thought you liked to spend Saturdays writing your reports to the Royal Geographic Society."

"Normally I do, yes. And I enjoy going out for supper usually, too. With you, I mean. Do you enjoy going out on Saturdays with me?"

"Of course I do, Perry," I said, then added, "I enjoy getting out."

Kira looked up at me over her coffee cup, a little baffled by my derisive tone, but she's sensitive that way.

"I should be home before suppertime. We can drive straight up to Inverness on the B852 if you'd like—and watch for the creature up and back."

"No, I don't mind. But we won't go to Inverness today. I don't feel like looking for the thing today. No, not today. Perhaps we could look together next weekend."

"All right," Perry said, as merry as a schoolboy, and kissed me on the cheek before collecting his papers and charts and heading out to the little pebbled beach and the Pelican's motor launch.

I retired to the chairs at the front of the house to finish my crossword after breakfast.

"Are you very unhappy?" Kira said from over my shoulder about an hour later.

"No, I'm not very unhappy. Did I seem unhappy to you?"

"You seemed—" she hesitated in her usual, polite manner. "To tell the truth, Mrs. Miggs, you seemed vexed at him."

I laughed. "That's just my tone. Perry isn't a sensitive man, you see. You can take any tone with him you like—you can bellow at him like an angry locomotive, but so long as all you are saying is 'pass the cheese,' that is all he will understand you to mean."

"Oh," she said and nodded, wiping her hands from the dishwater. "Still, you ken what your tone is, don't you?"

I suddenly felt ashamed of myself. It wasn't polite of me to behave that way in front of these two women. "I suppose I did feel a little—" I stammered, not really knowing how I felt anymore.

"Put upon?" Kira suggested.

"Well it is Saturday."

"Then you are vexed."

"Yes, Miss Shaw, I suppose I am vexed."

She sat wistfully beside me, swiveling like a painful corkscrew into the chair, because of her bad hip.

"I understand," she said once she'd settled, "that when you are long married you can allow little annoyances to become great ones. I have never been married, Mrs. Miggs, so I dinnae ken of my own personal knowledge. But I believe I would nae allow the little moments of anguish to bother me so."

"No?"

"Nae. No' today. I would nae allow such a thing to happen now." She pointed to an abandoned cottage beyond the road. It was overgrown and the glass was all gone. "I sometimes played foolish love games. Pouting, teasing games to make young Breton prove he loved me. It vexed me when he would nae play or didnae understand my rules. But living wi'out him all this time has changed all of that in me. I believe we could be as much in love today as we were back then. I feel that is true. I feel it here." She touched her breast lightly. "And," she continued quietly, with a mild tone of reproach that she aimed at me, "I believe I would nae play the love games. Games are made to win and to lose. I would nae stake my heart upon such a game today. I would nae risk the loss again."

"You still love him?"

She thought about it before answering. "I feel I could, yes. I canna say that I do just now, however, but I feel I could."

"And how do you think Mr. Trent feels?"

She smiled, reflecting. "Mr. Trent is coming only to add on the belvedere. He'll no' be interested in any of my foolish notions."

"You never know. He did come back, after all, didn't he?"

"Aye," she said with a deep satisfaction. In another moment, she patted my leg. "Thanks to you. Thanks to you and your generous husband. So dinnae be too vexed with him. Think of him as the man that you married, that darling, nervous man at the front o' the chapel that you promised to love. That should put the little vexations in their place."

Kira was such a romantic.

"Yes," I said, but I didn't bother to tell her how difficult it was to find that nervous little man at the "front o' the chapel" in Perry. So much was missing of him: the hair, the flesh, the fire. He had changed so much for the worse while Andrew Macgruer had changed so little and for the better.

"There's that done then," Kira said. "And you'll be happier for it."

The water of Loch Ness was smooth. The midmorning sun played on the surface, scattering bright rills across the loch's wide breast. In a tiny cove beneath the road the water swelled lazily, like the bosom of a comfortable sleeper when it rises and falls. The sunlight spread into wide sheets between the swells, and the water rolled peacefully between.

"Are you hungry this morning, my darling?" Adam Grant said to the slowly undulating water. "You've not hunted these waters for months, have you auld dearie? Aye, weel, the fish will be plentiful, I'll be bound, and you can swallow your fill this day."

It was just this sort of activity, talking to the wide, empty loch, that had earned Mr. Grant his nickname, Mad Adam. There was wisdom to Mad Adam Grant, if only one could strip away the eccentricities, the frivolities, and the thoroughly dangerous notions he held—not the least of which was the notion that he was cursed at birth to kill someone before he himself could die.

"We think none harm," he murmured across the swelling surface. "Do we, auld girl? We think none harm, do none harm, wish none harm. We canna help our natures, though, can we, dearie?"

He had a tattered basket hung over his elbow as he stood watching the water. He spoke with the animation of a stroller in Hyde Park who had just happened upon an old and well-loved friend.

"And what is this I have, my darling?" he said to the mid-distance. "Aye, now this is my lunch—and the pretty wife's. I have told you of her? Aye? Of course I have. She's a bonny lass, is she. And I'm courting her. Yes, I am."

The water swelled and sent a lazy rise rolling toward the shore. With the quiet contemplation of a dozing man, Adam watched the swell roll slowly toward him. It crested several yards from the shoreline and lapped upon the stones and grass with the gentle hiss and bubble of exhausted effort.

"Not in my own person, of course," he continued. "I'm gone courting to smooth the way for Andrew Macgruer. Have I told you of the conspiracy, auld darling? Of course I have, but mum, mum. Mustn't breathe a word of it. I sneaked flowers up to her room, ken, without a one the wiser. She was such a lovely thing in her bed, too, sleeping there like the angel she is. Am I a wicked auld kist o' whistles for creeping into a woman's bedroom? Nae, of course no'. I did it for him, didn'ah? He set me on, ken?

"What have I got in my basket? It's the French oozy-sort-o' cheese she likes and the ale and potted berries. But mum, auld love, mum. It's a secret sort of a repast. I have been the long way up to Dores to collect it this day, and now back I'm headed."

He watched the loch for a short time in a mesmeric trance, lulled by the gentle rise and fall of the wide waters. He sighed deeply, looked down the shore toward Iubhar, then smiled out at the water.

"It is a pleasant surprise to have met you along my way, my dearie, but I am expected at the else. Bid me safe hame and I'll bid you good hunting, auld girl."

Only a few cars passed Adam as he made his way along the B852 toward Iubhar. One carried Miss Shaw and Mrs. Reese on their way to Inverness. He waved at them and noted that Mrs. Miggs was not with them.

"Tha's a fair blessing," he said to no one along the road.

He met Andrew Macgruer walking toward Inverness.

"Struck out a bit late this morning, Macgruer."

"I'll be in fair time this day," Andrew replied. "I have bridges to build wi' Meg."

"You've been sorely missing the boy, I ken."

"Aye. She's not let me see him since I took him away for that week."

"A woman is a senseless creature at times. Senseless and cruel she can be when crossed."

"So are we all, Adam, so are we all."

"That may be."

Andrew eyed the basket over Adam's arm.

"Another picnic, then?"

"Aye," the old man said. "It's your job I'm doing wi' this, Macgruer. Well you ken she'd rather be out having her luncheon with a braw young man than a bruck old'un. She's like enough to come in time to thinking me a sleekit old shauchling sharger."

"Sleekit, is it? And what ulterior motives might you have that'd make her think you sleekit?"

"I've a fair grip of secrets, Macgruer, and well you ken. A woman senses secrets like a kitten senses cream. And I tell you again that I'm doing your office wi' this basket."

"Weel you may be, and you're doing a friendly office. God speed you, Adam Grant, for all your sleekit and secret ways—what's that?" Andrew had stopped suddenly, looking out over the loch. "Will you look at that." he said, pointing out into the water.

The *Pelican* motored across their field of view between a break in the trees. Adam watched the boat apprehensively.

"He's at the cove," Adam said.

"He is. That's him doing it himself. Is that important, that he's at the cove?"

"That's where she is today."

The two Scots listened to the motor after the cruiser had disappeared from their view. In a short time the engines sputtered to a halt.

"The cove," Andrew breathed.

Adam laughed. "There's payment for you."

"He canna work the equipment."

"Deil be paid if he needs to. She's at the surface this day. He'll see her wi'out the need o' cameras and such like."

Andrew tensed. He looked up the road toward Inverness, then back to his home above Iubhar.

"You go on to Inverness this day," Adam said, "and make all right with Meg. You canna stop the workings of what is meant to be."

"And what will you do, Adam Grant? You namore want the American to find her as I do. What will you do?"

"I plan to have some lunch this day. I have my obligations to you and to the pretty wife, so I have, and this day auld Nessie will have to fend for hersel'. She's able enough."

Adam patted Macgruer on the shoulder and continued his way toward Iubhar. He laughed as he left, and Macgruer heard him address the distant waters.

"Fend for yoursel' this day, auld dearie."

*Saturday is marketing day; Kira and Caitlin have taken their little car up to Inverness for the week's provisions. Caitlin had mentioned during the first few weeks that they did not usually go all the way to Inverness to market, but the arrival of Perry and me had required them to provision the house "much more grandly than is our personal wont."*

*That is Caitlin's way, imperious and direct. I like her the better for all of* her bluff and bluster. There is something altogether reassuring to be around a person who is not afraid to tell you precisely, no matter how abrasively, what she thinks, consequence be damned.

Caitlin was distrustful of Perry and quick to voice her suspicions. "A man who'd pay in cash for all, that's mischief afoot. That's a man covering his trail. I'd be asking myself what devilment and disquiet he would be up to now. Have you given a thought to him and his behavior? What is it he's been playing at?"

Of course, it is Caitlin's way, to be suspicious of men. She doesn't know poor little Perry at all. I could only wish he did have some devilment in him. Still, Caitlin says what she thinks, and there is a sort of solidity to that.

But today I am alone.

Perry is on the boat somewhere, and the sisters are off in Inverness for the day. Even Mr. Trent, who has begun measuring the roofline for a belvedere, is away somewhere, haggling for lumber.

I wandered down the main road and through the thin tendril of forest separating the loch from the hill. I found my gloomy place and settled down on the pebbly beach to watch the water lap and drag at my feet.

It is a peaceful bank of grass and a pleasant narrow of pebbles before the water takes over, and it does take me away from myself in an agreeable and diffident manner.

I closed my eyes after a while and daydreamed of horses.

"Mrs. Miggs?" the voice seemed to come from nowhere and broke onto my musings.

Adam Grant was at the edge of the woods above me, behind me, nodding deferentially and pinching his brow at me.

"Yes, Adam?"

"Only it's your husband, miss," he said. "Mr. Miggs."

"Has something happened?"

"He went out alone on that boat, miss."

"Yes, I know. What's happened?"

"Come with me, please."

My stomach twisted in me as I rose. I felt my heart lurch.

"What is it, please?"

*"I'll show you,"* he replied. *"I brought lunch."*

Mad Adam led me out along the path that followed the loch. We walked a very long way before he turned off the main trail and began up a steady rise. At length we came out upon a promontory where he sat down with me.

*"Tayberries and brie?"* I said as he set down the basket.

He only pointed in response out at the loch below us. About three hundred yards from shore, the Pelican rode on the water. Only the tiny ringlets that rolled from her hull where she met the water disturbed the smooth surface.

*"Macgruer's plan's for nocht. Your husband has the luck of fools and madmen."*

*"What do you mean, Mr. Grant?"*

*"Andrew Macgruer would nae take your husband to find the auld girl, but now your husband's taken himself."*

*"I don't understand."*

*"You will. It may take a bit o'time, but you will. Is there enough lunch for twae of us, do you think?"*

*"Of course."*

We opened the basket and ate together on the promontory overlooking the loch.

*"Your husband has led Macgruer a merry chase. There's Macgruer thinking to lead him off the track. Then comes your husband back wi' news that he's hunting for bones and not the auld girl at all. That's taken Macgruer aback, now. He namore kens where the bones lie than does your husband, so he canna lead him away from that. And now here's another joke on Macgruer."*

Again Adam pointed to the quiet boat on the water.

*"Andrew doesn't want Perry to find anything? Why not?"*

*"It's a difficult thing to explain. Once you see the auld darling, it sort of makes you protective like, and you only want to draw the ring aboot her to keep others oot. But now your husband has broken the ring, and there's the joke."*

*"I'm afraid I don't see the joke. Is it that Perry has learned to pilot the schooner by himself?"*

"Tha's a part of it, lassie. The other part's yet to come. We'll sit some more and drink a bit."

We finished eating and sat quietly sipping our ale until I grew sleepy, full of luncheon, in the warm sun. In a short time, I lay dozing on the rocks while the breezes played up the hill from the loch. I dreamed again of riding. What did I care of Perry's excursion? And Adam Grant was making no sense. I preferred the horses of my imaginings and the warm breeze of Scotland.

Adam woke me with a gentle touch on the arm.

"Now, I think," he said quietly to me. "Watch the boat."

The sky was overcast now and the water looked dark and gray beneath it. The Pelican, white and sparkling, was easy to watch without much effort. So I gave the activity little attention, rolling onto my side and looking through half-closed eyes.

There was nothing to see. The boat rode quietly at anchor. I could see that Perry was not at the helm. He was probably below, writing his report to the Royal Geographic Society. I watched for several minutes without seeing any point to it.

"What am I looking for?" I said finally.

"Her," Adam replied.

"Who?"

"Nessie."

I sat up. "You mean the monster?"

"Aye."

His reputation for seeing the monster, deserved or not, was enough to awaken me to full alert.

"How can you know she'll be here?"

"Rumgumption," he replied. "She has her patterns. I keep a watch on her and ken her odd ways. She'll be hunting here today. You watch."

I did watch. I watched for nearly an hour. Then I began to lose interest. I put the luncheon things back into the basket.

I was beginning to reconnoiter my surroundings and to think of a polite way to tell Adam that I would have to be leaving when he whispered, "There."

Almost involuntarily, my head whipped back to the view of the loch and boat. There was a decided commotion about fifty feet behind the Pelican.

It thrilled me to see it.

The smooth surface was broken; small rings radiated out toward the shores and tickled the Pelican's hull. Then I saw something break up from the water.

Silver, wild, thrashing slivers like shattering bits of glass flew up from the surface.

"It's only fish jumping," I said, dejected.

"Aye. But what is it they're jumping from?"

I had seen fish jump before. They didn't need the aid of a fanciful sea serpent for that. But I did not communicate my cynicism to Adam.

Then I saw her.

One fish made a mighty leap from the water and was followed into the air by a long neck surmounted by a tiny head. I would have said it looked like a snake, but the head of the thing was longer, like the head of a horse, grand and noble. She missed her catch. The fish fell sidelong into the loch, and the head splashed down after it. A moment later, I saw her large body break the surface. She was rolling over onto her side. A flipper appeared. It looked like the blade of a spear as it paddled against the air a moment before sinking again out of sight.

Imagine it.

I gaped for a moment, my throat dry, before I realized that I had stopped breathing. I exhaled a short burst of air, and the sound of my own breath brought me back to myself.

"No," my reasoning sensibilities echoed in my mind. "Imagination," it insisted, "you've been at it most of the day—and the ale for lunch—tipsy daydreams."

But just as I thought I had seen the last of her, just as I began rationalizing my own senses, justifying this mirage, this shadow of imagination, I saw a wide wake break the surface some eighty feet behind the boat. It was moving away at incredible speed, fish leaping in every direction before the mounding water.

Again the stately head rose up—rising several feet above the surface—searching the water the way a swan hunts for bread. It jabbed at something suddenly, unexpectedly, and disappeared beneath the surface. She disappeared in a rolling loll that made her back hump up above the water before it slipped away into a widening ring.

I sat, awestruck, on the promontory that moments ago had felt so ordinary, so solid and unexceptional; speechless, thoughtless, emotionless, bewildered.

"There," Adam said, startling me. "I told you she was hunting today."

I was suddenly filled with joy. I began to chuckle, a spasmodic, cleansing laugh, and involuntary tears ran down my cheeks.

"Aye. She affects most everyone like tha'."

It was all so natural, a wild creature out hunting, and yet she was unearthly, prehistoric, supernatural. Had she not surfaced the second time I could have denied her. I know I could have. But seeing her twice fixed her in my mind—real, irrefutable, absolute. I watched the marks she left across the water. Her widening wake tumbled to the shore below us; it set her in my mind, and she became as real as the crocuses in spring, as vital, as fragile.

"Looks like Macgruer's the lucky one," Adam said.

I looked back to the Pelican in time to see Perry coming out on deck. I could tell from his posture, idle and vaguely alert, that he thought he might have heard something. He was far too late, though. He hadn't even time now to see the wide pattern of her wake. It had already passed the boat, too large for him to make out, even though I could still see it clearly, rippling up the loch and across to the distant shore.

He leaned on the railings a moment and looked idly toward the shore, entirely the wrong direction even if she were still to be seen. I called to him, but, if he heard me, he did not recognize my voice. He went below a few moments later.

Adam laughed. "Ten thousand miles to roam and then miss by fifty feet. There's man's lot."

I had to laugh, too. It was a cruel thing to do, to laugh at dear Perry, but he had created this situation, this irony that allowed me to witness what he desperately wished to see and could not.

Moments before, I had searched for an excuse to leave, but now I wanted nothing better than to sit, to remain rooted to this magic place. We sat on the

promontory, the old madman and me, like familiar lovers, idling in after-
glow, and I pressed him to tell me his story.

"Is that your lot, too?" I asked Adam. "Have you traveled far to miss by
moments?"

"Aye. I am blessed with my curses," he sighed. "The good Lord has given
me much, health in age, a willing ear, the gift to see what is hidden, but he
has given me also the one gift I never wanted."

"What is that?"

"Long life."

He was like old Teiresias, I decided, though he wouldn't know Teiresias,
blessed by one god with foresight and cursed by another with blindness.
Adam Grant had a lot of strange notions about himself, not the least of
which was his firm belief that he was born to be a murderer and had somehow failed at his destiny.

"I must cause a death before I may die," he said. "I must cause the death
of a fellow being before death will release me."

"That is hard," I said, trying to sound serious.

"Aye," he said sadly and seemed to withdraw into himself. "And I'm not
the killing sort. I never have been, never have."


Perry returned, as promised, that evening before supper. I hardly had the
heart to tell him of my day, but I knew I could never keep this from him—
not in good conscience.

"You saw it?" he cried. "Where?"

I told him the circumstances.

He was overjoyed. "I heard it!" he exclaimed. "I did hear something. And
you saw me come to investigate. It was! I heard it!"

He made me describe her thoroughly while he sketched on his drawing
pad. He was not an inspired artist, but his rendering was accurate. He was
so excited.

He ate a nervous supper and asked me if I would ride with him up the
eastern shore and point out the promontory, which I did. He spent so very
much of the trip up looking off into the loch and running the car off the road

that finally I drove while he stared fecklessly across the wide, abandoned surface.

He looked out from the promontory and could only sigh and repeat "marvelous" into the wandering air that brushed around us. When he had marveled his fill, we went back to the lodging house.

This time of year, the sun does not set until quite late, and we were growing accustomed to going to bed in light that resembled late afternoon. Perry had difficulty sleeping deeply in the daylight, and this night was worse for him, agitated as he was by the sighting. He tossed in bed, unable to sleep.

"The transducers!" he said, suddenly sitting up in bed about an hour after we had snuggled down. "I had the beacons on all day while I was below decks. I was trying to get them to lock onto the bottom, just playing with them, trying to figure them out. If she was at the back of the boat heading away, maybe she passed under."

We were up and in our clothes, out the door and in the launch in minutes.

On the Pelican, Perry looked at the computer screen and did some calculations.

"The computer shows that the transducers locked onto something thirty-three times." He sounded doubtful. "Most of those times are just me playing around with the equipment, I know. There are a few here, though, a few I didn't do myself."

He wound the tape until it matched the counters on the computer screen, and played the image.

"Bottom rocks," he repeated over the first several images. "I did those."

They were only hazy images on the screen, they could have been anything.

"Fish," he said at another image.

It was a slightly better image than the rocks. At least one could make out movement and individual bodies in a group, but it looked no more like fish than it did a scanner's image of any moving group: balloons released into the sky, a snow flurry.

"Bottom rocks," he said at the next image. He stared at it a long time. I saw that he was disappointed.

"Is that all?" I said while he stared.

"No. But there's only one more on the tape that I didn't do myself. I don't think I got anything."

"Try it," I encouraged.

"If that isn't anything, though," he said, "then I didn't get it."

"But if it is—" I said and let the hope hang.

"I think I'd rather think I've got something than know I don't."

"That's silly. Look and see."

He nodded at me, an irresolute nod that indicated I had talked him into something he didn't want to do. He wound the tape to the spot, held his breath, and pushed the button.

A stream of white corpuscles wriggled about the screen.

"Fish," he said, disappointed, defeated.

We watched the dancing white blobs for a few seconds. They seemed to be floating in space against the black screen.

Perry sighed. "Nothing." Then, apparently to keep the outing from being a complete waste of time, he pointed to the number fifty at the bottom of the screen.

"They were fifty meters below the boat."

Then, as if his finger had shocked the fish into action, the mass of white blobs suddenly darted away toward every corner of the screen, scattering. The number began fluctuating from fifty to forty-seven, forty-two, forty-seven.

"The transducers are trying to get a lock again," Perry said.

In the next moment, they did. They suddenly locked at sixty-two meters.

A large white object came into view, materializing in the middle of the frightened, fleeing fish. The number rapidly dwindled to fifty meters, and the object grew in size on the screen. It was hazy and indistinct, a computer's idea of a thumbnail sketch, but it was clearly a wide-bodied, solid creature with a long, slender neck that rose into view through the snow storm of fish. Forty-five, forty, thirty-three meters, it rose rapidly, gracefully through the murky waters.

"She's hunting," I said.

We saw the clear outline of her at twenty meters, four diamond-shaped fins and a snub tail.

*"She must be thirty feet long!" Perry said.*

*She continued rising to nine meters, filling the screen until it showed nothing but a white mass crowded within its frame. Then she apparently darted toward the rear of the boat. The computer caught her back fins and tail, a highly detailed vision of agility as she stroked past the electronic beacons moments before I had seen her myself.*

*Perry turned off the machine, ejecting the tape. He marked the label with trembling hand.*

*"I've got it."*

# Chapter 16

✦

Meg's rooms were orderly, uncluttered, and attractive in a way that attested to her personal dignity and unobtrusive refinement. Meg's own personal reserve was strained on that Saturday morning when she opened the door to Andrew.

"Well then, Andrew Macgruer, you've clipped and trimmed yourself and no longer look so much like the wild man of Borneo," she said with an edge of sarcasm. "You'd better come in then."

Andrew had barbered himself. His long russet beard no longer fell to his collarbone, and his hair, still full, was bobbed to the middle of his ear. He seemed to her nautical in some way, and she was quick to say so.

"And so trawling the loch with the American has turned you into Captain Ahab, has it?" She waved him into the flat and shut the door behind him.

"Nemo," he responded quietly.

Wild man, Ahab or Nemo, though, Meg found her ex-husband more than a little attractive. But although she was pleased to see him again after so long an absence, she hid it well behind her anger.

Andrew walked to the middle of the room and stood, his back to Meg, looking toward the far windows. He did not speak.

"I've a fair load of words to say to you." Her words crackled like fire. "Where's Aidan?"

"Out playing with his mates. He'll be in soon enough."

"Then you'd best begin."

Meg shook her head. "What am I to do with you?"

"Like enough you'll tell me before the morning's out."

"Like enough," she said. "Will you have some tea then?"

Andrew turned. "You are a gracious and accommodating woman even in your fury, Margaret Macgruer. But I think it would be better that we sat and let me look you in the eye while you tell me what you have to say. Tea would only curdle in my stomach as I am feeling now."

Meg had not spoken to Andrew since he had returned Aidan from their excursion. She was too angry then to speak in front of Aidan, but now she had sent for Andrew and ordered Aidan off to play. It was time. They sat across the dining table from one another. Andrew knew his part was to keep quiet and let her have her say; he knew that anything she might say in these circumstances would be entirely justified.

He would only explain himself but would not ask her forgiveness. He had taken advantage and knew it.

"Have you anything to say to me?" Meg said, her anger welling anew.

"How did Aidan do on his comprehensive examinations?"

Meg's lips tightened and her eyes narrowed. "No' a word of explanation, then? Nae dash of contrition? Only a 'how did he do on his examinations'?"

"Aye," Andrew said quietly. "I am no' contrite, Meg, for I intended to do as I did, and it was all the best for the boy, I thought and still think. As for explanations, I left them behind in that note for you."

"And you never considered that I might no' find that note? Did it never cross your mind that it might go missing, fallen under the table? Never occur to you I might no' notice it for days and days while I wandered these rooms like a mother sheep bleating for her lamb?"

"Nae," Andrew answered.

"Nae!" Meg jeered. "Is that all you have to say in word of explanation? That my feelings never once entered your consideration?"

"I dinnae say that."

"Yes, you damned well did, Andrew Macgruer."

"Then I misspoke, Meg, and I apologize for that. I meant to say that it never entered my mind that you would nae find the note. You are just that organized in your habits. A blue envelope in the centre of your dining table is no' something you'd overlook for more than a few minutes at most. I know you that well, Meg, that I know you had read my explanation before Aidan and I were well and truly on the train from Inverness."

"And you never thought it might be lost before I could read it?"

"Was it lost before you could read it?"

Meg pursed her lips and glared into his eyes. She wanted to lie. She wanted to hurt him for taking Aidan away for the week without permission. She wanted to say that the note had been lost, that she had been frantic with worry. She wanted to see it register in his sensitive eyes, the realization of the betrayal. She had it in her power; she could hurt him. He would believe anything she told him. That was his way.

"Nae," she confessed, angered at having to admit it. "I did read it a few minutes after you'd left."

"And, had I asked permission," Andrew continued, "would you have allowed Aidan to come wi' me that week?"

Again she wanted to lie—again she did not. "Nae, I would no' have allowed it, no' with his examinations coming up that Friday."

"And do you blame me for wanting to show my son the world and taking advantage of my only opportunity?"

Meg kept quiet and continued to glare at Andrew. Of course she could not blame him, but at least she did not have to admit that, too.

Andrew sat and quietly returned her stare. It was her show, he knew. It was her turn to speak next. He would abide by her decision now to remain quiet and let the tension mount. She had, after all, a month's anger and resentment to vent. She would do it in her own good time, in her own good way.

"Damn," she spat before getting up and going into the kitchen.

She clattered around for some time out of Andrew's sight, rattling

pots, running water. Then came a long, tense silence. The kettle whistled at length, and Meg returned with a tea tray and poured them each
a cup. She set the delicate, feminine cups and saucers at their respec-
tive places before them, but she did not sit down. She paced to the
center of the room before turning angrily toward her former husband.

"I am no' having this, Andrew Macgruer. This is no' a question of
whether you answered to your higher conscience and did well or nae.
This is no' an issue concerning whether you left a note or nae. This is
no' aboot whether or no' you did well by the boy. The fact remains,
Andrew Macgruer, that you did no' consult with me in this matter.
You took it upon yourself to do a thing you knew I would object to;
you knew I would refuse you. But you did it anyway. Aye, I'll admit
you were considerate enough to leave your note and explain to me
where you were and when you'd be back. But this is no' a question of your consideration—aye, by God, it is a question of your
consideration—your consideration of me. Did you ever stop to think
that, no matter how noble and good your intentions, that you were
undermining my authority with the boy?

"I told him, didn't I? And I told you, too, Andrew, that I wanted you
back by that evening, that the Friday examinations were just that important. Didn't I make that clear? And you chose to ignore me. And
you chose to ignore me in front of the boy. So instead of doing as his
mother bade, Aidan went off on a junket wi' his father through En-
gland and the Irish Sea. And what position has that left me in, then?
What lesson has Aidan learned from it then? Hasn't he learned that he
can ignore his mother when it suits him to do so?"

Meg had whipped herself up and had to shut her eyes against the
angry tears that rose in her.

"Will you answer me that?" she choked out. "What have we taught
our son?"

"We have taught him a valuable lesson," Andrew said quietly. "We
taught it at your expense, and for that I am sorry."

"And what did we teach him?"

"We taught him that the difficult choices are not the choices we make between right and wrong, but they are the choices we must make between one right and another."

Meg stood glaring defiantly for another moment, shaking in her emotion, before she sighed deeply and sat down to her tea.

"And do you think," she said quietly while she resented herself for admiring him so much, "do you think he's learned that lesson?"

"It is up to us to make certain that he does."

"Aye," she said, nodding.

They sipped their tea in silence. Her anger abated as she drank the warm and soothing potion. His words lolled about her mind, and she realized that he was right. Despite her desire for it to be otherwise, Andrew had been right. She was a fair woman and saw that he had done well. It made her love him anew, as she had when they had first met.

"How did I let you slip away from me, Andrew?" Meg said after a time. "There's nothing in me that wants you away."

"You did nae more than love me, Meg, and you did what was best for me," Andrew said quietly. "And I went because I could no longer stay. I went alone because you could nae follow me. There was nae loss of love, Meg, please believe that."

"Will you ever come back, then?"

Andrew rested his cup on his saucer. "I dinnae think so."

"Why aren't men made more like you, Andrew Margiler? I do no' believe you have it in you to walk a wrong path. Oh, but you're a complicated one, aren't you? You were right to leave. And I was right to let you go. It's a hard lesson we are trying to teach Aidan, though, isn't it? One I'm not certain I've quite learned myself."

Meg sipped her tea and watched her handsome one-time husband across the table. God, he was a fine man. She suddenly felt petty and selfish for her former anger. In the end, she realized, she was angry only because she had lost control. He had taken it from her. That hurt her, irritated and insulted her, but in the end she knew he had done it for Aidan. There was nothing in Andrew to hurt her intentionally. He had hurt her deeply in their lives, but never intentionally, never maliciously.

He had hurt her only because he loved her. She had been hurt only because she loved him so deeply.

Andrew Macgruer was the perfect man, Meg knew, the ultimate mixture of strength and pliancy, intelligence and sentiment, love and wisdom.

But perfection is whole and needs no mate.

There was no empty spot that Meg could fill in his life. Andrew Macgruer had but one deficiency, but that was something from his past, a yearning that she had tried to fill but could not. She was a creature of the present and could not compensate his lost past.

"So," Andrew said after their long silence, "what's to be done?"

"About what?"

"You called me up here for a reason. You didnae want only to have a good bawl and feed me tea. That's no' your way. Am I no' to see Aidan again, then?"

He said it with such sincerity, such apprehension, that the long-held tears sprang to Meg's eyes. She went to him and held his head to her bosom.

"Of course I am not going to keep Aidan from you, you fool," she whispered. "How then could he ever grow up to be like you?"

She kissed the top of his head and laid her face against his soft hair, letting her tears dampen his brown-red curls.

"But there is something else," he said and wrapped his arms around her slender waist.

"Aye," Meg said, reluctant to let him go. "Gilliland Carlisle wrote you from St. Andrews."

"Carlisle's wife?"

"She wants you to call on her. She has something there for you that her husband left behind when he died."

"What could it be?"

"I'm sure I don't know," she said wryly. "I think you'll have to go to find out."

"Aye, well. I'll arrange it somehow."

"Let me know if I can help," Meg offered.

Andrew hugged her tightly and kissed her dress above her navel. His kiss sent an involuntary tingle through her and she gasped softly.

"Thank you," he whispered. "May I have Aidan for the rest of the weekend?"

Meg laughed.

"And when will you have him back home?" Meg teased. "When *exactly*, I'm meaning."

"Tomorrow night by the Julian calendar; eight forty-seven, thirteen seconds solar time."

"Aye, well, that's all right then. I'll set my solar watch to it. And if you are more than a second late, Andrew Macgruer, so help me—"

Andrew did not let her finish. He grasped her and lifted her as he stood, spinning with her about the room while she squealed in girlish delight.

"So help you," he continued her thought, "you'll pound fire-hot words through my soul a second time and drive my heart under the lash of your cruel tongue."

He stopped spinning and looked up at his attractive former wife. She cupped his face in her hands and looked him in the eye seriously.

"If I could do worse, I would. Now set my feet back on the ground if you please."

Aidan burst through the door a moment later, red-faced with play, and threw himself into his father's arms.

"Did you hear?" he said excitedly. "I took top marks at school on my comprehensive examinations last month!"

"Did you?" Andrew said with a keen look at Meg.

"Aye," Meg said sheepishly. "I was getting around to mentioning that, too."

# Chapter 17

✦

It was late afternoon before Andrew and Aidan left Inverness.

"Where did you tell Mother we're going today?" Aidan asked once they had reached the street.

"Back to the crofter's cottage in Iubhar, Son," his father replied.

"And where are we *really* going?"

Andrew smiled. "Back to the crofter's cottage in Iubhar, Son."

The boy laughed, grabbed his father's hand, and leaning back on his heels swung from his father's arm as from a rope.

"Nae, I mean *really*," he insisted.

Andrew bent his arm and lifted the boy effortlessly from the pavement.

"They used to hang traitors up by their arms, Son. Do you think I'd be after telling your mother we were going somewhere that we were no'?"

"We did it last time."

"We did nae such thing," Andrew said seriously, setting Aidan back down. "It was a stretch of the truth, but no' a lie I told your mother—and I left the whole truth behind in a note. Do you think I lied to her?"

"Nae."

"Why do you think I'm lying now, then?"

"I just want to go someplace today."

"Where do you want to go?"

"Edinburgh, Wales, I don't really care."

Andrew laughed again, and they began their journey out of Inverness.

"Is it no' enough to be wi' your father these days?"

"Aye, it is," the boy replied. "It's just you're that much more fun in Edinburgh, Wales, and on the Irish Sea. I'd like to sleep on the Isle of Man again."

"Plenty of time for that, lad."

Although the day was rapidly drawing to evening, the sun remained bright in the sky as the two Macgruers found the way out of town. They walked in silence for a while, and Aidan watched the countryside bloom around him as the city disappeared behind.

"Why is it you don't live back at the house with us?" Aidan said at last.

"Did your mother want you to ask that of me?"

"It's me asking."

Andrew stopped and stretched himself along the grass. Aidan sat beside him, tossing pebbles out into the loch.

"You have a right to know the answer to that," Andrew said. "I just dinnae know that I can explain it as you would understand."

"I'm old enough."

"No doubt, no doubt of that. It isnae you that's wanting, though. It's the explanation itself that is so difficult."

"You still love us?"

"Aye"

"Well?"

"Well? You're asking just like that. Oh, that it could all be so easy, lad. Do you know that big yellow tomcat that lives by the crofter's cottage?"

"The one that follows you aboot? Aye."

"I found him some time ago by the roadside, struck he was by a passing car and near enough to death to call it so. I kept him warm and fed and helped him to mend."

"Aye," Aidan said, "I know all that."

"So now he's strong and hale, fast he is like a rabbit, too, and quick enough to escape another car should he need to. But it's a strange thing aboot that cat, he will no' go near to the roadside. You ken, Aidan, when a body's been struck so hard, and the life's nearly run out of it, there's nae logic or reason or love can convince you ever to put yourself in that harm's way again—no matter that the danger's past. You carry it along wi' you, the fear of it. That's why that yellow tom keeps shy of the road. It isnae that he fears being struck again, ken? He fears having been struck the first time, and there's nocht to argue him oot of the fear of that fact."

He sat up and looked his son in the eye.

"It's even that way wi' me, Aidan. In another manner the life was nearly struck from me, and I canna live around people ever again because of it. I could nae live back there any longer, and your mother could nae come with me oot here. There's no more logic in it than there is in the cat, but the heart cares little enough for logic."

Aidan turned and threw another rock into the water.

"Do you understand that, Aidan?"

"Nae," the boy said. "But I didnae think I would. I wish we could just move out here with you then."

"I wish you could, too."

"Why can't I?"

"You'll have to ask your mother that."

"I have."

"And what did she tell you?"

"She said she had her work in town with the school, and I said it was no' such a long drive up from Iubhar."

"And what did she say to that?"

"She said it was a longer road than it seemed to me."

"Aye," Andrew said softly to himself, "perhaps it is at that. Perhaps it is a much langer road than any of us can know."

"Then we had best start walking," Aidan said as he stood up.

Andrew laughed at his son's casual insight, kissed him gently, and rose to his feet, too.

*That little boy unsettles me in the most pleasant way.*

*Aidan Macgruer came this morning for breakfast.*

*His hair is as fine as silk and as soft to the touch. It billows and glisters so. He wears it parted down the middle over an open, honest, and wholly devilish face that is so incredibly pretty that it is not hard to imagine the hearts he will break in another four or five years.*

*But still, seeing him makes me uneasy in a happy way. He is so like me: his hair, both in color and texture, is so like mine. And his eyes are so very like my own that even Perry noticed it that morning.*

*"To all the world, Perdie, he reminds me of you. Isn't that odd?"*

*"His manners are perfect," Kira noted for our benefit three or four times during breakfast; after each such comment, Aidan replied "thank you," as if it were the first time he had heard it.*

*"He's a most perfect little gentleman and nae doot," Mr. Trent observed. Breton Trent had taken to having breakfast with us now that he was well and truly working on the belvedere. It allowed him to get an earlier start, he claimed, and he was always to be found in the front room, no matter how early Perry and I rose to come down.*

*Caitlin suffered him at the table with as much good grace as she could muster. But even she seemed to take a genuine delight in young Aidan's presence. She made as much fuss over him as did her elder sister.*

*In fact, it was to Caitlin Reese that young Master Macgruer turned when he begged the favor.*

*"My father wants me to ask you a thing, Mrs. Reese, if I may," he said as Kira cleared away the porridge bowls and began bringing in the meats and breads.*

*"Does he?" Caitlin asked, her usual imperiousness flagging. "Well, then, you had best be asking this thing your father wants."*

*"It is a verra great favor."*

"Is it?"

"Aye."

"Isn't that just like a man?" Trent observed, leaning toward Caitlin. "Asking favors all the time, great favors and small."

Caitlin ignored the jibe and placed her hands on Aidan's.

"What is this great favor, then, lad?"

"He'll be needing to go across the way to St. Andrews." At the mention of my alma mater, my heart skipped a beat.

"And why will he be wanting to go all that lang way?"

"He's been called there by a widow woman."

Caitlin began to bristle. "Has he?"

"Aye, she was his old professor's wife."

"Oh," Caitlin relaxed. "I see."

"And she has a thing to give him, I think."

"And what favor is it your father wishes?"

"He needs to borrow a car for the trip and wonders if he might borrow yours and Miss Shaw's car."

"Does he?" Caitlin nodded sagaciously. I saw doubt creep in. It would be unlike Caitlin to do such a large favor for a man, but Aidan made it difficult for her to refuse. Andrew was a clever man.

"Aye," the boy said. "And he'll be taking me wi' him. I've never been to St. Andrews, and that's where he went to university. He said he would take me to see the old cathedral where there's a tower that looks out over the sea. It's over a thousand years old, and you can still climb up in it."

St. Rule's Tower, I knew it well. But to Aidan Macgruer it was merely a relic to be climbed. His eyes were bright with the wonder of it, and he worked a charm on Caitlin.

"And when would you be making this wonderful journey, then?" she asked.

"Tomorrow or the day after, he says. I'm no' in school this week. He has to ask Mother first because we never want to do anything wi'out her approval."

"Nae," Caitlin agreed with a steely tone, "we certainly do no'."

"What's this then?" Kira asked as she came in with a steaming pot of fresh tea. "Planning a trip all the way across to St. Andrews?"

"That's right," Trent replied. "Tomorrow or the day after, the lad says. Tell me, Aidan, how long will you be away?"

"All the week, I think. He has a thing or two to do wi' the widow first, he says, and it's a full day's drive to and another back, and we might stay the night in a castle, and he says he'll show me a place where soldiers dug mines to blow up a castle."

"All the week, do you say?" Trent said. "I wonder if auld Macgruer wud mind if I chummed him along. It's been a fair time since I was in St. Andrews, and I could help him wi' the driving."

"You've quite enough to keep you occupied on the roof, Mr. Trent," Caitlin snapped.

"All in good time, Mrs. Reese, all in its own good time," Breton Trent responded and then slapped the table. "By God, the more I think of it the better I like it. What do you say, Miss Shaw? Would you like me to take you along and show you auld St. Andrews? It's a fair bonny auld town it is. And we could watch young Aidan while his auld father is doing what he must for the widow—show the lad the town, eh?"

"Nae, Mr. Trent," Caitlin said, but no one seemed to hear her.

"Well, I dinnae think there's ocht stopping me. I think I can take the week in St. Andrews, Mr. Trent," Kira said.

"Nae," Caitlin said again, this time more firmly, and again she was ignored.

"Do you think your auld father would mind us for the company?" Trent asked Aidan.

"He'd like it, I'm thinking."

"Nae," Caitlin said.

"Then it's settled," Trent said.

"Nocht is settled, Mr. Breton Trent," Caitlin said. "And I'll thank you no' to be so free with lending out my automobile. As it happens, I will be needing the car this week for sundry purposes and canna spare it for so long a time. There's Mrs. Rose of Foyers whose daughter is ill. I'll have to be fetching her over myself for our Wednesday tea."

"But surely, sister," Kira said, "if I'm away and no one to cook, we'll simply leave the tea on Wednesday alone. It's a simple thing to cancel."

"I am quite looking forward to this week's tea," Caitlin said.

"Why this week's tea in particular?"

"I am anxious after Mrs. Rose of Foyers. Her health has been no' so good of late, and you canna tell how a person is by simply talking on the telephone. So I will need the car."

"Weel," Kira said a little sadly. "That's an answer to you then, Aidan."

The boy looked crestfallen, and my heart went out to him. He had so looked forward to the mines and the tower and the castles.

"There is no reason why they can't use our car, is there?" Perry suddenly said.

"Perry," I replied, "what a perfectly wonderful suggestion. No, there is no reason they shouldn't use our car at all. There's plenty of room and more besides for Aidan and his father, Kira and Mr. Trent."

"I canna do wi'oot my sister," Caitlin said.

"Whyever not?" Kira said.

"There's the tea, of course, and the cooking for Dr. and Mrs. Miggs. They have paid for suppers, and you know I'm no' a cook."

"There's plenty for the tea already made," Kira said.

"And as for suppers," Perry said, "let 1'em go this week. Besides, I'll be the only one here to miss his meal. Perdita needs to go along with you to St. Andrews."

Aidan, Kira, and Mr. Trent all expressed their immediate approval of the plan.

"Why?" I protested. "Why should I go?"

I couldn't tell him. How could I tell him? Everything in me wanted to slip into that little car beside Andrew Macgruer and glide away to St. Andrews. That was the problem precisely. The idea appealed far too much to me for my own good and certainly too much for Perry's own good if he would only know it.

"No. There's no reason for me to go."

"There's every reason in the world, dear."

"Why are you so anxious to get rid of me?"

"Because I know how you will enjoy yourself. You went to school there, didn't you? This might be your only chance to see it again. I will certainly be too busy to take you myself, and you hate to travel alone. This seems tailor-made. The perfect opportunity. You should go."

"No," I said firmly. "I don't believe I should."

The realization had struck me while Perry was talking; our anniversary fell in the coming week. I knew he was simply forgetting for the moment, but he would remember soon enough.

I knew Perry.

He'd insist that I go to St. Andrews until I was all packed and excited about it. Then he'd remember our anniversary. Then it would be a series of "you can go if you really want to" mini-martyrdoms until the very thought of St. Andrews would infuriate me.

"No," I repeated. "I'll just stay here. I think. That would be best for everyone concerned."

"Why?" Kira and Mr. Trent said at the same time.

"The car is too small." Now I was beginning to sound like Caitlin, making up excuses to get my way, but I was not going to remind Perry that our thirteenth wedding anniversary was coming up. He would remember. I derived great pleasure from having him remember every year.

"It isn't too small at all," Kira argued. "Why you and Aidan are such little creatures anyway that the pair of you barely make up one full adult person. There will be plenty of room and more besides, as you said yourself."

"Still," I said, "I don't think I should."

"You have to go," Perry said. "You know, if I remember our lease agreement, one of us must be with the car at all times. If anything should happen to it and it was discovered that we'd loaned it to someone, we could be responsible for the costs of repair."

"Really?" I said.

"Yes, it's either you go or no one goes. I can't get away just now, not after what we've got on the tape. I'll be all week studying it and writing up my report. You'll do everyone a favor if you agree to go."

"Well, all right, then."

The general cheer, all except from Caitlin, was very flattering.

Aidan called his mother from the house and received her permission to go. It was all set.

*I could hardly believe my good fortune—St. Andrews with Andrew Macgruer.*

✦

"Aidan," Perry said after breakfast, "would you like to come out to the boat with me today?"

"Father's taking me up into the Monadhliath today. We're going to look for deer."

"I think I can show you a more interesting creature," Perry said.

"What?"

Perry pulled the boy close to him and whispered confidentially, "I can show you Nessie herself."

Aidan's eyes grew wide.

"I have her on videotape," Perry explained. "And I need your help. Do you remember in the Irish Sea when we saw the haddock?"

"The ones with St. Peter's thumbprint?"

"Yes, those ones. You remember how you helped me, I read the instructions and you set the instruments for me?"

"Aye, I remember."

"I need your help again. The picture is very fuzzy right now, but I thought if you helped me to work the enhancement features, that you and I would be the first men ever to see the old girl in real detail. What do you say?"

"I'll tell Father," Aidan said and sprinted out of the door.

"Don't tell him everything!" Perry called after the boy. "Let's make it a real surprise."

Later that morning, Perry and Aidan sat in the *Pelican*'s crew cabin. They played the tape over and over, watching the blurry figure rise toward the transducers, almost come into focus, and then dart away after its prey.

"That's fantastic," Aidan repeated again and again, much to Perry's delight.

"Let's try to clean it up now, okay?" Perry said at last. "Try to make it something they can show on the evening news?"

"Yes," Aidan replied enthusiastically.

Perry slipped the tape into the machine, wound it to the appropriate place, and took out the manual.

"'Enhancement of Transducer Image,'" he read aloud. "Are we ready?"

"Ready," Aidan said.

"Press the RECORD and PLAY buttons beside the transducer control," Perry read.

Aidan did so.

"'Depending upon the depth and water quality,'" Perry continued, "'the transducers can create a resolution nearing photographic quality. If you are using the T387-V transducer array, you have the ability to switch to video enhancement, which will yield not only photographic quality but color as well.' What sort of transducer array do we have there, Aidan?"

Aidan read the metal plate above the transducer control, "T387-V."

"Then let's make a miracle, my boy."

# Chapter 18

❖

*There is nothing like a road trip for shaking oneself free from the quotidian habits that dig ruts through life and bog our wheels. I had done my utmost, of course, to avoid routines, but routines are insidious sorts of jailers. I need the freshness of a good airing out.*

*A road trip is just the tonic I need, just the refection for a soul fed full of dander and fluff, daytime and the dustings of dusk.*

*I will go with a glad heart and return with new eyes.*

*Perry is, of course, making it all so difficult. He has taken one of his moods, just as I thought he would. He puckered and pouted around me all this morning, watching me pack, regarding me with the woebegone look of a water spaniel.*

*It is no use talking to Perry when he gets like this, for it is always "nothing" when I ask what is wrong, and then the pantomime of surprise that I might think something was. It is always "yes, yes" if I ask whether he really wants me to go, but "yes, yes" is said with such reservation as to be the same as no. Then he sulks.*

*Having no sense at all for the subtleties of emotion and tone in others, Perry is not at all subtle when he has something to convey himself. But he is obstinate, too. No amount of wheedling will make him confess what he so obviously wants to say.*

"Don't you want me to go?"

"Yes, I think you should go."

"Because if you don't, you only have to say so."

"I know."

*It's galling.*

*So I packed my prettiest things, those things I had bought in Inverness, the ones I had not yet worn because we had not yet gone anyplace really nice, and let Perry brood like a disconsolate hen in the corner while I did.*

"It's just," he said under his breath, "the timing is bad."

*I pretended at first not to hear. What would be the point of my dredging it all up?*

*But I dredged at last.*

"Why is the timing bad?"

"Sorry?" *Perry acted surprised, a poor acting job.*

"You said the timing was bad, and I want to know why you think so."

"It's just that—" *he stammered,* "I'm just at loose ends this morning."

"Why?"

"Some decisions to make, you know, with the videotape and my report and things. You know, don't know what to do next."

"I see."

*Nothing about our anniversary.*

*He was good enough to insist upon lugging my bag down the stairs and into the car. There is a streak of gallantry in him, I know, but I often wish it would manifest itself in his mood as well as his actions.*

*Is there anything so vexatious as a pouting, self-indulgent man?*

*As he picked his way out of sight down the stairs, elbows high, craning my bag to the level of his breast, I had an inspiration—call it an anniversary surprise. I opened the top drawer of our bureau and lifted out the credit cards, still neatly bundled in rubber bands, and slipped them into my purse.*

*I hummed the "Anniversary Waltz" as I brushed past Perry at the car, kissing him lightly on the cheek as I went.*

*He didn't get it.*

*Kira and Mr. Trent climbed in, and we all rolled up to the roadway to meet Andrew and Aidan. We left Perry and Caitlin standing before the house, watching our departure with the dour disapproval of two Presbyterians watching a church burn.*

*Had Grant Wood wished to paint a scene and call it "Scottish Gothic," he would have painted the scene that retreated in my rearview mirror that morning.*

*"Your sister, Caitlin," Mr. Trent said to Kira in the back seat, "is no' the sourest woman God ever put on the earth, but she plays on the same team wi' her. I do believe she could lib a man wi' a single slice o' the tongue."*

*"She has her mind set within her, that's sure," Kira agreed. "And it's set dead against us." Then they laughed like naughty schoolchildren who had gotten away with a prank.*

*We drove about a mile down the paved track that served for our main road before we came upon the rest of our company. Andrew Macgruer looked like a postcard Highlander without the bagpipe. He had trimmed his beard and his hair, and looked keener somehow, more romantically poetic, with the Highland breezes fluttering the tartan around his waist and shoulder; I was glad to see him looking less like a dress extra from* Braveheart.

*"Here then," Trent said to Aidan as the boy climbed in beside me, "that's no face for a young lad out upon high adventure."*

*He was right. Aidan was glum as he crawled in and made room for his father.*

*"Good morning," Andrew said to me, holding my eyes with his for a moment.*

*"Morning," I managed to squeak back, my throat still morning dry. Damn it.*

*"What ails the lad?" Trent asked.*

*"Deil if I know," Andrew replied. "I can get no word of explanation."*

*"Don't you want to go to St. Andrews, Aidan?" I asked, but he only shrugged, a gesture that it made no difference to him what we did.*

*"Would you rather be aboot something else, then, lad?" Andrew said, teasing.*

*Again the boy only shrugged.*

"Catching rabbits, perhaps," Andrew suggested, grabbing the boy by the ribs and jostling him to make him laugh, "or plucking up the mushrumps and Munro-bagging the Highlands to Nevis and back." Every suggestion was accompanied by a gesture calculated to tickle Aidan in the ribs, the knee, under the chin.

It worked: Aidan squirmed and grimaced, trying to hide the delight. There was a petulance under the suppressed laughter, though, and he finally pushed his father's hands off of him and said. "Don't, Father, please," with an earnest sincerity that shattered all levity.

"Son," Andrew replied, "if you dinnae want to go, we dinnae have to."

"Let's just go," Aidan said peevishly.

Andrew shrugged at me with an apologetic smile that said "What's to be done? Let's go." I pulled the car back onto the narrow strip of roadway, and we headed up toward Inverness in silence.

At Inverness, we turned onto the A9 toward Aviemore and along the Glen Truim through the Pass at Drumochter over the Grampian Mountains to Glen Garry and Pitlochry beyond.

Kira and Mr. Trent insisted upon frequent stops, always with some innocent explanation. But it was clear enough that Kira was unaccustomed to car travel, and her poor hip could not suffer being cramped in our tiny back seat for long. So she and Mr. Trent strolled half an hour for each twenty minutes we spent driving.

Breton Trent told stories for part of the trip. They were mostly variations on the theme of the disastrous pranks he and his mates had played on a number of hapless, luckless laborers. His voice soon melded into the hum of the car's engine, though, and my mind wandered.

"The sun sets late in the Highland summer," Andrew said quietly while Mr. Trent regaled us.

"What?" I said to him under my breath.

"Have you noticed how late the sun goes down up here, stretching the days until there's hardly a night worth the name?"

"Yes."

"It makes the darkness blacker, as though all the dark hours of winter have to be squeezed together into the summer's night and balance out the bright day. The short and torrid hours of night."

My poor heart thumped against my ribs when I imagined all of the hidden messages implied in his observation. But Mr. Trent's story droned on from the back seat, and Andrew grew quiet for a time. At last he spoke again.

"So—" he said very quietly. "You're married long?"

"Thirteen years."

"Children?"

"Just Perry—I mean, no, no children. How long have you been dressing like a pikeman at the siege of Culloden?"

He smiled and changed the subject.

"I sometimes swim in the twilight—out in the loch—and watch the shadows grow deep and the waters black. At times like those a man may believe he is alone the only breathing creature of the earth. Do you know Ragnarok?"

Trent wasn't hearing us, and his story hid our words.

"No," I whispered over Aidan's head. Aidan was caught up in the backseat story.

"The Götterdämmerung. Twilight of the gods. The Teutonic people believed that at the end of time there would be a final, catastrophic battle between the gods and the powers of evil. Both would be destroyed; gods and evil, both gone, and all that would be left would be existence itself, life. Without the illusions of deity and morality, life would merely be."

He was staring through the windscreen with a dreaming, faraway look in his eyes, and I watched his reflection.

"That's how I feel out there, floating in the cold, black waters of the loch—freed of the evil that gods create and demons worship. Out there it is different. Just me, life, and the boundless, unbinding water."

He inhaled deeply and spoke again with deep feeling:

> "The winds of desire
> have blown the dark into stars,
>             my soul into ashes,
> And the moon under water—
> Where no winds blow."

"Did you write that?"

He turned to me and smiled. "You ought to come with me for a swim some night."

"I didn't bring a swimsuit."

"Och, well. That is too bad."

Breton Trent finished his story for Kira and Aidan, and all three of them laughed before he began another tale. Andrew turned and looked out of his window and away from me. He seemed to listen to the new story, distracted.

Aidan also seemed distracted. Nothing kept the boy happy for long, and his lapses back into gloom cast a pall across the rest of us.

It was fast approaching four o'clock when we reached Pitlochry, the midpoint in our journey. The stories began to irritate, and the laughter became forced. Soon we were all quietly listening to the rattling drone of the engine, the sort of grating quiet that fills a bus station between announcements of arrivals and departures. A sticky, need-to-have-a-shower silence.

"I hope we've guaranteed a room," Kira said. "We'll no' be in St. Andrews until midnight at least."

I sighed. It was no use pretending that the ride had become anything but a well-intentioned, optimistically expectant cruciation: a frigid, purgatorial, slow-roasting brazier of bonhomie.

"Let's do this again tomorrow," I said suddenly and turned off the road—heading north out of Pitlochry past Moulin. I had seen a sign, STAY THE NIGHT AT DUNCREAGDHUBH CASTLE BED AND BREAKFAST, PITLOCHRY'S OWN FIFTEENTH-CENTURY VERNACULAR CASTLE.

I followed the directions up the A924 and turned off along a winding, narrow path crowded about with shrubs and scrubby trees across a wide plain. I had driven a full fifteen minutes before anyone spoke.

"Where are we headed?" Mr. Trent said with quiet reservation. It wasn't until he spoke that I realized he had not spoken a word since Pitlochry. He had, in fact, paused in the middle of his story about a fellow named Chester reaching down into a bucket of hot rivets. I glanced into the rearview mirror and caught a glimpse of Breton Trent. He looked like a hamster with a toothache. Kira, too, was wide-eyed and purse lipped.

*"We are staying the night in Pitlochry's own fifteenth-century vernacular castle."*

*"Are we?" Kira breathed cautiously.*

*The Duncreagdhubh citadel rose from the near horizon, majestic and imposing, everything one might hope from Pitlochry's own fifteenth-century vernacular castle. The sight of it seemed to relieve much of the tension. Aidan sat up and showed real interest. He even became enthusiastic, which brightened us all.*

*"It looks gey dear," Kira said with the last vestments of apprehension.*

*By now I would happily pay anything to get out of that car and not have to think of looking for another roadside turn off "only to stretch our backs a wee bit, dearie."*

*I waved my credit cards about the interior of the car like a minister blessing a devil-haunted hollow and bumped my door open at the castle's front entrance.*

*"This one's on me."*

*I went alone into the charming little lobby. The walls were hung with ancient tapestries burnished tawny rose by time, and the stone floor was covered with a thin and worn-out rug. Dark woods, rich and shining, adorned the doorways and windows, and I knew I had arrived at my own personal Valhalla.*

*I laid my bundle of credit cards on the desk before a pretty young girl, blonde and blushing with the first hints of womanhood; I laid them out reverently, as though I were placing an offering on the altar of my own personal virgin goddess.*

*"I've had a trying day," I said, trying to disguise my strain.*

*I fingered the credit cards nervously, but she seemed to need more.*

*"Great Grandmother of all trying days, actually," I added and then smiled.*

*"I see," she said with a most unhelpful nod.*

*"Yes— " I went on, "well, it's complicated, really. Really, really complicated. I just—okay, it's like this, my husband has forgotten my anniversary, and, well, that's just the beginning. I really need a room for tonight."*

*"Oh, I'm sorry," she replied. "We're full."*

"Look," I pleaded. "I have driven eighty-seven-and-three-quarters miles in four-mile increments, watched about four dozen flocks of sheep crop about four dozen different fields in about four dozen different places. I have been trapped in a little circus car that no self-respecting clown would jam himself into, with a lame pensioner, a clansman from the first battle of Falkirk, and a ten-year-old boy with all of the joie de vivre of a penitent nun. The man in the back seat won't stop reciting the world history of humorous bodily mutilation, and for the past half hour I've been seriously contemplating the fact that the UK doesn't execute people for filleting their traveling companions. Now here I have five credit cards. I don't care about cost. Run them all to their limits if you must, but in the name of sweet bleeding charity and all that you hold dearest in life, let me have a room for tonight."

"I'm sorry," the malicious little cow repeated, "we're completely booked."

"Pleeeease?"

"I'd be happy to book your return trip." The vicious little heifer had the effrontery to smile.

Aidan wandered in just then and observed "Smashing," as he took in the grandeur of the place.

"Is there a ghost?" he breathed.

"They say Red Coinneach MacRovie walks the halls," she replied, widening the boy's eyes even further.

"Smashing," Aidan said again. "Really?"

"They say you can hear him some nights looking for his head."

"Can we stick to the point before we have to go looking for yours," I snapped. "Let's do book a room for the return at least. May we?"

I gave her the date we would be returning and booked four rooms.

"But," I explained, "I'll be paying cash for the rooms when we return." And I meant that the Royal Geographic Society would be paying cash. "I won't want to keep the rooms on my credit card, all right?"

"Yes, ma'am," the pretty little shrew replied.

"And I'll be back." It almost sounded like a threat. "And I'll be bringing them, too."

And with that I took Aidan by the wrist and led him from the sumptuous little foyer.

"Is the ghost always here?" he called over his shoulder to my blonde nemesis.

"Red Coinneach is often heard in the dark of the night," she called after us. "His wife sliced off his head, they say, that's why he's looking for it."

"Oh, smashing," Aidan observed a third time.

"Red Coinneach MacRovie gets lodgings," I muttered. "Of course Red Coinneach MacRovie gets lodgings. You have to die here to get lodgings."

I slid behind the wheel and turned to the party with my most winning face and said, "We all have lodgings for our return."

We had a late supper in Perth by the Tay and pushed on, arriving at our hotel in St. Andrews a little after ten o'clock.

Oh, there is nothing like a road trip.

# Chapter 19

❖

## St. Andrews

The Carlisle house was a small, slate-roofed bungalow down a quiet side street of St. Andrews, surrounded by trailing roses and climbing ivy, and encrusted with yellow and green lichen all along its steeply pitched and sloping roofs. Two tiny dormer windows peeked out from under heavy, moss-covered brows that gave the little cottage the look of a drowsy old man just beginning to nod.

Andrew Macgruer called just before tea, as he had been invited, and was met at the door by Gilliland Carlisle.

Carlisle's widow was a proper, well-bred woman, plump, with a patient face and penetrating, wise eyes. She smiled at the sight of Andrew, and her smile brought up dimples in her aged cheeks. She had been a beauty as a child, and the beauty had now slipped under the skin to perfume her soul.

"Dear Andrew," she said quietly, inviting him in with a gesture, "how long has it been?"

Andrew knit his brow, remembering that the last time they had spoken was at the funeral over a year past. He was ashamed for not having stayed in touch.

"Not since then," she said, reading his discomfort. "I mean how long has it been since you've come to tea here?"

"Och, I was a graduate student, I'm thinking."

"Well, that has been too long."

Gilliland Carlisle was not a Scot. She was from Devon, from Exeter, where she had met her future husband at university, and her accent sounded to Andrew like cream and buttercups.

Because Gilly was English and David a Scot, he had early on taken to calling her "the auld enemy," and there were few of his students who knew her real first name. "I was taking luncheon with the auld enemy just yesterday," Carlisle might say during a lecture, or "must be gettin' meself away on home, the auld enemy will be lookin' for me."

"I've put on the kettle already," Gilly said as she disappeared into the small kitchen to check its progress. "I hope you haven't already taken your tea."

"Nae, I hinnae."

Gilly laughed. "It's good to hear a Highland brogue in these walls again."

A moment later, she was at the door to the kitchen. She looked hard at Andrew, studying his face, assessing his costume.

"I look for David in you, Andrew, and I want to see him. You were the closest he ever came to having a son, and I would like to think he left some of himself behind in you. But all I see just now is the Highlands, and he'd tried to put that behind him. As though he could."

She disappeared around the corner again, to pour the boiling water into the pot. In another minute, she came carrying the tea tray laden with their tea things.

"Is it hard now for you," Andrew said, "here alone, I mean?"

Gilly sat and placed the tray on the table between them. She thought about his question before answering, taking her time to measure out the sugar and the milk before pouring.

"It was hard for some time," she said at last, "quite hard. He had been a part of this little house for over thirty years, part of me for over forty. It is hard to see it all just end, Andrew. I won't lie to you. It is hard to think back to that morning when I kissed him and put him on the motor coach to Inverness and realize now that those were the last words I would ever say to him, the last look of tenderness I would ever know. That's hard still.

"So much is left undone. So many plans unfulfilled. More than one life ends when a person dies. A whole world is stopped and another whole world takes over from there."

She stared absently into her tea, collecting her thoughts, remembering.

"It was hard for some time not to hear him calling me from the other room. I still made breakfast for two—out of habit—off and on for several weeks I made his breakfast—and it was hard to throw out his portion. But I've grown accustomed to the quiet, and it isn't so hard now.

"I have come to think that he is still here, just as he's always been, only quieter now and easier to deal with."

"He was a bit of a monk, I suppose," Andrew offered over his tea.

"Well," Gilly said slyly, "not in all things. But I know what you mean. That was the medievalist in him. And, except for the more obvious and important enticements of married life, I think David might have been very happy in a dark little cell with a quill and tonsure."

"He was a fair hand at his Latin and Greek."

"He was that," Gilly agreed. "And he believed in the strength of faith, Andrew. He truly believed that believing alone, and believing absolutely, was the only goal worth striving after."

"Aye, but believing in what?"

Gilly smiled. "Still our obstinate agnostic."

"I believe in a force greater than us, Gilly," Andrew said seriously, then added with a smile, "But like Voltaire I can no' worship a God I can understand."

"How you used to exasperate poor David," Gilly said, laughing. "He loved and despised that wicked, intelligent streak of scoffer in you."

"Aye, I know." It was Andrew's turn to laugh. "We were like the two Scots, your husband and me. He was the new Scot lured down from Gaidhealtachd to follow in the Christian ways brought in by the auld enemy."

"And you?"

"I'm the one who stayed behind and chose to cling to the auld ways, the auld gods, the auld land. It's peculiar we ever became friends."

"It would have been more peculiar had you not, I think. You were two halves of the same man. David always thought, and he thought as you do that somehow the two of you stood for something more than just the two of you. It is all a bit silly to me, but I have never had that academic turn of mind that could see metaphor and meaning in every little thing. And I thank *my* God to have been spared that particular form of trivial neurosis."

They laughed.

Gilly became serious and, laying down her saucer, looked Andrew in the eye.

"I hadn't the strength to ask you before, at the funeral, but you were with him. When he died, I mean, you were with him."

"Aye," Andrew said quietly, remembering that night.

"How—?" Gilly let the question remain unuttered.

"He'd been up the loch wi' me for the better part of the week, had he, and we'd collected up my lad, young Aidan, for David to get to know him. We had gone walking in the hills that day, and he was feeling tired; maybe he'd become ill, but he said he was only tired. Aidan wanted to go fishing that night. David said he knew a trick to bring the fish up in the dark by dangling a lantern from a pole, and Aidan was eager to try it.

"I was gey tired, now, because I'd hiked up to Inverness in the wee hours to collect the lad, but neither my fatigue nor my suggestions that David was no' feeling up to it could put the lad off. So we went.

"The sky and the water were so black they might as well have been shale or slate, for you could nae see through them any better. I rowed out to a place I thought the fish might be, and he put over the lantern while I curled up to sleep in the bow."

Andrew hesitated, remembering what had happened.

"Go on," Gilly prompted.

"There were nae fish to be caught even wi' the lantern, and David, no' wanting to wake me, tried to row the boat himself back to the shore. That's when he was taken. It was all too much strain for him."

Gilly nodded, taking it in. "You mustn't blame yourself. He was stubborn like that, polite, too, not to wake you. Did he—did he—?"

"No," Andrew said softly. "He felt no more than a pinch perhaps and then fell into my arms."

"Into your arms," Gilly repeated.

"Aye. I woke up a moment before."

"Then he died a happy man," Gilly concluded. "And I'm grateful that if he could not have been with me in his final hour that he was with you. He would have wanted to die in the Highlands, to go home. Yes, yes; that's appropriate and fitting."

Gilliland Carlisle wrapped herself in her thoughts while she served out a second cup of tea.

"David left something for you," she said at last.

"Left something?"

"Yes," Gilly said. "It isn't a legacy or a bequest, I'm afraid. I wish it were, and I'm certain he would wish so, too. But, nevertheless, I found something a few weeks ago that David wanted you to have."

She took a wide envelope down from the shelf. It was growing crisp with age, and the gum on the flap had begun to powder. She laid it in Andrew's lap quietly, staring him in the eye as she did.

"What's this then?"

In reply, Gilliland nodded quietly and watched him open the envelope. He pulled from it a collection of notes on mismatched paper and a neatly typed article. Andrew smiled to see it.

"The Archilochus poem."

"That's right," Gilly said. "He never published it. It was mostly your work, wasn't it?"

"I put in a fair bit of time on it. But David was the Greek scholar. He was the main translator."

"But the ideas and final expression are yours."

"Aye."

"David was very proud of your work on this. He was proud to have worked with you on it. He had a lot of belief in it and in you."

"Why was it never published then?"

"It wasn't his to publish, was it?"

Andrew grew solemn. "But he did try?"

"No," Gilly said gently, "he never did try. He had hoped for a while that you would come back for it. He never stopped believing that you would. In time, of course, he set it aside, and I had forgotten it quite until I came upon it again. I believe he would want you to have it."

"Aye," Andrew ruminated. "Thank you."

"So what are you going to do with it?" Gilly pursued.

"I dinnae know."

"Will you publish it?"

"Perhaps," Andrew said quietly. "I might do that for David."

"Why not do it for yourself, Andrew?"

Andrew only shook his head somberly.

"That is at the heart of the matter, isn't it?" Gilly replied to his dark mood. "What's driven you away from the comforts of society and made you this woodland wild man."

Andrew smiled wanly at her description of him but gave no reply.

"It's no good, Andrew," Gilly continued. "You must not live your life poisoned by self-doubts. We always knew, David and I, that you would come around in time. David never gave up hoping for you. But I must tell you, he was never able to understand how you could have given over so. It seems such a little thing, doesn't it, when you stop and consider it."

"It was no' just the loss of my position at university," Andrew said quietly. "I was cast long before then and made vulnerable. That just exposed it all and laid bare the bit of me buried down deep inside, the private bit of me. You see, Gilly, a man who fancies himself a poet keeps alive in him the little boy he always was, nurtures and sustains him and becomes his mother. It's the very lad that most men try their best to destroy, the weak and guileless parts of themselves they seek to kill as they grow. But he's also the wee lad wi' the tenderness of thought and unapologetic curiosity. He's that wee bit of a man that loves wi'out reservation and understands wi'out explanation.

"I cherish that lad and think him worth the saving. That's why I flew, Gilly, out of the town and down to the loch."

"Because you could not get a publisher to print your work?"

"It was no' *that* they would nae publish, Gilly, it's *what* they would nae publish," Andrew said quietly.

"The poems, you mean?"

"Aye."

Gilly regarded the handsome man with compassion. He was a strong, masculine, and appealing creature. And she saw in his eyes the wounded child he spoke of, frightened and huddling down deep inside of him.

"It has always seemed to me a drastic measure, Andrew," Gilly said sternly, "to give up your education, your marriage, your son simply because you could not publish your book. Forgive me if I say what I think, but it smacks of ego and self-indulgence."

"It does," Andrew agreed. "And if it were only that, a question of bruised pride and hurt feelings, I would be a reprehensible scoundrel. But there's more than just my pride that's blemished. Something dear, something precious, something more priceless and rare than I can say was threatened, and it was no' the galling pricks of pride that drove me. I was driven rather by the very essence that created me to do what I have done."

"The essence that created you, Andrew?" Gilly scoffed. "It sounds like you're speaking of God now."

"Aye," Andrew replied, "as well as I understand it, that is what it is."

Gilly smiled at him. "And you have retreated into the wilderness as some Old Testament prophet, have you?"

"Nae. They went in search of something," Andrew said. "But I've gone to preserve a thing."

"They all came back from their wandering, Andrew."

"They achieved their goals."

"And you cannot," Gilly completed his thought. "Andrew, Andrew. I have a secret little wish regarding you. I have long wished it, and it isn't that you should be reinstated and teach or publish or even find God. It's a simpler wish than any of that. I would like to see you go back to Meg. She's a good girl, and I liked her, Andrew. You two always seemed happy to me."

"Aye," Andrew agreed candidly, "we were happy until all of this. But, Gilly, your faith is as strong as David's. Can you tell me, by God's word, what is a marriage?"

"It is the knitting together of two souls within the pure and eternal love that flows from the everlasting."

Andrew nodded. "And that's what it is to me as well."

"They say that women are a puzzle, Andrew Macgruer, but you—" Gilly laughed lightly and took his face in her hands. "You are an unruly Scotsman and grow worse by the year, I think."

"You are genetically and geographically predisposed to think that, of course."

"Of course, yes."

They finished their tea amid the warmth of companionable conversation, but when the tray was cleared away, Gilliland grew serious again.

"I have another paper to give you, Andrew," she said, placing a thin envelope in front of him on the table.

"What's this then?"

"It's a letter David wrote several years ago," Gilly explained. "He was going to mail it to you when your 'time o' dandering aboot' was over. From what you've said today, I don't believe it ever will be over, and more's the pity, so I think I will go ahead and give this to you now. I also think I'd like you to read it before you go."

"My dearest Andrew," it read, "If you ever read this, my fondest hopes are realized and you have come back to us from your darkened and despairing way. Welcome back, my boy. You have so much to offer this weary old world, not simply your skill in poetry, which is vast, but also your skill in love, which is unequalled in all my experience. You have the ability to feel more deeply than any human being I have ever known. In large part, I believe that is why you have left us for a while. The world of men is too callous for beings such as you.

"I believe you were right to turn your back to us. I believe we have done nothing to deserve you. But I also believe you have done right to give up this escape from society. You have much that is good to teach us. We have much that is good to teach you.

"There is one lesson I would like to share with you upon your return, for it is a lesson you cannot learn from the forests and the meads. It is learned only through the acquisition of age, and it is simply this: Only the pastness of our past is past. What we have been, the important parts of us, remain always and forever who and what we are. It is in each of us to carry what we have been, and also what we are, into what we are yet to become.

"If, as I suspect, there is a regret you carry in your sensitive breast, let it never be a burden to you. Embrace it. It is what you are and always have been.

"Welcome home. We have missed you so. David."

# Chapter 20

❖

The little band of five travelers had arrived late in St. Andrews the night before. Perdita was, for reasons mysterious to Kira and Trent, strained after the drive and could not seem to settle down to rest. Breton Trent had sat up with her for a while, and they had talked.

"It is a romantic town, St. Andrews," Perdita had said.

"I've always found a large warm milk the verra recipe for sleep after a long, hard day," Trent offered, not being much interested in the romance of St. Andrews.

"You may keep Paris and Rome," Perdita continued in a steadily relaxing tone, falling into a state of internal peace, unwilling to be driven from the topic. "And the Riviera, too. Niagara Falls, New York, San Francisco. Keep them all; keep them all. St. Andrews is the single most romantic place on earth, Mr. Trent. And do you know why, Mr. Trent?"

"You're tired, lassie," Trent said in his own groggy stupor. "So tired you've gone tipsy wi' sleep. You should be in your bed now."

"I'll tell you why St. Andrews is the most romantic place on earth, Mr. Trent." She leaned across the back of the sofa in the common room where they were seated and whispered to him. "People fall in love here,

Mr. Trent. People may go to the Bermudas or—where else—Tobago and Bora Bora and Tahiti and—where else do people go that's romantic?"

Trent was paying little attention. "The wisest gae on and get themselves to bed," he said phlegmatically.

"I certainly can't argue with that. But you see, people in love go to all of these romantic places only *after* they've fallen in love, but this is the place where it happens. This is where people actually do it—fall in love, I mean. Isn't that lovely?"

"Drunk wi' sleep," Trent had said, pointing at her. Then he wiped his hand around his face. "Crivvens if I'm no' fair bleezin wi' sleep myself, girl."

"I think it's lovely," she said to herself. "Love is lovely. Do you want to fall in love, Mr. Trent? Here in St. Andrews, I mean. Would you like to fall in love in St. Andrews, Mr. Trent?"

"What is it you're asking me?"

"It would only take a stroll around this old town to do it—to make a girl fall into your arms and want to drown in your eyes and die on your lips," Perdita cooed. "Would you like a woman to die on your lips, Mr. Trent?"

"Weel, I don't know." Trent narrowed his sleepy eyes at her. "Can you speak plainly what you're meaning?"

"I mean stoke up the old flame, Mr. Trent. It wouldn't be difficult to make Miss Shaw fall in love with you, not in St. Andrews. Have I told you that it is the most romantic little town in the whole world?"

"I believe you might have mentioned it, aye." Trent rubbed his jaw and rolled his eyes thoughtfully before saying "Kira Shaw" quietly to himself.

Perdita heard him.

"Yep," she said. "It would only take a quiet stroll. Do you remember when you were children in Iubhar, Mr. Trent, you and Miss Shaw? Do you remember the moment you fell in love with one another?"

"There was a dance," Trent said wistfully, "all the way up in Dores. We were nae more than children, but I found enough to hire a horse and cart to take her—"

"No," Perdita growled, "she was already mad about you by then. She'd have walked up to Dores with you. Try again."

Trent's eyes widened with effort, as if attempting to stare back into the distance of his past. "Weel, I once bought her a muff for the cold—"

"No."

"Was it while we were in Drumnadrochit across the water for the auction of—?"

"No."

Trent ran his hand across his scalp and screwed up his face.

"When I came back from—"

"No."

"Sitting on her father's rooftop?"

"No."

"Weel, then, I'll be dampt if I know then."

"You walked with her down by the loch one afternoon. It was just after that big boy, I forget his name, knocked out your tooth in a fight."

"Sim Reese," Trent said. "Och, aye, there was a fight."

"You took her in your arms down by the big alder tree that since has fallen into the loch, and you kissed her. You later told her that it hurt your lip to kiss, but that was your first kiss and it made the pain of love the sweeter. That's when you fell in love."

"I remember the fight," Trent said. "That tooth grew back in straight enough."

"You remember the fight and forgot the kiss?"

"What was it we fought over?" Trent muttered to himself.

"Kira Shaw."

"Was it?" Trent said. "Oh, aye. I believe it was. Sim, oh he was a big boy, too. We fought a terrible battle, and I had him scared, though, big as he was."

"Kira said you lost the fight."

"Aye, true enough. I never could have beat big Sim—he was that big. But I had him scared all the same; oh aye— there was a bit o' time there when he thought he'd killed me. Och, there was a fight."

"And the next day," Perdita said, dragging them back to the subject, "the two of you went strolling, and you kissed her for the first time. That's when you fell in love."

"I'm willing tae take your word on it."

"And if you take her on a stroll in St. Andrews—"

"That lightning will strike twice. I ken what you're after."

They sat together in smug satisfaction, their conspiracy bubbling between them.

"She's no' a great one for strolling now, of course," Trent said. "No' wi' her hip bothering her. And the town is just that crowded in wi' people. I dinnae see a way to manage it."

"It only takes some imagination and a little willpower," Perdita said. She had found a city guidebook on the hotel's bookshelf. It was vintage 1923, but it had a map in the front and a poetic turn of description. "Here," she said, pointing to the area of the map marked *Magus Muir*, "three miles out of town through woodland parks along Lade Braes Walk, over the rustic Old Bridge; pull her to you under the hedgerow—by an ancient alder tree if you can manage it—and kiss her. Kiss her for every year you've kept her idling in Iubhar. Kiss her with every spark of passion you ever felt. If you want her, you'll do it. St. Andrews will work all the rest of the magic you'll need."

"Lade Braes Walk," Trent repeated as he examined the alluring photograph of the Old Bridge.

"The way is reasonably flat, too," Perdita said. "Kira won't have any trouble walking it. And it's out of the way of the day tourists."

"Aye," Trent said, considering, then again, with more force and conviction, "aye."

"Now I think I will have that glass of warm milk."

But the morning dawned and Perdita overslept. Andrew had appointments to keep before seeing Gilliland Carlisle that afternoon, and there was nobody to watch after Aidan.

"I'll take him," Kira offered over breakfast as Breton Trent blanched. But Trent was made of stern stuff and decided to take the boy along and do his courting as best he could. First he had to persuade Kira that a three-mile walk out to Magus Muir was just the outing every ten-year-old boy dreams of.

"It will be a holiday!" Breton Trent exclaimed.

"What? Taking a boy to an Episcopal prelate's grave?" Kira shook her head at the idea.

"Boys love to see dead churchmen. It's one of the great joys of youth."

Kira was skeptical.

"Aidan Macgruer," Trent said to the boy with the air of a conjurer about to produce doves from his pockets. "I ken a place no' too far from here where they hung up sixteen men from the trees—hung them up in chains—and kept them there until their flesh wore off and their bones fell into dust."

Aidan's eyes widened. "Are the chains still up?"

"We'd have to make a bit of a danner and see, some three miles or there aboot. Are you interested?"

"Aye, if the chains are still up."

Trent tossed a shoulder at Kira, to say "simplest thing" and "I know how boys think." "Then," he said, "we had best be on our way. And here's something I have no' told you, Aidan. I'll also show you, there under the trees where the sixteen men were hung up, the site of the murder of Archbishop Sharp. Would you like to see that site?"

"Aye," Aidan said, "I would. How do you come to know of it?"

"It's in the guide books. It tells you how to gae on to see the site of Archbishop Sharp's murder."

Aidan looked askance. "It says in the book where to see it?"

"Aye," Trent said.

"That's even better than seeing the chains in the trees!"

"I would have no' thought it," Kira said as the three of them walked through the crowded lanes of the old city, Aidan dashing on ahead in his zeal. "He is as happy about seeing that auld tomb as if you promised him a trip on a jet airplane."

"You have to ken the ways of boys," Trent said. "There is nothing so satisfying to a boy as the sight of a good, dead cleric—the more pontifical the better. I've seen boys wi' my own eyes lining up around a whole city block for a glimpse of a Methodist minister who'd had his brain knocked out wi' a nun's kneestone. I've heard tell of boys marching about like lost things—like lemmings or Jehovah's Witnesses—when the auld pope died, looking for a way to get to Rome. It's an odd thing to see, but they do grow out of it in time and settle themselves into more fruitful enterprises."

"I would have no' thought it," Kira observed again as they passed out of the town and into the woodland beyond.

Aidan checked the trees as they passed, looking for signs of chains and rotted corpses while Trent, with his glance divided between Kira and the woodlands, tried to identify an alder tree.

"How much further?" Aidan said after they had walked several miles.

"If you run along ahead you'll come to the picturesque Law Mill and a wee sort of a romantic stone bridge over the mill lade," Trent said, consulting the antique guidebook. "Carry on until you find the crossroads, turn to the right, there's a footpath. Aboot five hunner feet you'll come upon a rustic rough pyramid built of undressed blocks of stone. We'll catch you up there."

"Right," Aidan said and dashed away across the bridge and into the forest beyond.

"You'll find a granite tablet on the pyramid that tells all aboot the murder and how it took place in 1679," Trent called after him, waving the old book, but the boy was already out of sight. "Weel, no matter. The tablet is in Latin anyway, and I doot he could have read it if he knew to look for it."

"Do you think he'll be all right running ahead on his own like that?" Kira said.

"Nae boy in the whole lang history of Scotland ever came to harm while looking upon a martyr's grave, my dear, even an Episcopal martyr," Trent said. "The odds are running verra much in his favor."

Kira and Trent reached the little stone bridge that arched over the placid waterway. Trent stopped on the old bridge and took Kira's hands in his.

"Kira, darling," he whispered, suddenly feeling nervous.

"Breton?" she replied apprehensively. "What is it?"

"Can you tell me if any of these trees are alder trees?"

"And you a carpenter? Why would you be searching about for an alder tree, now?"

"I once kissed you under an alder tree, darling," Trent said with a shrug, "and I'd like to do it again this day."

"Just like that?"

"Aye."

"Wi' no word of explanation?"

"Kira Shaw," Trent carried on, pulling her hands to his breast, "do you think St. Andrews is the most romantic city in the world?"

"What?" Kira said, almost laughing. "Alder trees and kissing and romance, Breton Trent, what are you blathering aboot?"

"Do you remember the first time I kissed you? It was under that grand alder tree that has fallen into the loch—" Trent hesitated, "what explanation was it you meant?"

"Before I let you take any familiarities, Mr. Breton Trent, I would like to know what's kept you all these years."

"Oh," Trent groaned, suddenly looking sullen. "Is it that you want to know aboot? Weel, that's nae simple thing to tell you, Kira, darling."

"Nae," Kira agreed, "I supposed no'. It's a fair number of years you have to account for."

"Aye," Trent said and let go of her hands. "It's a fair good number of years, but they were no' fair years nor good."

Trent walked off the bridge and sat down along the bank, lost in solemn thought.

"What was it I promised you? To return to you wi' my pockets filled to bursting and marry you up on that house top of your father's. It was a fool's promise, Kira, a boy's boasting oath. I went off wi'oot an idea in my head as to how I would succeed, only the cocksure notion that I would succeed, succeed because I thought I would. No' once did I consider—the alternative. There was no' enough work to keep me in Inverness, Kira, and I failed there."

"Why did you no' write me then?"

"And tell you I was a failure?"

"Aye," Kira said sweetly, "and that you were coming back home."

"Pride, my dearie, youthful pride kept me from writing or coming home. Had I no' made you a promise that I'd come home a rich man?"

"That mattered little enough."

"Little enough for you. It is different for a man. So I took myself down to Aberdeen where I could ply my trade. The work was nae better there and the living worse. But it made nae difference to me then, I had sunk that far. I had nae estimation for myself at all by then. I had taken to drinking back in Inverness and kept at it in Aberdeen. I fell in wi' the worst sorts of people. I was one in the number of a dirty lot, Kira, and I say it to my shame. I was nae kind of man for anybody's company, least of all a guid woman's."

Trent looked away down the narrow course of water, turning from Kira. She frowned at him, pitying him and not knowing how to express it.

"So?" she said at last, "what happened to you then?"

"After those years I was shaken out of it all—youth, the wounded pride, and drink—and I grew myself up. But look what it did to me, Kira, just look. I gave myself a bit of a look in the mirror one day and said, 'That's your lot, then, lad. You've done yourself,'—skin all dried out like parchment and my face lined wi' an old man's wrinkles. My eyes were clouded up. That fresh-faced lad by the banks of the loch was gone, darling, sucked down into a bottle.

"I could no' show you this face then, nor the rags on my back, nor this broken and twisted body. I could no' bring this back to you when I had promised riches. I just gave it up, packed it off, and counted it all lost."

He glanced over to her still on the bridge, a glance filled with abject suffering and humility that sunk deep into her tenderest feelings.

"But you did no' marry?" she said quietly.

"Weel," he said before sighing and shrugging. "Some promises are left unbroken."

"And why did you come back now?" she asked.

Trent looked at her again and smiled.

"I had to bring you back your money. And I wanted to build you that belvedere and look out over the loch one more time, just for friendship's sake if for nae other cause worth fighting for. And—"

"And what, Breton?"

"And to show that I had changed from those wild and reckless days. I came back to make amends for it all, to build back those bridges I'd broke."

"I see."

"And what have you done these years?"

Kira shrugged. "Skittered aboot mostly. I won a contest for pies."

"Did you?"

"Aye, but that was some years ago. When we buried Father, and Caitlin left the house, I turned it toward the boarding trade, but it's no' been a success to speak of—being on the wrong side of the loch for tourists. When Caitlin came home again, I spent a fair amount of time wi' her; she was that injured. And the rest of the time I've waited for news from you or of you, however it came."

"Can you ever forgive me?"

"I've never blamed you. It's all been in the way of life, hasn't it?"

"Aye, that it has."

They stared at one another from across the flat water, each trying to read the other's emotions. At last Trent spoke again.

"So, what's now?"

"I could meet you under that alder tree just beyond you there."

They spent the remainder of the morning strolling around the green, talking of familiar old things, and catching up on decades of Iubhar gossip. They laughed and kissed like nervous children under more kinds of trees than either could identify.

"I am no' the man I was," Trent said at last. "I've mended all those ways that took me frae you. I swear to you I am no' the man I was."

"You need only be in part the boy who left me coming home, and I'm content."

"I am that boy."

"The boy!" Kira suddenly cried. "We sent Aidan up the path ages ago. Come, we have to find him."

Their joy turned to anguish as they gained the footpath and made their way through the fine old wood toward Mount Melville. They shouted the boy's name, but he did not respond.

They came to the crossroads and called, but there was no reply.

Kira remained at the tiny car park while Trent hurried down the footpath into the trees. He traced the five hundred feet to the pyramid of Sharp's monument, but Aidan was not to be seen.

"Aidan!" Trent called. There came no answer.

"Aidan!" he heard Kira call from beyond the woods. Still there was no answer.

"Aidan," Trent called again, "are you lost then?"

"Nae, sir," came the small reply from the area about Trent's knees. The boy was crouched in the bushes.

"What are you doing hiding down there, lad?"

"I got tired of hiding behind the pyramid, Mr. Trent."

"And why were you hiding at all, lad?" Trent demanded. "We were that worried; account for yourself now."

"When I saw no chains aboot in the trees, I settled myself down for the other thing and to wait for you."

"Aye," Trent said, suddenly embarrassed, "we were a fair time meeting you, sure. But why were you hiding in those bushes all the same? Did you come to play foolish tricks or to see the site?"

"I came to see the sight, and I stayed crouched behind that rough stone pyramid for hours—until my legs got sair—then I moved into the bushes, but I think the murder must have been called off. I saw no sight of the archbishop or nae murderers neither. The next time they want to plan on murdering the archbishop, I think they'd better not advertise it in the guidebooks."

# Chapter 21

✦

I am discovering St. Andrews anew. Summer in St. Andrews; her crimson robes of schooling cast away, her jaunting togs put on, she is lithe and vivacious, quite a smart girl still for all the years she's seen.

The first day I had slept late. The young woman who brought my tea with scones and butter told me that Mr. Trent had taken Miss Shaw strolling and that they had taken Aidan along. She also told me about the hectic morning in the kitchen. An old man, probably a beggar, had found his way in when nobody was there, and the staff had been obliged to show him out.

That day I went to the West Sands and watched boys throw sticks into the surf. I had once ridden these sands on horses Andrew had hired.

I wandered down past Witch Hill, "where strong women used t'be martyred for knowing their own minds," according to Pippa, one of my suite mates here. Pippa was the militant one—the one with a weekly and unrequited crush on a different and undeserving boy. Peevish Pippa, the undated.

I had three suite mates when I was living in the dormitory, Fraser House 39, David Russell Hall, off Buchanan Gardens: Peevish Pippa, Irish Judith, and Terese. Terese's best friend, Diana, was so much in evidence in our suites that we all came to think of her as a suite mate as well.

Terese, Diana, and I were called the Three Graces of the hall, and some-times Diana and her disciples. We were members of the V Club, as we called it, the V standing for "virgin."

Thinking of Diana that first day made me want to go to the castle. I looked down into the crowded bathing pool, crammed in now with the late-June holiday horde, and remembered dear Diana. She was not the prettiest girl on the Scottish coast. She was, in fact, rather plain, but she had a trim figure and a big chest, and for that reason she enjoyed a certain popularity with the boys, especially the American boys.

"What is it about American boys?" Diana used to beg me to explain. "They canna seem to keep good eye contact, and they're forever on about my bosom. Dinnae they have bosoms in the States?"

"Yes," I replied, "we have bosoms in the States, but there's a growing cri-sis in the weaning industry."

"It's all testosterone," Pippa would comment. She had developed the opinion that testosterone was some sort of genetic mutation or hormonal poisoning in the makeup of boys, which impaired intelligent conversation, rationality, and the simple ability to remember a telephone number.

Seeing the castle bathing pool reminded me strongly of dear Diana and her ample bosom. We had all gone down that May Morning to dance eight-some reels on the castle courtyard and take the ritual plunge into the icy sea. Diana had gone down with determination, her swimsuit under her dress. At the final moment, however, she had decided to go into the bathing pool in-stead of the sea.

Lots of people were taking their lap in the pool by the time we all got down there, just one quick splash across before climbing out into the waiting warm towels that their friends held out.

Diana determined to be brave. She tossed her towel to Terese and stripped down to her swimming costume the color of tropical birds. The boys were all attention. It was a strapless, tight, and alluring outfit. When dear Diana dived in, the water peeled the top all the way back to her midriff.

I do not know if it was the cold or her concentrated resolve to prove brave, but poor Diana, the soul of modesty, was wholly unaware that she was completely bare-breasted in the cold, saltwater of the castle pool. And, *to our horror, she chose not to do anything like an Australian crawl but rolled slowly to her back, bare chest held high out of the water, and took a languid, leisurely, even sensuous backstroke across the pool, baring her ample delights to an awestruck, suddenly silent gathering.*

*She reached the end of the pool and turned a slow circle, attempting to prove that the cold water had no effect on her (though we all could plainly see that it had), and stroked slowly back past the captivated multitude for a second look.*

*She was nearly to the closest wall before she noticed and instantly bobbed underwater. She stayed under for a very long time, apparently hoping that she might just drown.*

*At last she strode up from the water, her costume in its proper place and her jaw set in firm resolve. She marched to where Terese stood with the waiting towel, turned, and addressed her gaping fans.*

*"Blessings and benedictions!" she bellowed heroically before stalking off toward Buchanan Gardens amid spontaneous and raucous applause.*

*She was even more popular with the boys after her May Day salute.*

*Standing above the castle pool in the warm June sunshine, remembering Diana's chilly swim, I realized that today was my own anniversary.*

*My lip trembled and my eye burned for a moment, but with an effort I swallowed the pain of being alone on my thirteenth anniversary.*

*"Good for you, Perry Miggs," I said to myself. "Play with your videotape and charts if that's what makes you happy."*

*I believe that was the first time in my life I looked upon shopping as an assault, an attack leveled at an enemy, but I went shopping then with a very definite idea that I was mounting an offensive against Perry's insensitivity. I would quite literally make him pay for abandoning me today.*

*I fished out the credit cards and peeled off the prophylactic rubber band that shielded them from the world.*

*I searched for hours for the sexiest, most expensive bathing suit to be had in St. Andrews. I settled for a one-piece suit with a sunburst on the abdomen. It was ridiculously overpriced, though, and I took real delight in using Perry's credit card to purchase it. I then arranged to have it shipped back to Iubhar—just to make it more expensive.*

*Later I also bought Perry a handsome brass sextant I found in a maritime shop. To confess the truth, though, I paid for it with Royal Geographic cash, and I did not have it shipped but took it with me. Guilt had not given way to forgiveness.*

*On the second morning of our stay in St. Andrews, I met Kira and Breton Trent for breakfast.*

*The young serving woman told us that the troublesome old man had been found again in the kitchen and again been bustled out. This time, she said, there were some words passed between him and the manager and the whole affair was very unpleasant.*

*"But what's he doing in the kitchen?" Kira asked.*

*"Just skittering aboot as well as I can tell. He takes nocht that we've seen or accounted for."*

*"He'll soon be on his own way, lassie," Mr. Trent assured her. "It is the way of wanderers. They fix on things. They are like dogs that way, ken. I knew of a terrier over in Aberdeen made a career of studying a cricket ball, carried it wi' him everywhere. Queer thing, that. Dinnae worry yourself, though; these gangrel auld wandering men take a notion for a while, but they never stay any one place for long.*

*"If he does come back another time," Trent continued, "just give him a stick o' butter and a few coins. That is the universal sign among the races of wandering souls and speaks of generosity and dismissal. He'll understand your meaning well enough and leave wi' a glad and charitable thought, never to trouble you again."*

*I left the hotel by midmorning without a thought to destination or design. I would merely wander like that poor wretch of the kitchen, like the wanderers Mr. Trent invented over his butter and buns. I would fix on things today, I thought, as the notion would strike. Let memory and moments have their sway, I would abandon myself to hap and give my day to chance.*

*The world is a merry sort of busy, useless spin when one is not bound up in it. It is all a merry, ungainly, purposeless sort of tangle, a vainglorious illusion of activity without end. And I wandered through it, drinking it in,* glorying in it, until I found myself standing in a familiar garden of benches and grassy plots winding through squat flowers and twisting vines.

I was standing at an arbor, an old, familiar spot I had not thought of in nearly seventeen years. But now—how the memories came flooding back!

"This is Andrew Macgruer," Melanie Torrence had said to me under this arbor early in our first term. She hung from the young Scotsman's arm.

She was a horrible little bitch, Melanie Torrence, with a reputation little better than a prostitute, a tarty sort of creature that I was embarrassed to acknowledge an American.

We were the only two Americans on the hall. So the vicious vixen from Virginia and I were insufferably and inescapably linked.

"He's going to be a poet," she simpered like a cheap knock-off Scarlett O'Hara under that garden bower.

It was the first time I had ever set eyes on Andrew Macgruer. He was in his starchy-shirt-and-creased-trouser stage then, tall and lean and muscled like an eau de toilet model. He was clean shaven back then but had the same penetrating, perceptive eyes.

I hardly noticed him, though. I wanted only to deflate Melanie's pretentious smirking.

"A poet?" I replied with a wickedly dulcet spin on the word. "There certainly isn't much future in that, is there?" Melanie's father was a car dealer with dealerships in four cities, and she had more than once made clear her intentions of marrying money. "I mean," I finished, "there can't be much money in it—outside of greeting cards."

I didn't mean it. Of course I didn't. I was the English major. I was the budding Phi Beta Kappa. I was the one sitting up nights with Wordsworth and Tennyson and Byron and Keats and Shelley and Shakespeare and Marlowe and Marvell. I was the one who valued poetry above money and position, but I knew she didn't. That was the point.

Melanie Torrence blanched visibly. She had only been showing off her next conquest, and I knew it. What did she care about poetry?

But the boy-toy trophy Scot, it turned out, had a brain and a pride.

"If every man worked only for bread and the lining of his pockets," he replied in a gentle, moderate tone that crushed me with its sincerity, "then the race of humanity would be little better than a stodgy murder of crows. Wi'out the use of their wings and no beauty in their hackle, they would hop frae spot to spot, devoid of reason, wi' no purpose, no future. If you would marry a man for the love of his money, miss, prepare to breed wi' him a species of worker drone unfit to call human. Beasts wi'out love or sense. And look for nocht more from that man's passion than the cold luster of the gold you wed."

He had thrown in my face my very sentiments, using them against me, defending not only himself but Melanie Torrence as well. Her supercilious smirk galled me.

He piqued my interest, this mild-spoken Scot with the wide shoulders and poetic passion. He wasn't for the likes of Melanie Torrence, and I decided on the spot to see that she didn't have him. I apologized sincerely and beat a calculated, flustered retreat into this arbor, tangling myself momentarily in the vines just there.

I can smile at it now. It was a juvenile beguilement, playing suddenly the distracted woman-child in need of rescue or indulgence at least. Men love that; women grow out of such tricks, or at least grow into better beguilements.

I disentangled myself, brushed back my hair, careful to hazard a coy glance up at the lovely young Scotsman as I did, and hurried off along my way. Just out of sight of them, I slowed to a smug saunter and brushed the grit of the arbor trellis from my hands.

That was well played, I thought. Very convincing. I knew I had trumped an ace from the look of bemusement on Andrew Macgruer's face and of loathing on Melanie's.

The arbor was being well kept, and I was glad.

When the allure of the arbor subsided, I drifted back into the stream of humanity circulating through the town.

For a while Pippa had thought that Andrew Macgruer was interested in her and that was why he spent his teatimes in our suite. Later, when she found out that Andrew liked me, she was livid and thought that I had stolen him. But we made up when she found another boy to interest her.

"Fish enough here for my tackle," Pippa would say when she wasn't *deriding the whole gender or wondering aloud why she had not been born a lesbian "so ah'd never again have to be bothered with this wretched botch o' men."*

*"So why not just go for it?" Terese once asked Pippa in her wide, flat accent somewhere between Derry and Brooklynese. "Just go gay."*

*"Och, I canna," Pippa had lamented. "I reckon I fancy the willies and the wankies just that much."*

*That was Pippa.*

*Delightful memories aside, a very peculiar thing happened to me on that second day. I was crossing South Bell Street, window-shopping, when I glimpsed a familiar face in the reflection. He was a few feet behind me, jostled in a flurry of pedestrians.*

*"Mr. Grant?" I called, turning. "Adam Grant."*

*I could not locate the knot of people I had seen reflected in the glass. Look as I might, I did not see Adam Grant anywhere in the throng. I called his name again, but no one answered.*

*I had an early supper and spent the evening sitting out on the end of the pier imagining the students parading out along the high, narrow jetty with the North Sea crashing and growling below. I sat out until the sun was almost set and then walked through the sleeping little town to find the hotel by the last faint rays of day.*

*I slept well that night and dreamed quiet dreams filled with old friends.*

*Our third morning brought news that the old wanderer had returned, and far from offering him butter and coins, the manager had summoned the police and had the man taken forcibly from the kitchen.*

*"He would neither tell us his name nor his business," the young woman reported.*

*"So what became of him?"*

*"I believe they're aboot putting him in jail. Poor auld fellow. I suspect he was looking for a bit o' bread or maybe some tea. He was caught messing aboot wi' the teapots this time. That's what set off Mr. Griggs that made him call for the police. Poor auld fellow."*

*"What will happen to him?"*

*"Nocht, I'm thinking. Mr. Griggs is a soft-hearted sort. I dinnae think more will come of it than keeping the auld thing in jail for the day and then a stern warning to move on along wi' himself."*

*I set out again after breakfast and caught sight of a lovely woman in the street, reflected in the shop windows, smiling back at me with eyes I used to know. She was like this little town, made lovelier by the gentle touch of time, her rough edges tumbled smooth in the dashing millrace of days. She had waited here for my return, and as I touched her reflection in the glass, her hand reached back to rest her fingertips against mine.*

*I smiled and saw that smile reflected in the glass, sweet and uncomplicated.*

*Had this girl been away for seventeen years? Surely not, seventeen days, perhaps months, not years. Her face was not seventeen years worn, her figure was still trim, eyes bright, hair sleek and full of color. No, had I aged seventeen years in the States, those years had been returned to me here untarnished and unused.*

*"Flatterer," I murmured to the glass and to my puckish imagination. "Welcome home."*

*I turned away and went to the Britannia Pub. Something in me wanted to think that it had not changed, was frozen in time as it was in my thoughts, with Jamey Chandliss beating out time at the counter while impromptu tunes broke out from the merrymakers. I looked for the old throng, but of course they were no longer there. The fare was different, too, and the atmosphere had changed. The faces were changed.*

*I suddenly felt very lonely.*

*I felt like a child who should have boarded the train but had remained on the platform. And I stood there watching the retreating faces of my old friends, faces pressed against the back glass of the train as it gained speed out of the station: Diana and Terese, Irish Judith and Peevish Pippa, even Melanie Torrence and Moira Givens.*

*I felt abandoned by them all. They'd gotten on with their lives. Only I was left behind. I felt it sharply there in the Britannia with big Jamey Chandliss absent and the music flown away.*

*Even the sun had abandoned me today and sulked behind the leaden veil of the approaching summer storm.*

*School friends leave. That is the way of life. We are meant to go our ways, separate and grow, transplanted from the classroom like rootbound plants into ever-larger worlds, ever-richer soil.*

*But husbands, no, not husbands.*

*The sinking certainty then chilled me. I had been abandoned indeed. This was not bittersweet remembrance—not merely the desire to recall good old days. This was not the teeming regret of retreating youth. I had lost something that I should not have lost. I had lost the care, the affection, the love and attention of Perry.*

*Pippa, where are you now?*

*I needed Pippa's love-hate relationship with men just now. "Just put a knee up his orchids and move on, dearie." I needed a sense of her outrage, the stinging certainty that I hurt so badly because I loved too much, believed too strongly, trusted too absolutely.*

*But these thoughts have no place in St. Andrews, where the air is always sweet. I know that. I wanted to drift away from them with my few coins and butter. I wanted them to dismiss me so I could dismiss them—knee up the orchids. But my melancholy thoughts followed me out of the Britannia and into the street.*

*The day was glutted with moody storm clouds, and the air grew heavy.*

*The crowd thinned, abandoning the streets, as it grew dark under the mounding clouds.*

*When the rain did come, it broke suddenly and fell in large, warm drops. It was not a downpouring but rather a steady, soothing rainfall that drove the bustle of shoppers and stragglers from the lanes.*

*I did not quit the street, though.*

*I stopped at the end of South Street under the left arch of the West Port and leaned there in the solitude of the rain.*

*"I knew if I waited long enough, you'd find your way back here." The voice came from around the edge of the arch behind me. I turned.*

*"Andrew," I breathed.*

*Andrew Macgruer stood in the rain, the long portion of his tartan draped* over his head like a monk's cowl. He slipped in under the arch with me.

"Have you had your lunch?" he said, pulling back his woolen hood and resting it over his shoulder.

"I had—" I started to tell him about the Britannia Pub but changed tacks midsentence, "—been planning to have a bite when the rains came."

"If you'd like," he said quietly, "we could go together and have something when the rains have done. This wetting will no' last long. It's only enough to lay the dust."

"Yes."

"Do you wonder what I'm doing here?"

"I know why you are here. You've been waiting for me."

He smiled sweetly at me. "And after all these years. How can you still know me so weel?"

"You haven't been easy to forget, Andrew Macgruer."

"Nor you."

I took my eyes from his, hoping he was not now lying to me. I couldn't stand that: not now, not here.

He then whispered to me:

> " 'Tis said 'out of sight, out of mind'
> But, no, believe it not.
> I've tried at length its power to prove,
> But thou art not forgot."

I leaned back against the wall, my hands behind me, and closed my eyes. My fingers bent into the rough stone at my back and suddenly I was twenty years old again and waiting for the warm breath and then the gentle touch of his lips upon mine.

It didn't come.

I opened my eyes to find him standing there, one hand resting on the wall beside my ear.

"Why tell me this now?" I said, recovering.

"Because," he breathed softly, "only the pastness of our past is past. What we have been is what we always are and what we can only be. Come wi' me."

*We dodged through the rain to our favorite little shop, Pepita's, for lunch.*

*"I've been wandering," I told him over a jacket potato. "All over town, just wandering and thinking."*

*"Thinking aboot what?"*

*"Everything, nothing. Nostalgia."*

*"Nostalgia," Andrew said with a sympathetic smile. "It's a word from the Greek. It means the pain of homecoming. It's a strange word to use for a pleasant activity."*

*"I didn't say it was pleasant. Not all of it, anyway. I have been 'all alone beweeping my outcast state'— 'summoning up remembrance of things past' and 'sighing the lack of many a thing I sought.'" He used to like it when I quoted poetry. He still did, and smiled.*

*He replied:*

> *"Why didst thou promise such a beauteous day,*
> *And make me travel forth wi' out my cloak,*
> *To let base clouds o'ertake me in my way,*
> *Hiding thy brav'ry in their rotten smoke?"*

*I laughed. "So," I said, "we both remember our Shakespeare."*

*He laughed in return, but we both understood. We had each spoken more than we had said, more probably than we could have said in the street dialects of linen drapers, petrol boys, and shop clerks.*

*We had spoken from the redemption sonnets of Shakespeare—poems of love and parting, of rejection, forgiveness, and renewal—while our hearts cracked with the pain of pleasure. I placed my hand on his cheek, and he returned the gesture. A thousand pains of longing tingled in our fingers and rippled through our eyes.*

*How sweet it felt, that pain.*

*"You've a wide eye and a huge soul," he whispered.*

*"Then I'd better skip dessert."*

*We strolled out along the Scores after lunch, the rain having stopped, and we laughed at our foibles as awkward children in college.*

*"Whatever became of that girl who swam nude in the castle pool?"*

Andrew asked as we stopped to look over the quiet waters, deserted by the bathers now since the rains had come.

"Diana?" I had to laugh. "She wasn't nude; she was naked. That was an accident. Her suit got pulled down when she dived in."

"Did it? I thought she meant to do it. I always thought she was a wee bit randy."

I laughed. "She married well and has twin girls."

"And that friend o' yours with the tight nap o' hair, the one who was always aboot to put her hand in my trouser pockets and guess how much change I had."

"Oh, you mean Pippa."

"What became of her?"

"She went to work for the BBC as a copywriter and married a producer. Last I heard they'd moved to the south of London somewhere."

"We swam here once, you and I," he said, still looking out over the quiet pool.

"Yes."

"It was that same day—that May Day."

Andrew and I had dipped into the cold waters. He'd held me as we treaded water, and our bodies were warm in the icy pool. We'd kissed and allowed ourselves to sink under the surface. It had been wildly stimulating, the cold, the warmth, the embrace, the silence.

I wondered now if Andrew was thinking about that part of our swim. I wondered how close he had come to asking me to make love with him that day. I wondered if he suspected how close I had been to accepting the invitation if he had. But he kept his thoughts of that day to himself now, and so did I.

In the late afternoon we walked on the West Sands where we used to ride at full gallop. The sand was the color of mocha and beaten flat by the rain until it appeared that we were the first ever to cross it, the first to leave a perdurable print on the earth's gentle face. He reached out to me and took my hand gently. I let him, and we walked along the seaside without speaking.

"It's a fair, fine thing," Andrew said quietly as the evening drew on, "to find what you've lost."

"Never lost. We only left it here so we could come back to it."

He slipped his fingers through my hair and whispered, "Soft and sweet as silk." He laid his arm tenderly over my shoulders and walked us quietly home.

The next day I awoke early and met the company for breakfast. It was our first time together since we'd arrived. Mr. Trent and Kira were glowing and jabbering about their plans. Andrew was stoic, as usual, but we had planned to show the town to Aidan that day, Andrew and I, and I was excited about that.

"Nae sight o' your kitchen goblin this day?" Trent asked the manager, Mr. Griggs, as he passed.

"No' today," Mr. Griggs said. "But he wouldn't be here today, would he? I left him the night in jail to give him a lesson and two or three good meals before they send him on his way. I'll go by after breakfast time to drop the charge of vagrancy. That'll be the end o' that."

Mr. Trent gave a doubtful grunt and muttered, "Butter and coins'd do the trick. That'd set him on his way."

"And we should be on ours," Andrew said, tousling his son's hair.

On our walk, I showed Aidan where we'd gathered on the second Monday in November, Raisin Monday, for our festivities.

"Your father dressed like a triffid," I told Aidan.

"A what?"

"Triffid. It's a large, carnivorous snapdragon sort of plant from the movies."

"Did you?" Aidan sought the affirmation of Andrew.

"Aye," Andrew admitted tersely, then added to me, "Thank you verra much."

"Actually," I added, "it wasn't a very good triffid costume."

"It was."

"Andrew Macgruer, you looked like a bad-tempered tulip in a baby bonnet."

"I won a prize for that costume, I'll have you know."

"The girls on our hall gave him an old iron hipbath we'd painted up," I explained to Aidan. "We told him it was a prize and made him carry it everywhere he went until midnight, as a condition for winning."

"And I did it, too." He seemed so proud of the accomplishment that I had to laugh.

We visited the mine and countermine and toured the castle, almost everything Aidan had been promised. The day proved too short for Aidan. It was too short for me, too.

The next day was to be our last in St. Andrews, and it began with a bit of excitement.

"He's been back," the young woman told me as I sat, the first at breakfast this morning for a change. "The old beggar man, I mean. Mr. Griggs caught him in the kitchen as before, and this time he was certainly at the teapots. Mr. Griggs says we can serve no tea this morning until he has everything looked into."

"But it's my last day here, and I want my morning tea."

"I'm sorry, ma'am, Mr. Griggs will no' allow it."

"Is he here?"

"No' now."

"Then bring me one cup, that's all, just one. I'll risk it. We'll never tell Mr. Griggs."

"It isnae wise, ma'am."

"Never mind wisdom. I don't think much harm can come of it if the water is well boiled. It will be our secret. Please. I may never be here again."

She clearly did not like the idea, but she said, "Very well, ma'am," and brought out one cup for me.

"What happened to the beggar?" I asked her when she returned.

"He got away. That's where Mr. Griggs is off to. He's called the police and promised to press charges this time. He's just that angry."

We had planned to leave by midmorning, but Mr. Trent and Kira wanted to go into town and buy something for Caitlin by way of an appeasement, and Aidan was invited along with them.

"Nae doot they'll be aboot buying him sweeties for the trip," Andrew said. "Will you come someplace wi' me now?"

"Where?"

"I'll show you."

He led me down to the ruined cathedral.

"Do you remember the last time you met me here?"

"Yes. Of course I do. We said good-bye here."

"I want to bid you a welcome back here now, Pær."

"Thank you, Andrew," I said, not knowing how I felt or what I wanted him to mean by it. "That's sweet of you."

He led me to a bench under St. Rule's Square Tower, and we sat.

"I sat here, right at this spot where we are now, and I wrote. I spent three days writing some of the worst poetry a man had ever set to paper, really awful stuff it was. I'd write all day and then put it all in the bucket there before heading home—for three days."

"Why? Why throw it all away?"

"Because it was only verses really, no' poetry at all. It was just me scribbling, you see, out o' my head—all meter and clever turns and nothing else, nothing real. It was safe poetry—the kind o' greeting-card stuff you once said I was fitted for."

I began to protest, but he touched my lips with his finger and smiled.

"I know you didnae mean it, Pær. But that's the sort o' thing I was writing for those three days.

"The Greeks used to think that a place can have a personality, you ken? Like a man can have charisma, a place can have what they called numen. It's what makes one place comfortable and another uneasy. I wanted to capture the numen of this place, where you had been. This is where you inspired me that day, do you see?"

"But you couldn't write here."

"Not on those three days, no' when I wrote safe poetry. On the fourth day that all changed. I sat down here and wrote no' from my head, but from my love of you."

I looked away, overwhelmed by the confession. My mind raced as I looked out to where the dark and chopping North Sea muscled its way toward shore. We had often kissed. We had touched one another and held one another in the gaze of love, but we had never actually said the words. How could we? I was destined to leave and he obliged to stay.

He continued to speak in his soft, tender tones while I looked over the priory field.

"It is never enough for a poet to say I have felt love or I feel love. Love is too rich and complex. Words alone are weak. There is a love inherent in nearly all things; there is love in the beauty of life but also in its ugliness, love in revulsion as well as attraction. It's that hard lesson a poet first learns. If he can survive the purging fires of that realization—that there is love in lamentation as surely as there is love in passion or in discord or even in hatred and indifference—then can he set ink to paper. Only then may he attempt the hard task of wrapping those extracts of the soul in the satin flesh of speech.

"For in each love, in each fragment of emotion, is the mix of all the other loves. The passion and attraction, of course, but also the misery and sting of neglect in love; and there's the tension of sex and the allure of flesh, the doubt, the ecstasy, and even the selfishness of giving and the generosity of taking. And at the centre of it all is the apprehension of love."

"'The apprehension of love,'" I repeated. "I like that; you mean both the understanding and fear of love. Did you write that in one of your poems?"

"Aye," he said softly, "words to that effect. But they are no' my words. They are yours. You used that verra phrase, 'the apprehension of love,' just there." He pointed to the top of St. Rule's Tower. "And it opened the whole world before me, Pær. I took you to me and pressed your lips to mine, and they tasted to me as the warm fresh mint tastes on the tongue, and in my mind raced a half a hundred thoughts. My only desire then was to keep you wi' me, to find a way to keep you from climbing aboard that plane in Glasgow. The whole mystery of the world lay bare before me then, and I saw it clearly, as I'd never seen before: the whole simple reason we are alive. And it all seemed to me unjust and unfair that we should part—that we even could part—when we had intertwined so perfectly, mind and soul, heart and sense. And you remember what you told me?"

"No," I admitted.

"There,' you said, 'there, Andrew Macgruer, is the love for the unfathomable. There's my gift to you to carry wi' you when I am gone. It's the same gift you are giving to me to take away home.' Och, Pær, how it tore at my heart to love you and lose you all in the same moment. How it haunted me then and still does so today."

As he spoke, a single tear slipped from his deep eye and coursed down his cheek, disappearing into his beard. It left a silver trail on his face, a trail that spoke of an arduous and yearning love, and it filled me with pity and self-satisfaction.

"When I wrote then—on that fourth day—wi' your words and love in me, I wrote poems that could make gods weep and nature dance. I wrote not wi' ink but wi' the distillation o' my soul until I had no soul left but what I had scratched out on that paper and dedicated to you."

He ran his hand along my cheek sweetly, and I returned the gesture, wiping away the tear that had fallen.

"I tried to get on in life. And I thought the emptiness I felt would be filled wi' other loves, perhaps, or activity at least. It sounds like the foolishness of love, but even now I believe I left something of me wi'in those pages, something important and vital, that only you can understand. And only you can give back to me. Will you come wi' me?"

"Where?"

"To the tower's top."

I did not want to go back there until that moment, that place that only reminded me of all I had left, all I had lost, but now I wanted to see it again, to see it with Andrew. My heart raced at the thought of it and would not slow again as we traced the few yards to the tower's gateway.

Inside, a set of stairs circled up the hollow corridor to the heavens, and we began the long, steep climb up through the dank and humid air.

"I have to stop," I said when we had gone halfway up the tall tower.

"What's wrong?"

I was suddenly sick. My heart beat so loudly that I was certain Andrew could hear it, and my breath caught. It was like anxiety closing in upon me, fear and foreboding, as though my whole body rebelled at the thought of seeing that place again, where I had last been entirely happy and perhaps would not be so happy ever again.

"I don't know," I managed to say. "A little faint, I think."

The world inside the tower seemed to spin slightly, and sparkling flecks danced about the periphery of my vision, closing it into a narrow tunnel. My head grew light.

I must have tottered, because Andrew suddenly caught me around the waist and ordered me to sit on the stairs.

My heart continued to thud within my breast for some time, but it slowed finally and I felt better. I was exhausted but rapidly recovering by the time Andrew led me back out onto the field and we found a place to sit.

"Is it pregnant you are?" Andrew whispered delicately.

"I doubt it. Are three men on camels approaching from the east?"

"What was that then?"

"I really don't know. Nothing like that has ever happened before."

Even as I said the words, I thought of the morning tea. What had the stranger done in the kitchen this morning? What had he put in the tea?

"No matter," I said to Andrew with a bright smile, feeling recovered. "I'm much better now. I'm sorry we couldn't—" With a gentle gesture, Andrew quieted me.

"It is nae matter. 'Tis only a place."

He reached down and picked two flowers from the base of the bench, one red, one white, and laid them delicately upon my palm.

"Fáilte," he said, "is maith an t-anlann an t-ocras."

"I don't speak Gælic."

He smiled. "Hunger makes good sauce."

I smiled at him and said, "We had better start home."

We walked out from under the shadow of St. Regulus Tower, and I thought of Andrew's comment under the West Port:

Only the pastness of the past is past.

The two little flowers crouched between my fingers as we walked. Their roots twisted into the roots of all past flowers, red and white. Remembrance warmed into feeling, present and new, and all the pastness of our past was gone indeed.

# Chapter 22

✤

Aidan was better during the drive to Pitlochry and Duncreagdhubh Castle, though still I thought he acted gloomier than a ten-year-old ought to act. I wondered what troubled him. Kira and Mr. Trent had bought him jelly bears for the trip, and he seemed content with those.

Kira was not a good traveler. We again found ourselves stopping every half an hour or so to take the view and stretch our legs. Twice Kira and Mr. Trent went strolling off hand-in-hand to sit and overlook a vista while Andrew and Aidan played impromptu games with a stone or stick in the field.

I was impatient with such delays, necessary though they were. Ever since Andrew pressed close against me under the old arch at the West Port, my mind and heart had raced forward, seeking some unthinking tomorrow. And each delay, each moment spent on some useless or utilitarian necessity, filled me with a sense of futility and rubbed at my nerves.

We arrived at the castle B and B in about the same time it would have taken us to jog there.

I got ready for bed. The hollow corridor of the castle bed-and-breakfast whistled slightly and filled me with misgiving. It was just nerves, of course. But I could not help thinking of Red Coinneach MacRovie searching for his head.

I believed I did hear something shuffling in the hallway outside my door, a sound like someone brushing the wall with paper. I haven't heard it now for a bit.

It was as though something stopped at my door a minute ago and is standing there, listening.

I was not long in such thoughts, the deep pillow wrapped around my face, when I thought I certainly heard the door open.

The paper-on-the-walls sound advanced to my bed, and I felt a tiny, cold hand slip under the sheets and grasp my hand.

"Mrs. Miggs?" it murmured.

It was Aidan. He was in his pajamas, face freshly scrubbed for bed.

"I have to speak with you," he said.

"What's the matter?"

"I wanted to tell you before we get back. No one else can know. But you already know, so I can tell you."

He had begun to pucker up as though he might cry.

"That's all right, Aidan, love." I held him to me and comforted him. "What is it?"

He began to blubber quietly in my arms, deeply tormented.

"I dinnae mean to do it," he said at last.

"Do what?"

"He told me to push the buttons."

"Who told you to push what buttons, Aidan?"

"Mr. Miggs," he moaned. "We were aboot to enhance the tape he had of her, of Nessie. You know aboot the tape, so I can tell you. Mr. Miggs didnae want anyone to know aboot it, but you know."

"What about the tape, Aidan?"

"We were aboot to enhance the tape the way we enhanced the St. Peter's haddock in the Irish Sea. He read the book, and I pushed the buttons. But the book said that you cud no' enhance a tape. You can only enhance the real thing. I already had the buttons pushed, though, the RECORD and PLAY buttons."

"What happened?" I asked, growing cold at the pit of the stomach.

"I erased it. I erased it all."

"The videotape of Nessie rising?"

"Aye," he managed to squeak before he began to bawl.

I hushed him and dried his tears, rocking the dear child quietly against my bosom.

"Is that what's been bothering you all along?"

"Aye."

"Hush, then. It wasn't your fault, Aidan. Mr. Miggs told you to do it. It isn't your fault. You couldn't know. Was Mr. Miggs angry with you?"

"Nae."

"No, of course not." Whatever else Perry might be, he was not a man to lose his temper. He had no temper to lose.

"He said it was all his fault."

"Well, there then," I cooed. "What's done is done. We cannot undo what is meant to be, and this was certainly meant to be. Nobody's angry with you, Aidan dear. If you hadn't pushed those buttons, Mr. Miggs would have pushed them himself. It would have happened no matter what."

"But he looked so woeful and unhappy."

"That's because this meant a lot to him, Aidan, but that is all his concern, isn't it? We might feel sorry for him, but you must not reproach yourself. He asked for it, dear—that is, he wanted to do it. All right? Run on back to your room now. Your father will be wondering what's happened to you."

He left much relieved to have unburdened himself.

Perry had said this was a bad time for me to be leaving. He wouldn't tell me why. He had been foolish, and he had handled it all so badly.

He should have told me. He should have never let me go.

Perry was right, though. He was right when he told Aidan that this was all his own fault.

It was—all of it. It was his fault.

I dangled for a while between pity and irritation. Poor unbearable Perry.

I whispered a soothing "damn" while I lay in my bed, repeating it like a mantra as I fell off to sleep.

# Chapter 23

❖

## INVERNESS

We completed our journey as far as Inverness by late the following morning. We had taken a lovely breakfast at Duncreagdhubh Castle, but I was eager to complete our trip, and so we left early.

Kira wanted to stop in Inverness and shop for groceries. She was certain Caitlin had bought all the wrong things during marketing day, and she was not about to cook food she had not purchased herself.

"It is such a pleasure to travel," she announced as we entered the outskirts of Inverness, "and I do so love to have someone else cook, but I must repair the damage done to my pantry."

I had been marketing with Kira before, and knew that it could be a painstaking process, filled with the nuance and detail of an Arabian auction. So I told Andrew that we probably should plan for lunch in town.

He wanted to return Aidan home first, so we made plans to meet for lunch. He promised to return within the hour, so I window-shopped awhile before finding my way to a cozy little double bench. I sat there for nearly a quarter of an hour watching the gulls floating like corks on the river Ness.

I sat back on the little double bench—on the side facing the river—and *thought whimsically that St. Andrews was more a state of mind than a place really.*

*"Perdita?" I heard a woman's voice behind me. "Perdita Leal?"*

*I turned and saw a young woman standing in the crowd, staring.*

*"Oh, my God," she said as I turned. "It is you."*

*She looked familiar somehow, and I searched my mind for where I might have known her.*

*"Perdita Leal?" she said again, this time seeking confirmation.*

*"Miggs," I responded, trying to hide my misgivings. "It's Perdita Miggs now. I've been married." I don't know why I didn't say "I am married," but that's the way it came out.*

*She seemed both bemused and overwhelmed at the sight of me sitting there like a prim schoolgirl on my little back-to-back bench. She spun herself around and sat on the other side of the double bench. She stared into the crowd, gaping astonishment played on her face.*

*"I'm sorry," I said at last, "do we know each other?"*

*"Nae," she said in her daze. "We don't know each other, but I know you. I know you verra well." The admission seemed to amuse her. She laughed and turned to me, placing her elbow over the shared bench backs. She opened her eyes wide and took me in. She seemed pleased, even delighted to see me. "I am Margaret Macgruer, Aidan's mother. I think you'd better call me Meg."*

*I suddenly realized why she had looked familiar. She looked like me, maybe not enough to have been my twin, but very similar indeed. Except for her hair, which she wore cropped close instead of flowing, like mine, we might have even passed for one another to a casual acquaintance: eyes, height, figure, face, hair color, all the same.*

*No wonder Aidan reminded me so much of the child I had never had. He had inherited most of his mother's qualities and few of Andrew's.*

*"I could nae believe it when I saw you sitting here. I knew it was you. I just had that feeling. Imagine. I haven't thought of you in weeks, perhaps months, and then I saw you here, just out of the corner of my eye, and you would have thought I had been touched wi' a wire, it was just that quick. And I knew it was you."*

She put her hand across her mouth in gesture of critical assessment, ap-
praising me for a second time in the few moments since we had met.
I was flattered and bewildered and laughed out of my bewilderment. Her
eyes danced merrily at the sound of my laughter and she joined me.

And there we sat, two complete strangers, laughing into one another's
faces like long-parted friends.

"My lord," she said through her merry laughter, "we even laugh alike,
don't we? Hello, Perdita Miggs."

"Hello, Meg Macgruer."

"Miggs?" Meg mulled over the name for a moment. "You're the one Andrew's been taking out on the loch, aren't you?"

"My husband."

"What are the chances?" she said, still shaking her head in rapt disbelief.

"What are they?" I echoed.

She stood abruptly.

"Have you had your lunch?"

"No."

"Nor I. I think we'd best take lunch together today."

She put out her hand, and I accepted it. Something about her made me
feel at once comfortable and content. I had never had a sister. I had never
had a sibling. Now, without warning, I had acquired one, and I liked her immediately. I liked the very thought of her.

"I know of a place," she said, "all hanging plants and textiled walls,
where they serve aubergines like heaven and six different kinds of chocolate
for afters."

"That does sound like heaven, but I was just waiting for—" I hesitated,
but she seemed to understand.

"Andrew, is it?"

"He was taking Aidan back home."

"Was he now?" she said. "That's early for him. I hadn't expected them
much before supper. That's well as it may be, though. When he sees me no'
home, he'll find something to do with Aidan. They're never lost for a thing to
keep them occupied. Come on, then, if it's only them we're worrying after."

"But then they'll come here looking for me," I stammered.

"And then they won't have found either of us. It's a lark. Come on."

Lunch was a delight. The food was excellent, and we dawdled over the desserts and coffee, neither of us eager to see the afternoon end.

"You know," Meg said with a serious pucker of the brow. She was toying with her fork around the chocolate torte but seemed suddenly preoccupied "I didnae always like you much."

"No? I suppose that's understandable."

She winced, grappling with some internal idea that discomfited her. "It isnae only that. It went a bit beyond the simple jealousy of a wife for a past girlfriend, quite a good bit beyond it, really, I'm afraid. I mean I really didnae like you at all."

"No," I confirmed, seeing that there was much more to it.

"It was really rather difficult," she said awkwardly, "living the part of your high priestess."

"Sorry? My what?"

"That's how I came to think of it," she said quietly, not making eye contact with me. "And it was hard for me. I honestly loved Andrew, and for a good, long while he loved me. We were happy. More than that. Andrew is the perfect husband. Sorry. He was the perfect husband—caring, honest, just everything that makes a person a pleasure to be around. He was too honest, perhaps, and that's what brought it all crashing down."

"You know, Meg," I said tactfully, "I'm really not following this."

"Sorry," she said, regaining herself. "Of course not. How stupid of me. I only meant to say, and I want to say it candidly and tactlessly at first, if I may—I want to get it oot into the air just like that and then explain it all to you after."

"But that's just not necessary if you don't want to."

"But I do. I want to tell you. You really should know, I think. And I want to tell you in my own way. I want to be candid and tactless to you. But then I want to explain it so you can understand what I mean by it all."

"Very well."

She nodded to me before steeling herself to the moment. Her eyes narrowed. Meg Macgruer suddenly became another woman, dark and vengeful. She spoke with venom and vitriol.

"Candidly and tactlessly, then," she said, "you ruined my marriage, Perdita Miggs, and I could find it in me to hate and resent you for that until I draw my last, dying breath."

She said it quietly, not causing a scene, but she said it with depth and anger. Rage filled her and painted itself across her pretty face.

A flash of anger flared in me—her rancor seemed so very unfair. But in the next moment, I realized that it was not unfair at all. She had suffered much because of me.

I was shocked by the realization, embarrassed. Meg sat for a long moment, continuing to stare me in the eye, blazing with the years of gnawing bitterness. Her words continued to echo about my imagination: "I could find it in me to hate you and resent you until I draw my last, dying breath."

My contrition must have registered, for I felt my face flush. She was visibly relieved to see my reaction. The tightness of her own features relaxed at once.

"There's that said then," she sighed in a deep, soul-felt satisfaction, and lifted her cup to her lips.

She was suddenly herself again. In a twinkle, the anger, the animosity, the scorn all vanished—subsiding as quickly as they had erupted. She smiled suddenly, and I saw what she had done, saw what she had needed to do.

I dabbed the napkin to my lips and returned her bright smile. I collected a deep sigh and blew it out.

"Does that pay back some of it?"

"Aye, a great good deal of it. Thank you for taking it so weel."

"My pleasure."

She reached across and squeezed my hand.

"You're a treasure, you are. No wonder Andrew loved you as he did. You cannot know the weight that is off of me. Are you all right?"

"I think so."

"Good," she said, dropping some cash onto the table. "Let's go round to my place. I owe you that explanation now."

Andrew and Aidan had, as Meg expected, left when they found she was not at home, and we had her apartment to ourselves. She took a stepladder from a narrow cabinet in the kitchen and set it up in a hall closet. She spent some time rummaging in the upper shelves of the closet before producing a narrow book hand bound in white leather.

She sat on her sofa beside me with the book facedown upon her lap and demurely folded her hands across it.

"He's a fine, good man," she said earnestly to me, "but he's also a deeply feeling and sensitive one."

"I know that."

"This nearly cost him his sanity, I think," she said as she massaged the book with her fingertips, "and it certainly cost us our marriage."

She sighed and again patted the book. She turned it over on her lap, and I saw its title, Unpathed Waters, Undreamed Shores, stamped in gold across its face.

"I bound it for him," she said. "I found it a few years after we married and thought it would make a nice gesture. I probably should have left it alone. It would be a different day today if I did no' know about this book. But I'll come to that in the fullness of time."

She lay the attractive little book on the table in front of us and leaned back in her place.

"I met Andrew a few years after university. He was teaching literature then, classical languages and literature, and he had made inroads to be named poet in residence. He was such a serious man, I thought, and I loved him perhaps from that verra first day.

"He was attracted to me as well, I could tell. My hair was long then, and I wore it aboot my shoulders as you do. He used to tell me how lovely it was. We fell in love that quickly and were married. Soon after that I was pregnant wi' Aidan, and all was better than I could have planned it. Andrew was a wonderful husband, and, when the time came, he became a wonderful father.

"There was never a hesitance in his kiss, and I never caught glimpse of a quiet discomfort or a secret regret in him in all the years we were married. How could I have known such a thing existed in the man I loved so well? And God knows, Perdita Miggs, I loved Andrew Macgruer with all the love I had.

"So that was us, solid and secure as well as happy.

"Then a thing happened that seemed such a little thing. The universities gave up on the tenure system. Andrew need never worry. He was secure in his job. But, wi'out tenure, Andrew was told he would have to publish a full book of poems if he wanted to be considered for the poet-in-residence position.

"It seemed a little thing. Such a little thing.

"He was a fine poet, of course, and had published individual poetry here and there. Quite a lot of it. So he set himself upon a book, but nae book would come out of him. Night after night he tried, but nothing he wrote pleased him. He threw away the main of it. And no book would come. He felt the pressure keenly, of course, and the more it worried him the less he could do in the way of writing, and he at last despaired.

"Then I made my mistake. 'You've a fine book of poetry already,' I said and reminded him of these poems I had bound up for him years before. He was desperate by then, or I believe he would never have done it, for these poems meant that much to him. I encouraged him, though, and he took them around to publishers.

"Poetry is difficult to publish in the best of times, but those were not the best times. The publishers were verra sympathetic in rejecting him, but their words bit him cruelly. That's when I realized how much these poems meant to him. They were no' written for a public but only for himself. I told him to stop, but it was too late by then, of course.

"One publisher had called them old-fashioned and sentimental in the worst way, and those words worked hard upon Andrew. They dredged up a wellspring of remembrance in him, and he seemed to drift away from me from that day.

"That's the first I realized that the poems were not written to me. You see, they all speak of his love for a girl he calls Vesta. This girl is described so well throughout the poems that I had always thought he meant Vesta to be me. But when I could no' soothe him, I realized the truth of the matter. We had opened an old wound, and it would bleed afresh and nothing would close it this time.

"He told me aboot you then, and I realized how he had replaced you with me. I was hurt and angry and foolish. I accused him of loving you and not me. I told him I'd no' share my bed wi' a teenaged phantom.

"He is a good man, though, and an honest one. He told me the truth—he still loved you and would never stop loving you. That's the way he is made, do you see? That is why I loved him as I did. I was no' able to see that he could love you and still love me.

"I was no' an understanding wife to him then. I was only a wounded woman, thinking only of my pain, inventing a world of deceit and betrayal that never was. I had my hair cut off and did whatever I could to erase any trace of Vesta from me. I think then I might have stopped and seen that he loved me still, that Vesta and Perdita Leal were but his memory of love.

"But what did I do? I made him choose between me and the memory. There's foolishness. A memory is as much a part of a body as a hand or a finger. I drove him out in my way. I held the church and his vows over him. I waved morality before him. And he retreated away from it all.

"What else could he do? I gave him nae other choice. The university and the publishers gave him nae other choice. He reverted to the simple life. He moved away from society and embraced that never-never world of Highland romance, off to become the wildman poet o' the wood.

"He asked me to come wi' him and bring young Aidan, that we'd live a simple life oot of man's world. And I said nae. I forced him into a divorce we neither one wanted, and he gave it to me as sweetly as he'd given me the rest of his love, but I was too stupid and angry and selfish to see it.

"So off he went to be alone wi' his thoughts and alone wi' those high standards of his that the foolish auld world was poorly equipped to meet.

"And, I think, a part of him went off to be alone wi' you. The memory of you that is."

Meg returned from her reverie and looked me in the eye.

"I would have given anything to have found you today fat and toothless, Perdita. But look at your pretty, young self. I am flattered that he saw you in me now that I have a good look at you.

"I suppose you'd better have your look at this, then."

She took up the book of poetry and opened it on her lap. We spent the next hour reading Andrew's poems. They were the poems he had written on that fourth day under St. Rule's Tower. They were miraculous—rich and filled with yearning and the happy pain of memory.

Vesta was "the breath of beauty's flower" and the "brief glimpse of eternity frae which man's mind can no' return." They were good poems, even great.

In them, Andrew spoke of "the final cause of love" and said, "nae heart can hold the world nor can the world the heart." They were tiny lyrics, deceptive and simple seeming. I recognized at once why the publishers would not print them. They were not really simple at all.

They spoke of love—real love—romantic love: unrequited, pure, sensual, undying, and deep.

In the poem he called "Transformation," he imagined that he dreamed and in the dream saw Vesta become Αθηνη, the Greek goddess of wisdom and purity. She rose from his bed, where she had refused him carnal love, and with a kiss that fell on his face like a teardrop she changed him into a roebuck and herself into a huntress and chased him through the Highland woods. The poem ended as the dreamer awakes to find a teardrop still clinging to his cheek where the kiss had fallen.

No wonder they would not print—could not be mass-produced—written as they were with Andrew's soul; the ink was too precious, too rare.

"They're beautiful," I managed to say through tears. Such an insufficient word.

"He never showed them to you, then?" Meg sniffed.

"No, he wrote them after I was gone."

The news made Meg cry again, and her tears prompted fresh tears in me, and we laughed and cried at once.

"Aye," she said, chuckling through her tears. "Then I see that weeping is the only proper response to them. I wonder now how I never saw the sadness in them. It is so plain in every word. What is it to be loved like that by such a man?"

"You would know better than I."

Meg was serious now. "Nae. I've shared his bed and known his love, and he loved me as much as I may know love, but I never inspired anything like this in a man before, no' even in Andrew. I think I would begin hating you all over again now if I weren't so fascinated by you. What is it in you that inspires this kind of love?"

*"I don't know, Meg. I honestly don't know."*

*"Then I would move heaven and hell to find out, Perdita. This is no' natural, no' in the normal path of man and woman, I mean. I never knew until this minute how foolish I was to make Andrew choose between us. I can see it now, though. My Lord, I can see it. There are people we love, as Andrew loved me, and then there are people who must be together. That's what he means when he says, 'Vesta is to me as life to flesh and my soul to the rampant eternal.' This is a love beyond love."*

*"Yes."*

*"And it is also the way you feel aboot him."*

*"It is."*

*"He's lost to me," she said with resolve. "I had him and threw him away. But he is not entirely lost to you; perhaps you can reclaim him for one of us at least. It's always been you he wanted."*

*"I am married, Meg."*

*"Aye," she breathed softly, "well. I fancy myself a good woman, Perdita, a moral person, and I believe in the teaching of the Church. But my Bible says a man and woman marry in their souls and not in the church. It's a question you must answer for yourself, but if God is love, how can He but bless a union founded in love?"*

# Chapter 24

# July

✤

Adam Grant sat disconsolately amid the loud hum of diesel engine and heavy tire upon rugged road.

He might have been happy that he was on the early and uncrowded coach or that he sat nearly alone. He might have rejoiced to have the long bench along the coach's back all to himself and the wide, clean window at his shoulder. He might have delighted himself to think that he was released from jail again, all charges dropped, after only three days—or that the kindly Mr. Griggs from the inn had pressed a few pounds into his hands while warning him to stay out of the inn's kitchen in the future.

Instead he brooded upon his failure. He placed his face against his hand, his hand against the glass, and stared without seeing out of the window.

It had been simple enough to make his way to St. Andrews, simple enough to find the girl and her lodgings. It had even been a simple task to enter the kitchen; a pebble—tiny as a secret—slipped against the doorjamb had kept the latch from catching. And, with a little shuffling, Adam had been able to creep in while the world slept.

He had little difficulty with his plan. It was simple enough: wait for her to appear for breakfast, watch which pot of tea would be prepared for her, and slip the powder into the pot while the staff was not looking.

But he had been caught. That was not part of the plan. And they took away his envelope filled with the powder.

That all-important, dusky orange powder was gone. Perhaps he could get more.

But it was gone now, and Adam sat listlessly on the back bench of the motor coach, his old head rattling on his hand, musing upon his failure.

"Och, weel," he murmured to the glass, "there's the trick of it, auld girl."

He closed his eyes and imagined, not for the first time, the cold, bottomless waters of Loch Ness. And he longed to plunge into the murky cold depths of death, to release his unhappy spirit and cease his wandering.

"No use," he whispered, his eyes still closed. "No use, auld girl. There's some just not meant for it. There's some men born to it, the evil. There's some can do the bad thing, but no' I, auld girl, no' I. There's the trick of it."

There was a woman on the bus with Adam, sitting a few seats ahead of him and on the opposite side of the coach. She turned casually to regard him, to see whom he might be addressing.

"Destiny is a tricky auld devil," he said to her in his aimless, casual way. "It sets each man a path and takes away the feet to walk it."

She nodded warily at him before turning again to mind her own business.

"And damn me for the saint of sinners," Adam said quietly again, "that man Miggs will be gone by now, and where does that leave me?"

Adam Grant closed his eyes again and fixed his mind on the distant loch. He would walk, he decided, from Inverness, and take the old circuit around the loch. He calculated where he would stop, where She might be. He drifted into sleep as he imagined the great, gray creature diving gracefully down through the darkness, cutting the peaty depths of Loch Ness.

He smiled at that.

✦

*The strangest thing has happened. Perry is gone.*

*We arrived in Iubhar to the news. Caitlin told me. Two men came asking for Perry. He nodded to them, according to Caitlin, packed his bag (the large one with the strap), took his portfolio of sketches and notes, and left.*

*There was a note from him on our bed. He had been called away to London, and he was required now, halfway through his grant period, to deliver a report on his progress.*

*That is strange.*

*He has been sending progress reports all along. I know. I have seen him. I have read a few he has left lying about—all about viability and acidity and other such -idities that stop the mind and paralyze curiosity. And I have seen them dutifully mailed off every Saturday, dropped in the box, the large yellow envelopes carefully sealed and clasped and taped for good measure.*

*So it seemed odd to me, after all of those dreadfully dull reports, that the Royal Geographic Society should call for him to come to London personally. It seemed odd to Caitlin, too.*

*"The English," she said in exasperation after telling me about the two men who came to collect Perry. "Och, the English." She was no warmer to the English than she was to men in general.*

*I was alarmed at first by the news of Perry's departure. I felt abandoned initially and wandered my room like a newly caged animal, panicked and wild. But within hours the nascent shock wore off. And as my confusion subsided, it was replaced by a bizarre sense of elation and release.*

*My room remained just as I'd left it. Only Perry's things were gone. It was as if the memory of a husband haunted me like a fantasy, a colorless sort of dream that I had carried with me from America.*

*Everything else was as it had always been.*

*The only real difference was me. I was suddenly as much a part of the landscape as the sheep, as much a part of that world as the breezes that ruffled across the loch and up the shore to set Kira's flowers bobbing in the garden.*

*How the world seemed to spin into place for me then, like Kira's little tables on Wednesday morning. Dozens of little bits and pieces all slipping easily into their predetermined places: St. Andrews, my reawakened feelings for Andrew Macgruer, Meg's words, Perry's disappearance. I could suddenly sense the higher power at work in my life.*

*Enchantment.*

*It filled me with old, familiar sensations, all the colors of candies wrapped for Christmas and the scent of cloves that hung in the warm summer air. It rushed in upon me, seized me like a lover, and made my heart gallop.*

*There is a plan in life, yes there is. There is a pattern to it all so delicate and obvious that it often escapes notice; but there it is, lying like a seed on the ground, filled with its blueprints and purpose. Meg is right. Life isn't about moralities and laws and divine retributions. Life is about living. Life is about getting on with it all.*

*I lay drinking in the morning until Kira cried, "Breakfast!" up the stairs. I dressed and went down filled with my new sense of sensuality and living in the moment.*

*How sweet the meal tastes when it is all there is; when each bite is the sum of all experience, how sweet. Kira had surpassed herself that morning and filled our table with fresh fruits and berries, baked things with surprising centers, jams and creams, thick-flowing porridge and amber tea with cream and the polite little lumps of tawny sugar that nest in the bowl like finches. How good it all tasted; how good it all smelled—how good to step down into that scene. To see the lazy steam lolling up from plates piled high with all the delicacies of Kira's kitchen—how good.*

*The food of a contented cook, that's what it was, morsels filled with serenity and the peace that comes from knowing.*

*We ate our fill, we three, and talked of light matters while above our heads Breton Trent sawed at a board and whistled a sprightly tune. He had eaten very early indeed, having arrived with the sun and set to work, up the ladder at the back door, after "just a bite of bun" and "no more than a swallow of tea" over the threshold of the kitchen while Kira cooked.*

Kira cleared the table after breakfast, and while she clattered merrily about the kitchen Caitlin fixed me with a stony glare.

"They seem verra cheerful," she said with no cheer in her own voice. "Those twae."

"I think they are cheerful," I replied.

"I believe that's what comes of a week away together." Caitlin tried to sound conversational, but it was no use. I enjoyed sipping my tea innocently while she worked around her curiosity like a cat circling a bowl of milk too hot to taste. "It is an agreeable place, St. Andrews, I believe."

"It is that."

"Of course," she continued, "I have never been there. I have never had a reason to go to such a place as St. Andrews. Still, I hear it is agreeable."

"Mmm, yes."

She watched me pointedly, trying to ferret behind my amiability. She clutched her fists in her lap and tightened her jaw.

"Did you," she said, "that is did the group of you, stay together the whole long while?"

"Hardly at all," I said casually and took another sip of my tea.

"Nae," she agreed with a hidden triumph I could not comprehend. "Nae, the twae of them, my sister and that carpenter were quick to steal off, I dinnae doot."

"Actually," I said as I scraped a drop from the bottom of my cup into the saucer, "we all went our separate ways for most of the time."

"Aye," she confirmed, still reveling in whatever secret she thought she had uncovered. "And the twae of them together the while?"

I chose to leave it an open question and did not answer.

"Did they speak of anything in particular?" she said so transparently that I smiled, but she turned to me just then, and I had to hide my smile behind the teacup.

"Nothing in particular," I replied. "Nothing that I remember in particular, that is."

"Nae," she assented in the tone of a physician taking a case history. She puttered about for a while longer before picking up the thread again. "Nae mention of Aberdeen, for example?"

*"No. Not that I can recall."*

*"Nor of Inverness?"*

*"Nothing particular about Inverness, no."*

*She folded her hands on the table and leaned toward me.*

*"I'm nae woman to play at catch-the-mouse," she said, suddenly brusque and businesslike. But behind her candor I could see the signs of strain and worry. "I'll tell you directly what is on my mind and ask of you the courtesy of direct answers."*

*"I have no intention of betraying any trust."*

*"Have you a trust to betray?" she said apprehensively, her eyebrows raising.*

*"No, I've expressed myself poorly. I mean I am not comfortable being questioned as if I were sent along to play informer on Mr. Trent and your sister."*

*"But you're saying you could inform upon them if you'd a mind to do it," she said, her anxiety deepening.*

*"No," I protested. "I mean I'm not comfortable talking about people behind their backs. It isn't seemly."*

*Caitlin sat back and collected herself.*

*"You're right. Of course you are right. It isnae seemly at all, and she my own sister. But it is for her sake I'm asking. My sister is a romantic fool of a woman even as she was a romantic fool of a young girl, and Breton Trent is a man. Och, he's nae ordinary sort of a man, is he. He's done enough harm to the world, and I'll no' have him making Kira Shaw's life bitter for her."*

*She leaned toward me again in a conspiratorial manner.*

*"He was no' altogether unknown to me when I went to live with Mr. Reese in Inverness. And tales of him have I heard of the days he's spent in Aberdeen. It is true he promised my sister that he'd never take a wife, and weel he didnae. But that was neither hindrance nor hobble to him taking on a girl in his home to act the part of a wife to him. And by habit and repute if not by law they were as well as married. She was a fine girl from good family by all account, but he was hard to her and broke her tender spirit.*

*"He drank, and it was the common talk of the street that he would reel home to his wife more often than he would walk the way. He spent what*

little money he would earn and so leave that poor girl in a home no better than a hole with her belly pinched for the want of a scrap or a crust.

"He fisted her, too, both drunk and sober, and many a day she was left on the dirty floor to wipe up her own blood when he went away to work or drink.

"And I would hear these terrible tidings of Mr. Breton Trent long after he had moved away to Aberdeen and taken the poor creature wi' him there. And I would fall to my knees, pitiful as my own lot was and cruel as Mr. Reese was to me. No less a beast than Breton Trent, and I would thank Almighty God that my sister had been spared such a life with such a man.

"You canna know what a girl she was, in every way but birth my younger sister, that callow and open was she. How a life among men would have changed her for the worse, broken her, hardened her, hurt her in more ways than wit can count. And I used to thank dear merciful God that He had spared her. She would nae have lived to this day had she lived that life; her dear, sweet ways would have been crushed and wi' that her verra life I'm sure. Breton Trent would have ruined her, killed her, too, I think, in his time."

Her passion was too intense. I saw more, I think, than she meant to say.

I then spoke like a woman in a dream, without thinking, hardly believing myself as I did. "Is that why," I said, "you lived with him under the name of Reese? You were protecting her?"

She froze with an inscrutable look upon her face.

"That girl was you, his wife by habit and repute?"

She did not look up at me but stood slowly and turned away. She walked quietly to the door and seemed to consider turning back to me, but her better judgment apparently took control. She listened for a moment at the kitchen, and when she had satisfied herself that Kira had heard nothing she walked from the room with her accustomed bearing, dignified and prim.

I sat in embarrassed silence for a long time and collected myself only when Kira came in to remove the few remaining tea things I had commandeered from the breakfast table.

She smiled sweetly at me, and I could see that she had never guessed how she had been deceived, what betrayals had shifted about her like unresolving squalls. She smiled, and I wanted to throw my arms around her, to protect her, but I could not determine if I wanted to protect her from the terrible past or from the threatening present. I could not shield her from both. She would soon know of Caitlin's perfidy or Breton's brutality, and one would likely reveal the other.

And I had been the matchmaker.


I fretted over the news all that day. Then, in the evening, Caitlin appeared at my door. She was in her nightclothes and carried a candle to light her way secretly to my room.

"You've right enough to have an answer," she said. "I went away wi' Breton Trent because I loved them. I loved them both. I knew what a man he was. He had sexed me on the hillside, in the scrub and barley, when I was not yet full seventeen. Sweet Savior on the cross, how I wanted the lad and set myself for him. It was no matter to me that my own sister loved him, nor that he had his cruel and rough ways that left me sore and staggering even from that first time. What matter? I loved the lad.

"And I loved my sister. She saw him as a kind of wee god, but I knew him better. Her virgin idea of the lad was nocht like the lad himself. It would have crushed her, the discovery of him as he was. So I went off wi' him as much to feed my lust as to save my sister. We are so little alike. And I had it in my way to save the great good in her by giving away the little I found in me.

"It was a secret sacrifice and love's abomination. I'll no' have it come to nocht now. I'll tell her the truth if need be. Hurt her though it will, it would be nocht compared to a life wi' that monster. Now we will speak nae more of it. Let me take this to my grave if I can find the way clear to do it. It is the only favor I'll ask of our acquaintance, Mrs. Miggs."

"People change," I offered. "They mellow, see their errors, and are sometimes redeemed."

"Aye, that may be," she whispered in a tone I had never heard from her, a sound tinged with hope. "But can I risk that chance on a man's redemption? It is too great a gamble."

# Chapter 25

✤

*I have turned the matter over in my mind now, looked at it during the inter-*
*vening days and nights with all the fascination of a kitten with a cricket.*

*Caitlin is wrong. The evil, if that word is not too strong, is not that Kira*
*and Mr. Trent are together now but rather that they had not always been*
*together.*

*That is the omission, the dereliction of design, that I'd intended to rem-*
*edy all along. That plan has not altered.*

*How different, I wonder, would they all have been had Breton Trent not*
*run away with Caitlin? I would like to think that Kira could have exercised*
*her sweet influence upon him, mellowed him, sustained him in adversity,*
*soothed his young and angry spirit. And Caitlin, too, freed of the painful in-*
*dignation of remembrance, how different might her life be today, how differ-*
*ent might all their lives have been?*

*No. It is right and proper to soldier on in the causes of love. I have not*
*been wrong to encourage love, to nurture the tender shoots of this plant*
*grown of ancient seeds. No effort can be too great, no consideration too*
*small.*

*But I had to make sure of Mr. Breton Trent first. Had he changed?*

*The sky threatened rain all day, but none came. I'd listened to Mr. Trent's* hammerings and scrapings for days, alternately resenting him and fearing what he might do once he had finished his work up there.

Then the sky grew thick with rain clouds and the rooftop grew quiet. He had gone up early, as usual, and hammered for nearly an hour. Then all became still, menacing.

He did not come down the ladder.

For the whole of the morning I sat in watchful apprehension, fearing foolishly that he might have finished. I dreaded that he would appear on the ladder with his kit of tools in hand, ready to suggest to Kira, who was all too willing, that they should make away together, patch up the old times, marry on that rooftop, and be gone.

By early afternoon, I could stand it no longer and climbed the ladder leading from the upper window. There, where I had first set eyes on Breton Trent, he had constructed a tight flooring surrounded by a decorative rail, less a belvedere as I knew the word, more like a widow's walk out across the shoulder of the house.

He sat under the low sky with his knotty hat pulled over his brow, deep in concentration over a narrow angle of wood that he carved with a penknife. Tiny flakes of curled wood heaped themselves across his lap and around the stool on which he perched, piling up like snow on a windless day. On his right were three wooden triangles carved in intricate filigree like the trim of a gingerbread house, on his left four other angles lay marked in pencil awaiting the carver's knife. The one in his lap neared completion.

He seemed to know I was standing behind him, watching, for he spoke without looking up.

"Afternoon, lassie," he said, bobbing the point of his knife up to his ragged brim in cursory salutation before applying it again to the wood.

"How did you know I was here?"

"Because Kira Shaw could nae come and Caitlin Reese would nae. That leaves only you to whisper up behind me on woman's feet."

"What are you making?"

"Just dithering," he said, then he set himself to a labyrinthine portion of his work. He carved at it silently for a long time before finally finishing and, with a beam of satisfaction, holding it up for my approval, blowing on it as he did.

"Very pretty."

"Is it? Aye. I think so, too. I could have cut the corners, made them wi' dowels and a wee bit of scrolling, but that's no' how they were done there."

He gestured with his knife as he bent and deposited his work on the pile of completed carvings. He pointed to the filigree on the roof's corners. It was identical to his work.

"Victorians," he scoffed. "Nocht but trouble, the whole lot of them. All lead solder and dickey pipes."

"But they are exquisite." I was in a mood to gainsay him.

"Oh, aye, they're attractive enough; I grant that. Still, they are a fair deil of trouble to keep."

"So why not cut corners? Why not do it with the dowels and scroll work? Would anyone know the difference?"

"I would."

"Are you such a perfectionist, Mr. Trent?"

He looked up at me, puzzled by the question or perhaps hearing the reproach I intended. He cocked a brow for a moment before returning to the next piece of carving.

"I didnae used to be such a perfectionist, miss, no. It was all just slather and push for the longest while. Slather, push, and get it done, move on, slather, push. That's all. We'll call that the Aberdeen years."

He chuckled, a note of dismissal in the sound.

"Was that while you were living with Mrs. Reese or after?"

He paused before going on with his work. "She told you, then?"

"I figured it out."

"Aye, weel. That was during that time and after."

He carved awhile longer before either of us spoke again.

"And now?" I said.

"Nae," he replied quietly. "No' now. I've left all that behind me."

"Why did you come back, Mr. Trent? Why did you decide to come back to Iubhar? Why now?"

He continued whittling as he spoke, not seeming to mind or even to notice my intrusiveness.

"You awake one day, lassie, and look into the glass and see that sad and *wrinkled face looking out at you, and you say 'Jocko, you've gone auld'—and you hardly believe yourself, for you feel no different than a lad of sixteen or maybe twenty years. It's just the odd ache aboot the knee and the rattle in the chest that was no' there before tells you—as the face in the glass tells you—that you've gotten on and nearly done your best years.*

"Something calls to you then and tells you that you'd best repair what damage you've done to the auld world before you leave her behind. The damage I've done was here, and so here I've come wi' my tools and skills and a wee bit of hope in my rattling auld breast that I can do enough repair before my greetie auld knees can nae longer carry me up the ladder."

"What damage?" I said with quiet accusation. "The damage you've done Miss Shaw or Mrs. Reese?"

"They're still both Miss Shaw, truth be told. Reese was just a name she came home by. I've done them both a world of hurt, though. I'm here to repair all I can as best as I can."

"And if it isn't good enough?"

He looked up at me, his eyes filled with steady sincerity.

"It won't be," he said. "It canna be. There's no' just the hurt done, there's the life passed as weel. I can never make that up to either of them."

His candor surprised me.

"What sort of man do you see here?" he asked suddenly. "Take away forty years and as many pounds, wipe smooth the face, and lift off a decade or three of disappointment and worry and frustration, what would I be? Look at me hard, lassie, and use some imagination. That's what I was when I left these green hills."

His eyes were kind. They had a warmth and depth behind the bedeviled sense of humor. I could see the allure he might once have held for two lonely sisters.

"I'm no' asking for you to understand," he said. "I understand it all little enough myself. I went out to be a conqueror. But I did no' leave alone. I would take a woman wi' me, one of the Shaw sisters. That much I knew from an early day. But which one? Which one?"

He returned to the wood and slipped the knife gently along the long edge, peeling off a thin shaving as deftly as if he had planed it.

"Have you ever considered them? Kira and Caitlin, I mean. What kind of girls they once were? What were they as children, young girls, and women? Can you find me an answer to that?"

I stood quietly. In another moment, he went on.

"Kira was the elder and had the fairer face. She's always run to the weight and was even as a child plump as a ripe persimmon. Och, but she had fair apple cheeks, like a painting they were. Her manner was much the same as weel, shy and quiet and loving; like a fawn she was back then, tender and wide-eyed in this narrow world. And I loved her, Mrs. Miggs. I loved young Kira Shaw with a thing like idolatry and wanted only to please her. But I was young and a fair way leaning to witless, I ken. And as I grew I noticed the other girl of the house.

"Caitlin Shaw was as little like her sister then as she is now, only she was a different sort of a girl. She's gone tough now, like an iron corbie, but she was no' always as dour and cold as a Lenten church under a fresh fall of snow. Nae, she was no'."

Breton Trent stopped stropping the blade along the wood and looked out across the side yard to the trees, his mind wandering back, remembering.

"She was the bold girl, was Caitlin, always the one oot on the prow of the fishing boat, posing like a pinup girl in the magazines. She was the girl wi' the quick smile and sharp word.

"Her face was no' so pretty as her elder sister's, no' so round and wholesome, so fresh as ripe fruit. But it was a bonny face for all of its mischief, and where Kira's eyes sparkled wi' joy, Caitlin's danced wi' devilment. She appealed to my vanity, did Caitlin Shaw, back when she was a willin' young girl wi' breasts like buds and her legs and hurdies strong and shapely from her tomboy ways. She raised something in me that was no' idolatry, and to a teenaged boy there is nocht so important as the flutter in the breeches when a young, firm girl fancies him and presses herself against him in the warm night.

"It was after a dance. We were hot wi' the skip of it, we'd been drinking besides—no' much, but just enough to fill the lungs wi' the golden air of malted vapor and make us feel like gods, deathless, daring, and sure—too gallus by half. She pressed close against me beyond the weak light of the hall and tickled me in all the secret places God gave a man to please himself and a woman besides.

"I tore at her, and she at me, and we tumbled into the bushes together, a pair of slobbering, half-drunken teenagers wi' nae business to be naked together. And she said 'nae' to me even as she grabbed me by my exhilaration and guided me into her.

"Warm and soft she was inside, and I rocked in the delight of her. There wi' the guelder rose and holly scratching at ma back and her clutching up ma behouchie, and the partymakers from the dance walking on the path no' four paces from us, never seeing us in the dark there. What did I care? What did we either of us care for them that passed beyond us? Never hearing, never knowing, while all my insides were flooding into her like a fountain and she drinking me up. How could we care? It was a fine sort of grappling madness upon us, and we cared for nocht besides the game."

Breton Trent swallowed hard just then, and I thought he might have fought back a surge of regret. He applied himself to the woodcarving again and stroked it gently under the knife.

"My God she was good," he whispered. "And she took to me as weel. We were like addicts wi' it. That's youth. And when I went to make my way and set myself to leave this place, I had the choice: fair Kira or my fond and frolicking Caitlìn.

"It was no simple matter to decide, for I loved them both. In the end it was Caitlìn, of course. She was the more headstrong and as much as made up my mind for us both. Besides, the mother was ailing and needed Kira at home. So I went off to Inverness, and for a while Kira would visit me some weekends wi' baskets of things, and Caitlìn would sneak up during the week for a tumble. In time, Caitlìn stayed wi' me there and didnae bother going home. The imaginary Mr. Reese and the phantom wedding came soon after to explain it all, for never a word of marriage passed between us. We both knew my promise to Kira and could neither of us bring ourselves to hurt that dear soul, never mind how lust slipped by behind her.

"You know the rest, I ken. I came to resent that girl in my bed, love her though I did. Resented her for nae fault of her own, nae fault but that she came to live wi' a man too young and foolish to handle his disappointment like a man.

"I did terrible things.

"But, as I told you before, I have no' lived my life to feed on regret. A man can be happy and still take no pride in the things he's done or the way he's been.

"But none of that was the handsome lad who left this little world. Something came between his nature and himself. It was no' Caitlin or love or lust but only his own belief that he was a better man than he was. And frae that he came to act a worser man than he should."

He continued to whittle and observed, "Och, weel," several times while he did. In his resolve I could see the contrition that had brought him back. He had changed. Of course he had.

I no longer feared him. I no longer saw in him the beast Caitlin saw. She had suffered under him as only a woman in love could suffer.

"And what of you?" he suddenly said. "Why did you come here?"

I had to laugh. It was a fair question, and he had been so frank with me that I now felt obliged to return his candor. I slid down the wall and wrapped my arms around my knees. I collected my thoughts while watching the clouds scud and drift.

"I'm running toward something," I said. "And away from something, too, I think. I want to throw away the conveniences of choice that pass for thought. I came to discover which of my assumptions can hold and make it to port and which will founder under the waves."

"And?" Breton Trent continued carving.

"I don't know yet."

"Still tempest tossed, Perdita Miggs?"

"Still tempest tossed, Breton Trent."

"Aye, weel. There's life for you."

"There's life," I agreed, feeling much closer to the round little man in the battered clothes than I ever had.

"There's more mystery in a single heart than in all the deep waters," he said quietly.

"It's very pretty," I said, meaning the belvedere. "You've done a lovely job."

"Funny sort of things, these," he said. "The auld sea captains would have them built at the top of their hames so they could look out and dream of returning to the sea. And when they did finally go out into the sour reek of the salty ocean's depth, their women would repair to these posts and dream of their men returning from the sea. They're little worlds of dreaming, the belvederes of the world, men's dreams and women's dreams, where never the twain do meet."

I gazed across the side lawn and down into the thick canopy of birch, oak, and roan trees, when I suddenly saw, to my horror, that the loch was completely hidden.

"Aye," Breton Trent said, "I noticed that, too. They've let the forest grow up along there."

"But," I stammered, "that's why Kira wanted this belvedere built—to look out at the loch."

"So she says."

"What do you mean?"

"She only wants it built, lassie. It's the doing of it that matters and no' its use at all. Still, I'd call it a favor if you would nae tell her the view has gone."

"She'll find out soon enough."

"She might." He shrugged as he continued the intricate job of whittling and carving. "Then again, she may never learn of it."

# Chapter 26

✤

## LONDON

Perry Miggs stood before the imposing Georgian building with his meager supply of notes in a cardboard box, a small box that only served to accentuate how very paltry Perry was. He looked thin and weak before the wide, solid edifice. He felt thin and weak.

He was heartsick, too.

The trip to London had been a misery. Not only had he been sick most of the way on the train, for he was not a good traveler, but also he had been filled with anxiety, which did nothing to help him along his way.

He knew well enough what this was all about. It had nothing to do with what his wife expected. This was a very different building, a different sort of panel. It was time to account for himself. The committee he was about to face held in their hands the power of life and death for him, the continuation or the termination of his long-thought-out project.

It was not completed.

They would care little enough about that. They would only want to know what he had been doing up on the banks of Loch Ness all summer. They would want a full accounting. They would want detailed explanations. They would want him to justify himself, his actions.

Of course he had no justification, nothing tangible. Nothing, he was certain, that would satisfy their demands upon him.

How could he satisfy them? These were civil servants. They understood little enough about hopes and ideals, love and idolatry. They wanted figures, evidence. They wanted the cold accounting, the facts, the valuations, the columnal scrolling of achievement set down with arithmetical precision.

Aspiration counted for nothing here.

Good intention is uncipherable. Perry did not understand much about the wide world, but he certainly understood that.

His whole life experience had taught him that meaning well counted for little.

Virtue is not a contribution.

That was what Dexter had said at the second tenure review all those years back. "Good fellow, good *sort* of fellow, Miggs, but we are looking for effective teaching, not good sorts of fellows. This department doesn't need or want the shirt off his back; we need a contribution. He means well, I know, and can plan like a field marshal—well enough—but what happens *on* the field trip—the actual learning, you see? That is so very much more important than having the bus show up on time or packing up enough insect spray, isn't it?"

Of course it was. Perry had had no defense for Dexter. He probably had no defense today for the committee that had called him to account.

He crossed the street and climbed the wide stone steps leading to the imposing doors, announced himself at the front desk, and was ushered to his appointment by a stern-looking underclerk.

He kept his mind riveted on his one hope as he traced the wide marble hallway. They would not be satisfied with his explanations, his approach. He knew that well enough. If he could convince them of his sincerity, he thought, they might be willing to give him some latitude—he only needed a bit of time to see it to its conclusion, just a bit of time. That is all he asked now, just a bit of leeway, not carte blanche—certainly not freedom—but only a little room, a little more time.

He had done it once before, convinced an antagonistic panel, that is. He had won a reprieve when he had been up for tenure the third time and it had mattered absolutely that he get it. Three strikes and you are out, with tenure reviews.

He had lain his meager résumé before the college tenure board and proceeded to impress them with his sincerity, his unqualified commitment. He broke down and told them why he needed tenure, why he must have it. He called upon their pity, and they had allowed him tenure. People like to pity people. He had done it then, why not once again?

He knew he had to do it again, to do it now.

"P-p-please," he muttered to himself as he placed his hand on the brass knob, "if there is a God someplace out there, and You approve of this—what I am doing, I mean, up there—in Scotland, I mean—let it be a committee of women in there."

Perry felt better about women. Men frightened and intimidated him.

So, again he murmured "please" very quietly and twisted the knob, opening the door timidly.

"Do come in."

He stepped into the room.

There were only three people at the highly polished table. Two middle-aged women and an elderly man. He looked like a sympathetic sort of fellow.

Perry smiled with relief and placed the small box of papers on the table in front of them.

"How can I satisfy you?" he said steadily.

# Chapter 27

✤

Late in the evening, Andrew led me to the small beach of pebbles. We watched the sun set over the western hills.

"She's a deep split in the earth," Andrew said, staring across the loch as the sun slowly vanished. "They used to think that Loch Ness was bottomless, as deep as the world itself. She's more special than that, though. The great plates that move the continents meet at her bottom. Here to the south and east we are sitting on the last few inches of the European plate. And over there, the castle and the violet hills, that's the beginning of North America: the New World not a mile away."

I had made us a snack and piled it into a basket for a midnight picnic: tayberry conserve, warm brie, nutty brown ale, and two tea roses, one red, one white.

We ate in the comfortable silence of twilight while the loch lapped up on the shore in a murmur filled with satisfaction.

I told him of my anxiety about Mr. Trent, and he listened.

"I'd like to think that I can trust him," I said at last.

"You can trust him to be himself," Andrew observed. "That's as much as we can expect from any man. You may trust Mr. Trent to be human, nothing more. Humans are capable of wonders when left to themselves."

He leaned back against his little boat and let the last rays of the sun paint his face a brilliant golden red. In another moment, the sun set and slipped us into night. The western horizon blazed for another few minutes, and the trees above us flamed. Then the darkness came. The stars shone brilliantly in the raven sky where dark clouds drifted like cargo steamers along a black sea.

As the roads of the world grew dark, a bagpipe began to play in the near distance.

"Listen," I said. "It's a forlorn sound. Sad and shrill, sharp as a woman's tears."

"Adam Grant. He does that of a night. Playing to the auld girl. He is sad, maybe the saddest of men."

When the moon climbed into the sky, it lighted the loch in a light like sifted flour, hazy and indistinct yet pure. I could see clearly to the castle on the far shore, and above the clouds glowed like feathered ivory in a jeweler's front window.

The moon's reflection bobbled on the loch.

"There's a tale of a lad," Andrew said, "who saw the moon's reflection and thought she had fallen into the loch. Thought the rippling was her struggling to swim up."

"What happened to him?"

"Och, he loved the moon, this lad, but the moon is a virgin goddess and loves nae man. And so he dived in to save her—hoping so to win her love. But she disappeared. As soon as his head was under the water, the reflection was gone, and it was the lad who died. Drowned in the depths while staring up at her in her sky."

"That's too sad."

"No. There's a happy sort of an ending. You see, the moon, she was so touched by his sacrifice that she gave him her love—her valiant, drowned hero—that is why she is a virgin still. She is a true lover is the moon, and love will never be fully realized until the moon can slip under the water."

It was a warm night. I slipped out of my little sundress. My new swimsuit showed me to good advantage.

"Let's have that swim," I said.

*Andrew stood and began undressing.*

*Back at university, I had often fantasized what Andrew Macgruer might look like, back when he wore trousers and I tried to imagine him out of them. I thought back then that he would be shy.*

*Perhaps he would have been back then—self-conscious and maybe even a little diffident—but not now.*

*For here he was, unaffectedly stripping off his long wrap of plaid, his jacket, his linen shirt, until he stood on the small pebbled world naked, unblemished by the fantasies I'd spun. He was even more ravishing than my adolescent imagination had crafted, thick armed and bare chested, muscled across the breast and thigh like some Celtic god of fertility.*

*He dipped into the loch up to the shoulders before beginning the slow, rhythmic strokes that carried him out to the deep. There he rolled lazily onto his back, displaying himself to the cool moonlight, allowing the crisp waters to lap around him and dance across his skin in tiny rivulets, like capering water sprites at play upon their river lord.*

*"My God," I said, "you are fine."*

*"Get in," he replied and swept the water around him with wide and confident strokes.*

*The water was chilly. I waded as far as I could, but the bottom dropped away quickly, and I was up to the chin in a few steps, paddling out to Andrew with quick, desperate strokes, trying to build up some warmth.*

*"You aren't afraid of the monster?" he said.*

*"No," I said in a chilled vibrato, "she seems harmless enough, even peaceful I think."*

*"She is peaceful," Andrew said. "And why not? This is where she belongs."*

*"You've seen her?"*

*"Touched her. Twice."*

*"Twice?"*

*"Aye," he said quietly over the water. "At first she startled me. But the second time, when I laid my hand against her gentle flesh as cool and smooth as midnight—that made her somehow real to me, and I lost all fear."*

*"I'm freezing," I said.*

*He slipped across to me and wrapped his arms around me. He was* warm. He pressed himself against me and pressed his lips to mine. We stopped swimming and disappeared beneath the surface. I was suddenly warm, and all was quiet and peaceful.

I hung suspended in the great wide loch, in the blackness of the water, in the blackness of the night, my arms wrapped around my broad, strong Scotsman. We kissed as we had in the castle pool, in the salt of St. Andrews, until our bodies ached for air.

We kicked upward into the night now and sucked up the warm, damp darkness. The taste of the peat water, like garden earth, trembled against our lips, and we drank in the fresh air with greedy, laughing gasps, as young as we once had been. Seventeen years were stripped away in the moment, washed off in the waters of Loch Ness, and only the pastness of our past had passed.

"I have a surprise for you," Andrew said as he held me against his naked body. I was still trembling though I hardly felt cold. "Will you meet me again in the morning?"

"Of course I will."

I tangled my fingers in his wet hair and pulled him to me again. Again we kissed and again drifted down into the wide silent lethe of that mysterious loch, sinking away from the sifted moonlight, the ivory-feather clouds, and the skirl of Mad Adam's sad pipes.


In the morning, with Mr. Trent on the roof gently tapping his gingerbread carvings into place, Andrew came to the front of the house.

He brought with him two hunters. His steed was a leggy, mahogany bay stallion, and he ponied along with him a dappled mare, gray as steel, with fire in her eye and an arch in her thick neck.

"I've hired them from a man. Fancy a ride?"

I planted my foot in the bright chromium stirrup and swung up lightly into the saddle. "I haven't ridden in years."

"It'll all come back to you in no time," he said and wheeled his horse up the road and into a gallop.

I squeezed my mare and found her willing. She bounded forward after Andrew's stallion, and in a breath we were galloping up the hill, disappearing *into the dark forest toward craggy peaks and the Monadhliath beyond.*

*We rode south into the ancient woodlands of Glen Mor where the world is draped in the rich aroma of wet earth and sphagnum and the trees twist up from a deep carpet of sward, wildflower, and sandstone. Andrew knew the trails and paths. We picked our way up through antediluvian splendor until we came at last upon a high stream, or burn, where we let our horses drink.*

*"It starts up high in the Carn Easgann Bàna, this burn," Andrew said, "and falls all the way into the loch; come on, I'll show you."*

*We followed the waterway at a slow trot, moving always toward the rushing sound of the burn until, suddenly, we rode out upon a wide green bank suspended under a dazzling cascade. The waterfall dropped hundreds of feet from a narrow cleft in the rocks high above, widening like a horse's tail where it tumbled past us. The wide plume of mist drifted like cobwebs across our promontory and stuck to our hair and eyelashes, spangling our horses with tiny droplets that glittered against their velvet coats like stardust.*

*And below us the water thundered into a chasm with a force that vibrated all the earth around us and rumbled deeply within our breasts like a symphony of cannon fire.*

*"It's wonderful!" I shouted through the damp and roaring air.*

*"This is the Fall of Foyers. Bobby Burns wrote of it. It's been largely ruined by the aluminum works now, but it's still worth a look. The whole region takes its name from here. In the auld tongue, Loch 'an Ess means 'the lake of the cataract.'"*

*I was reminded of Coleridge:*

> *But O, that deep romantic chasm which slanted*
> *Down the green hill athwart a cedarn cover!*
> *A savage place! as holy and enchanted*
> *As e'er beneath a waning moon was haunted*
> *By woman wailing for her demon-lover!*

*" 'Kubla Khan,'" I shouted. "The most erotic poem ever written."*

*"Perhaps," he said with a grin. "Then again, there may be others."*

He turned his horse and we traced our way back and off of the splendid, mist-swept promontory. By midday, we were far from the falls and stopped in a leafy glade where our horses could graze. We unsaddled and let them roam while Andrew set about picking wild things for us to eat—berries and tiny, early ripening fruits.

We drank clean water from the little stream that bubbled by, and after lunch I lay resting my head across his chest by a glade where the horses nuzzled grass.

"What is the most erotic poem?"

"English is no language for passion. For pure eros, there's no language like the Greek and no poet like Archilochus."

"Archilochus?"

"Some lads found a poem of his in Egypt in 1973; wrapped in among the binding of a mummy it was. Truly it was. 'Young men,' he says, 'know many delights of the Love-goddess, quite apart from that sacred affair of generation.' There's true eroticism: Guiltless it is and guileless, all unmolested by the expectation of society."

Andrew placed his wide, gentle hands on my shoulders, staring deeply into my eyes. His face was warm, sincere, and inviting. He looked much as he had at the West Port of St. Andrews when first he kissed me.

I thought he was about to kiss me again. I hoped he would.

But instead, I felt his hands slip slowly down my arms, pulling my thin blouse away as they went, stripping me gently, tenderly. My blouse clung for a maiden's moment to my breasts and then fell away, exposing me to him: tingling sweet delirium.

I unfastened my jeans and let them slide down my legs to gather on the soft forest floor. He unbuckled his belt, and I bent and put my tiny hands under his kilt, onto his fine, thick thighs. I brushed them swiftly up his naked body, carrying away the wool and linen that separated us, stripping Andrew Macgruer with the deftness and delight of seventeen-years-pent-up foreplay. I was bold, and ran my hands along the body I had dreamed of for so long, outlining his muscular chest and abdomen with my fingertips, stroking his erect penis gently, before I pressed myself to him, wrapping myself around him, feeling at once desperate and safe.

He lifted me to the ground so skillfully that for a moment I felt as though I had lost all weight and floated.

He placed me on the forest floor on top of his thick woolen tartan and pressed his weight upon me with a gentle, yielding kiss. In another moment he was deep inside of me. It was all so natural, so delicate and serene, so deliciously, deliriously fulfilling.

"The ground is too rough for you," he whispered, and his strong, soft voice echoed like thunder deep in my imagination.

He held me firmly against him and with nimble, athletic courtesy rolled onto his back, bringing me effortlessly up and astride.

"And there, my darling," he said quietly, sliding his hands up across my breasts to fondle my throat and face.

And there, for the better part of the afternoon, we joined, gently enthusiastic, and appeased the demanding gods of love that animated us.

We lay afterward in the wet grass, the warm sunshine filtering through the trees, the steady rise and fall of his wide, hard chest under my cheek, the cool dew soaking through the linen shirt he had wrapped loosely about my naked body.

It felt nourishing somehow, that damp grass, refreshing and restorative. It strengthened me like a Sunday morning misting before the dawn.

I was youthful again, filled with the wild and wandering emotions of childhood, adolescence, womanhood: feminine and warm, human and real. I was at once myself, just me: my seventeen-years-absent me.

This was not selfishness. I was once again the wonder-filled, romantic, long-lost schoolgirl of St. Andrews.

"So," I whispered across his chest without opening my eyes, "they found Archilochus's poem wrapped around a mummy."

Andrew breathed a quiet chuckle.

"You know the Egyptians," he murmured low. "Reading material for the hereafter. They didnae believe in death."

"Still," I said as I felt my mouth draw up into a satirical grin, "it seems a nasty thing to do, I think, leaving erotic poetry around for someone who's just lost his body. Not a friendly thing to do."

Andrew laughed. "Torment."

*"Eternal torment."* I added.

*"Unceasing."*

*"Interminable."*

*"Unendurable,"* he said and bent to me, pressing his lips to mine.

It was such an after-kiss as I have never known—filled with passion unspent; contentment, yes, that, too. But there was something else there, something familiar and pleasant: friendship.

It was pleasant, yes, but more; it was uncomfortably pleasant.

It reminded me of Perry. Perry's friendship had made life worthwhile, not exciting, not exhilarating, but worthwhile.

*"You are thinking of your husband."*

How he knew, I cannot say, but it made me love him all the more that he did know and had the tenderness to struggle down and find me in my emotional coil.

*"Yes."*

*"Do you regret—?"* he began, but I would not let him finish.

*"No. Not for a moment. I am only sorry for Perry."*

*"Sorry for? That's an odd way to think."*

*"He could never understand this. I'm not certain I do. But this has nothing to do with Perry or how I feel for him. Nothing has changed."*

I rolled over and folded my arms upon Andrew Macgruer's wide chest, resting my chin on my hands.

*"I wonder what you mean by that,"* he said, looking deeply into my eyes.

I could only smile and say, *"It's feminine mystery. You aren't meant to know."*

He raised his eyebrows and sighed deeply.

*"Nothing has changed, then,"* he said. *"You dinnae love me, but love your husband instead. Aye, well, that is how it should be."*

*"Foolish and simple,"* I said and kissed his breast. *"I love you both. That is how nothing has changed. I always have loved you, Andrew.*

*"We've only done now what we should have done back then, at university, except I was too young and timid. It would have been all the same to Perry when I finally met him. I would have still been me. I would have loved you no more, I would have loved you no less, when I met him. And I would*

*have married him. I would have loved him as I did and as I do. And I would still have loved you as I have, as I always have. That's what I mean when I say that nothing has changed. Only—"*

"Only what?"

"Only I feel fulfilled now, and I think perhaps I might not have felt so empty all of these years had I been less—what is it I am trying to say?—less—I know what I mean, but I can't say it so it makes sense."

"Ach, weel, it must be that feminine mystery again."

"Scoundrel."

"It is a fair, rare thing to find a creature such as you, Pær. You know your mind. You always have known your own mind—whether you can actually express it or no'."

*I rolled over and used his chest for a pillow, rested my head there and stared into the trees above us.*

"Sometimes I do. But there are times I don't at all."

*Andrew smiled and kissed me gently.*

"I want a thing that I can't describe, and it irritates me not to be able to. I don't want to be, just now, not today. I've spent too many days being irritated. I want to be—"

*I searched for the word.*

"Enchanted?" *Andrew suggested.*

*I smiled at him.*

"Yes," *I whispered,* "that's it exactly."

"That only comes wi' contentment. Life is for burning, and fire is never contented. I want to hold you, Perdita, and never let you out of my arms. I want to make up for these years, these thousands of miles of separation. There's how I burn."

"So do I, Andrew."

"But we canna," *he whispered.*

"No. We can only go on from here."

"There's the fire of life. It cannae be content."

*We caught our horses in the early evening and rode along the loch back to Iubhar.*

# Chapter 28

✤

It was my idea to take out the Pelican. It seemed such a waste to have a good boat and a man who could pilot her and yet leave her floating unused.

We motored out in the early mornings and spent the days cruising the twenty-four miles of Loch Ness.

I like the Great Glen from the water, like it even better than I do from the shore. It all makes better sense from out here; the topography is shown to better advantage from the water than it is from the rough and narrow asphalt paths ringing the loch.

Every morning, Ness throws up great vapors and mists that cling to the summits and mountainsides—the hills sweep up, majestic and peaceful, cupped in the white velvet haze of early gloamin', gray crags like ancient skulls rising out of a twilight morning vapor all white and downy.

"Your Nessie," I said to Andrew. "I think she has a good thing going for herself here."

"Aye," Andrew said. "If she were no' there, I think we'd have to invent her. This world wants mystery."

"If there aren't more things in heaven and on earth than are dreamt of in man's philosophy, there certainly should be."

"We've a full larder and a tank of petrol. We only want some draught or two for a picnic. We'll go up the canal today to Loch Oich and try to see the great elevation of Ben Nevis."

"Why not?"

If only life could drift as peacefully by as we did, sailing down the loch toward Fort Augustus and the Caledonian Canal that day, man would have never a thought of heaven and never a dream of the Elysian fields. Eden's apples would be hanging, still untouched.

We cruised through the quiet, sapphire waters that cut through the emerald vales of the great Glen Albyn, and in a short time cruised out into Loch Oich, the most splendid of the lochs. We did not stop there but rather passed through the second series of canal locks and entered Loch Lochy, where Andrew raised sail. We gained speed through the grandeur of the Highlands and found a secluded inlet where we anchored under the distant majesty of Ben Nevis.

"How are you getting on with Mr. Trent now?" Andrew asked.

"Not as well as Kira is," I said smiling. "The early morning bedsprings have had quite a workout this whole week. It's really better than having an alarm clock on the side table."

"Really?"

"Oh, yes. They're at it ferociously."

"There's what forty years' wait will do."

"Where do they find the energy? And then afterward, he spends the day on the roof—he's working on the catwalk to the belvedere now. I think perhaps he isn't applying the hammer and saw with that same vigor he once used."

"Aye," Andrew concluded. "A man should apply himself to nae more than one rigid practice a day. Weel, I'm glad for them both, then. How is Caitlin Reese taking it all?"

"Difficult to say. She keeps her distance, hardly speaks a word at breakfast. I don't think she's aware it's going on."

We laughed delicious, open laughter. I put my head on his hard chest, my hand around his neck as we did. In a moment he had slid his hand under my blouse while lifting my chin with the other. He kissed me tenderly on the lips. I pulled him to me again and kissed him heavily, darting my tongue quickly between his yielding lips, flicking against his, and retreating. He followed me back.

We made love there in the little cabin on the heaving loch.

We went topside in the late afternoon, and Andrew turned us back into the canal and toward home.

I grasped the guy wire in both hands and swung from it listlessly, staring into the wide blue water. The canal was as flat and delicate as porcelain, as blue as a jewel. My mind wandered, and a melancholy tremor washed across me.

"You're thinking aboot him again, aren't you?" Andrew said before I realized that he had been watching me, "aboot your husband."

I was thinking of Perry just then and said so.

"Aye, well," he sighed. "Now you're discovering regrets in you."

"Nothing of the heart is easy. I can't hurt Perry. Not even now when I am angry with him. But we are in love's limbo, somewhere on the line between infatuation and indifference. We are nudging ever closer to indifference, though, sliding uncontrollably closer. It once moved just a fraction at a time; now it comes in leaps."

The wind slid across the canal just then. I watched it tousle the surface as it advanced toward me, and waited for it to caress me and toss my hair about my face.

"I don't know," I said when it had passed, brushing the hair back. "It's as though my heart's been cut in half."

"Then throw away the worser part of it, and live the purer with the other half."

"But which half is the worser?" I teased.

Andrew only scowled in concentration, so I continued seriously. "Darling Andrew, it isn't as though I can just purge myself of one or the other of you, just put one of you in the basket and move along to the checkout line. If my heart is halved, then each half has grown whole again and left me two hearts, one each to love each one of you wholly."

Andrew was still concentrating, not listening to me at all.

"It was never my thought to bring you to this confusion, Pær."

"If I am confused, I am confused over Perry—not you. He's fallen away—all that's left of him is the shell of the man I married. Everything else is gone: his youth and looks, his passion, even his personality—and only the name 'husband' remains."

"Perhaps you hinnae lost him so much as you've found yourself."

I don't know why his words affected me as they did, but I felt my heart thud within my breast, and hot tears rushed into my eyes. Andrew Macgruer pulled me to him and held me tenderly, whispering, "Shhhush, shhhush now, lassie mine," until I gave myself over to sobbing, purging myself of all the heartache and worries of my life, rebaptizing myself in my own remorseful tears.

Andrew held me as I wept, rocking me gently, comfortably, until he had to let me go.

"Here now," he whispered. "Still your greetin, Pær. The lock is opened, and we must be on our way."

We passed through Neptune's Staircase and slid through the magnificent vistas of the Glen Albyn beyond. This is the most sublime land on earth, I thought again, soothing and healing like a pagan god, ancient and fertile and beckoning, enigmatic and embracing.

"What will you take with you from today, Andrew?"

"A man can never know the importance of the day till it is passed. Remember your Solon, 'Count no man happy until he is dead.'"

"Tuck away the Greek philosopher and try again. What would you like to take with you?"

"You, Pær. I would like to take you into tomorrow and forever."

"Well done. That's so much better than dead and happy Greeks, isn't it?" I kissed him for it.

We arrived at Fort Augustus in the late afternoon. There, where the narrow canal opens into the vast loch, I wrapped my arms around my gallant Scotsman and kissed him. I kissed him for all the yestertime of thought he had peopled for me. I kissed him because I wanted to commemorate this moment while the great loch heaved and rolled and the seabirds wheeled like confetti tossed across the sky.

"This," I murmured to him. "I want to hold this moment, and in it this kiss, forever."

In another moment, a dapper young man on the quay hailed us.

"Hallo, Pelican!" he shouted out to us. "Could you put in? I have to talk to you."

His name, as it turned out, was Richard Halifax.

"You'd be Perry Miggs's . . . ?" he hesitated.

"Wife," I said, "why?"

"Perhaps we need to sit down."

Halifax was about twenty-three years old, English, with an uncertain complexion and teeth like an elderly picket fence.

"So," Andrew said, "what's this aboot, then?"

"It's about the boat, the Pelican," Halifax said. "I'll have to take charge of it now."

"Take charge of it?" I said.

"And who are you to be taking it?" Andrew asked, a challenge in his tone.

"I'm the person they sent up, actually. No one told you I was coming?"

Our silence was his answer.

"Mr. Miggs didn't—no, apparently no one did. How awkward. I do beg your pardon. It's just that, when I heard the Pelican had been taken up the canal, I thought—well, I thought it was rather in the nature of a farewell excursion on her, you see? But you were apparently—that is, the two of you were just out together to—oh, dear, this is awkward."

"Get on with it, man," Andrew demanded. "Who is it sent you up after the boat?"

"The Royal Geographical Society. I'm taking it back today. You see, it's only the lease hasn't been paid up in some time."

"There is a mistake," I said. "Dr. Miggs was not leasing the boat; it was given to him as part of the grant he received from the Royal Geographic Society. He's conducting research on the loch this summer."

Richard Halifax dug an envelope from his jacket pocket and unfolded the papers in front of us.

"Here's the lease agreement for the Pelican signed by Dr. Miggs. You see *where it stipulates a weekly payment of £350 due and payable a week in advance? Dr. Miggs has missed his last two installments."*

"But I thought that this was part of his grant from the Royal Geographic."

"Dr. Miggs doesn't have a grant from us, miss," Halifax said. "The Royal Geographical Society has no research on Loch Ness at all this season. It is just a lease."

"That isn't possible," I said. "Where did the money come from? You awarded him something like twenty-five thousand pounds."

"We don't have any grants of that size outstanding just now, miss. This lease is forfeit, and I've been sent along to collect the Pelican and take her back to Penzance."

I recognized Perry's signature on the lease agreement. Halifax showed us his credentials. At last I was satisfied, though bewildered by it all.

"I understand that you are staying up the loch a bit," Halifax said.

Andrew scowled deeply at him, and he continued quickly. "That is, they said so in the pub. Not that I've been prying—I was only inquiring after the boat—the Pelican—trying to locate—that is—what I mean to say is I would be happy to take you home before setting out. That's the least I can do. Who knows? We might even spy the Loch Ness monster as we go."

It seemed to him a silly suggestion. He apparently had not guessed that Perry had taken the Pelican for that very reason.

Halifax took us up the coast to Iubhar and ferried us to shore in the motor launch. Andrew helped him cast off from the pebbled beach, and we watched him take the Pelican back down the shore toward Fort Augustus and the Caledonian Canal.

She cut the loch's surface proudly as she sailed from view; proud she was and yair, and I felt sorry to see her go. I had not thought how attached I had become to her.

"I think," I said after we had watched the wide, empty water for a while, "that this is what I'll take with me from today."

I cupped some cold water out of the loch with my hands and watched it trickle through my fingers.

"Perry's never lied to me before. At least, not that I've ever known."

*I rubbed my cool hands onto my face. I dipped some more water up and splashed it against me. It was chill and took my breath, but the shock felt good and stable, somehow, bracing and real.*

*"Och," Andrew said decisively. "Someone has made a mistake."*

*"Yes," I replied. "I wonder if it was me."*

# Chapter 29

✤

Wednesday arrived. The tables were slipped into place, the chairs pulled up, the house swept clean, and by midmorning, the steaming largess from Kira's kitchen began to appear.

The gathering had grown larger since the return of "Breton Trent from years ago." Everyone apparently remembered or knew of him and his affection for Kira—remembered vaguely a promise to return for her.

There were even some confidential rumors, the best-meaning sort of trivial slanders really, that Caitlin—when she was still a Shaw—had fancied Breton Trent herself.

That always drew smiles. Caitlin, indeed.

It added to the romance, though, and the history of Mr. Trent and the Shaw house enticed many occasional members of the Wednesday Tea to become regulars this summer. They all cast furtive looks onto the rooftop, hoping to see the man himself, as they either arrived or departed for the day.

It was a congenial gathering, the Wednesday Tea at the Shaws'. A dozen and a half women, sometimes more than a score, of varying ages, a handful of meek children, the pleasant hiss of gossip over cards, and the aroma of baked goods. There was an unspoken and inviolable rule that any child to be found without a biscuit or jam flip in his hand was to be labeled immediately a "scantling" or "scarecrow" and plied with scones and shortbread in an emergency effort to keep the waif from expiring upon the carpet.

There was a familiar scenario to these meetings. Mrs. Waller would doze at some point and trickle her tea. Mrs. Rose would be discussed if she was not in presence, and her daughter would be discussed if she were.

Someone would be sick.

And through it all, the steadfast Wednesday women would fare forward. They called bids and trumps at one table, pegged out at another. And all the while, they delicately probed for details of Mr. Trent, the American couple, and all of the summer circumstances that had breathed the sweet marjoram fragrance of romance into the Wednesday Tea.

They brought their own idle gossip, of course. Mrs. Rose of Foyers's daughter had taken to her bed now, very ill, and there was talk of sending her to hospital. Mrs. Rose of Foyers's own condition seemed better, then worse, very much depending upon the day and whether or not her fibrous diet had done her some good. "Nocht but blackness in that hoose," they all agreed.

Eibhlin's boy, Niall, her youngest, was promoted in the constabulary, or did she mention that last week? Some thought she had, others that she had not, but all agreed in the end that it certainly bore another mention.

They were, of course, all very curious about the strange happenings surrounding the Americans. Some had heard that the husband, Dr. Miggs, had gone to London. Was he to return? He seemed to have been gone a very long time, hadn't he?

Mrs. MacAlasdair, an infrequent member from the near end of Loch Mhór, had heard that Mrs. Miggs and Mr. Andrew Macgruer were seen riding horses together.

"And if they were?" Kira said with unaccustomed severity. "It happens that Mrs. Miggs likes to ride, but I dinnae think they would have been found all the long way over to Lochgarthside, Queenie MacAlasdair."

Mrs. MacAlasdair agreed that of course not, that would be too great a ride, and allowed that her information was most unreliable.

Séana Baran had been so long absent from the Wednesday meetings that she had not yet heard the now-famous story of the trip to St. Andrews. It was a popular tale among the gathering, and Kira was pressed to tell of the lovely drive, the comical incident of the boy Aidan at the martyr's grave, and the haunted castle they lived in for a night. She ended, as she always did (now accustomed to telling the tale), with the statement that of all the pleasures of the week the greatest was getting away from cooking—martyrs and ghosties notwithstanding.

Mention of St. Andrews reminded Eibhlin Chattan of a peculiar bit of news.

"My son, Niall, says there's a search on for auld Mad Adam Grant. The police want to question him aboot his activities in St. Andrews. He was arrested, or have you no' heard? Arrested and held for a time in the jail."

"What? In St. Andrews?"

"On what charge?"

"Oh, loitering, I shouldn't wonder." one suggested.

"Aye, that'd be it," another agreed. "Adam Grant is the one for dandering aboot."

"Did Niall say what the charge was?"

"Och, loitering sure. But the police took some powder frae the auld man. It turned out to be rat poison he'd been carrying. Didnae discover what it was until after he'd been released."

"Rat poison?"

"Why would auld Adam Grant gae the long way over to St. Andrews wi' rat poison in his pocket?"

"Aye, now," Eibhlin said, "that's what Niall and his boys are eager to learn as weel."

Once the gathering had scattered and only Kira and Caitlìn remained behind, alone in the clutter, the sisters sat—against their custom—without cleaning up the room. They both had the same thought in their minds.

"I was the one who put him onto the motor coach," Caitlin said. "What might he have been thinking? What might I? It was that verra morning that you left yourself for St. Andrews. But he never said he was going to St. Andrews. I never made the connection."

"There was a man in our kitchen, too," Kira said. "Whatever would he be doing in that kitchen wi' rat poison?"

"He's mad, Kira Shaw, and weel we have always kent it."

"Aye," Kira said, "but now I think back on it, he was aboot my kitchen, too, for a while. Do you remember those months ago when Dr. Miggs went up the loch and stayed away by day and slipped back by night? Adam Grant was coming around those nights as weel, and I fancied things had been moved about in my kitchen though I never thought to mention it at the time."

"I wonder," Caitlin said. "Is he finally after—you ken—doing that deed?"

"Rat poison—Mrs. Miggs?"

"It'd be auld Grant's way, sure."

"What should we do?"

Caitlin collected herself for a long moment before speaking.

"What can we do with suspicion and hard thoughts alone? Sure Mrs. Miggs would think us a pair of dafties."

"We can certainly do more than nothing."

"We can keep Mad Adam Grant frae the kitchen as best we may," Caitlin concluded. "And we might worry him frae the door if he calls. What else can a woman do wi' a man?"

"But this man has poison about him."

"They all have their poisons, Kira Shaw."

# Chapter 30

## The Royal Geographical Society
### LONDON

25 July

Dear Perdie,

I have been a long time writing, dear, and I am sorry for the delay.

I was sick on the train coming down. I'm sure that can't surprise you. Travel is so unpleasant for me that I have had some difficulty working up the courage to come back to Scotland. That may be the main reason I am still in London, really. I'm sorry.

There have been other difficulties, too, with the Royal Geographic Society. My presentation went well enough. I did not have the video to show them, though. But I had taken some bottom soundings with the transducers and was able to give an accounting of sedimentation. I was pleased with that. If I do not deceive myself, I believe the society was pleased as well.

But to my point.

As there are only a few weeks remaining of the grant, I think it best that I launch into my studies as soon as I return. I will not come directly home to see you. I will begin working my way down from Inverness along the opposite bank from Iubhar. I have hardly given that area a look, and I do think it an oversight on my part.

I hope you understand.

There is another little trouble. I imagine you already know of it. The society is recalling the vessel, the *Pelican*. There have been storms in the Caribbean, a hurricane as I understand, and several of their research craft have been damaged there. They need the *Pelican* to go there at once. If they haven't come around to take her back they soon will. Don't be disturbed about that.

I do hope you understand.

I will be back in Iubhar in about a month, in enough time for us to catch our return flight anyway.

Say hello to Miss Shaw and Mrs. Reese for me and tell Mr. Macgruder that I won't need a guide any longer. If Adam Grant comes around, he may have the meals I've paid for at the house, otherwise tell Miss Shaw not to worry about them, as we won't expect a refund.

Give yourself a hug for me,

Perry.

*It is the length of time that bothers me. A full month nearly, and he isn't going to come see me from Inverness—not for another month at least. He's always been one who had to be in the same room with me, a handholder in public, always attentive.*

*Now this.*

*How does one fight against the intangible obsessions that drive the heart from love?*

*Meg knows how. Meg learned the hard way.*

*One accepts it, lives with it, or loses everything.*

# Chapter 31

# August

Late at night, as the clouds crowded in around a waning gibbous moon, I lay awake in my bed. There was a movement in my room, and when I looked up I saw a figure poised at the foot of my bed, outlined by the faint window beyond.

"Will you turn on your light," came the old voice.

Adam Grant squinted against the brightness as I pulled the cord beside the bed.

"Would you listen to an auld man?"

"This is an odd time to come calling, Mr. Grant."

"It is an odd thing I am to say."

"Go ahead."

He found a chair and pulled it up to the bed and sat beside me. He was pained, and I waited while he composed himself. His hesitation worried me.

"Your husband—" he choked out before stopping. He looked me in the eye for a long time. His chin trembled and eyes filled with tears.

"What about him?" I said at last.

"He sent me."

"Yes?"

"He sent me after you."

*"Tonight you mean?"*

*"No' tonight. Before."*

*"Before?"*

*"To St. Andrews."*

*"Mr. Grant, what is this about?"*

*"I didnae know it was rat poison, miss."*

*"What?"*

*"The police are after looking for me now," his voice trembled. "They think I—but it was your husband sent me. He called it medicine. Back before, when we were up the loch together. He would come sneaking back wi' the powder and showed me how to put it in the pots. The teapots. He said if ever there came a time that he could nae do the job that I should take it over for him. He gave me the powder and some money."*

*"You've been putting rat poison in my tea?"*

*"Maybe I shouldnae hae taken it. The money, I'm meaning. But he gave me money before, too. That seemed harmless enough."*

*"Tell me about the rat poison, Mr. Grant. Exactly how much—"*

*"For the lunches, the picnics, miss, he gave me money for that—and to collect up flowers for you."*

*"Forget about the money, what's this about rat poison?"*

*"It isnae right that a man would give money to have his woman looked to like that. I had my doubts, miss, but I did it all the same. Can you forgive me?"*

*"Of course, Adam. I forgive you. Don't worry about the money—really."*

*"I would no' hae done it, but he said it would be the best for you."*

*"Just how much rat poison, Adam?"*

*"Och, no' but a wee pinchy or twae of a morning." Adam was clearly feeling better about it all now that he had been forgiven. "He told me we were to look after you, himself and I, and see between us that you had enough every morning. That's why I went up to St. Andrews."*

*"See to it that I had enough rat poison?"*

*"Aye, for your wee heart."*

*"There's nothing wrong with my heart."*

*"His words, his words. 'She needs this medicine to take care of her*

heart,' says he. 'She has a problem wi' her heart, Adam Grant.' His words."

"And I needed rat poison?"

"Aye. You weren't to know. It was a holiday for you but a care only for him. That's why the two of you came." Adam became suddenly circumspect. "Now, I want you to tell the police it was all a mistake. Then they will stop looking aboot for me. If you tell them what has happened—about your heart, about your husband—and the money—they'll stop soon enough and leave me in peace."

He smiled in the uncertain light. I was suddenly furious.

"You put rat poison in my tea in St. Andrews?"

"Aye."

"Adam Grant," I said firmly. "Do you know what you put me through? I nearly passed out halfway up the stairs at St. Rules. What would have happened, do you suppose, if I had? I might have fallen—might have been killed. Had you considered that?"

"Your husband—" he began with an air of conciliation.

"No," I interrupted. "Stop that now. Did you never stop to think what rat poison would do? You could easily have killed me. What then?"

"I dinnae know it was rat poison, miss. Not until the police—"

"What if I had died?"

"Then I would be free, miss," he said sadly. "It's the one thing I've lived to do and feared to do. It would have been a sad day, sure, and I would have wept the bitter tears, but in the end you might hae released me at last."

"That's what you were really doing there in St. Andrews. Chasing that superstition of yours, weren't you?"

"Nae, miss—"

"I do not have a heart condition, Mr. Grant. My husband would not tell you that I had a heart condition. Furthermore, Perry is incapable of doing what you are suggesting. He is my husband, and I know him."

"Do you?" he whispered with a menace that made my flesh creep. "Do you know then that he is back and living across the water now? Do you know he's been watching you and has done for over a week now?"

The news astonished me, but I maintained my composure. "I think you'd better go, Mr. Grant."

*"You'll do me nae good, then?"*

*"I don't believe I can."*

*"Then I can do you none, neither," he nearly hissed. "But think on this: if your heart is well, then Mr. Miggs is up to nae good. Good night, miss. I never meant no harm."*

*In another moment, he was gone, padding down the stairs quickly and quietly. He left angrily, and for a moment I worried about his ire. But what would he do now? What could he do?*

*"Not much," I muttered as I pulled the cord and plunged the room back into the Scots night. Still, I decided it might be wise to switch to instant coffee for the rest of the trip.*

# Chapter 32

✤

"Meg," Perdita Miggs said at Meg's front door. "I wonder if we could speak."

"Of course."

Meg Macgruer showed Perdita into her neat little apartment, put the kettle on, and sat down with her. Perdita Miggs spoke at length and told an extraordinary tale.

"There's adventure for you," Meg said when she had finished. "Do I understand you, then, that your husband has deserted you, and Adam Grant has tried to poison you all in the course of a month?"

"Incredible, isn't it?" Perdita replied with a sardonic air that Meg found at once puzzling and attractive.

"How can you be so calm about it, Pær? I'm sure I'd be in shambles."

"I suppose it's because I've surrounded myself with such an improbable cast. Perry is an unlikely runaway husband; he gets motion-sick pushing the shopping cart—for any trip farther than the supermarket, he requires Maalox and cool cloths. And just look at Adam Grant. An octogenarian stalker? That's my lot, I suppose, and I just don't see myself in any danger."

"I see," Meg said, finally laughing at it all. She became serious, though, in the next moment. "And Andrew," she said tentatively, "how are you getting on wi' him?"

"He's well and happy, I think."

"I am glad of that." Meg let the topic die as she went to make the tea and collect together some biscuits on a plate.

"I need a friend," Perdita said.

"Oh?" the tension showed in Meg's voice. She was at once pleased, for she liked this American woman who looked so much like herself, but she was also uncomfortable. She did not want to be confided in, not if it meant listening to Perdita's plans concerning Andrew. That would be too hard.

"It isn't that." Perdita sensed Meg's misgivings. "It's about me. I need an ear. Do you mind?"

"No' at all."

"All of this has got me to thinking. What is it all about? Why am I here in Scotland? Why now? Why Iubhar? What has led me here?"

"I don't understand, surely your husband's work—"

"Yes," Perdita said without conviction, then shook her head. "No, that's just it. I can't shake the feeling that there's something else going on—here in Scotland, I mean, and in my life, too. I may have just gone crazy, Meg, and I need a friend who'll tell me if I have, someone who will tell me the truth."

"Very well."

"I have lived in the world of women all my life. I went to live with my grandmother when I was eight. After that I lived with roommates, always other girls, of course, and went to a women's college—Sophie Newcomb in New Orleans. I never knew a man until I married Perry. That is, never really knew one."

Meg nodded and smiled. "And you've never been able to understand the creatures?"

"I've never even tried."

"I consider that verra wise. It's a bit like making up your mind no' to disembowel yourself. Verra wise indeed. Men are a tricky lot to know."

Perdita continued, concentrating and missing the joke. "I'm not certain I know what I want. That's not what I mean. I mean, I know what I want and I know what I cannot have—"

"—and they're the selfsame thing," Meg interpreted.

Perdita shrugged helplessly.

"Aye, well," Meg said. "We're in the same boat, then, aren't we? You want what you canna have, and I canna have what I want."

"Not exactly. I want what I cannot want and have what I cannot have."

"Ah, then we're in the same boat still, but it's only you've got the paddle, eh?"

They laughed.

"But this isnae about Andrew, is it?" Meg said.

"It's about me."

"Go on then."

"All this business with Adam—the rat poison and his trying to blame Perry—" Perdita began.

"You mean telling you that he said it was medicine for your heart and that it was your husband set him on?"

"Yes. It all got me to looking back over my life, reevaluating everything. What if it's true? What if I don't know myself at all? It means—" Perdita said with difficulty. "It means I have never really known myself. And that frightens me, Meg."

"We don't any of us really know ourselves, Pær. That is in the will of God. We are all of us such a great lot of sinners that if we ever got a really clear look at ourselves in the mirror we just could nae go on. It's the horror of ourselves God protects us from. That's the main purpose of religion."

Perdita smiled. "I always called it art."

"Aye, that's what I said, isn't it? I call it religion. You call it art. Andrew calls it beauty or nature or some other such. But in the end we're all talking to the same purpose. God, virtuosity, Nature: it transcends us, hides us, perfects us. And it's all the same thing."

"I thought you taught geography."

It was Meg's turn to shrug. "I was married to Andrew Macgruer long enough to pick up a twist or twae."

"I'm worried, Meg. A few years after our wedding I got sick—more weak than sick really. Perry insisted I go to the doctor. There were tests, lots of tests.

"On the morning we went in to hear the results, I was petrified. I told Perry I didn't want to know if it was bad news. It was silly, but I was young. The last thing I said to him before he went through that door was 'if it's bad news I don't want to know, don't ever tell me.' I didn't want to know if I were dying, didn't want to spend my life dwelling on it—dwelling on death.

"Everything was fine. I had a heart murmur. It was a problem, they said, but if I didn't get worse I'd get better. I got better. We celebrated and went on with the business of living. But now I wonder. Ever since Adam told me about my heart, I wonder. I told Perry to lie to me if the news was bad. What if he did? What if he's been lying all along—out of love for me?"

"I think you're buying trouble, Pær. How long ago was this?"

"Ten years maybe."

"Aye—and if you were dying then, why haven't you gotten on wi' it? You don't look sick to me. You're beautiful in fact. Do you feel sick?"

"I get tired easily, can't exercise. Perry's never let me work."

"But the murmur isnae life-threatening?"

"No."

"Then there you are."

"I've come back to that myself, Meg, every time I've looked at it. But something seems to be missing. Everything almost makes sense. It all almost fits together. Too much is happening—too much wrong, too much right. Perry's staying away, Andrew's coming back, the *Pelican* and Mr. Halifax, Adam Grant, the poison, coming to Scotland now after so many years, the whole grant from the Royal Geographical Society—just everything. I thought if I could talk it out that maybe it would make sense. But it doesn't, does it?"

Meg smiled sweetly. "Nae. But that's all right. Life isnae supposed to make sense to us any more than the sky makes sense to the birds. It just is."

"That's my problem."

"You've yet another problem?"

"No, this would be the main-rubric problem."

"Ah, that problem," Meg snickered. "What is that?"

"I have always expected my life to mean something. Even when I was a child I thought I had a purpose."

"You do have. As have we all."

"I've always thought I could figure it out. I've always thought I was meant to know why I am where I am, who I am."

"Aye, that's a problem. We can none of us know, suspect how we will."

"These last months it seems as if I've been working at it. My mind hardly ever stops. You know the old saying, 'a little learning is a dang'rous thing; drink deep, or taste not the Pierian spring'? I believe it. I believe it with my whole heart. And now, just recently, I drink it all up—everything—like a sponge. It's like I'm living to excess, crowding myself with experience, flooding myself with emotion until I don't know whether I'm making up for my empty past or drawing down my stock of a happy future. Perhaps both. I'm just filling the present with all of it."

Meg nodded quietly at her. "You depress me unutterably, Pær. Do you know that? What you're describing is living—living life as I can only guess at. Do you think I like envying you? Och, if only I didnae like you so bloody much. I was happy enough hating you before I met you. Happy enough coming to terms wi' the thought of you off in America.

"Do you know what I did that night after we first met? I stared at the ceiling and asked myself why I wasn't you. I finally convinced myself that I was idealizing. Nobody could be so wholly complete as you, content and able to know life. I convinced myself that I had misjudged, had overvalued you."

"Content? Me?"

"But then you come again to sit and drink my tea and tell me that you're living with all of the depth, all the color and passion life has to offer. And it disturbs you. Can I help? You're living at such a pitch that you've almost seen into the mind of God Himself, you're saying. And you're wondering if you've got it all in perspective. You're asking me. And all this while I'm thinking how I'd like to tell you that nae human being can think and feel as you describe, that it would drive a mortal mad. But crush me into hell itself if I dinnae believe you. Andrew always said you were a kind of a goddess. I dinnae believe that, but you are some kind of a woman. And I will be staring up at my ceiling again tonight. So, are you insane, you want to know. If that's insanity, I only wish I were as insane as you, Perdita Miggs. I only wish we all were."

Meg placed her hand on Perdita's. "So what is it you want from me? Do you want me to tell you to be happy wi' Andrew and make yourself happy in doing it? I have and I do. Shall I tell you to get back your husband? Do that as well. Or is it that you want me to tell you what to do if you're aboot to die? I'd say live. Live as you are living, completely. That's how I'd wish to do it myself if only I had the knack for life that you have."

# Chapter 33

✦

Speaking with Meg the other day helped. I think I am seeing more clearly now.

It is time for Perry to come home. I decided this morning that I would drive around to the other side of the loch to find and collect him.

He must be there by now. Even Perry could have found his way back from Newcastle by this time.

Here was a test for a wife. I had only Mad Adam's mention that he was across the water to guide me. But the Loch Ness Research Centre was there, and the Monster Museum. It would be so like Perry to head somewhere familiar.

I reasoned it out before I left; "It is merely a matter of driving down the A82 until I spot a man bent double in the loch."

I found him on the first try.

I drove onto the grassy siding and stopped the car. Perry was up to his thighs in water; the loch slapped playfully against his olive drab bottom as he peered into its shallows.

"Any luck?" I called down to him.

"A bit, I think," he replied before looking up. He raised his head and saw me on the shore.

"Oh!" he exclaimed, a bit surprised but not displeased, perhaps even a bit exhilarated.

He said "Hello" in his docile way, quiet and submissive, and I returned a bemused "Hello."

He held up the jars he was just then filling, raising them high for me to see, and said cheerfully, "I have had some luck."

"Good for you. Come up and talk to me."

Perry sloshed up from the water and, depositing his muddy kit in the grass, shambled across to me in his awkward boots.

"Hello," he repeated sheepishly and wrapped me in a friendly embrace.

I lay my cheek against his shoulder and held him gently to me.

"I'm getting your pretty things wet and muddy," he said.

"Never mind. It's not the first time."

"I've missed you," he said, and I felt his arms tighten around me.

"I should hope so."


As we skirted the loch, heading up toward Inverness, Perry kept his eyes firmly fixed out of the driver's window at my shoulder, looking at the loch. He didn't seem to mind my line of questioning. He seemed, in fact, oblivious to everything I said, as though I were speaking Gælic. I had asked very broadly about where he'd been keeping himself, what had happened with his lease on the Pelican—I even managed to slip in the phrase "rat poison." He was wholly unresponsive. So thoroughly Perry.

It was all some great, godawful, ghastly misunderstanding, surely. The Royal Geog people were muddled. Adam Grant was mistaken. Perry had caused all of the confusion, probably, but he wasn't aware of it, that seemed certain. He was busy with his slimy water and gummy boots. There was no world beyond that for him. That was world enough—perhaps even too much world—for Perry.

He seemed sad.

"What do you see out there?" he asked me after we had been on the road awhile.

"Loch Ness," I replied.

*He nodded, still ruminative, and again watched the passing parade through my window.*

*"You're used to being uncomplicated for me," he said. "But I want to know what you see when you look out there."*

*"What I see?"*

*"Yes."*

*"Are you trying to take my mind on a subject, Perry Miggs?"*

*"I suppose I am."*

*It pleased me. We very seldom really talked to one another.*

*"What do you see," he continued hesitantly, "when you look out there?"*

*"Everything."*

*"What do you mean by that? What do you mean by everything? The water, the trees?"*

*"I see that, yes. And I see recent memories, too: a half a hundred sunsets and the thick rainless clouds that stampede across the sky; the mists that rise like dreamers. I sense the peace and serenity, the hopes, too, the ambitions of every wayward soul that has ever wondered in idle fascination on her secrets. And I see the mystery itself that is so much a part of every breath. I see Scotland, Perry, and everything Scotland has ever been to me. That's what I see when I look out there."*

*Perry nodded again, quietly, pensively, and turned away from the view and from me to gaze at the floorboards.*

*"What do you see, Perry? You're the marine biologist."*

*"The water and the trees." He shook his head. "Look at it. It's sixteen or seventeen times the size of Niack—maybe more—and so much deeper. I couldn't do it in a lifetime. And even if I charted every meter of it, found everything there was to find, it would never be all those things to me. I could never see a tenth of what you see out there. It is just beyond me."*

*I patted his knee and said, "Never mind that," but I saw that he did mind it. It seemed to me just then that he minded it very much.*

*"How did your report go?" I asked.*

*"Report?"*

*"To the Royal Geog people—the reason you went to London, remember?"*

*"Oh," he said quietly. "That. You know reports."*

"Yes, I suppose I do." They were nasty, dry talks about nothing that would ever really matter to anyone.

"Did they like it?"

"Who?"

"The committee or whoever it was you went to see."

"I satisfied them." Perry answered, his mind elsewhere, looking out across the loch again.

"I must be a disappointment to you, Perdie," he said with the guilty surrender of a schoolboy caught cheating.

I patted his knee again. It was no use contradicting him. I loved him too much to lie to him now, so I patted his knee and let my hand remain there to comfort him.

"You're a good man."

"Would you marry me again?" he said suddenly. It was not a proposal, merely a question.

"Drumnadrochit's made you broody."

"Would you?" he persisted. "If we were only meeting now, I mean. Would you marry me now if you had the choice?"

"Not until after you got out of those muddy things, certainly," I joked.

"I'm serious, Perdie. Would you want me to be your husband if you had it to do over?"

My first reaction was to say yes, of course I would marry him. That is what one does with husbands, after all. But I hesitated—the question was so utterly unexpected. It was not a question Perry was likely to ask, and I was surprised, even amused a little, that he asked it now. Still, I wish I had not hesitated, because in hesitation came contemplation, and suddenly I was not certain that I would marry Perry Miggs if I had the choice today.

I wished he had only asked whether I loved him. That was the easy, unreserved answer. Dear man, who wouldn't love Perry?

So, instead of an answer I evaded the question.

"Would you ask me to marry you today?" I replied. "If you had the choice, would you give me the option of accepting you?"

Perry frowned deeply, and tears came up in his eyes.

"Not if it meant giving up the last thirteen years with you."

*It was a strange, sweet response, even romantic in its way. Not my Perry at all.*

"I've missed you," he said for the second time.

"Apparently."

*Poor Perry, alone in London. How it must have shaken him. It was all suddenly like driving home a stray puppy or collecting up the runaway child, frightened and abashed by his experiences in the world.*

"Nothing is more important to me," he said a moment later, "than you, than our marriage, Perdie."

"Oh?" I said, not angry but nettled.

*I don't know what I heard in his voice, but suddenly all of my sympathy drained away. His tone carried in it the hollow echo of a lie.*

"It's true," he said.

"Have a look in the back seat."

*Perry looked and saw the anniversary present I'd bought in St. Andrews for him.*

"What's this?"

"Your anniversary gift." *I put a sardonic spin on the "your," but of course he didn't catch it at all.*

*The fact that he had done nothing himself to mark the occasion completely eluded him. He saw no irony. Instead, he tapped his fingers on the pretty wrappings and muttered "Oh my, my" in his self-satisfaction.*

"I— I missed it, didn't I?" *he whispered.* "Our anniversary."

"One out of thirteen is a pretty good record," *I replied caustically. It was actually pretty bad, but he took me at my word and not my tone.*

*He peeled open the paper carefully, folding it into a neat square before turning to the box. He unfastened the brass catch and opened the lid slowly, with delight, and stared into the case.*

"A sextant!" *he exclaimed.*

"It's an authentic antique."

"And all here: Index mirror, shades, horizon glass, good telescope, even the tangent screw—all, all here. Tangent screws are notorious for falling off."

"The shopkeeper said it would still work. Can you use one?"

"Yes."

"Good," I replied. "Then you might keep it with you for the next time you get lost. It should help you get straight home in the future."

He didn't perceive the rebuke. I knew he wouldn't. It is refreshing to say what one thinks without the risk of hurt feelings. There is something therapeutic in the exercise.

Perry played with the new toy for a few moments before stopping, suddenly rigid.

"Did you—" he said indelicately, "did you use a credit card for this?"

"No, the Royal Geog bought it for you."

"Ah, that's all right then. This must have cost a fortune."

"Only a small one."

"Thank you, darling."

Perry leaned across and touched my cheek with his lips.

"You're welcome." I gave the "you're" a twist, but he didn't catch that, either.

He tried to work it out of the side of the car with the midday hillside rushing past until he became motion sick and had to put it back in its case. He became quiet, thoughtful, and soon I saw he was morose. No doubt the sextant reminded him of his nautical attempts on the loch.

We drove on in silence for a while before he sighed: "I haven't done a thing here."

"You've done something, though," I encouraged him. "What about the tape? There's proof if only for your own curiosity."

"Yes," he sighed. "There's some consolation in that, I suppose. But then, you've actually seen her, haven't you? I mean actually seen her—with your own eyes."

He sounded almost reverent.

"Yes."

We drove on in silence before he spoke again. "It was a bad trip to London."

"I gathered as much from your letter."

"Did you?" He was impressed. He was forever impressed by the ability everyone else seemed to have of reading between the lines.

"But it's no use hiding away in Drumnadrochit just because London was unkind."

"No, I suppose not. Still—"

"That's like hiding in the oven because you found the stove too hot. You have a car here. You can stay in Iubhar and drive around the loch by day. That's the most I can spare you."

"Yes," he brightened. "I suppose I could do that."

"And you'll have Kira's homecooked meals to see you on, won't you?"

"I'd like that."

He fidgeted in his seat and then said, "We're out of money now, you know."

"I thought we might be."

"It all just got away from me."

"Well," I said reassuringly, "money has a way of doing that."

"We won't be able to go out around the lake on Saturdays anymore."

"Never mind. That will give you more time to work, won't it?"

"I am sorry, Perdie."

"There is nothing to be sorry about, Perry Miggs." I employed that tone wives take when defending their husbands against their own foolishness.

"Yes," he protested, "there is. I am supposed to be such a good planner— the one thing I can really do—and look at the mess I've made."

"You were farsighted enough to pay out everything in advance—meals, rooms, the car, return passage, and the airline tickets. You have provided for us very well, I should think."

"Do you? Do you really think so?"

"Of course I do. Besides, I've seen the Loch Ness Monster Exhibit often enough. I don't believe I'll miss it come Saturday, and, if I do, I'll just recite it to myself, won't I? I'm sure I must have it memorized by now."

"Yes," Perry chirped back. "And you won't be disappointed if I leave for the day—weekends included?"

"Providing you come back every night, I have no objection at all."

"I'll need the car."

"That's settled then."

It made Perry happy. So much so that he began to hum a tune, something

*I had almost never known him to do. It was not a recognizable tune, of course, but it gladdened me to see him so happy.*

"Is that the anniversary waltz you're humming?"

"I don't think so."

"No. Neither do I."

# Chapter 34

✤

I heard the sounds of love downstairs again this morning.

Perry left early to drive to the opposite shore. Caitlin is gone, too. I heard the kitchen door closing some time ago. I did not go downstairs. Not immediately. Not for a while. Not until there was sufficient time for Kira to comb back her hair and smooth the wrinkles in the bed and straighten her dress.

Discretion is the handmaiden of desire.

I might linger in my room, I thought. Or, better still, I decided to idle about on the new belvedere.

I made myself a strong tea with the aid of the hot pot in our room and the tea bags I'd bought in Inverness for just these sorts of mornings—mornings when I longed for solitude.

The belvedere is a tidy affair now. A catwalk leads across the roof from one gable.

I enjoy it now that it is complete. Breton Trent raised a conical roof above it and shingled it like the false turret on the opposite side of the house. The addition blends perfectly, as if it has always been meant to be.

Trent is some sort of genius, I think, in his craft. He has managed to raise the conical roof above the belvedere without the use of posts, by building it out from the existing roof. It seems to float above the belvedere's floor almost by magic if you look at it from the garden—I have seen pulpits in episcopal churches that give the same impression. It reminds me also of the overhanging precipice at the Foyers Fall—natural and yet somehow premeditated.

It is a wonder, this promise fulfilled. I love to stand out here in the richness of the morning above the garden, in the canopy of trees, away from the world that habituated me to tedium, greed, and petty prejudice: far away from the States and that world of waste.

Of course, I cannot see the loch from here, and Trent hasn't yet told Kira that the view is gone. There is still that obstacle to overcome in their relationship, one last disappointment in love. But I can imagine now, standing here even without the view, how it might have been when a boy and a girl sat on the rough shingles, on this dangerous pitch, and watched the wide waters. I can almost feel the sense of wonder, the sense of surprise at the world, the sense of danger that stiffens the sinews and strengthens the resolve as those two sat here, promising devotion and never dreaming what a time forty years might be.

I wonder, was the loch bluer then? Were the days fresher? The hours richer? I doubt it. Youth is a magnifying glass under which all things were bigger, better, more splendid and abundant than ever they could be again. It is only the age of men that dulls the world and not the age of the world at all.

My tea grew cooler, drinkable, while I stood waiting. The herbs from Kira's garden are in full bloom at this time of year, and their mixing aromas pack the air like memory. Even up here one can smell them dancing and whirling about as færies about an oak, mingling with my steeping tea and cavorting with the warm vapor rising to the narrow pitch of the belvedere's roof.

This is the world built of love, of devotion: the world of promises kept.

Perhaps I am finding contentment at last. Perhaps this is it. Perry is back now.

And Andrew.

Together they are my present life, the life I have always wanted. My balance.

My days are filled with Andrew now, and my nights belong to Perry.

*They have become as the sun and moon to me, so different and yet so vital to my universe. They each rise at their appointed hours and keep their steady orbits, and my life, that is my Scottish life—this pagan world of mine suspended somewhere between the fantastic and familiar, between wonder and convention; floating midway in the murky realm between the ancient and new worlds—is quite perfect.*

*But the summer is growing short now. The fleeting nights are lengthening again toward winter, and soon we will be on an airplane for Larchmont and that other world where the sun seldom shines and the nights are invariably cold.*

*Enough of that.*

*There is time enough to grieve this passing when it has passed.*

*It is enough to drink my tea and watch the sparrows bob and weave through the branches in their morning ballet. It is enough for now.*

*It is enough to close the eyes, fill the lungs, and listen in silence to bedsprings below, imagining ancient lovers embracing, whispering, planning to meld long lives into one while the sweet scents of woodbine and wild thyme twine the air where bees hum and sparrows skip.*

*My tea was quite finished before Breton Trent met me on the belvedere. So far he and I were the only two to visit his minor masterwork.*

*"I didnae know you were here, lassie," the squat Mr. Trent said from the catwalk. "Guid morning."*

*"Good morning, Mr. Trent. How are you feeling this morning?"*

*He beamed brightly and I caught a faint blush creep across his features.*

*"Och, weel, weel. I doubt a man has felt better since the fall itself, lassie."*

*I observed that he seemed to glow this morning with an unusual light.*

*"Weel," he replied bashfully, "I'm just that proud to be done wi' the work up here."*

*"What's next?"*

*He puckered his lips in thought, looking out across the side yard to the trees.*

*"I suppose I'll have to tell Miss Kira Shaw aboot the view—or lack of it."*

*"And then?"*

*"I'm going back to Aberdeen, Mrs. Miggs." He propped one of his*

haunches up on the railings and mused contentedly. "It's a braw, bonny world here—and it is grown too sweet for the likes of me. I'm no great lover of Aberdeen, but it suits me now somehow. I fancy I suit it as weel. We've both grown bowff wi' age, and I'll dree my weird there."

"But before you go," I prompted, "isn't there something else to do?"

He nodded. "Aye, there is one other thing." He seemed bleak somehow, cheerless at the prospect.

"Don't you want to?"

"I dinnae know. I'm frankly feart."

"What are you afraid of?"

He did not reply. Instead he looked away into the forests beyond the garden. It was by now late morning, and Caitlin was making her way back to the house from her errands. He watched her slow progress through the dark woods, and I followed his gaze, watching her idly myself, waiting for him to reply in his own good time.

Then Caitlin stepped from the woods and onto the twisting rock path that ran through the garden, and I saw. It was not Caitlin at all but Kira returning from the woods. Caitlin came out of the door below and met her.

I felt the blood draining from my face and nausea churning in me. The sounds. I had heard the sounds of lovemaking when Kira was not here and Caitlin was.

"Oh, not that."

"Now you know," he replied. "The leopard's spots, lassie."

"Oh, you bastard," I breathed in my confusion, more amazed than angry.

"Aye."

He watched me for a long time, perhaps hoping I would let him explain. But I only stared into the empty garden where the truth was revealed. He turned away and went back into the house across the catwalk.

Breton Trent and Caitlin announced their intention to leave together that day.

It could have been a miserable time, the days that followed, but Kira wouldn't let it. She greeted the news with aplomb and hugged them both for luck. The dear woman, she hid her misery well.

———

*Those next days were given to planning and packing. Caitlin packed a suit-case only, small enough preparation for a lifetime together. And I think I no-ticed that something was changed in her demeanor, too.*

*Of course Perry didn't see it at all.*

*She seemed a woman resuscitated, I imagined, dragged from the swollen rivers of her own bile and breathed into afresh. It is difficult to describe the alteration. It was so subtle. No chirping about the house like a canary, of course, not Caitlin. But there was less weariness in the eye, more blush in the cheek, I think. Her breath came deeper and her jaw softened, until the tight, weasel look of suspicion mellowed into a muted, world-wise sense of equilib-rium.*

*She brought my breakfast up to my room one morning, much against all custom and tradition, and spent so much time preparing the table by the window that I soon realized she wanted something of me.*

*"Your husband is enjoying success, I hope?" she said. It was the first kind word about a man I think I had ever heard from Caitlin.*

*"I am not sure I would call it success," I said. "Will you join me for some of this toast?"*

*"I've had my breakfast already. My sister and I ate wi' your husband afore he went this morning. But I'll sit wi' you for the company if you wish it."*

*"That would be very nice."*

*She watched me butter my toast and prepare my tea with distracted fas-cination, as though her mind wandered paths other than those offered by the table and view.*

*"You are happy in your marriage?" she said suddenly.*

*"I beg your pardon?"*

*"Och, I dinnae mean to pry."*

*"Of course you didn't. Yes. I think I am happy in my marriage. Of course, marriage isn't a goal in itself. A person must be happy in herself be-fore she ever may be happy as a wife."*

*"Aye. Aye, that's true enough. It's only your husband said the queerest thing at table this morning. I think he must love you verra much."*

"What did he say?"

"He said that we should see to you and see you were to want for nocht."

"Well, that is nice, isn't it?"

"It is. And it makes me wonder what you do to make a man that caring after you."

"I really don't know. I think it probably greatly depends upon the man. And don't forget he's going to be gone all day again today. That's hardly doting, is it?"

"True," she said. "Still, there's the thought behind it all. There's a kindness in that."

"I don't know what makes men love us, Caitlin. I wish I did."

"So do I." She said it with such sincerity, such depth of feeling, that I suddenly saw her in a different light altogether.

Hardness and cynicism had made her seem mannish to me; nothing about her had ever suggested femininity until then. She was suddenly transformed, just in that moment, and I saw her as the frightened girl she had probably been all along. There was beauty in her fragility, her uncertainty. I think it grew from her willingness to be vulnerable, the trust she displayed at that moment, that made me want to embrace her and welcome her back into this unsure world.

"I do know this, though," I said. "The less we regard gender and the more we treat one another as human beings, just as friends, the closer we grow. There's a lot of harm done in the name of manhood, sisterhood, and sexuality; a lot more harm than good, I think."

"Mr. Trent and I are leaving today. He's to take me back to Aberdeen wi' him."

"Yes."

"And you know Mr. Breton Trent now. You've spoken to him often, I think. And I want to know frae you, in your own good opinion. Does he seem to you a stable sort of a man, like Professor Miggs?"

"Not like Perry, no," I said, "but stable nevertheless. He won't act like Mr. Reese."

"Can you be sure of that?"

"No. We can only be sure of love. Everything else is life's illusion."

*She collected up my empty things on the tray, thanked me for my time, and went downstairs. I think she felt better for our discussion. I really do think it.*

*By afternoon Mr. Trent and Caitlin were prepared to go away together again. Again they prepared to leave Kira behind. But it was different this time.*

*Kira met them at the door and placed her arms around them each in turn, kissing her sister on the cheek.*

*"Promise me," she said to Breton Trent, "that you will marry my sister as soon as you can in Aberdeen and that you'll invite me up. And promise me you will always be good to her and see that she is never unhappy."*

*"I promise you that, Kira Shaw," he replied with conviction. "I promise it all."*

*"Then get off wi' you both and be happy."*

*Later, I found Kira in the front room. She stared out of the window in the direction her sister and Trent had gone, remembering the sight of departure.*

*"I think," she said to me, without turning from the glass, "perhaps I will ask Mrs. Rose of Foyers to come up to live in Caitlin's room. Her daughter, poor dear, is verra sick. She will do weel up in the guestroom where you and Professor Miggs are living just now. Mrs. Rose will do weel enough on the stairs and will be able to watch after the girl. I can tend to the poor auld dearie herself down here. It will make Wednesdays all the easier, too. I like to have a bit of help wi' the tables come Wednesdays."*

*"Do you want to talk about it? Caitlin and Mr. Trent, I mean."*

*"I think maybe nae."*

*She continued to stare out of the window like a saint, no tears, no sighs, only the resignation of suffering renewed.*

*"I'll have a time in the garden, though," she continued. "Mrs. Rose is nae great hand in a garden, and Caitlin was always a help wi' the weeds. Weel, I have my creepie stool and can get doon low enough wi' that for the weeds and trimmings, I ken. And maybe when Mrs. Rose of Foyers's daughter feels weel some days she can come doon and watch me and maybe hold my basket. That will be a comfort to us both. A body needs to feel useful."*

"Would you like to see the belvedere?" I said. "Would you like to come up and see it with me?"

Kira smiled and turned to me. "No," she said. "The stairs are too much for me."

"I think you would like it."

"No, all the same. It was always the view I loved frae there, and that's been gone now ages."

I was surprised. No one had told her. "You know there is no view?"

"Aye," she said and turned back to the window. "I've kent it all along."

"Then why call him back—?"

Kira laced her fingers in her lap and squeezed her hands together for a moment. "A body canna live wi' things left undone. I couldnae let Breton Trent die in Aberdeen unfulfilled, no' when it came into my hands to see to him."

"You love him."

"Aye. I always have, and so has Caitlin."

"How long have you known about them?"

"I think," she said, "since I was eighteen, perhaps nineteen. Och, Caitlin never knew, of course. I knew also that she lived wi' him under the name of Reese. She never knew that, either. It's that secret that bound us together. They were doing a thing they thought would hurt me and chose from love to keep it frae me. I had the choice to condemn the act or laud the secret. The act they did for themselves, the secret for me. The secret was love, and I took it as love. I can find nae blame in love."

"But you were hurt?"

"Aye. Weel, disappointed anyway. When two women love one man, one must do wi'out him. That's the way of it. It's better for me. Hate is like a rust, and Caitlin would have let hate eat into her soul in time. They both need this time for the healing. They punished each other wickedly for what they did to each other and what they think they've done to me. There are no' so many years left to them for the forgiveness they both need. Tha's why I called him back. Tha's why I sent the money along and called him back."

"You meant for this to happen?"

"No' at first." She smiled wistfully out of the window. "At first I fluttered *like a young girl and thought to recapture that handful of summers when he was mine and no' hers. I did that, too, I think—I had him for a wee timey then and for a wee timey now. He's paid me everything he promised me. Only the marriage in the belvedere has gone undone, and I could nae make the walk up now. So I've released him. Finally released. I was never meant for marriage, but Caitlin loves men too much—so much she resents them at times for overfilling her kind heart. She needs to be married to a kind man who'll undo the damage done to her trusting soul.*

*"But no, Perdita, I didnae plan this. I only opened the doors and hoped."*

*"They're both afraid, I think."*

*"Weel, they should be. They've a wicked history to undo, and there's nae small task in that."*

*"I think they're both afraid it will be the way it was."*

*"Then it will no' be the same as it was, and thank the good Lord for that. Fear is a powerful instrument for good. Wi'out fear we are capable of terrible things."*

*"Then you think it will be different this time? Do you think he will be good to her?"*

*She smiled at me with the grace of an angel.*

*"He's never yet broken his promise to me."*

# Chapter 35

✤

*They've been gone now for days, Caitlin and Breton Trent, and in the mellow times of this new silence I have found myself thinking even more than before, working through the labyrinth of my mind and heart.*

*The summer's nearly died away. I feel the draining of the year, the drying up of time.*

*Kira has spent these intervening days clipping up the few remaining blossoms from her garden and draping them head-downward along a string she's strung before her window. They look like children at play, knees caught over tree limbs, these beautiful dried remembrances of the blooming time. She stares at them now, those crisp summer buds, like a woman reading her life. Her scrapbook.*

*She looks into her flowers and I into my heart. Two women alone in a world grown quiet from absence. Summer's ending is lifeless, I think, and a time for languid recollection.*

*Where does contentment go? Joy, pleasure, delight, where do they fly once they have been felt? Are they dried up by memory, preserved along the window casing of the soul?*

*I once asked my grandmother, that old Scotswoman I can blame for my* desires, where the wind went, and she said, "I dinnae know, but if we wait long enough it'll come back."

I think contentment must be like the wind. It shifts across me without warning and disappears again, carried over the distant hills like a retreating flock, leaving only the ruffle and frisson of experience behind.

But it always returns, winding back on unexpected wings, swooping up from the blind glens and hidden shadows of quiescence: the thrill of serenity, the explosion of tranquility that surprises the soul and soothes the heart. It always does return.

I want to hug tranquility to my breast like a thing stuffed full of feathers and fluff.

That is what I want.

And that is what I see slipping from me. August is too near the end of it all. August speaks too loudly of autumn and death, of Larchmont and return. Return speaks too forcefully of retreat. Retreat sounds too much like defeat.

And I wonder what will become of the me I am rediscovering, this me I wish to be.

"I've been so close," I told Andrew that midmorning.

We had ridden the horses into the wilderness and had spread our cloth on the high hills under the Monadhliath and above the loch.

The red sandstone is rugged here; it seems real and unchangeable. And the heather wafts like dreaming across the hill face.

"But I'm not part of it. You are, though, Andrew Macgruer. It is like you."

"Is it?" he said.

"You know it is."

He did not reply but rather rose and walked to the edge of the precipice. He looked away across the distant loch. The breeze came rolling up from the glen just then, tattering his hair and whipping his kilt back against his hard legs.

That is the picture of him I want always to carry with me. Andrew Macgruer on the boundary of the world, his wise and sensitive face beaten by the Highland wind, his body unmoved, his hair like wildfire whipping around his face—his spirit melding into that landscape he seemed once to transcend.

"I want to come home," I said suddenly.

Andrew looked puzzled.

"Not to Larchmont," I explained. "America isn't my home. It isn't any-body's home that I know of. It is only the holding place for the landless and forsaken children of wandering parents, the waylaid seed of a vagrant and confused race."

"Scotland has her problems, too, Pær."

"I don't want to grow drab again, tired, watching my clothes become fa-miliar. But Perry could never live here. He's too much like Larchmont and America."

"It is a difficult situation," Andrew said. "I couldnae leave this for the hurly-hustle of America nor walk where the air is too thick to breathe."

"You're wrong to hide out here," I suddenly said.

"What's that?"

"No, it's wrong. There is no use arguing about it, I know you're wrong. I may have to be stifled, locked up and put away like a summer frock, but you don't. I don't have the choice, but you have, Andrew, you have. The world needs your sanity, your kindness, your love."

"You're the one, Pær," he said sweetly. "You are what's needed."

"But I cannot turn back the hands. I cannot reverse the choices I've made."

"Yes you can," he replied.

The suggestion stunned me. I felt it strike me hard, tightening my chest like love or regret, washing through me like nausea.

I wanted to stay. God how I wanted to remain here, to stay here and be always filled with the Scots summer, but not at Perry's expense.

"No," I replied. "That would be too selfish."

Andrew nodded gently and sighed.

"So you canna stay here, and I canna leave."

"That, too, is too selfish."

He winced at that, stung by my reproof, then nodded.

"It may be at that."

*Andrew and I spoke little of the immediate future after that. The days drove ahead, and we avoided speaking of the parting we knew must come. It only depressed me and seemed to worry him. But though we never spoke of it, the thought of returning to Larchmont troubled me still and began to drain me. The nausea that had struck me on that midmorning stayed with me, shadowing my every thought, my every action.*

*I felt too sick at heart finally to ride out with Andrew, to be reminded of everything I would soon have to leave behind me, so I arranged with Perry to meet him across the water below the great castle.*

*"But I'll have the car," he protested.*

*"Never mind, I'll ask Andrew to row me across to you."*

*Perry tried to protest, but my mind was made up. I wanted to have Perry and Andrew together with me. It just seemed natural to me, somehow intended.*

*It was a calm, cool day, and, being midweek, there were no other boats in sight on the loch. It was the perfect day to try the crossing.*

*I put the basket into the little boat, and Andrew pushed us from the pebbled beach. Andrew pulled at the oars while I dragged my hand through the cold waters of Loch Ness. The time passed slowly, and we were in the middle of the wide water before either of us spoke.*

*"Are you feeling better today?" Andrew said.*

*"Not really."*

*"What do you think is wrong wi' you?"*

*"It's something Kira said a long time ago. We can't sweep away the shadows. I think that's what's wrong with me. I can cast only the shadow I've made, and I'm not certain I like the shape of it."*

*Andrew continued to pull at the oars. He hummed in response, a noncommittal sound.*

*"That is," I said, "I think I'd like you to go back to Meg."*

*"I could see you thinking that."*

*"I've been thinking about monuments these last few days and wondering what mine will be. We leave monuments behind us wherever we go. I'd like to be remembered for something when I leave here. You said I inspired you. I want to be remembered for that; I really would like to be remembered for*

*that. But it will never happen if you stay here. Go to your home and write me as I am, not as you would have wished me to be. Let me be your muse. You already have a wife. Meg's a good woman."*

*"Aye."*

*"And Aidan needs his father."*

*"Aye."*

*"And I am responsible for your leaving her in the first place."*

*He did not say "aye," but neither did he say "nae," so I continued, "You can't run away from disappointment. It's part of your life and makes you who you are."*

*"And if I dinnae like the look of that shadow?"*

*"You still can't sweep it away, Andrew. Looking away doesn't make it go away. Think about it, though, for me. What will be your monument? And, if you do decide to go back to Meg, go back to Meg."*

*Andrew stopped rowing. The small wake we had trailed caught up to us and lifted the little boat briefly before sinking into the center of the loch. Andrew stared into the dark waters. His penetrating eyes seemed to scan the bottom of that bottomless depth.*

*"Tell me," he said quietly, "aboot the old times."*

*He looked up and fixed me in his eyes. "Tell me aboot St. Andrews."*

*I knew what he wanted.*

*"It was the clarifying time of my life," I said, "as I think it was for you. I remember when I met you and later when I first really noticed you. You made that incredibly high eighty-three on that impossibly difficult Latin composition. You were apotheosed then, anointed by Athena in my mind and made somehow more handsome and attractive, beautified in all the manly forms. I wanted to know you better, but I had no thought of falling in love with you. Not then."*

*"When?" he asked. "Remember for me when we fell in love and then tell me to return to Meg."*

*My mind raced back, looking now for a moment I had so long thought of as tangible, a moment like a jewel, many-faceted and real. But now it slipped sideways in my mind, that moment. It became all moments: the kiss at the West Port, Melanie Torrence's introduction in the garden, the pub songs while Jamey Chandliss beat out rhythms on the counter, Raisin Monday, Maundy Thursday, our May Day swim, and all the moments before and since.*

*"I have always loved you," I said as the tears rushed from me. "Before I knew you, there was an empty, longing, loving place in me for the part of me that was already you. I have never not loved you but only not known you."*

*"And those words echo in me, Pær, for, gods love me, it is how I have always felt for you."*

*That's when the pain came. The pinch in the chest I had felt so often over the past months caught me again, but this time it held on and became a tight, gripping sensation.*

*At first I thought it was some emotion in me struggling to break free. It was profound, but whether it was joy or sorrow I could not say. It didn't hurt much, but I knew it was my heart.*

*My color must have changed, for Andrew suddenly looked concerned and said, "Are you all right?"*

*"Yes," I said. "No. I don't know."*

✦

Andrew stopped rowing as she spoke.

Her face paled visibly and her eyes slipped shut, but her lips retained the gentle smile, filled with warmth and compassion. She laid herself down in the boat, her head in Andrew's lap, and would not be awakened. Her breath became labored, and her brows knit together in pain.

He had seen it before: the pallor, the stillness, the nadir expression. Davey Carlisle had looked like this when his heart had gone.

"Not this," Andrew said as he cradled her head in his arms. "Not now. Not again."

The Scotsman looked about him for help, but there were no vessels on the loch. He grabbed up the oars and turned the little boat around in the center of the wide water and began pulling for the shore. Even with all of his strength he was half an hour from land.

"Please, Pær," he repeated again and again, "dinnae leave us."

He pulled desperately for the water's edge, anxiously watching her breath shallow until it scarcely raised and lowered her slender arm where it lay across her.

"Jamey Chandliss?" he said to her as he stroked hard at the water. "Aye, I know what happened to Jamey Chandliss. He did no' pass his year-ends and didnae sit for the summer examinations. He became a bartender at last in Dundee. He's there still, as far as I know, grown fat and happy I believe, and will spend his last days beating out the music's rhythm on his counter. It's what he loved at university. We all have our own paths to learning, Pær. That was his."

He continued talking, recounting times they had known, people they had enjoyed, and he fancied his words held her with him as he pulled the little boat as mightily as his great strength allowed. Her breathing remained shallow, but she was still breathing.

He turned to gauge his progress and saw a figure standing on the high shore.

"There's luck, Pær." He could make shore now, closer to Iubhar, and would not have to make for the little beach still ten minutes up the bank.

"Gae us a hand! We need help!" he cried to the figure above the water.

The figure heard and answered by raising an arm.

Andrew pulled toward the high bank where the man stood patiently. In another minute, the figure called down to him.

"What's wrong, then?" It was Adam Grant.

"She's taken ill, man," Andrew explained across the narrow strip of water that separated them. "Tie off my ropes for me. I need to get her to the doctor."

Andrew threw the mooring line up to Adam, and the old man caught it. He stood on the bank with the rope in his hand and looked sorrowfully down into the boat.

"It's Mrs. Miggs, then, is it?" he said softly.

"It is, man," Andrew hissed in his desperation, "tie off the line."

"Is it her heart then?"

"I dinnae know, but I think it might be."

"So you believe me now," the old man said. "You believe I was no' trying to kill the wee lass."

"Tie off, man, tie off. She's dying."

Adam Grant's face twisted in agony, and he pinched his eyes closed for a moment. He opened them sadly and looked despairingly at Andrew.

"What, man? Tie off!"

The old man released the rope and watched it snake down the embankment and into the loch. The little boat slid back into the wide water.

"Are you completely mad?" Andrew yelled at his old friend. "Help me."

Adam turned from them, his face contorted in the anguish of resolution. He did not turn to look back but only shambled away into the woods.

Andrew's arms ached now and the muscles across his chest shivered with the exertion as he fought the little boat around to the pebbled beach. He dragged the craft ashore and lifted the petite figure from it.

"We're back, Pær," he said weakly. "Back to dry land and help."

The late morning was filled with bird song and the sweet smell of moss.

Her eyes fluttered open just then and turned to regard the soil. She knit her brows in an effort, as if she wanted to speak, but said nothing. She merely gave the world a glance, and, seeming to approve what she saw, closed her eyes again.

Her reaction heartened Andrew. He rushed on, carrying her through the woods.

He found the house empty and took her up to her room where he laid her in her bed.

By now his arms were numb with the moil; his chest and legs felt weak. He wanted to collapse on the floor beside the bed and weep across her body, but there was still a dim hope if the doctor could be found.

"It's happening," came a voice from the door.

Andrew turned to see Perry Miggs there.

"Isn't it?" the professor said.

"How did you know to come?" Andrew said.

"I saw what happened out on the loch and drove around as fast as I could."

"You *saw?*"

"Yes," Perry stammered, fingering his little brass telescope. "I'm afraid I've been watching all along."

# Chapter 36

✤

When I opened my eyes, I was in my room. The bowl of flowers and fruit were in the other room, but I could still smell them. Andrew was there. I knew he was there. I sensed his presence in the room, but I did not look for him. Knowing was enough just then.

My eyes were fixed on Perry. Somehow he had known to come, now that I needed him and no longer merely wanted him. He was standing in the door wearing those boots, his face was a horrible thing to see, filled with fear, filled with knowing, unexpected fear.

His face told me all I needed to know and already knew. It had happened so quickly, with all of the surprise of a sudden spring shower. I was glad to have it come like this and embraced it. Scotland had given me all of herself; now I was required to repay her in kind.

"Perry, darling," I said to him as he came into the room.

"Hello, chuck," he said from the doorway. I had forgotten how he used to call me that. He stood pale and trembling at the threshold. Poor lamb.

"Something's happened, my love," I whispered. It was as if I were trying to explain this horrible thing to a child, only a few moments to distill for him all that I was. The great, impossible task.

"Your heart is too full," he said with a quaver in his voice that threatened tears, and my concerns were suddenly all for him.

"Come here, my sweet," I said. "I must tell you—"

"—about you and Andrew," he completed my awkward sentence without hesitation or heat.

"Yes," I told him, determined to show him my love for him but also my desire for Andrew. I wanted him to understand, to see the complications of the heart. "There is more."

"You mean the liaison?" he said in his simple way, unhurt. I was so glad he did not say "affair." "You have yearned for Scotland all this time, and feeding nourishes and sustains only to increase the appetite."

I was astounded by his sudden poetic urge. I must have looked surprised, for he laughed.

"Your words," he said. "I have never forgotten a word of you. Have you drunk as deeply as you desired, as you needed?"

"I have," I said, amazed and appreciative. I had not thought Perry capable of seeing so clearly or so quickly. He was such an innocent. "How do you know—about Andrew and me?"

"I know," he said. "Of course I know. I've always known. I knew it on the dock in Pembroke. I knew it back on Lake Niack, all of it; I planned it last September. It is the only reason we came here. I told you we had come for you. I told you all along."

Then he bent over me, stroking my hair, and kissed me. It was a warm kiss with no heat, a passionate calm.

And, as he kissed me, my world was filled with crocuses again, and the colors of Christmas candies, and the welcoming aroma of cloves in a summer garden. The struggle is but the game of life. What endures is the captivation of contentment—gently rocked boats on black seas, the confident power of horses, and the cool-burning devotion of Perry.

# Postlude

# September

Andrew Macgruer had not been here for over a year. He had sworn he would not return. Not at night, as he had before. Not ever.

But he pulled at the dry, cracked oars of his little rowboat on that cool, dark September night, and sent the black water swirling and gulping under the lantern light. The tiny craft slid like a skater across the surface of the loch, and the deep, impenetrable waters parted only slightly to allow him passage to that secret, hallowed place.

There had been three of them on that June night that now seemed so long ago: himself, Aidan, and David Carlisle.

Now there were only the two in the boat.

So much had changed. The nights lengthened. The days grew cooler. Kira Shaw had gone away to Aberdeen for the wedding, and Mrs. Rose of Foyers and her daughter were making immediate preparation to move into the quaint Victorian home.

"This is just my way of saying good-bye," Andrew said, his only word of explanation for the curious nocturnal journey.

The boat glided into the stillest place on the loch, and Andrew stopped rowing, allowing the little boat to slow and stop in its own good time.

He swung the lantern on its pole out in front of the rowboat.

"What now?" Perry asked.

"We wait," Andrew said heavily before pulling a blanket around his shoulders and nestling into the bow to rest.

"You're going back, aren't you?" Perry said after a few minutes of silence.

"Back?"

"Back to your wife, I mean. Adam Grant said you were packing up your things to move back up to Inverness."

"Meg said she'd have me. It is enough in life to have love. It is better, though, to have memory. Memory is the gift of love."

"Yes," Perry said through a feeble smile.

The interior of the boat was dark; the lamplight beamed into Perry's eyes so that he could not see the muscular Scotsman's face at the bow. He wished he could. He thought Andrew's eyes might tell him what he meant. The words were sweet and calm, and he wished he could understand them.

"What about your cat?" Perry asked after a few more quiet minutes had passed.

"He's no' my cat. He's just a close friend."

"What will happen to him when you're gone?"

"Like in all things, he'll remake his way and carry on. I'll no' take him back to Inverness wi' me. There are too many streets in the city of men. He would nae be happy there. He lives for the chase and the taste of cool water frae the loch. He wants a free heart to anchor him, one that allows him his wandering and still keeps the cream bowl filled at home. He asks little enough, a kind word frae time to time and a wee tickle aboot the chin to keep his spirits up. The rest he can furnish for himself. And then, some day when his wee bones ache wi' the chase and the mice are running faster than once they did, he'll ask no more than a bit of sheep's fleece by the fire and the warmth of words. I fancy he'll take to Miss Shaw. They've a fondness for each other and share a hatred for the road."

Perry nodded his understanding and the two again lapsed into silence. Only the sound of water lapping at the old boat filled the air around them.

Andrew shifted uncomfortably in the bow. He began struggling with his conscience.

"Miggs," he said at last, then corrected himself, speaking more gently, "Perry. I have something I really ought to tell you."

"I don't think you do."

"I think I need to," Andrew insisted. "When Pær told you—started to tell you—aboot us—that is, she didnae tell you everything."

"She told me enough."

"Then," Andrew said, "you do know that she and I—we—"

"Were once in love? Yes. Fell in love again? That, too. Finally consummated that love? I don't know that, but I do hope so."

"Hope so?"

"It's why we came out here, Andrew. It's why I brought her to Scotland."

"What?"

"Once, after we'd married, on one of those wistful sorts of evenings I suppose I never really got the hang of, she was in a mood to talk. She told such a lovely story about the two of you—St. Andrews and the West Sands and, well, everything. She said that there was still a part of her that would always love you, and she hoped that didn't hurt me. I thought at the time that perhaps it did—hurt, I mean. But I used to think about it quite a bit—you, St. Andrews, Perdie—and came to think of you less as a rival and more as an ideal, her ideal, to be precise.

"She was like that, idealistic. She would be happy no matter what."

Perry sighed deeply, and the sigh stuttered out of him on a flood of quiet emotion. "Her optimism is all that kept us going in Larchmont sometimes. I hate Larchmont."

He hesitated before continuing. "There always seemed to be something she held out in front of her, some secret thought of happiness she always strove toward. It was you, of course. It just came to me one day that it was you. She dreamed of returning here to Scotland and finding you.

"She could never come back here, of course—not on my salary. She knew that. She'd never find you. She knew that, too. So she filled in those missing parts of me with what she liked best of you. She could be happy with me only because she had once been happy with you. Does that make any sense to you at all?"

Andrew smiled in the darkness. "Nae."

Perry knit his brow and searched for a way to express himself better, but he knew he never could.

"Most men," Andrew said, "and I include myself, would feel a gnawing sort of jealousy."

"I did in the beginning, but then of course everything changed. It all came into perspective then."

"How did it change?"

"She had primary pulmonary hypertension. The capillaries in the lungs collapse, won't let the blood in to get oxygen. It's like a traffic jam in the heart, and there is no cure. So the vessels leading out from her heart closed off a little at a time and backed up into her heart.

"After she was diagnosed, anything that made her happy, anything that sweetened her precious life, became precious and sweet to me, too. You had given her such happiness."

Perry stared out across the still, dark waters.

"I only wanted her happiness then. I powdered medicines into her food so she'd never know. I never knew until I came here that warfarin is also used as rat poison. You'd think I would. I made such a study of it all.

"I had to stay in Larchmont, at the college, for the medical benefits."

Perry rubbed his hand absently through the thin hairs of his scalp and looked momentarily lost.

"Then, last summer, the newsletter came from St. Andrews telling of Professor Carlisle's death. He'd been out fishing with Andrew Macgruer on Loch Ness, it said. She tried to hide it, but I saw how she lighted up to read your name. She'd found you, and so had I. It just came to me all at once. She was dying, and I could give her you."

"Tha's when you applied for the grant?"

"There was no grant," Perry said. He continued to look out into the darkness. He was distant and inscrutable. "I tried, but I didn't get it."

Andrew laughed. "No? Then how did you get all the way over here for the summer?"

"I sold everything, even the house, for this summer."

"What?"

"We packed everything away in boxes. I took out loans I'll never be able to repay and paid for everything in cash. They'd never take this summer away from me—from her. They would be looking for me. They would try to stop me.

"It's all been a lie, the Royal Geog, everything. I mailed the reports to a post box that I rented in London. Planning is the one thing I am really any good at."

"Then how did they catch you, the mortgage people from America?"

Perry knit his brow. "I don't really know. The only trail we could have left was credit card purchases, and I was careful to keep the cards all wrapped up and tucked away. Cash, you see, is untraceable. I really don't know how they caught me."

"What were you planning to tell her?" Andrew said after the quiet of the night had intruded for some time.

"Tell her?"

"When she got home and she didnae have a house. How were you planning to explain it?"

"She only had this summer left. This is what she wanted most, to mix herself into the roots and soil of Scotland."

"You knew she was dying?"

"Oh yes, all along."

"But how—how could you bring her to me, man?"

"Charity does not envy, and love is never jealous."

There was a long silence before either moved.

It was Andrew who broke the moment. He reached into the floor of his little boat and lifted out a book he had put there, *Unpathed Waters,*

*Undreamed Shores.* He lay it on the surface of the loch, as if trying to float it, and let it go. It drank up the cool water and slipped away gradually, disappearing under the dark waters of the night.

"What was that?" Perry said.

"Just a wee piece of the moon. It belongs to the other myths of this auld loch."

They looked for a long time at the spot where the book had disappeared before Andrew spoke again.

"She didnae want to—to love me," Andrew stammered. "To love me again."

"I think she did."

"That isnae what I mean. I mean she never meant to be untrue to you."

"She never was," Perry croaked through emotion. "She never was."

Andrew saw Perry's tears glint in the lamplight. They coursed freely down his gaunt face.

"You foolish auld darling, Miggs," Andrew murmured to himself, then said aloud, "You're a better man than I could ever be, Miggs, a better lover, too. I thought I was guiding you."

Andrew put his hands on both sides of Perry's face and looked deeply into his eyes. "She loved you verra much, Perry Miggs."

"Thank you, Mr. Macgruer. I would like to think she did. I would really like to think so."

"Aye, she did—verra much indeed."

Perry sniffed and rubbed his face. "Thank you. I never really knew."

"How could you not know, man?"

"People are a mystery to me, Mr. Macgruer."

They grew silent for a long time and let the little boat sway gently in the water beneath them.

"I loved her for that too, I suppose," Perry broke the silence. "The mystery of it all, of her love. Some people are just meant to be content in darkness. I am one of those people."

"I have tae know," Andrew said quietly. "I didnae know that until she came back, but it's the way I truly am."

"You," Perry agreed, "and Perdie. There is strength in facing the world as it is—knowing and not being afraid. Not being disappointed. I have to have mystery."

"That's why you hunt your monsters, is it? Are you hoping not to find them?" Andrew teased.

"Is that what we're doing out here tonight? Looking for her?"

"Aye."

"I think," Perry said carefully, "I think I want to know that she exists. I think I do know that she exists. But I'm afraid to know it."

"Daft," Andrew laughed.

"It is. It thrills me and frightens me to think of it, though. The mystery, I mean."

"This is where she hunts by the dark of the moon," Andrew whispered.

"Is that what Adam Grant told you?"

"Adam Grant has never seen her oot here."

"But . . ." Perry could barely form the question. "But you have?"

"Aye." Macgruer hesitated before continuing. It was his one secret. He decided after a brief internal struggle to share it with the frail man. "On the night Professor Carlisle died, I saw her. I touched her."

"Touched?"

"Aye, twice."

"What was she like?"

"Och, she was smooth as any dream and soft as fantasy itself on the first touch. The second time she was real and beautiful."

Their voices trailed off into the darkness. They sat in the tiny boat quietly, moved only by the gentle rise of the water that lapped against the fragile hull.

The boat rose softly on a wide, black swell. Macgruer sat up quickly but quietly; he had felt it before.

"She's here," he barely whispered. Had Perry been sensitive to tone, he would have recognized the suppressed excitement in Andrew's voice as he repeated, "She's here."

Somewhere in the starboard gloom, the water splashed sharply, the sound of a large animal breaking the surface.

"Hear that?" Andrew whispered in his zeal.

"Y-yes, I did." Perry's heart began to race. He knew what it was they heard. He understood the significance of it all.

Macgruer squinted into the darkness.

"There!" he nearly squealed under his breath, being careful not to frighten the timid, wild creature he could barely discern. "There off starboard some twelve metres, maybe fifteen, you can just see the glint o'the light on her wet skin. D'you see her? She's swimming this way. The light! It is the light that draws her. Damn Carlisle for a prophet! He knew the light would draw the fishes from the deep. He knew. Can you see her, Miggs?"

Perry placed his head between his knees, breathing heavily.

"N-no," he croaked, his hands pressing his eyes beneath his spectacles.

"Look at her, Miggs!" Andrew whispered. "Look at her not six feet from you now and coming on."

"Can't," Perry mumbled, "I can't."

The sleek, beautiful monster sailed past the lamp, slowing to examine it as she paddled by. Andrew saw her clearly this time, saw her long, elegant neck and the head that reminded him vaguely of a horse's, strong and noble and wonderful.

"Look, look!" he breathed, barely audible, as she circled the boat.

"N-no," Perry muttered back.

"God damn it, man," Andrew grabbed Perry by the collar, frenzied with euphoria. He pulled him upright in the boat and hissed, "she won't stay on the surface forever!"

"I can't," Perry pleaded, his eyes clamped shut.

"Damn you," Andrew barked in his zeal.

Macgruer struck Perry. In his excitement and frustration, he struck the plodding man, slapped him sharply on the scalp. Perry's glasses clattered into the bottom of the boat.

"Look at her!" Andrew ordered, shouting, grabbing Miggs under the jaw in a passion, trying to crane Miggs's head around, forcing him to see the miracle. His voice rebounded in the echoing midnight, "Look at her!"

A wild commotion of water arose at the side of the boat. The creature whipped the loch into froth and bolted under the water like a startled deer retreating into the woods.

Andrew stared into the subsiding foam by the side of his craft.

"Och," he murmured, releasing his grip on Perry's jacket and trying to smooth the creases he had squeezed into it, "now see what I've done."

Andrew touched Perry lightly on the shoulders, kindly.

"I'm sorry I struck you, Miggs."

"I can't look."

"Nae," Andrew agreed. "She's gone now. She won't be back, no' tonight, maybe never now."

Miggs slowly opened his eyes; he was as timid and frightened as the creature had been. Andrew smiled at him, reassuring him, and patted him lightly on the cheek.

"She won't, you know," he whispered to Perry. "She won't come back again. She can never come back."

Perry nodded sadly as he fished his spectacles up from the floor of the boat. He rocked them into place on his nose and looked earnestly at the Scot.

"She's not really gone, though," Miggs said. "She's here—where she's meant to be."

Andrew laid his arms around the meek little man and hugged him close to his breast as he whispered, "Aye."

Perry sniffed and wiped his cheek where a tear had slid.

Andrew laid his face against Perry's scalp and murmured gently, "Damn you for all foolishness."

# About the Author

✤

Brian Jay Corrigan was born in Kansas City, Missouri. He now divides his time between the States, London, and Amalfi, Italy. He studied law and Renaissance literature at Tulane and is or has been a professor of literature, theatrical director, and a professional actor. He has acted with Katharine Hepburn and auditioned for the part of Luke Skywalker. He is married to the classical scholar, Damaris Moore Corrigan.

# Special Thanks

✧

To the genius who invented Bosentan and to the FDA for approving it: You have spared my beloved wife Perdita's fate, and me Perry's. Now let's find the cure for PPH.